Innocent Surrender

ANNE McALLISTER
ROBYN DONALD
CHANTELLE SHAW

OMILLS

Published in Great Britain 2014
by Mills & Boon, an imprint of Harlequin (UK) Limited,
Eton House, 18-24 Paradise Road, Richmond, Surrey, TW9 1SR

INNOCENT SURRENDER © 2014 Harlequin Books S.A.

The Virgin's Proposition, *The Virgin and His Majesty* and *Untouched Until Marriage* were first published in Great Britain by Harlequin (UK) Limited.

The Virgin's Proposition © 2010 Barbara Schenck
The Virgin and His Majesty © 2009 Robyn Donald
Untouched Until Marriage © 2010 Chantelle Shaw

ISBN: 978-0-263-91199-2
eBook ISBN: 978-1-472-04494-5

05-0914

Harlequin (UK) Limited's policy is to use papers that are natural, renewable and recyclable products and made from wood grown in sustainable forests. The logging and manufacturing processes conform to the legal environmental regulations of the country of origin.

Printed and bound in Spain
by Blackprint CPI, Barcelona

THE VIRGIN'S PROPOSITION

BY
ANNE McALLISTER

Award-winning author **Anne McAllister** was once given a blueprint for happiness that included a nice, literate husband, a ramshackle Victorian house, a horde of mischievous children, a bunch of big, friendly dogs, and a life spent writing stories about tall, dark and handsome heroes. 'Where do I sign up?' she asked, and promptly did. Lots of years later, she's happy to report the blueprint was a success. She's always happy to share the latest news with readers at her website, www.annemcallister.com, and welcomes their letters there, or at PO Box 3904, Bozeman, Montana 59772, USA.

CHAPTER ONE

SOMEDAY HER PRINCE would come.

But apparently not anytime soon, Anny thought as she glanced down to check her watch discreetly once again.

She shifted in the upholstered armchair where she'd been waiting for the past forty minutes, then sat up even straighter, and craned her neck to look down the length of the Ritz-Carlton lobby for any sign of Gerard.

There were hundreds of other people milling about. In fact, the place was a madhouse.

It always was, of course, during Film Festival week in Cannes. The French seacoast town began overflowing with industry moguls, aspiring thespians, and avid filmgoers toward the end of the first week in May.

By now—three days into the festival—the normally serene elegant area near the hotel bar, where small genteel groups usually met for cocktails or apertifs, was now a sea of babbling people. The usual polite hushed voices of guests had been replaced by raucous cracks of masculine laughter and high-pitched flirty feminine giggles.

All around her, Anny heard rapid intense conversations rumbling and spiking as producers talked deals, directors flogged films, and journalists and photographers cornered the world's most sought-after actors and actresses. Everywhere she looked curious fans and onlookers, not to mention the hopeful groupies, milled about trying to look as if they belonged.

A prince would barely have been noticed.

But unless he was masquerading as a movie fan, which of course was ridiculous, there was no sign of tall distinguished Prince Gerard of Val de Comesque anywhere.

Anny was tempted to tap her impatient toes. She didn't. She smiled serenely instead.

"In public, you are serene, you are calm, you are happy," His Royal Highness, King Leopold Olivier Narcisse Bertrand of Mont Chamion—otherwise known as "Papa"—had drummed into her head from the cradle. "Always serene, my dear," he had repeated. "It is your duty."

Of course it was. Princesses were serene. And dutiful. And, of course, they were generally happy, too.

Privately Anny had always thought it would be the worst ingratitude if they weren't.

Being a princess certainly wasn't all fun and games as she knew from twenty-six years of personal experience. But princesses, by their mere birthright, were entitled to so much that none of them had a right to be anything but grateful.

So Her Royal Highness, Princess Adriana Anastasia Maria Christina Sophia of Mont Chamion, aka Anny, was serene, dutiful, determinedly happy. And grateful. Always.

Well, almost always.

At the moment, she was also stressed. She was impatient, annoyed and, if she were honest—with herself at least—a little bit apprehensive.

Not scared exactly. Certainly not panic-stricken.

Just vaguely sick to her stomach. Edgy. Filled with a sort of creeping dread that seemed to sneak up on her when she was least expecting it.

Except she had felt the dread so frequently over the past month that now she *was* expecting it. Regularly.

It was nerves, she told herself. Prewedding jitters. Never mind that the wedding was over a year away. Never mind that the date hadn't even been set yet. Never mind that Prince Gerard, sophisticated, handsome, elegant, and worldly, was everything a woman could ask for.

Except here.

She stood up so that she could scan the busy lobby once more. She'd had to dash to get to the hotel by five. Her father had called her this morning and said that Gerard would be expecting her, that he had something to discuss.

"But it's Thursday. I'll be at the clinic then," she had protested.

The clinic Alfonse de Jacques was a private establishment dedicated to children and teens with paralysis and spinal injuries, a place between hospital and home. Anny volunteered there every Tuesday and Thursday afternoon. She had done it since she'd come to Cannes to work on her doctoral dissertation right after Christmas five months ago.

At first she'd gone simply to be useful and to do something besides write about prehistoric cave painting all day. It got her out of the flat. And it was public service—something princesses did.

She loved children, and spending a few hours with ones whose lives were often severely limited seemed like time well-spent. But what had started out as a distraction and a good deed quickly turned into the time she looked forward to most each week.

At the clinic she wasn't a princess. The children had no idea who she was. And when she came to see them it wasn't a duty. It was a joy. She was simply Anny—their friend.

She played catch with Paul and video games with Madeleine and Charles. She watched football with Philippe and Gabriel and sewed tiny dolls' clothes with Marie-Claire. She talked movies and movie stars with eager starry-eyed Elise and argued—about everything—with "cranky Franck," the resident fifteen-year-old cynic who challenged her at every turn. She looked forward to it.

"I'm always at the clinic until five at least," she'd protested to her father this morning. "Gerard can meet me there."

"Gerard will not visit hospitals."

"It's a clinic," Anny protested.

"Even so. He will not," her father said firmly, but there was a sympathetic note in his voice. "You know that. Not since Ofelia…"

He didn't finish. He didn't have to.

Ofelia was Gerard's wife.

Had been Gerard's wife, Anny had corrected herself. Until her death four years ago. Now beautiful, charming, elegant Ofelia was the woman Anny was supposed to replace.

"Of course," she'd said quietly. "I forgot."

"We must understand," her father said gently. "It is hard for him, Adriana."

"I do understand."

She understood that there was every likelihood she'd never replace Ofelia in Gerard's affections. She only knew she was supposed to try. And that was at least part of the reason she was feeling apprehensive.

"He'll meet you in the lobby at five. You will have an early dinner and discuss," her father went on. "Then he must leave for Paris. He has a flight in the morning to Montreal. Business meetings."

Gerard was a prince, yes, but he owned a multinational corporation—several of them, in fact—on the side.

"What does he want to discuss?" Anny asked.

"I'm sure he will tell you tonight," her father said. "You mustn't keep him waiting, my dear."

"No."

She hadn't kept him waiting. It was Gerard who wasn't here.

Now Anny did tap her foot. Just once. Well, maybe twice. And she shot another surreptitious glance at her watch, while in her head her father's voice murmured, "Princesses are not impatient."

Maybe not, but it was already almost quarter til six. She could have stayed at the clinic and finished her argument with Franck about the relative merits of realism in television action hero series after all.

Instead, when she'd had to leave early, he'd accused her of "running away."

"I am not 'running away'!" Anny told him. "I have to meet my fiancé this afternoon."

"Fiancé?" Franck had frowned at her from beneath his mop of untidy brown hair. "You're getting married? When?"

"In a year. Maybe two. I'm not sure." Sometime in the foreseeable future no doubt. Gerard needed an heir and he wasn't prepared to wait forever.

He had agreed to wait until she had finished her dissertation. Barring disaster, that would be sometime next year. Not long.

Not long enough.

She shoved the thought away. It wasn't as if Gerard was some horrible ogre her father was forcing her to marry. Well, yes, he'd arranged it, but there was nothing wrong with Gerard. He was kind, he was thoughtful. He was a prince—in more than one sense of the word.

It was just— Anny shook off her uneasiness and reminded herself that she was simply relieved he understood that finishing her dissertation was important to her and that he hadn't minded waiting until she had finished.

Apparently Franck did mind. He scowled, his dark eyes narrowed on her. "A year? Two? *Years*? What on earth are you waiting for?"

His question jolted her. She stared at him. "What do you mean?"

He flung out a hand, a sweeping gesture that took in the four walls, the clean but spartan clinic room, his own paralyzed legs. He stared at her, then at them, then his gaze lifted again to bore into hers.

"You never know what's going to happen, do you?" he demanded.

He had been playing soccer—going up to head a ball at the same time another boy had done the same. The next day the other boy's head was a little sore. Franck was paralyzed from the waist down. He had a bit of tingling now and then, but he hadn't walked in nearly three years.

"You shouldn't wait," he said firmly. His eyes never left hers.

It was the sort of pronouncement Franck was inclined to make, an edict handed down from on high, one designed to get her to argue with him.

That was what they did: argued. Not just about action heroes. About soccer teams. The immutable laws of science. The best desserts. In short, everything.

It was his recreation, one of the nurses had said to Anny back in January, and she'd only been marginally joking.

"So what are you saying? That you think I should run off and elope?" Anny had challenged him with a smile.

But Franck's eyes didn't light with the challenge of battle the way they usually did. They glittered, but it was a fierce glitter as he shook his head. "I just don't see why you're waiting."

"A year's not long," Anny protested. "Even two. I have to finish my doctorate. And when we do set a date there will be lots to do. Preparations." Protocol. Tradition. She didn't explain about royal weddings. Ordinary everyday weddings were demanding enough.

"Stuff you'd rather do?" Franck asked.

"That's not the point."

"Of course it is. 'Cause if it isn't, you shouldn't waste time. You should do what you want to do!"

"People can't always do what they want to do, Franck," she said gently.

He snorted. "Tell me about it!" he said bitterly. "I wouldn't be locked up in here if I didn't have to be!"

Anny felt instantly guilty for her prim preachiness. "I know that."

Franck's jaw tightened, and his fingers plucked at the bed-clothes. He pressed his lips together and turned his head away to stare out the window. He didn't say anything, and Anny didn't know what to say. She shifted from one foot to the other.

Finally he shrugged his shoulders and shifted his gaze back to look at her. "You only get one life," he said.

His voice had lost its fierceness. It was flat, toneless. His eyes had lost their glitter. His expression was bleak. And seeing it made Anny feel wretched. She wanted desperately to provoke him, to argue with him, to say it wasn't so.

But it was.

He wasn't ever going to be running down the street to meet

Gerard—or anyone else—again. And how could she argue with that?

So she did the only thing she could do. She'd reached out and gave his hand a quick hard squeeze. She had wished she could bring Gerard back with her. Meeting a prince might take his mind off his misery at least for a while. But her father was right, Gerard wouldn't come.

"I have to go," she said. "I'm sorry."

Franck's mouth had twisted. "Go, then." It was a curt dismissal. He looked away quickly, his jaw hard, his expression stony. Only the rapid blink of his lashes gave him away.

"I'll be back," Anny had promised.

She should have stayed.

Another look at her watch told her that it was ten to six now and there was still no sign of Gerard.

But the moment she glanced down at her watch, a sudden silence fell over the whole room, as if everyone in the entire lobby had stopped to draw in a single collective breath.

Startled, Anny looked up. Had they noticed her prince after all?

Certainly everyone in the room seemed to be staring at something. Anny followed their gaze.

At the sight of the man now standing at the far end of the room, her heart kicked over in her chest. All she could do was stare, too.

It wasn't Gerard.

Not even close. Gerard was smooth, refined and cosmopolitan, the personfication of continental charm, a blend of 21st century sophistication and nearly as many centuries of royal breeding.

This man was anything but. He was hard-edged, shaggy-haired, and unshaven, wearing a pair of faded jeans and a nondescript open-necked shirt. He might have been nobody. A beach bum, a carpenter, a sailor in from the sea. He seemed to be cultivating the look.

But he was Somebody—with a capital S.

His name was Demetrios Savas. Anny knew it. So did everyone else in the room.

For ten years he'd been *the* golden boy of Hollywood. A man descended from Greek immigrants to America, Demetrios had started his brilliant career as nothing more than a handsome face. And stunning body.

In his early twenties, he'd modeled underwear, for goodness' sake!

But from those inauspicious beginnings, he'd worked hard to parlay not only his looks, but also his talent into a notable acting career, a successful television series, half a dozen feature films, and a fledgling but well-respected directing career. Not to mention his brief tragic fairy-tale marriage to the beautiful talented actress Lissa Conroy.

Demetrios and Lissa had been Hollywood's—and the world's—sweethearts. One of the film industry's golden couples—extraordinarily beautiful, talented people who lived charmed lives.

Charmed at least until two years ago when Lissa had contracted some sort of infection while filming overseas and had died scant days thereafter. Demetrios, working on the other side of the globe, had barely reached her side before she was gone.

Anny remembered the news photos that had chronicled his lonely journey home with her body and the shots of the treeless windswept North Dakota cemetery where he'd taken her to be buried. She still recalled how the starkness of it shocked her.

And yet it had made sense when she'd heard his explanation. "This is where she came from. It's what she'd want. I'm just bringing her home."

In her mind's eye she could still see the pain that had etched the features of his beautiful face that day.

She hadn't seen that face since. In the two years since Lissa Conroy's death and burial, Demetrios Savas had not made a public appearance.

He'd gone to ground—somewhere. And while the tabloids had reprinted pictures of a hollow-faced grieving Demetrios at first, when he didn't return to the limelight, when there were no more sightings and no more news, eventually they'd looked elsewhere for stories.

They'd been caught off guard, then, to learn last summer that he had written a screenplay, had found backing to shoot it, had cast it and, taking cast and crew to Brazil, had directed a small independent film—a film that was getting considerable interest and possible Oscar buzz, a film he was bringing to Cannes.

And now here he was.

Anny had never seen him before in person though she had certainly seen plenty of photos—had even, heaven help her, had a very memorable poster of him on the wall of her dorm room at university.

It didn't hold a candle to the man in the flesh. The stark pain from those post-funeral photos was gone from his face now. He wasn't smiling. He didn't have to. He exuded a charisma that simply captured everyone's gaze.

He had a strength and power she recognized immediately. It wasn't the smooth, controlled power like Gerard's and her father's. It was raw and elemental. She could sense it like a force field surrounding him as he moved.

And he was moving again now, though he'd stopped for just a moment to glance back over his shoulder before he continued into the room. He had an easy commanding stride, and though princesses didn't stare, according to her father, Anny couldn't look away.

A few people had picked up their conversations again. But most were still watching him. Talking about him, too, no doubt. Some nodded to him, spoke to him, and he spared them a faint smile, a quick nod. But he didn't stop, and as he moved he scanned the room as if he were looking for someone.

And then his gaze lit on her.

Their eyes locked, and Anny was trapped in the green magic of his eyes.

It seemed to take a lifetime before she could muster her good sense and years of regal breeding and drag her gaze away. Deliberately she consulted her watch, made a point of studying it intently, allowed her impatience full rein. It was better than looking at him—staring like a besotted teenager at his craggy hard compelling face.

Where in heaven's name *was* Gerard, anyway?

She looked up desperately—and found herself staring straight into Demetrios Savas's face.

He was close enough to touch. Close enough that she could see tiny gold flecks in those impossibly green eyes, and pick out a few individual grey whiskers in rough dark stubble on his cheeks and jaw.

She opened her mouth. No sound came out.

"Sorry," he said to her, a rueful smile touching his lips. "Didn't mean to keep you waiting."

Me? she wanted to say, swallowing her serene princess smile. Surely not.

But before she could say a thing, he wrapped an arm around her and drew her into his, then pressed hard warm lips to hers.

Anny's ears buzzed. Her knees wobbled. Her lips parted. For an instant she thought his tongue touched hers!

Her eyes snapped open to stare, astonished, into his.

"Thanks for waiting." His voice was the warm rough baritone she'd heard in movies and on television. As she stared in silent amazement, he kept an arm around her waist, tucked her firmly against him and walked her briskly with him toward the shops at the far end of the lobby. "Let's get out of here."

Demetrios didn't know who she was.

He didn't care. She was obviously waiting for someone—he'd seen her scanning the room almost the moment he'd walked in—and she looked like the sort of woman who wouldn't make a fuss.

Not fussing was at the top of his list of desirable female attributes at the moment. And amid all the preening peacocks she stood out like a beacon.

Her understated appearance and neat dark upswept hair would have screamed practical, sensible, unflappable, and calm if they had been capable of screaming anything.

As it was, they spoke calmly of a woman of quiet composed sanity. One of the hotel concierge staff, probably. Or a tour guide waiting for her group. Or, hell, for all he knew, a Cub Scout den mother. In other words, she was all the things that people in the movie industry generally were not.

And she was, whether she knew it or not, going to be his salvation. She was going to get him out of the Ritz before he lost his temper or his sanity or did something he would no doubt seriously regret. In her proper dark blue skirt and casual but tailored cream-colored jacket, she looked like exactly the sort of steady unflappable professional woman he needed to pull this off.

He had his arm around her as he walked her straight down the center of the room. It was as if they were parting the seas as they went. Eyes widened. Murmurs began. He ignored them.

In her ear he said, "Do you know how to get out of here?" Even as he spoke, he realized she might not even speak English. This was France, after all.

But she didn't disappoint him. She didn't stumble as he steered her along, but kept pace with him easily, turning her head toward him just enough so that he could see a smile on her face. She had just the barest hint of an accent when she said, "Of course."

He smiled, then, too. It was probably the first real smile he'd managed all day.

"Lead the way," he murmured and, while to casual observers it would appear that he was directing their movements, he was in fact following her. The murmurs in the room seemed to grow in volume and intensity as they passed.

"Ignore them," he said.

She did, still smiling as they walked. His savior seemed to know exactly where she was going. Either that or she was used to being picked up by strange men in hotel lobbies and had a designated spot for doing away with them. She led him through a set of doors and down another long corridor. Then they passed some offices, went through a storeroom and a delivery reception area and at last, when she pushed open one more door, came to stand on the pavement outside the back of the hotel.

Demetrios took a deep breath—and heard the door lock with a decisive click behind them.

He grimaced. "And now you can't get back in. Sorry. Really. But thank you. You saved my life."

"I doubt that." But she was smiling as she said it.

"My professional life," he qualified, giving her a weary smile in return. He raked fingers through his hair. "It's been a hellish day. And it was just about to get a whole lot worse."

She gave him a speculatively raised brow, but made no comment other than to say, "Well, then I'm glad to have been of service."

"Are you?" That surprised him because she actually sounded glad and not annoyed, which she had every right to be. "You were waiting for someone."

"That's why you picked me." She said it matter-of-factly and that surprised him, too.

But he grinned at her astute evaluation of the situation. "It's called improvisation. I'm Demetrios, by the way."

"I know."

Yes, he supposed she did.

If there was one thing he'd figured out in the past forty-eight hours it was that he might have fallen off the face of the earth for the past two years, but no one seemed to have forgotten who he was.

In the industry, that was good. Distributors he wanted to talk to didn't close their doors to him. But the paparazzi's long memory he could have done without. They'd swarmed over him the moment they'd seen his face. The groupies had, too.

"What'd you expect?" his brother Theo had said sardonically. He'd dropped by Demetrios's hotel room unannounced this morning en route sailing from Spain to Santorini. He'd grinned unsympathetically. "They all want to be the one to assuage your sorrow."

Demetrios had known that coming to Cannes would be a madhouse, but he'd told himself he could manage. And he would be able to if all the women he met were like this one.

"Demetrios Savas in person," she mused now, a smile touching her lips as she studied him with deep blue eyes. She looked friendly and mildly curious, but nothing more, thank God.

"At least you're not giddy with excitement about it," he said drily with a self-deprecating grin.

"I might be." A dimple appeared in her left cheek when her smile widened. "Maybe I'm just hiding it well."

"Keep right on hiding it. Please."

She laughed at that, and he liked her laugh, too. It was warm and friendly and somehow it made her seem even prettier. She was a pretty girl. A wholesome sort of girl. Nothing theatrical or glitzy about her. Fresh and friendly with the sort of flawless complexion that cosmetic companies would kill for.

"Are you a model?" he asked, suddenly realizing she could be. And why not? She could have been waiting for an agent. A rep. It made sense. And some of them could contrive to look fresh and wholesome.

God knew Lissa had.

But this woman actually looked surprised at his question. "A model? No. Not at all. Do I look like one?" She laughed then, as if it were the least likely thing she could think of.

"You could be," he told her.

"Really?" She looked sceptical, then shrugged "Well, thank you. I think." She dimpled again as she smiled at him.

"I just meant you're beautiful. It was a compliment. Do you work for the hotel then?"

"Beautiful?" That seemed to surprise her, too. But she didn't dwell on it. "No, I don't work there. Do I look like I could do that, too?" The smile that played at the corners of her mouth made him grin.

"You look…hospitable. Casually professional." His gaze slid over her more slowly this time, taking in the neat upswept dark brown hair and the creamy complexion with its less-is-more makeup before moving on to the curves beneath the tastefully tailored jacket and skirt, the smooth, slender tanned legs, the toes peeking out from her sandals. "Attractive," he said. "Approachable."

"Approachable?"

"I approached," he pointed out.

"You make me sound like a streetwalker." But she didn't sound offended, just amused.

But Demetrios shook his head. "Never. You're not wearing enough makeup. And the clothes are all wrong."

"Well, that's a relief."

They smiled at each other again, and quite suddenly Demetrios felt as if he were waking up from a bad dream.

He'd been in it so long—dragged down and fighting his way back—that it seemed as if it would be all he'd ever know for the rest of his life.

But right now, just this instant, he felt alive. And he realized that he had smiled more—really honestly smiled—in the past five minutes than he had in the past three years.

"What's your name?" he asked.

"Anny."

Anny. A plain name. A first name. No last name. Usually women were falling all over themselves to give him their full names, the story of their lives, and, most importantly, their phone numbers.

"Just Anny?" he queried lightly.

"Chamion." She seemed almost reluctant to tell him. That was refreshing.

"Anny Chamion." He liked the sound of it. Simple. But a little exotic. "You're French?"

"My mother was French."

"And you speak English perfectly."

"I went to university in the States. Well, I went to Oxford first. But I went to graduate school in California. At Berkeley. I still am, really. I'm working on my dissertation."

"So, you're a…scholar?"

She didn't look like any scholar he'd ever met. No pencils in her hair. There was nothing distracted or ivory towerish about her. He knew all about scholarly single-mindedness. His brother George was a scholar—a physicist.

"You're not a physicist?" he said accusingly.

She laughed. "Afraid not. I'm an archaeologist."

He grinned. "*Raiders of the Lost Ark*? My brothers and I used to watch that over and over."

Anny nodded, her eyes were smiling. Then she shrugged wryly. "The 'real' thing isn't quite so exciting."

"No Nazis and gun battles?"

"Not many snakes, either. And not a single dashing young Harrison Ford. I'm working on my dissertation right now—on cave paintings. No excitement there, either. But I like it. I've done the research. It's just a matter of getting it all organized and down on paper."

"Getting stuff down on paper isn't always easy." It had been perhaps the hardest part of the past couple of years, mostly because it required that he be alone with his thoughts.

"You're writing a dissertation?"

"A screenplay," he said. "I wrote one. Now I'm starting another. It's hard work."

"All that creativity would be exhausting. I couldn't do it," she said with admiration.

"I couldn't write a dissertation." He should just thank her and say goodbye. But he liked her. She was sane, normal, sensible, smart. Not a starlet. Not even remotely. It was nice to be with someone unrelated to the movie business. Unrelated to the hoopla and glitz. Down-to-earth. He was oddly reluctant to simply walk away.

"Have dinner with me," he said abruptly.

Her eyes widened. Her mouth opened. Then it closed.

Practically every other woman in Cannes, Demetrios thought grimly, would have said yes ten times over by now.

Not Anny Chamion. She looked rueful, then gave him a polite shake of the head. "I would love to, but I'm afraid I really was waiting for someone in the hotel."

Of course she had been.

"And I just shanghaied you without giving a damn." He grimaced. "Sorry. I just thought it would be nice to find a little hole-in-the-wall place, hide out for a while. Have a nice meal. Some conversation. I forgot I'd kidnapped you under false pretenses."

She laughed. "It's all right. He was late."

He. Of course she was waiting for a man. And what difference did it make?

"Right," he said briskly. "Thanks for the rescue, Anny Chamion. I didn't offend Mona Tremayne because of you."

"The actress?" She looked startled. "You were escaping from her?"

"Not her. Her daughter. Rhiannon. She's a little…persistent." She'd been following him around since yesterday morning, telling him she'd make him forget.

Anny raised her brows. "I see."

"She's a nice girl. A bit intense. Immature." And way too determined. "I don't want to tell her to get lost. I'd like to work with her mother again…."

"It was truly a diplomatic maneuver."

He nodded. "But I'm sorry if I messed something up for you."

"Don't worry about it." She held out a hand in farewell, and he took it, held it. Her fingers were soft and smooth and warm. He ran his thumb over them.

"I kissed you before," he reminded her.

"Ah, but you didn't know me then."

"Still—" It surprised him how much he wanted to do it again.

But before he could make his move, she jerked, surprised, and stuck her hand into the pocket of her jacket.

"My phone," she said apologetically, taking it out and glancing at the ID. "I wouldn't answer it. It's rude. I'm so sorry. It's—" She waved a hand toward the hotel from which they'd come. "I need to get this."

Because it was obviously from the man she'd been waiting for. His mouth twisted, but he shrugged equably. "Of course. No problem. It's been—"

He stopped because he couldn't find the right word. What had it been? A pleasure? Yes, it had been. And real. It had been "real." For the first time in three years he'd felt, for a few brief moments, as if he had solid ground under his feet. He squeezed her hand, then leaned in and kissed her firmly on the mouth. "Thank you, Anny Chamion."

Her eyes widened in shock.

He smiled. Then for good measure, he kissed her again, and enjoyed every moment of it, pleased, he supposed, that he hadn't entirely lost his touch.

The phone vibrated in her hand long and hard before she had the presence of mind to answer it in rapid French.

Demetrios didn't wait. He gave her a quick salute, pulled dark glasses out of his pocket, stuck them on his face, then turned and headed down the street. He had gone less than a block when he heard the sound of quick footsteps running after him.

Oh, hell. Was there no getting away from Rhiannon Tremayne?

He badly wanted Mona for a part in his next picture. To get her, he couldn't alienate her high-strung, high-maintenance, highly spoiled daughter. But he was tired, he was edgy and, having the sweet taste of Anny Chamion on his lips, he didn't relish being thrown to the jackals again. He spun around to tell her so—in the politest possible terms.

"I seem to have the evening free." It was Anny smiling, that dimple creasing her cheek again as she fell into step beside him. "So I wondered, is that dinner invitation still open?"

CHAPTER TWO

PRINCESSES DIDN'T INVITE themselves out to dinner!

They didn't say no one minute and run after a man to say yes the next. But she'd been given a reprieve, hadn't she? The phone call had been from Gerard, who was going straight to Paris to get a good night's sleep before his flight to Montreal.

"I'll see you on my way back," he'd said. "Next week. We need to talk."

Anny had never understood what people thought they were doing on the phone if not talking, but she said politely, "Of course. I'll look forward to seeing you then."

She hung up almost before Gerard could say goodbye, because if she didn't start running now, she might lose sight of Demetrios when he reached the corner. She'd never run after a man in her life. And she knew perfectly well she shouldn't be chasing one now.

But how often did Demetrios Savas invite her out to dinner— at the very moment her prince decided not to show up?

If that didn't confirm the universe's benevolence, what did?

Besides, it was only dinner, after all. A meal. An hour or two.

But with Demetrios Savas. The fulfillment of a youthful dream. How many women got invited to dinner by the man whose poster they'd had on the wall at age eighteen?

As a tribute to that idealistic dreamy girl, Anny couldn't *not* do it.

He spun around as she reached him, his jaw tight, his eyes hard. It was that same fierce look that had made his name a household word when he'd played rough-edged bad-ass spy Luke St. Angier on American television seven or eight years ago.

Anny stopped dead.

Then at the sight of her, the muscles in his jaw eased. And she was, quite suddenly, rewarded by the very grin that had had thousands—no, *millions*—of girls and women and little old ladies falling at his feet.

"Anny." Her name on his lips sent her heart to hammering. "Change your mind?" he asked with just the right hopeful note.

"If you don't mind." She wasn't sure if her breathlessness was due to the man in front of her who was, admittedly, pretty breathtaking, or to her own sudden out-of-character seizing of the moment.

"Mind?" Demetrios's memorable grin broadened. "As if. So?" He cocked his head. "Yes?"

"I don't want to presume," she said as demurely as possible.

"Go ahead and presume." He grinned as he glanced around the busy street scene. Then his grin faded as he realized how many people were beginning to notice him. One of a gaggle of teenage girls pointed in their direction. Another gave a tiny high-pitched scream, and instantly they cut across the street to head his way.

For an instant he looked like a fox with the hounds baying as they closed in. But only for a moment.

Then he said, "Hang on, will you? I'm sorry but—"

"I understand," Anny replied quickly. No one understood better the demands of the public than someone raised to be a princess. Duty to her public had been instilled in her from the time she was born.

That hadn't been the case for Demetrios, of course. He'd become famous in his early twenties, and as far as she knew he'd had no preparation at all for how to deal with it. Still, he'd always handled fame well. Even in the tragic circumstances of his wife's death, he'd been composed and polite. And while he might have gone to ground afterward, as far as Anny was concerned, he'd had every right.

He'd come back when he was ready, obviously. And while he clearly hadn't sought this swarm of fans, he welcomed them easily, smiling at them as they surged across the street toward him

Confident of their welcome, they chattered and giggled as they crowded around. And Demetrios let them envelop him, jostle him as he laughed and talked with them in Italian, for that was what they spoke.

It wasn't good Italian. Anny knew that because she spoke it perfectly. But he made the effort, stumbled over his words and kept on trying. If the girls hadn't already been enchanted, they would be now.

And watching him, listening to him, Anny was more than a bit enchanted herself.

Of course he'd been gorgeous as a young man. But she found him even more appealing now. His youthful handsome face had matured. His cheekbones were sharper, his jaw harder and stronger. The rough stubble gave him a more mature version of the roguish look he'd only begun to develop in the years he'd played action hero Luke St. Angier. Hard at work on her university courses, Anny had rarely taken the time to watch anything on television. But she had always watched him.

Demetrios Savas had been her indulgence.

Looking at him now, admiring his good looks, mesmerizing eyes, and easy grin, as well as that enticing groove in his cheek that appeared whenever the grin did, it wasn't hard to remember why.

But it wasn't only his stunning good looks that appealed. It was the way he interacted with his ever-so-eager fans.

He might have run from the sharklike pursuit of some intense desperate starlet, but he was kind to these girls who wanted nothing more than a smile and a few moments of conversation with their Hollywood hero.

Actually "kind" didn't begin to cover it. He actually seemed "interested," and he focused on each one—not just the cute, flirty ones. He talked to them all, listened to them all. Laughed with them. Made them feel special.

That impressed her. She wondered where he'd learned it or if it came naturally. Whichever, it didn't seem to bother him. Somehow he'd learned the very useful skill of turning the tables and making the meeting all about them, not him. For once she got to simply lean against the outside wall of one of the shops and enjoy the moment.

It was odd, really. She'd barely thought of him in years. Responsibilities had weighed, duties had demanded. She'd fulfilled them all. And she'd let her girlish fantasies fall by the wayside.

Now she thought, *I'm having dinner with Demetrios Savas*, and almost laughed at the giddy feeling of pleasure at the prospect. It was as heady as it was unlikely.

She wondered what Gerard would say if she told him.

Actually she suspected she knew. He would blink and then he would look down his regal nose and ask politely, "Who?"

Or maybe she was selling him short. Maybe he did know who Demetrios was. But he certainly wouldn't expect his future wife to be having dinner with him. Not that he would care. Or feel threatened.

Of course he had no reason to feel threatened. It wasn't as if Demetrios was going to sweep her off her feet and carry her away with him.

All the while she was musing, though, the crowd around him, rather than dissipating, was getting bigger. Demetrios was still talking, answering questions, charming them all, but his gaze flicked around now and lit on her. He raised his brows as if to say, *What can I do?*

Anny shrugged and smiled. Another half a dozen questions and the crowd seemed to double again. His gaze found her again and this time he mouthed a single word in her direction. "Taxi?"

She nodded and began scanning the street. When she had nearly decided that the only way to get one was to go back to the Ritz-Carlton, an empty one appeared at the corner. She sprinted toward it.

"Demetrios!"

He glanced up, saw the cab, offered smiles and a thousand apologies to his gathered fans, then managed to slip after her into the cab.

"Sorry," he said. "Sometimes it's a little insane."

"I can see that," she said.

"It goes with the territory," he said. "And usually they mean well. They're interested. They care. I appreciate that." He shrugged. "And in effect they pay my salary. I owe them." He flexed his shoulders against the seat back tiredly. "And when it's about my work, it's fine. Sometimes it's not." His gaze seemed to close up for a moment, but then he was back, rubbing a hand through his hair. "Sometimes it's a little overwhelming."

"Especially when you've been away from it for a while."

He gave her a sharp speculative look, and she wondered if she'd overstepped her bounds. But then he shrugged. "Especially when I've been away from it for a while," he acknowledged.

The driver, who had been waiting patiently, caught her gaze in the rearview mirror and asked where they wanted to go.

Demetrios obviously knew enough French to get by, too, because he understood and asked her, "Where do we want to go? Some place that's not a madhouse, preferably."

"Are you hungry now?" Anny asked.

"Not really. Just in no mood to deal with paparazzi. Know any place quiet?"

She nodded. "For dinner, yes. A little place in Le Soquet, the old quarter, that is basically off the tourist track." She looked at him speculatively, an idea forming. "You don't want to talk to anyone?"

A brow lifted. "I want to talk to you."

Enchanted, Anny smiled. "Flatterer." He was amazingly charming. "I was thinking, if you're really not hungry yet, but you wouldn't mind talking to a few more kids—not paparazzi, not journalists—just kids who would love to meet you—"

"You have kids?" he said, startled.

Quickly Anny shook her head. "No. I volunteer at a clinic for children and teenagers with spinal injuries and paralysis. I was there this afternoon. And I was having a sort of discussion—well, argument, really, with one of the boys…he's a teenager—about action heroes."

Demetrios's mouth quirked. "You argue about action heroes?"

"Franck will pretty much argue about anything. He likes to argue. And he has opinions."

"And you do, too?" There was a teasing light in his eye now.

Anny smiled. "I suppose I do," she admitted. "But I try not to batter people with them. Except for Franck," she added. "Because it's all the recreation he gets these days. Anything I say, he takes the opposite view."

"He must have brothers," Demetrios said wryly.

But Anny shook her head. "He's an only child."

"Even worse."

"Yes." Anny thought so, too. She had been an only child herself for twenty years. Her mother had not been able to have more children after Anny, and she'd died when Anny was twelve. Only when her father married Charlise seven years ago had Anny dared to hope for a sibling.

Now she had three little half brothers, Alexandre, Raoul, and David. And even though she was much older—actually old enough to be their mother—she still relished the joy of having brothers.

"Franck makes up for it by arguing with me," she said. "And I was just thinking, what a coup it would be if I brought you back to the clinic. You obviously know more about action heroes than I do so you could argue with him. Then after, we could have dinner?"

It was presumptuous. He might turn her down cold.

But somehow she wasn't surprised when he actually sat up straighter and said, "Sounds like a deal. Let's go."

The look on Franck's face when they walked into his room was priceless. His jaw went slack. No sound came out of his mouth at all.

Anny tried not to smile as she turned back toward Demetrios. "I want you to meet a friend of mine," she said to him. "This is Franck Villiers. Franck, this is—"

"I know who he is." But Franck still stared in disbelief.

Demetrios stuck out his hand. "Pleased to meet you," he said in French.

For a moment, Franck didn't take it. Then, when he did, he stared at the hand he was shaking as if the sight could convince him that the man with Anny was real.

Slowly he turned an accusing gaze on Anny "You're going to marry *him*?"

She jerked. "No!" She felt her cheeks flame.

"You said you had to leave early because you were going to meet your fiancé."

Oh God, she'd forgotten that.

"He got delayed," Anny said quickly. "He couldn't come." She shot a look at Demetrios.

He raised his brows in silent question, but he simply said to Franck, "So I invited her to dinner instead."

Franck shoved himself up farther against the pillows and looked at her. "You never said you knew Luke St. Angier. I mean—*him*," he corrected himself, cheeks reddening as if he'd embarrassed himself by confusing the man and the role he'd played.

Demetrios didn't seem to care. "We just met," he said. "Anny mentioned your discussion. I can't believe you think MacGyver is smarter than Luke St. Angier."

Anny almost laughed as Franck's gaze snapped from Demetrios to her and back again. Then his spine stiffened. "Could Luke St. Angier make a bomb out of a toaster, half a dozen toothpicks and a cigarette lighter?"

"Damn right he could," Demetrios shot back. "Obviously we need to talk."

Maybe it was because he, like Anny, treated Franck no differently than he would treat anybody else, maybe it was because he was Luke St. Angier, whatever it was, the next thing Anny knew Demetrios was sitting on the end of Franck's bed and the two of them were going at it.

They did argue. First about bomb-making, then about scripts and character arcs and story lines. Demetrios was as intent and focused with Franck as he had been with the girls.

Anny had thought they might spend a half an hour there—at

most. Franck usually became disgruntled after that long. But not with Demetrios. They were still talking and arguing an hour later. They might have gone on all night if Anny hadn't finally said, "I hate to break this up, but we have a few more people to see here before we leave."

Franck scowled.

Demetrios stood up and said, "Okay. We can continue this tomorrow."

Franck stared. "Tomorrow? You mean it?"

"Of course I mean it," Demetrios assured him. "No one else has cared about Luke that much in years."

Franck's eyes shone. He looked over at Anny as they were going out the door and he said something she thought she would never hear him say. "Thanks."

She thanked Demetrios, too, when they were out in the hall again. "You made his day. You don't have to come back. I can explain if you don't."

He shook his head. "I'm coming back. Now let's meet the rest of the gang."

Naturally he charmed them, one and all. And even though many of them didn't know the famous man who was with Anny, they loved the attention. Just as he had with Franck and with the Italian girls, Demetrios focused on what they were telling him. He talked about toy cars with eight-year-old François. He listened to tales about Olivia's kitten. He did his "one and only card trick" for several of the older girls. And if they weren't madly in love with Demetrios Savas when he came into their rooms, they were well on the way by the time he left.

Anny, for all her youthful fantasies about Demetrios Savas, had never really imagined him with children. Now she thought it was a shame he didn't have his own.

It was past nine-thirty when they finally stepped back out onto the narrow cobbled street in Le Soquet and Anny said guiltily, "I didn't mean to tie up your whole evening."

"If I hadn't wanted to be there," he said firmly, "I could have figured out how to leave." He took hold of her hand, turning her so that she looked into those mesmerizing eyes. She couldn't see the color now as the sun had gone down. But the intensity was there in them and in his voice when he said, "Believe me, Anny."

How could she not?

She wetted her lips. "Yes, well, thank you. It hardly seems adequate, but—"

"It's perfectly adequate. You're welcome. More than. Now, how about dinner?"

"Are you sure? It's getting late."

"Not midnight yet. In case you turn into a pumpkin," he added, his grin flashing.

Was she Cinderella then? Not ordinarily. But tonight she almost felt like it. Or the flipside thereof—the princess pretending to be a "real" person.

"No," she said, "I don't. At least I haven't yet," she added with a smile.

"I'm glad to hear it." Then his voice gentled. "Are you having second thoughts, Anny? Afraid the missing fiancé will find out?"

He still held her hand in his, and if she tugged it, she would be making too much of things. She swallowed. "He wouldn't care," she said offhandedly. "He's not that sort of man."

He cocked his head. "Is that good?"

Was it good? Anny knew she didn't want a jealous husband. But she did want a husband to whom she mattered, who loved her, who cared. On one level, of course, Gerard did.

"He's a fine man," she said at last.

"I'm sure he is," Demetrios said gravely. "So if I promise to behave in exemplary fashion with his fiancée, will you have dinner with me?"

He held her hand—and her gaze—effortlessly as he hung the invitation, the temptation, dangling there between them. He'd already asked before. She'd said no, then yes. And now?

"Yes," she said firmly. "I would like that."

She wasn't sure that she should have liked the frisson of awareness she felt when he gave her fingers a squeeze before he released them. "So would I."

* * *

He wanted to keep holding her hand.

How stupid was that?

He wasn't a besotted teenager. He was an adult. Sane, sensible. And decidedly gun-shy. Or woman-shy.

Which wasn't a problem here, Demetrios reminded himself sharply, determinedly tucking his hands in his pockets as he walked with Anny Chamion through the narrow steep streets of the Old Quarter. She was engaged and thus, clearly, no more interested in anything beyond dinner than he was.

Still, the desire unnerved him. He'd had no wish to hold any woman's hand—or even touch one—in over two years.

But ever since he'd kissed Anny Chamion that afternoon, something had awakened in him that he'd thought stone-cold dead.

Discovering it wasn't jolted him.

For as long as he could remember, Demetrios had been aware of, attracted to, charmed by women. He'd always been able to charm them as well.

"They're like bowling pins," his brother George had grumbled when they were teenagers. "He smiles at them and they topple over at his feet."

"Eat your heart out," Demetrios had laughed, always enjoying the girls, the giggles, the adulation.

It had only grown when, after college where he'd studied film, he'd taken an offer of a modeling job as a way to bring in some money while he tried to land acting roles. The modeling helped. His face became familiar and, as one director said, "They don't care what you're selling. They're buying you."

The directors had bought him. So had the public. They had found him even more engaging in action than in stills.

"The charisma really comes through there," all the casting directors were eager to point out. And it wasn't long before he was not just doing commercials and small supporting parts, he was the star of his own television series.

Three years of being Luke St. Angier got him fame, fortune, opportunities and adulation, movie scripts landing on his doorstep, plus all the women he would ever want, including the one he did—the gorgeous and talented actress, Lissa Conroy.

The last woman he had felt a stab of desire for. The last one he'd cared for. The last one he would ever let himself care for.

But this had nothing to do with caring. This was pure masculine desire confronted with a beautiful woman. He couldn't expect his hormones to stay dormant forever, he supposed, though it had been easier when they had.

He glanced up to see that the distraction herself had stepped over to talk to the waiter in a small restaurant where they'd stopped. The place was, as she'd promised, no more than a hole in the wall. It had a few tables inside and four more, filled with diners, on the pavement in front.

She finished talking to the waiter and came back to him. "They know me here. The food is good. The moussaka is fantastic. And it's not exactly on the tourist path. They have a table near the kitchen. Not exactly the best seat in the house. So if you would prefer somewhere else…"

Demetrios shook his head. "It's fine."

And if not perfect because the table really was right outside the kitchen door, no one paid any attention to them there. No one expected a film star to sit at the least appealing table in the place, so no one glanced at him. The cook and waiter were far too busy to care who they fed, but even though they seemed run off their feet, they doted on Anny. Menus appeared instantly. A wine list quickly followed.

"You come here often?"

"When I don't cook for myself, I come here. They have great food." And she ordered the bouillabaisse without even looking at anything else. "It's always wonderful."

He was tempted. But he was more tempted by the moussaka she had mentioned earlier. No one made it like his mother. But he hadn't been home in almost three years. Had barely talked to his parents since he'd seen them after Lissa's funeral. Had kept them at a distance the entire year before.

He knew they didn't understand. And he couldn't explain.

Couldn't make them understand about Lissa when he didn't even understand himself. And after—after he couldn't face them. Not yet.

So it was easier to stay away.

At least until he'd come to terms on his own.

So he had. He was back, wasn't he? He had a new screenplay with his name on it. He had a new film. He'd brought it to Cannes, the most public and prestigious of film festivals. He was out in public, doing interviews, charming fans, smiling for all he was worth.

And tonight moussaka sounded good. Smelled good, too, he thought as he detected the scent mingling with other aromas in the kitchen. It reminded him of his youth, of happier times. The good old days.

Maybe after he was finished at Cannes, he'd go see Theo and Martha and their kids in Santorini, then fly back to the States and visit his folks.

He ordered the moussaka, then looked up to see Anny smiling at him.

"What?" he said.

She shook her head. "Just bemused," she told him. "Surprised that I'm here. With you."

"Fate," he said, tasting the wine the waiter brought, then nodding his approval.

"Do you believe that?"

"No. But I'm a screenwriter, too. I like turning points." It was glib and probably not even true. God knew some of the turning points in his life had been disasters even if on the screen they were useful. But Anny seemed struck by the notion.

The waiter poured her wine. She looked up and thanked him, earning her a bright smile in return. Then she picked it up and sipped it contemplatively, her expression serious.

He wanted to see her smile again. "So, you're writing a dissertation. You volunteer at a clinic. You have a fiancé. You went to Oxford. And Berkeley. Tell me more. What else should I know about Anny Chamion?"

She hesitated, as if she weren't all that comfortable talking about herself, which was in itself refreshing.

Lissa had commanded the center of attention wherever they'd been. But Anny spread her palms and shrugged disingenuously, then shocked him by saying, "I had a poster of you on my wall when I was eighteen."

Demetrios groaned and put his hand over his eyes. He knew the poster. It was an artistic, tasteful, nonrevealing nude, which he'd done at the request of a young photographer friend trying to make a name for herself.

She had.

So had he. His brothers and every male friend he'd ever had, seeing that poster, had taunted him about it for years. Still did. His parents, fortunately, had had a sense of humor and had merely rolled their eyes. Girls seemed to like it, though.

"I was young and dumb," he admitted now, ruefully shaking his head.

"But gorgeous," Anny replied with such disarming frankness that he blinked.

"Thanks," he said a little wryly. But he found her admiration oddly pleasing. It wasn't as if he hadn't heard the sentiment before, but knowing a cool, self-possessed woman like Anny had been attracted kicked the activity level of his formerly dormant hormones up another notch.

He shifted in his chair. "Tell me about something besides the poster. Tell me how you met your fiancé?" He didn't really want to know that, but it seemed like a good idea to ask, remind his hormones of the reality of the situation.

The waiter set salads in front of them. Demetrios picked up his fork.

"I've known him all my life," Anny said.

"The boy next door?"

"Not quite. But, well, sort of."

"Helps if you know someone well." God knew it would have helped if he'd known more about what made Lissa tick. It would have sent him running in the other direction. But how could he have when she was so good at playing a role? "You know him, at least."

"Yes." This time her smile didn't seem to reach her eyes. She focused on her salad, not offering any more so Demetrios changed the subject.

"Tell me about these cave paintings. How much more work do you have to do on your dissertation?"

She was more forthcoming about that. She talked at length about her work and her eyes lit up then. Ditto when he got her talking about the clinic and the children.

He found her enthusiasm contagious, and when she asked him about the film he'd brought to Cannes, he shared some of his own enthusiasm.

She was a good listener. She asked good questions. Even better, she knew what not to ask. She said nothing at all about the two plus years he'd stayed out of the public eye. Nothing about his marriage. Nothing about Lissa's death.

Only when he brought up not having come to Cannes for a couple of years did she say simply, "I was sorry to hear about your wife."

"Thank you."

They got through the salad, their entrées—the moussaka was remarkably good and reminiscent of his mother's—and then, because Anny looked a second or so too long at the apple tart, and because he really didn't want the evening to end yet, he suggested they share a piece with their coffee.

"Just a bite for me," she agreed. "I eat far too much of it whenever I come here."

Demetrios liked that she had enjoyed her meal. He liked that she wasn't rail-thin and boney the way Lissa had been, the way so many actresses felt they needed to be. She hadn't picked at her food the way they did. She looked healthy and appealing—just right, in his estimation—with definite hints of curves beneath her tailored jacket, scoop-necked top and linen skirt.

The hormones were definitely awake.

The waiter brought the apple tart and two forks. And

Demetrios was almost annoyed to discover he wasn't going to be able to feed her a bite off his. *Almost*.

Then sanity reared its head. He got a grip, pushed the plate toward her. "After you."

She cut off a small piece and carried it to her mouth, then shut her eyes and sighed. "That is simply heaven." She ran her tongue lightly over her lips, and opened her eyes again.

"Taste it," she urged him.

His hormones heard, *Taste me*. He cleared his throat and focused on the tart.

It was good. He did his best to savor it appreciatively, aware of her eyes on him, watching him as he chewed and swallowed.

"Your turn."

She shook her head. "One bite. That's it."

"It's heaven," he reminded her.

"I've had my taste for tonight." She set down her fork and put her hands in her lap. "Truly. Please, finish it."

He took his time, not just to savor the tart but the evening as well. It was the first time he'd been out on anything remotely resembling a date since Lissa. Not that this was precisely a date. He wasn't doing dates—not ones that led anywhere except bed now that his hormones were awake and kicking.

Still he was enjoying himself. This was a step back into the normal world he'd left three years before, made easier because of the woman Anny was…comfortable, poised, appealing. He liked her ease and her calmness at the same time he felt a renegade impulse to ruffle that calm.

The notion brought him up short. Where the hell had *that* come from?

He forked the last bite into his mouth and washed it down with a quick swallow of coffee.

Anny shook her head in gentle sadness. "You weren't treating it like heaven just then."

He wiped his mouth on the napkin, then dropped it on the table. "I realized I was making you wait. It's nearly midnight," he said, surprised at how the time had flown.

"Maybe I will turn into a pumpkin." She didn't smile when she said it.

He did. "Can I watch?"

"Prince Charming is always long gone when that happens, remember?"

He remembered. And he remembered, too, that however enjoyable it had been, unlike the Cinderella story, it wasn't going anywhere. He didn't want it to. She didn't want it to. That was probably what made it so damn enjoyable.

"Ready to go?"

She nodded. She looked remote now, a little pensive.

He paid the bill, told the waiter what a great meal it was, and was bemused when the waiter barely looked at him, but had a smile for Anny. "We are so happy to have you come tonight, your— You're always welcome." He even kissed her hand.

Outside she stopped and offered that same hand to him. "Thank you. For the dinner. For coming to the clinic. For everything. It was a memorable evening."

He took her hand, but he shook his head. "I'm not leaving you on a street corner."

"My flat's not far. You don't need—"

"I'm walking you home. To your door." In case she had any other ideas. "So lead on."

He could have let go of her hand then. He didn't. He kept her fingers firmly wrapped in his as he walked beside her through the narrow streets.

In the distance he could still hear traffic moving along La Croisette. There was music from bars, an occasional motorcycle. Next to him, Anny walked in silence, her fingers warm in his palm. She didn't speak at all, and that, in itself, was a lovely novelty. Every girl he'd ever been with, from Jenny Sorensen in ninth grade to Lissa, had talked his ear off all the way to the door.

Anny didn't say a thing until she stopped in front of an old stuccoed four-story apartment building with tall shuttered French doors that opened onto narrow wrought-iron railed balconies.

"Here we are." She slipped out a key, opened the big door.

He expected she would tell him he could leave then, but she must have understood he meant the door to her own flat, because she led the way through a small spare open area to a staircase that climbed steeply up the center of the building. She pressed a light switch to illuminate the stairs and, without glancing his way, started up them.

Demetrios stayed a step behind her until they arrived at the door to her flat. She unlocked hers, then turned to offer him a smile and her hand.

"My door," she said with a smile. Then, "Thank you," she added simply. "It's been lovely."

"It has." And he meant it. It was quite honestly the loveliest night he'd had in years. "I lucked out when I commandeered you at the Ritz."

"So did I." Her eyes were luminous, like deep blue pools.

They stared at each other. The moment lingered. So did they.

Demetrios knew exactly what he should do: give her hand a polite shake, then let go of it and say goodbye. Or maybe give her a kiss. After all, he'd greeted her with a kiss before he even knew who she was.

But now he did know. She was a sweet, kind, warm young woman—who was engaged to someone else. The last sort of woman he should be lusting after.

But even knowing it, he leaned in and touched his lips to hers.

Just a taste. What the hell was wrong with a taste? He wasn't going to do anything about it.

Just…taste.

And this one couldn't be like the first time he'd kissed her. That had been for show—all determination and possession and public display.

Or like the second when he'd left her on the street corner with her phone buzzing in her hand. One quick defiant kiss because he couldn't help himself.

This time he could certainly help himself. But he didn't, because he wanted it.

He wanted to taste her. Savor her. Remember her.

And so slowly and deliberately he took Anny's lips with his.

She tasted of wine and apple and a sweetness that could only be Anny herself. He savored it more than he'd savored the tart. Couldn't seem to stop himself, like a parched man after years in the desert given the clearest most refreshing water in the world.

He would have stopped if she'd resisted, if she'd put her hands against his chest and pushed him away.

But she put her hands against his chest and hung on—clutched his shirt as if she would never let go.

He didn't know which of them was more surprised. Or which of them stepped back first.

His hormones were having a field day. After so long asleep, they were definitely wide-awake and raring to go.

Demetrios tried to ignore them, but he couldn't quite ignore the hammer of his heart against the wall of his chest, or keep his voice steady as he said, "Good night, Anny Chamion."

For a moment she just looked stunned. She barely managed a smile as she swallowed and said, "Good night."

There was another silence. Then he tipped her chin up with a single finger, and leaned down to give her one last light chaste kiss on the lips—the proper farewell kiss he should have given her moments ago.

"I owe you," he said.

She blinked. "What?"

"You rescued me, remember?"

She shook her head. "You fed me dinner. You went to see Franck."

And you brought the first evening of joy into my life in the last three years. Of course he didn't say that. He only repeated, "I owe you, Anny Chamion. If there's ever anything I can do for you, just ask."

She stared at him mutely.

He reached in his pocket and pulled out a business card, then scrawled his private number on it, tucking it into her hand. "Whatever you need. Whenever. You only have to ask. Okay?"

She nodded, her eyes wide and almighty enticing. She had no idea.

"Good night," he said firmly, deliberately—as much to convince his hormones as to say farewell to her. But he waited for her to go inside and shut the door. Only when she had did he turn and walk toward the stairs.

He had just reached them when the door jerked open behind him.

"Demetrios?" she called his name softly.

He stiffened, then turned. "What?"

He waited as she came toward him until she stood bare inches away, close enough that he could again catch the scent of the apple tart, of a faint hint of citrus shampoo.

Her eyes were wide as she looked up at him. "Anything?"

"What?" He blinked, confused.

"You said you'd do anything?"

He nodded. "Yes."

She wetted her lips. "Whatever I ask?"

"Yes," he said firmly.

"Make love with me."

CHAPTER THREE

SHE COULDN'T BELIEVE she'd said the words. Not out loud.

Thought them, yes. Wished they would come true, absolutely. But ask a man—this man!—to make love with her?

No! She couldn't have.

But one look at his face told her that, in fact, she had. Oh, dear God. She desperately wanted to recall the request. Her face burned. Her brain—provided she had one, which seemed unlikely given what she'd just done—was likely going up in smoke.

What on earth had possessed her?

Some demon no doubt. Certainly it wasn't the spirit of generations of Mont Chamion royalty. They were doubtless spinning in their graves.

"I'm sorry. I didn't mean—" She had always thought people who fanned themselves were silly and pretentious. Now she understood the impulse. She started to back away.

But Demetrios caught her hand. "You didn't mean…?" Those green eyes bored into hers.

She tried to pull away. He let go, but his gaze still held her. "I…never should have said it." She wanted to say she didn't mean it, but that wasn't true, so she didn't say that.

"You're getting married," he said quietly.

She swallowed, then nodded once, a jerky nod. "Yes."

"And you'd have meaningless sex with me before you do?"

That stung, but she shook her head. "It wouldn't be meaningless. Not to me."

"Why? Because you had my poster on your wall? Because I'm some damned movie star and you think I'd be a nice notch on your bedpost?" He really was furious.

"No! It—it isn't about you," she said, trying to find the words to express the feeling that had been growing inside her all evening long. "Not really."

"No?" He looked sceptical, then challenged her. "Okay. So tell me then, what is it about?"

She took a breath. "It's what you made me remember."

His jaw set. "What's that?" He leaned back against the wall, apparently prepared to hear her out right there.

She sighed. "It's…complicated. And I—I can't stand here in the hallway and explain. My neighbors don't expect to be disturbed at this time of night."

"Then invite me in."

Which, she realized, was pretty much what she'd already done. She shrugged, then turned and led the way back down the hall and into Tante Isabelle's apartment. She nodded toward the overstuffed sofa and waved a hand toward it. "Sit down. Can I get you some coffee?"

"I don't think either of us wants coffee, Anny," he said gruffly.

"No." That was certainly true. She wanted him. Even now. Even more. Watching him prowling around Tante Isabelle's flat like some sort of panther didn't turn off her desire. In fact it only seemed to make him more appealing. She had plenty of experience dealing with heads of state, but none dealing with panthers or men who resembled them. It was a relief when he finally crossed the room and sat on the sofa.

She didn't dare take a seat on the sofa near him. Instead she went to the leather armchair nearest to the balcony, sat down and bent her head for just a moment. She wasn't sure she was praying for divine guidance, but some certainly wouldn't go amiss right now. When she lifted her gaze and met his again, she knew that the only defense she had was the truth.

"I am not marrying for love," she said baldly.

If she'd expected him to be shocked or to protest, she got her own shock at his reply.

He shrugged. "Love is highly overrated." His tone was harsh, almost bitter.

Now it was her turn to stare. This from the man whose wedding had been touted as the love match of the year? "But you—"

He cut her off abruptly. "This is not about me, remember?"

"No. You're right. I'm the one who—who suggested...*asked*," she corrected herself, needing to face her foolishness as squarely as she could. "I was just...remembering the girl I used to be." She studied her hands, then looked up again. "I was thinking about when I was in college and I had hopes and dreams and wonderful idealistic notions." She paused and leaned forward, needing him at least to understand that much. "Today when I saw you, I remembered that girl. And tonight, well, it was as if she was here again. As if I were her. You brought it all back to me!"

She felt like an idiot saying it, and frankly she expected him to laugh in her face. But he didn't. He didn't say anything at all for a long moment. His expression was completely inscrutable. And then he said slowly, almost carefully, "You were trying to find your idealistic youth?"

He didn't sound as if he thought she was foolish. He actually seemed intrigued.

Hesitantly, Anny nodded. "Yes. And then, when you said you'd do anything..." Her voice trailed off. It sounded unutterably foolish now, what she'd wanted. "I thought of those dreams and how they were gone. And I just...wanted to touch them one more time. Before—before..." She stopped, shrugging. "It sounds stupid now. I didn't mean to put you on the spot. But it was like some fairy tale—this night—and..." She felt her face warm again "I just wished—" She spread her hands helplessly.

He was the one who leaned forward now, resting his elbows just above his knees, his fingers loosely laced as he looked at her. "So why are you marrying him?"

"There are...reasons." She could explain them, but that would mean explaining who she was, and she'd ruined enough of her fairy-tale evening without destroying it completely. She didn't want Demetrios thinking of her as some spoiled princess who couldn't have her own way. For just one night she wanted to be a woman in her own right. Not her father's daughter. Not a princess.

Just Anny.

Even if she looked like an idiot, she'd be herself.

"Good reasons?"

She nodded slowly.

"But not love?" His tone twisted the word so that it still didn't sound as if he believed in it.

But Anny did.

"Maybe it will come," she said hopefully. "Maybe I haven't given him enough of a chance. He's quite a bit older than I am. A widower. His first wife died. He—he loved her."

"Better and better," Demetrios said grimly.

"That's another of the reasons I asked," she admitted. "I just thought that if I had this one night…with you…then if he never did love me, if it was always just a 'business arrangement' at least I'd…have had this. It's just one night. No strings. No obligations. I wasn't expecting anything else," she added, desperate to re-assure him.

He was silent and again she had no idea what he was thinking. And he didn't tell her. There was nothing but silence between them.

Seconds. Minutes. Probably not aeons, but it felt that way. Millions of years of mortification. What had been a magical night had become, through her own fault, the worst night of her life.

Outside she heard the muffled sound of a car passing in the street below and, nearby, the ticking of Tante Isabelle's ornate French Empire brass-and-ebony mantel clock. Finally she heard him draw in a slow careful breath.

"All right, Anny Chamion," he said, getting to his feet and crossing the room to hold out his hand to her. "Let's do it."

She stared.

At his outstretched hand. Then her gaze slid up his arm to his broad chest, to his whisker-shadowed jaw, to that gorgeous mouth, to the memorable groove in his cheek, to those amazing green eyes, dark and slumberous now, and more compelling than ever. She swallowed.

"Unless you've changed your mind," he said when she didn't speak or even more. He looked at her, waiting patiently, and she knew he expected that she would have changed it.

But she couldn't.

Faced with a lifetime of duty, of responsibility, of a likely loveless marriage, she desperately needed something more. Something that would sustain her, make her remember the passion, the intensity, the joy she'd believed in as a girl.

She needed something to hang on to, her own secret.

And his.

She reached up and took Demetrios's hand. Then she stood and walked straight into his arms. "I haven't changed my mind."

When she slid into his embrace, Demetrios felt a shock run through him.

It was like the sudden bliss of diving into the water after a burning hot day.

It was pure and right and beautiful.

He could almost feel his body reawaken, as his eyes opened to Anny's upturned face as she lifted her lips to his.

He took what she offered. Gently at first. With a tentativeness that reminded him of his first fumbling teenage kisses. As if he'd forgotten how.

He knew he hadn't. He knew he'd been burned so badly by Lissa that he'd learned to equate kisses with betrayal.

But this wasn't Lissa. These lips weren't practiced.

These lips were as tentative as his own. Even more hesitant. Infinitely gentle. Sweet.

And Demetrios drank of their sweetness. He took his time, settling in, soaking up the sensations, remembering what it was like to kiss with hope, with joy, with something almost akin to innocence.

That was what they were giving each other tonight—a

reminder of who they had been. Not to each other, but as a young man and a young woman with dreams, ideals, hopes.

He didn't have hopes like those anymore. Lissa had well and truly ground those into the dust. But right now, kissing Anny, he could remember what it had felt like to be young, hopeful, aware of possibilities.

It was as powerful and intoxicating a feeling as any he could recall.

So why not enjoy it?

Why not celebrate the simple pleasure of one night with this woman who tasted of apple tart and sunshine, of citrus and red wine, and of something heady and slightly spicy—something Demetrios had never tasted before.

What was it? He wanted to know.

So he deepened the kiss, trying to discover more, trying to capture whatever was tantalizing him. He touched his tongue to hers and a second later felt the swirl of hers touching his.

At its touch his whole body responded with an urgency that surprised him. He might have deliberately forgotten these things, but his body hadn't.

It knew precisely what it wanted.

It wanted Anny. Now.

But as much as he was willing to take her to bed, he resisted his body's urgent demands to simply have his way with her right then and there.

Granted, this was going to be a one-off. But it wasn't a sleazy one-night stand, a quick mindless exercise in sexual gratification.

She wanted it for reasons of her own. And Demetrios, understanding them, decided she had a point. Yes, he was older and wiser now. But he could still appreciate the hopeful young man he'd once been. There was something satisfying about paying tribute to that man.

But it wasn't just about the past. It was about the present—the woman in his arms and making it beautiful for her as well. If he was going to be her memory, by God, he wanted to be a good one.

So he drew a deep breath and told himself to take his time as he let his hands slide slowly up her arms and over her back as he molded her to him.

She was warm and soft and womanly—and wearing far too many clothes. Demetrios couldn't ever remember seducing a woman who had been wearing so many clothes. Anny was still wearing her jacket, for heaven's sake.

Of course, he wasn't actually seducing her. He was enjoying what had been offered, and giving pleasure—and memories—in return.

In doing so, Demetrios discovered how much pleasure there was in removing all those clothes. First he eased her jacket off, slowly peeling it off her shoulders and down her arms, then tossed it aside. His fingers eased themselves beneath the hem of her silk top and brushed her even silkier skin.

He caressed it with his fingers as he kissed his way down to nuzzle her neck. He traced the line of her bra beneath, brushed his fingers over her nipples, and smiled at the quick intake of her breath and the way her fingers clutched at his back.

He drew back to share the smile with her. She stared up at him, her lips parted in a small O that made him bend his head and touch his lips to hers.

This time her tongue was there first, tasting, teasing. And he felt his body quicken in response. The last thing he wanted now was to go slow. He wanted to rip their clothes off and plunge into her as fast and furiously as he could.

He couldn't. He wouldn't. But he wanted to do more than kiss her. Soon.

"Have you got a bed somewhere, Anny Chamion?" he murmured against her lips.

She smiled as her tongue lingered against his lips for a second longer before she took his hand in hers. "Right this way."

In all her years as a princess Anny had never identified with Cinderella.

That made sense, of course, because Cindy hadn't been a princess in the beginning. She'd become one by taking a risk—

daring to do what she wasn't supposed to do—not for a happy ending, but for the joy of one single beautiful night.

And that Anny could identify with completely.

She, too, wanted a single beautiful night. A night that she could remember forever—a night that would get her through, not the endless drudgery of Cinderella's pre-prince future or even the endless succession of royal duties and obligations that were hers, but a passionless, loveless marriage.

Oh, she supposed there was a tiny chance that Gerard might come to love her the way he had loved Ofelia. But the instant Anny allowed its theoretical possibility, she knew that in truth it was never going to happen.

If Gerard had been going to fall in love with her, he would have done so before now. He'd had years, literally, to do it. As had she. It wasn't going to happen.

But Gerard had at least known love. Anny hadn't.

And she wanted to. Once. Just once. She wasn't asking for forever. Only for tonight—with Demetrios Savas.

Making love with him wouldn't be the deep abiding love that Gerard had shared with Ofelia. Anny knew that. Besides good conversation and dinner, she and Demetrios had shared nothing at all.

But she had memories of him that their meeting today brought back to life. Ever since he'd swept her out of the hotel this afternoon, she'd felt the same sort of heady enchantment she had known from the years when everything had seemed possible.

When he'd asked what on earth she was thinking, she had told him the truth. She wanted to recapture the young woman she'd been—just for this night—and give her a taste of the joy she'd longed for. And the young Demetrios she hadn't really known, but had only dreamed of, had been part of that young woman's life.

All she could think was that today, when he'd walked into the Ritz, kissed her and swept her out again, it was as if God or serendipity or fate or—who knew what?—had dropped him into her life for a reason.

This reason, she thought as she lay back on her bed and took hold of his hands and drew him down beside her.

That Anny wasn't a practiced lover was pretty much the understatement of the year. Her spine usually stiffened whenever Gerard slipped an arm around her or pressed a kiss to her cheek or lips. But now, when Demetrios kissed her, she felt as if she had no bones at all.

His lips were warm and firm and eager. And so were hers.

His had followed his fingers, kissing her shoulders, as he'd peeled off her jacket on the way to the bedroom. Now those same fingers slid beneath her silk top and his lips followed again, right up to the edge of her lacy bra.

He drew her top up and over her head with the skill of a man who knew exactly how to undress a woman. And for a brief moment Anny thought about all the beautiful women he must have known intimately—women far more practiced and appealing than she was.

And yet he didn't seem distracted by those memories. He was focused only on her. He made Anny feel as if she were the only woman in the world.

Demetrios's eyes, so green in the light, were dark now in the shadows. The skin seemed taut across his cheekbones. And Anny thought she felt a faint tremor in his fingers as they skimmed across her ribs, then pulled her up against him while he deftly unfastened her bra and drew it off.

He knelt on the bed beside her and pressed kisses along the line of her bare shoulders, then moved lower to her breasts, cupping them in his hands, and kissing them. The feel of his mouth on her heated flesh was more erotic than anything Anny had ever experienced. She clutched at his arms, hung on.

His hair tickled her nose as he nuzzled her. It smelled of the sea and of pine, and Anny drew a deep breath, as if she could capture the scent and save it forever. The memory would be more tangible that way.

And then he was kissing his way down the valley between her breasts all the way to her waistband. Only when his fingers sought the fastening, she caught her breath, then shook her head.

He pulled back, his brow furrowed, his hair tousled. "No?"

Anny wanted to smooth his brow. "Yes," she assured him.

"But…I don't want to be the only one undressed." She gave him a hopeful look, at the same time wondering if she was stepping out of bounds. She knew all the royal protocol in the world, and not a bit about whether she should be asking to take an active role in undressing the man she was in bed with. Maybe she should have been busy with his buttons already.

Demetrios's mouth quirked briefly and she wondered if he would tell her so, but he didn't. He just smiled and settled back on his heels, then dropped his hands to rest on his thighs. "Be my guest."

Anny swallowed. Then she levered herself up to sit against the headboard of the bed. She felt awkward as she reached out to touch him, but her hands didn't. They knew precisely what to do, taking hold of the buttons of his shirt, undoing them one by one, exposing his bare chest to her gaze.

And as she parted his shirt, the tips of her fingers brushed against the wiry curling hair that arrowed down from his chest to the waistband of his jeans.

Demetrios's jaw tightened as he watched her every move, breathing shallowly, his eyes hooded, his body totally still, as if he were steeling himself to endure some sort of pain.

"Are you all right?" she asked him worriedly.

He gave a hoarse laugh. "Oh, yeah. More than all right." Then abruptly he shrugged his shirt off, tossed it aside, took her hands and pressed them against his chest.

His skin was hot and damp and she could feel his heart thundering beneath her palm. Instinctively Anny leaned forward and touched her lips to his chest. Kissed him there, loved the feel of his heated flesh beneath her lips. She moved higher, kissed his collarbone, then his shoulders. She kissed his neck, nuzzled against his stubbled jawline, nibbled his ear, then traced it with her tongue and felt him shudder.

His response made her smile with a heady sense of power and excitement as she understood that he wanted her every bit as much as she wanted him.

And then he was bearing her back on the bed, where he made quick work of the zip on her linen trousers, hooked his thumbs in the waistband, skimmed them down her legs and dropped them onto the floor.

She should have felt self-conscious when he settled back to let his eyes roam over her. But all she felt was desire. And need.

Anny reached for his belt eagerly, but her hands weren't expert now and she fumbled with it.

Demetrios stilled her fingers. "Let me." He had it undone and was skinning out of his jeans in a matter of seconds. And then he was settling between her knees, running his hands up her thighs. Anny stroked his, too.

Demetrios tried to take it slow. He understood that she wasn't in the habit of propositioning men. Her touch was tentative, but no less tantalizing for being so.

The truth was that her unpracticed touch was more erotic than anything he'd felt in years. Of course, Lissa had been a skilled lover. But knowing she'd got her skills from sleeping with dozens of men was something he'd done his best to blot out of his mind.

Anny's touch was nothing like Lissa's. As her fingers skimmed over his body, he felt as if she were learning him and reawakening him at the same time.

It was almost like being reborn.

After the drama and trauma of his life with Lissa, he'd deliberately and determinedly shut off that part of himself. He'd refused to touch. Refused to feel.

Until tonight. Now, tonight, with her warm smiles, her gentle demeanor and soft touch, not to mention a certain artless allure that he doubted she was even aware of, Anny had unwittingly opened that door.

She made him feel again. Need again. Ache with desire in a way he hadn't since he was barely more than a boy. Both of them were connecting with their youthful selves tonight, Demetrios thought as he ran his hands over the line of her ribs, the slight swell of her hip, her long, lovely thigh to her knee, then slowly traced a line up the inside of that same thigh.

She quivered. So did he.

She lifted a hand and drew her fingers lightly down his

chest. Lower. And as she did, the heel of her hand brushed against his erection, a simple unintentional touch nearly sending him over the edge.

His breath hissed between his teeth. "Careful," he said, his voice shaky. "I'm a little overeager tonight. It's been a long time."

Her eyes widened. She looked stricken. "Oh! Oh, I'm sorry," she said, putting the meaning he hadn't said into the words he had. She started to sit up, to pull away. "I didn't mean—I should never have—"

But he caught her and held her right where she was. "It's fine," he assured her. "More than fine," he added truthfully. "I'm…looking forward to it."

And there was an understatement for you.

But Anny didn't look convinced. "I never thought—"

He shook his head. "Now's not the time to think."

He tugged her panties down her endless legs, then stripped his boxers off as well. Her gaze went at once to his erection. She swallowed, then reached out a hand to stroke him.

"Wait. Hang on." He was gritting his teeth as he reached down to snag his jeans and pull a condom packet from his wallet. With clumsy fingers he sheathed himself quickly, then settled between her thighs.

He wanted to simply dive in, to lose himself in her heat and her softness. But he knew better, knew that as much as he wanted this, really it was for her. And so he forced himself to slow down, to draw a line from her navel south, dipping his fingers between her thighs, watching as her eyes widened and her breath caught in her throat.

She was damp, ready. Her body moved restlessly as his fingers probed her. She bit her lip and her fingers knotted in the bed clothes. Her breaths were quick and shallow. His were, too. He was dying with need, but still he waited, touched. Stroked.

And then suddenly Anny ground her teeth and reached for him. "Yes! Now. I need—" The words caught in her throat. She tossed her head.

"What do you need?" Demetrios could barely get his own words past his lips. His voice was as strained an desperate as his body felt.

"Need…you!"

No more than he needed her. He'd reached the end of his endurance, and now he drove into her, felt her stiffen, heard her gasp.

His whole body froze. She couldn't be! Surely she wasn't a virgin! For God's sake! Why on earth would she have thrown her virginity away on one night with him?

It didn't make sense. He couldn't think. He could only feel. And want. Still. Then she shifted her body, accommodated him, settled against the mattress and dug her heels into his buttocks, driving him deeper.

He groaned. He had to be wrong. Of course he was wrong. But he tried to move slowly, carefully, to control his desperation.

But Anny's fingers gripped his shoulders. "It's all right," Anny said fiercely through her teeth. "It's all right," she said again when he still didn't move.

"You're sure? You're not— I thought you were—" But then she moved beneath him, her body seducing him, driving him insane, shattering the last of his control.

His world splintered as he buried himself inside her. He knew he had left her behind. He had failed.

"Oh!" There was a sudden delighted breathlessness in her voice that made Demetrios lift his head to stare at her.

"Oh?" he echoed warily.

Her face seemed to light up. "It was…wonderful." She was smiling at him. Even in the dim glow of the streetlamp beyond the window he could see her beaming. He didn't understand it at all.

"It wasn't wonderful," he told her abruptly.

Her smile vanished. "I'm sorry. I thought you…"

"I did. Obviously. And it was amazing for me," he assured her. "Absolutely." Mind-blowing in fact. "But that doesn't excuse my lack of control."

She smiled and touched a hand to his arm. "I…liked your…lack of control."

He stared at her. She liked it? He gave a quick disbelieving shake of his head. "I don't see why," he muttered.

"Because…because…" But she couldn't explain it. It was

simply enough to know that he'd wanted her, had lost himself in her. "You made me happy," she told him.

"Yeah?" He still couldn't quite fathom that. "I'll make you happier," he vowed.

And he set about doing just that.

If their first lovemaking had been short and, for him, desperate, this time Demetrios had considerably more finesse. More control. He kissed her thoroughly, taking his time, enjoying the soft sounds she made as he roused her desire. He let her slip the condom on him this time, and tried not to shudder with the desire her soft hands provoked.

She was perfect, fresh, beautiful, and responsive. And Demetrios was determined to give her the memories she'd asked him for.

As he made love to her he thought about the young woman she must have been then, and found himself wishing that he'd known her. At the same time he didn't imagine she'd changed much. There was an innocent sweetness about her even now. He didn't let himself think about the future she had predicted for herself. That was her choice—her life—not anything to do with him.

What he could do for her was what she'd asked—give her a night to remember.

He loved her completely, thoroughly, made her need his touch so that finally she clutched at his hips and drew him in.

"Yes." The word hissed through her teeth as she shattered around him. And as he brought her to climax, he understood her satisfaction at his own earlier loss of control.

It meant as much—even more—to give pleasure as to receive it, he thought even as his own climax overtook him and he buried himself in her body and felt himself wrapped in her arms.

Making love with Demetrios was everything Anny had ever dreamed of. More. It was as perfect as Cinderella's night at the ball.

She wanted to cry and at the same time she'd never felt happier—or more bereft—in her life because it was so wonderful and she knew it couldn't last.

Had always known, she reminded herself. Had gone into it with her eyes wide open. It was what she'd wanted, after all.

Memories.

Well, now she had them. In spades. She would remember this night always. Would savor it a thousand times. A million. All her life and the eternity that stretched beyond it. She would never forget.

Even now as she lay beneath Demetrios's sweat-slicked body and ran her still trembling hands down his smooth hard back, she focused on every single sensation, storing up the sound of his breathing, the weight of his body pressing on hers. She memorized the feel of his hair-roughened calves beneath her toes, the scent of the sea that seemed inexplicably so much a part of him, the scrape of his jaw against her cheek.

She catalogued them all, wishing she could create some tangible reminders to take out whenever she wanted to relive these moments. She was in no hurry at all to have him roll off her, create a space between them, smile down at her and say he had to go.

And when at last his breathing slowed and he rolled off, she felt an instant sense of loss. She wanted to clutch him back, to cling, to beg for more.

She didn't. He had given her what she asked for. He had given her the most memorable night of her life. Anny told herself not to be greedy, but to be grateful. And content.

"Thank you," she said quietly.

He seemed surprised. He raised up on one elbow and regarded her from beneath hooded lids. His mouth quirked at one corner. "I think I'm the one who should be saying thank you." For all that he smiled, his words were grave.

Still, they made her happy. She was glad he'd enjoyed their lovemaking. She didn't expect he would hang on to the memories forever as she would, but she hoped he might have occasional fleeting fond thoughts of this night—of her.

"You gave me wonderful memories," she assured him.

He opened his mouth, as if he might say something. But then he closed it again and simply nodded. "Good."

He didn't move. Neither did she. They stared at each other. Under Demetrios's gaze, for the first time Anny felt self-conscious. None of the royal protocol she'd ever learned—not even her year in the Swiss finishing school—had prepared her for the proper way to end this encounter.

Perhaps because it hadn't been proper in the least.

But she didn't regret it. She would never regret it.

"I should go," Demetrios said.

She didn't hang on to him. She stayed where she was in the bed, but she watched his every move as he dressed. This night was all she was going to have—she didn't want to so much as blink.

He didn't look at her or speak until he had finished dressing and was slipping on his shoes. Then his gaze lifted and his eyes met hers.

"You…should maybe rethink this marriage you're planning," he said.

She didn't answer. Didn't want to spoil the present by thinking about the future. Silently she got out of bed and wrapped herself in the dressing gown she'd left hanging over the chair. Then she crossed the room to him and took his hands in hers.

"Thank you," she said again, refusing to even acknowledge his comment. He opened his mouth as if he would say something else, then shut it firmly and shook his head. His gaze was steely as he met hers.

"It's your life," he said at last.

Anny nodded, made herself smile. "Yes."

She didn't say anything else. She needed him to go while she still had the composure she'd promised herself she would hang on to. It was only one night, she told herself.

It wasn't, she assured herself, as if she was in love with him.

That would teach him, Demetrios thought when he got back to his hotel. He flung himself over onto his back and stared at the hotel room ceiling. Though what he'd learned this evening he wasn't exactly sure.

Probably that women were the most confusing difficult contrary people on earth.

He should have known that already, having been married to Lissa. But Anny had seemed totally different. Sane, for one thing.

And yet all the while they'd been sitting there and he'd been thinking she was simply enjoying dinner and his company and having a good time she'd been thinking about inviting him into her bed.

It boggled the mind.

Still, when she explained, he'd understood. God knew sometimes over the past three years he'd yearned for the days when he'd believed all things were possible.

He didn't believe it anymore, of course. He wasn't looking for a relationship again. He'd done that with Lissa. He'd been the poster boy for idealism in those days—and look where it had got him.

No more. Never again.

From here on out he wanted nothing more than casual encounters. No hopes. No dreams. No promises of happily ever after.

Exactly what he'd had tonight with Anny.

Who was getting married, for God's sake! Talk about mind-boggling. But he supposed she was more of a realist than he had been. Though why the hell a beautiful, intelligent young woman was marrying some elderly widower was beyond him.

And why was the elderly widower marrying her?

Stupid question. Why wouldn't any man—who still believed in marriage—want to marry a bright fresh beautiful woman like Anny?

But if he had been the marrying kind and engaged to her, Demetrios knew damned well he wouldn't leave her feeling luke-warm and desperate enough to invite another man into her bed!

He was sure she didn't do that very often. Or ever.

For a minute there, when he'd entered her, he'd thought she was a virgin. But that didn't make sense.

He wished he knew what was going on.

Was her family destitute? Did they owe money to this man? Was Anny being bartered for their debts?

It certainly didn't look as if they had money worries from the apartment she was living in. Of course she'd told him at dinner that she was staying in the flat of her late mother's best friend, Anny's own godmother, a woman she called Tante Isabelle. While Isabelle was in Hong Kong doing something for a bank, she'd lent Anny her apartment for the year.

So why wasn't Tante Isabelle, who obviously cared enough for Anny to provide her a place to live, objecting to her god-daughter's loveless marriage?

Did she even know it was a loveless marriage?

Where was Anny's father? He was still living, Demetrios knew that. Anny had mentioned him in the present tense. He was married again. She'd mentioned a stepmother and three little stepbrothers.

Was she doing it for them?

Whatever the "good reasons" were, she didn't seem to be doing it for herself. So who was she doing it for? And why?

Stop it! he commanded himself roughly. It wasn't his problem. *She* wasn't his problem.

He'd done his part. He'd taken her to bed. He'd made love with her and had, presumably, reminded her of the idealistic girl she'd been. He'd given her the memories she wanted.

He had a few himself. Not that he intended to bring them out and remember them. And yet, when he attempted to shut them away, they wouldn't go. He could still see her in his mind's eye—bright-eyed and laughing, gentle and serene, eager and responsive.

They were far better memories than those he had of Lissa.

They should have relaxed him, settled him. His body was sated. It was his mind that wouldn't stop replaying the evening.

He tossed and turned until eventually the bed couldn't confine his restlessness. He got up to prowl the room, to open the floor-to-ceiling window that opened overlooking La Croisette and the sea.

To the west he could see the shape of the Palais du Festival beyond the boulevard. Past that was the harbor where Theo was on his sailboat. Beyond that the hill and buildings of Le Soquet rose against the still dark sky.

Anny was there.

He could be, too, he thought. He was sure she would have let him stay the night.

But he didn't want to stay the night, he reminded himself. He wanted brief encounters. No involvement. He shoved away from the window and shut it firmly.

He wasn't going to care about any woman ever again. Not even sunny, smiling Anny Chamion with her upcoming loveless marriage, her hidden dreams and her memories of the lovemaking they'd shared.

It was going on five. He had a breakfast meeting at eight with Rollo Mikkelsen, who was in charge of distribution for Starlight Studios. He needed to be sharp. He needed to have his wits about him. He didn't need to be thinking about Anny Chamion.

He yanked on a pair of running shorts and tugged a T-shirt over his head. Maybe running a few miles could do what nothing else had done.

He pocketed his room key and went downstairs into the cool Cannes morning. He crossed La Croisette and bounced on his toes a few times, then he set out at a light jog. The pavement was nearly deserted still. In a couple of hours it would start to get busy. The day would begin.

He would meet with Rollo. There would be more meetings after that. Lunch with a producer he hoped to work with down the road. And late this afternoon the screening.

Afterward he'd go see Franck. He was tempted to see if Franck wanted to come to the screening, but it wasn't an action hero story. It was a dark piece—the only sort of thing he had been capable of writing in the aftermath of his marriage and circumstances of Lissa's death. It was a cautionary tale.

Not exactly fodder for a teenager who still had his life ahead of him. No. Better that he go see Franck after.

Would Anny be there?

It didn't matter if she was.

Demetrios picked up his pace, refusing to let himself think about that. He didn't care. They'd had one evening. One night of loving. One night in which they'd each recaptured a part of the young idealistic people they'd once been.

They'd given that to each other. But now it was over.

Time to move on.

CHAPTER FOUR

ANNY DIDN'T SEE Demetrios again.

She didn't really expect she would.

But as she went about her business, as she walked to the clinic, did her grocery shopping, worked on her dissertation, and actually went to a screening or two at the Palais du Festival over the next ten days, she couldn't help keeping an eye out to see if she could spot the tall dark-haired man who had so startlingly swept into her life.

He had gone back to the clinic. She knew that because Franck had been full of the information. And he hadn't only come the next day as he'd promised, but also several times over the past week and a half.

Yesterday, Franck had told her gleefully this afternoon, he had commandeered a wheelchair and taken Franck down to the dock.

"A wheelchair? You went to the dock?" Anny, who had never been able to get Franck to go anywhere because he was too self-conscious, could barely believe her ears. "Whatever for?"

"We went sailing."

Then she really did gape.

Franck nodded eagerly. "We went in his brother's sailboat."

He recounted his amazing day, his eyes shining as he told her how Demetrios and his brother Theo—"a racing sailor," Franck reported—had simply lifted him out of the wheelchair and into the boat, then set out for a sail around the Îles de Lérins.

Anny was still stuck imagining Franck allowing himself to

be lifted, but apparently, as far as Franck was concerned, Demetrios and his brother could do anything. "Didn't he tell you?" Franck demanded.

Anny shook her head. "I haven't seen him."

He looked surprised. "You should have come in the mornings. He always came then."

Of course he did. Because he knew when she went to see Franck. She'd told him. If Demetrios had wanted to see her, he could have. He knew where she lived.

He hadn't. And she hadn't sought him out, either.

She'd had her night. She'd relived it ever since.

Of course she couldn't deny having wished it had lasted longer—even wishing it had had a future. But she knew it didn't.

So it was better that she not encounter him again. So even though she had kept an eye out for him over the following week and a half, she'd carefully avoided attending any parties to which he might have gone.

Of course, she knew he'd come to Cannes to work, not to party. But she also knew that sometimes going to parties *was* part of the work. Some years it had even been part of her own. Fortunately her father had decided not to host one this year.

And now the festival was over. Demetrios, she was sure, was already gone. He'd got what he came for. News stories early this week had reported that he'd landed a big distributor for the film he'd brought to Cannes. And yesterday she'd read that he'd found backing for his next project.

She was happy for him. She almost wished she had seen him again to tell him so. But what good would that have done, really?

It would only have been embarrassing. He might even have believed she was stalking him.

No. She'd already had her own personal fairy tale with Demetrios Savas. One night of lovemaking.

That was enough.

But when Gerard had called her that afternoon and announced, "We will be hosting a party on the royal yacht this evening," she wasn't quite as sanguine as she'd hoped.

She'd told herself that she would go to her fate gracefully and willingly. He was a good man. A kind man.

But the truth was, she'd barely given him a thought since the night she'd had dinner with Demetrios.

Now she felt oddly cold and disconnected as she repeated, "We?" Did he meant the royal "we" or "the two of them"?

"My government," Gerard clarified briskly. "The party was planned to occur whether I was here or not. We hoped to attract film companies, you know. The revenues are an excellent boost to the economy."

"Yes, of course." Her father believed that, too.

"And since I've finished my work in Toronto, I'm able to be here. And it will be a wonderful opportunity for us to host it together." He sounded delighted.

Anny wasn't certain. "Are you sure I should host it with you?" she asked. "I mean, we're not married." As if he needed reminding.

"Not yet," Gerard agreed. "But soon. That is something we need to discuss, Adriana."

"What is?"

"The date of our wedding."

"I thought we agreed we'd wait until after I finished my doctorate."

"Yes, but we can make plans. It will not be an elopement, you know."

"Of course not. But there will be time—"

"Yes," Gerard said cheerfully. "Tonight. After the party."

"But—"

"So, no, you will not be my official hostess," he went on, "but we have waited long enough. I've missed you, Adriana."

"I've—" Anny swallowed "—missed you, too."

He heard the hesitation in her voice. "You are upset that I wasn't here last week."

"No. I—"

"I'm sorry I couldn't be," he explained to her. "Duty called. It often does," he added wryly. "You understand. Better than anyone, you understand."

"Yes."

"But I am here now. And I'm looking forward to seeing you tonight. I will be there for you at eight." He rang off before she could object.

Object? Hardly. Gerard had the same ability to command that her father did. It came from a lifetime of expecting people to fall in with his plans. And even if he had stayed on the phone, what possible objection could she have made?

Of course he had sprung it on her at the last minute. But it wasn't as if she couldn't pull herself together, find a dress, be prepared to leave at eight.

Princesses were always prepared. It was part of their job description.

She just wished she felt more prepared to marry him.

"His Highness regrets that he is unable to come in person," the driver said respectfully as he bowed, then helped Anny into the back of the black sedan that had arrived outside her flat at precisely 8:00 p.m. "He is hosting a dinner meeting. He will be on the yacht when you arrive."

Anny tried to look regretful, too. But what she felt was relief. While she could make conversation with anyone anywhere, thinking about being alone with Gerard in the confines of the car had made her edgy for the past three hours.

He would be all that was proper and polite. And so would she. They would make small talk. Discuss the weather. His trip to Toronto. Her latest chapter notes on her dissertation.

Or their upcoming wedding.

She flashed a quick smile at the driver. "*C'est bien. Merci.*"

He shut the door, and immediately the silence enveloped her. Sometimes riding in cars like this suffocated her. She felt as if she were buffered from the real world, isolated, with the sounds and commotion beyond the doors held firmly at bay.

But right now, for a few minutes, she welcomed it. The short ride to the harbor would give her a chance to compose her thoughts, to prepare herself, to become the princess of Mont Chamion she would have to be this evening.

But as the car approached the harbor, she became distracted by the rows of yachts and sailboats, thinking about how Demetrios and his brother had brought Franck here. Now she scanned the multitude of boats as if, just by looking, she might be able to tell which one was Theo's.

Of course chances were very good Demetrios's brother was already gone. And it didn't matter anyway. The memories of her night with Demetrios had been intended for her to take out and savor, yes. But they weren't intended to distract her from the obligations at hand.

Now, though, even when she turned her gaze away from the harbor and stared resolutely straight ahead, it wasn't the driver she saw. In her mind's eye she still saw Demetrios making love with her.

"Go away," she muttered under her breath.

The driver glanced around at the sound of her voice and met her gaze in the rearview mirror. "I beg your pardon, Your Highness?"

"Nothing." Anny pressed her fingers to her temples, feeling a heachache coming on. "I was simply thinking aloud."

And she needed to stop. Now.

A small launch carried her to where the royal yacht lay at anchor. As they approached the yacht she could see tuxedo-clad staff scurrying around. She caught snatches of the lively sounds of live music. Maybe she and Gerard would dance. He would hold her in his arms and they would find love together. It had happened that way for Papa and Mama. Her father had assured her it was so. Their marriage had been arranged and it had been wonderful. It could happen.

Determinedly Anny lifted her chin and made herself smile at the prospect.

She even made a point of minding her royal manners and staying primly seated until the crew brought the launch alongside the yacht when she would have preferred to stand up and let the wind whip through her hair or, worse yet, be the one to throw the line and clamber aboard the way she always had on her father's smaller yacht when she was a child.

So she was definitely in princess mode when she heard Gerard say, "Ah, wonderful. Here you are at last."

He was waiting on deck and gave her his hand to help her aboard, then let his gaze travel in slow admiration down the length of her navy blue dress with its galaxies of scattered silver sequins for a long moment before he kissed her on both cheeks.

Then, to her surprise, he wrapped her in a gentle embrace. "It's so good to see you again, my dear."

He truly did look pleased.

He was a lovely man, Anny reminded herself guiltily. Kind. Gentle. Capable of love. He had after all, by all accounts, loved his first wife very very much.

"Gerard," she greeted him warmly, and smiled not only with her lips but her voice as well.

He linked his arm through hers and drew her onto the deck beside him. "I'm so sorry I wasn't able to come and get you in person. But I had a dinner meeting with Rollo Mikkelsen. Come. I want you to meet him. Rollo is the head of Starlight Studios. He's interested in possibly setting future projects in Val de Comesque."

Anny smiled. "What wonderful news."

"It is." Gerard opened the door to the main salon where a table had been set for perhaps ten people. The meal was over now and the dinner guests had left the table to chat in small groups. "Rollo." He drew Anny with him toward the nearest group of men. "I'd like you to meet my fiancée."

They all turned as Gerard slipped an arm around Anny's waist and said proudly, "Her Royal Highness, Princess Adriana of Mont Chamion, may I present Rollo Mikkelsen, head of Starlight Studios."

A man took her hand.

Anny didn't see him at all. He was nothing but a blur. Her heart pounded. She smiled perfunctorily, murmured politely, "Mr. Mikkelsen, a pleasure."

"And Daniel Guzman Alonso, the producer," Gerard said, introducing the next man.

Another blur. Another hand shook hers. Now her ears were ringing as well. Her voice worked, though, thank God. "Mr. Guzman Alonso, I'm delighted to meet you." Years of social deportment practice had something to recommend it, after all.

"And of course you must recognize Demetrios Savas," Gerard was saying jovially, "whose latest film Rollo has just agreed to distribute."

Demetrios was not a blur at all. Sharp and clear, tall and imposing. And, judging from the hard jade glare in those amazing eyes, somewhere between stunned and furious. His gaze raked her accusingly.

Anny could barely breathe. Nor could she stop her own eyes from fastening on him, hungrily, devouring him. Wanting him again so badly that how she could ever have thought one night would be enough, she hadn't a clue.

"Mr. Savas." She held out her hand to him, polite, proper, sounding—she hoped—perfectly composed.

Demetrios crushed it in his. "Your Highness," he said through his teeth. "Imagine meeting you here."

A princess?

Anny Chamion was a *princess*?

She was the "delightful fiancée Princess Adriana" that Gerard had mentioned over dinner?

His fiancée would be joining them later, the crown prince of Val de Comesque had said. She was busy with her day job—unspecified—and since he hadn't given her any warning, he'd only asked her to come to the party, not appear for dinner.

"Even we royals have to work hard these days," he'd joked. "You will meet her tonight."

Now here she was, with Gerard's arm around her, looking serene and elegant and every bit as royal as the man she was marrying.

Which made Gerard her "elderly widower"?

Demetrios's teeth came together with a snap. Maybe she hadn't used the term "elderly," but that was what he'd thought.

The slim fingers he was crushing between his were trying unsuccessfully to ease out of his grasp. For a moment he didn't even realize he was still gripping them.

Then, still staring into Anny's—no, *Princess* Adriana's— wide eyes, he dropped them abruptly, took a step back and shoved his hands into his pockets.

It was probably some sort of social solecism, to have his hands in his pockets in front of a princess, but short of strangling her, he could think of nothing else to do with them.

Besides, as far as social gaffes went, it was no doubt a bigger one to have slept with her!

He shot her a glare. He doubted she noticed. She wasn't looking at him. She was smiling at Rollo Mikkelsen, answering a question he'd asked her, her voice low and melodious, steady and completely at ease—just as if she were not standing between the man she was going to marry and the man she'd taken to her bed!

And he'd thought Lissa was a lying cheat!

Abruptly he said, "Excuse me. I see someone I need to speak to." And he turned and walked out of the room as fast as he could.

It was no bigger lie than hers. And almost at once he did see someone he knew. Mona Tremayne was standing on deck by herself, looking at the sunset, and even if it meant listening to her extol the virtues of her darling starlet daughter Rhiannon, he was determined to do it.

It was better than standing there listening to the lying *Princess* Adriana charm all and sundry while her fiancé looked on!

Mona was delighted to see him. She kissed him on both cheeks, then patted his arm. "It's lovely to see you, dear boy. I'm glad you're back among the living."

Demetrios took a careful breath and tried to focus solely on her. "It wasn't that bad," he told her. He liked Mona, always had. She called a spade a spade, and she couldn't help it if her daughter was a ditz.

"Maybe not for you. But we can't afford to let talent go to waste," she said with a throaty laugh caused by too many years of cigarettes. "You do good work. You've been missed."

"Thanks." His heart was still pounding, but he refused to look back toward the salon. He didn't gave a damn where the princess was. He slanted Mona a grin. "Does that mean I can toss an idea at you?"

"You want to marry my daughter?" Another wonderful husky Mona Tremayne laugh.

Demetrios managed a laugh of his own as he shook his head. "I'm through with marriage, Mona." Truer words had never been spoken.

"I'm not surprised," Mona said briskly, her eyes telling him that she knew more than he had said. Then she smiled and added, "Well, if you ever change your mind, you've got a fan in my household. More than one."

Demetrios smiled, too. "Thanks."

She leaned against the railing and stared out across the water before slanting him a sideways glance. "So toss me the idea," she suggested. "I'm listening."

It was the sort of chance he'd been waiting for all week. Mona at his disposal, her daughter nowhere to be found. And he did have an idea for her. He tried to pitch it.

He'd have done better if, a few minutes later, he hadn't been instantly distracted by the sound of Anny's voice nearby and the knowledge that she and Gerard had come out onto the deck.

He lost his train of thought as he glanced over his shoulder to see where she was. His fingers strangled the railing because he still wanted to grab her and shake her and demand to know why the hell she hadn't bothered to tell him who she really was. Not to mention what she thought she'd been doing inviting him into her bed!

He was still steaming. Still furious.

And not paying any attention at all to whatever Mona was saying in reply to his movie pitch.

"—think I'll jump overboard," Mona ended conversationally and looked at him brightly.

In the silence Demetrios recollected himself and tried to get a grip. "Huh?"

"Oh, my dear." Mona patted his cheek. "We should talk another time—when you can focus."

"I'm focusing," he insisted.

But only, it seemed, on Anny. He couldn't seem to make sense of anything beyond her soft voice somewhere behind him, followed by the melodious sound of her laughter. Then he heard Gerard, too, chiming in, speaking rapidly in French to whoever they were talking to, and then Anny switched to French as well. Their conversation went too quickly for him to have any idea what they were saying.

She sounded happy, though. Was she happy? What about her loveless marriage?

"But if I drowned, I couldn't be in your film then, could I?" Mona was saying.

He stared at her blankly.

She laughed, again. "Never mind, dear." She gave him air kisses and began to move away. "Another time. I think I'll find another drink."

"I'll get you a drink," he said hastily.

"No, dear boy. I'm fine. You stay here and entertain royalty." And giving his cheek one more pat, she swept away.

He turned to protest again—and came face-to-face with Anny.

Her wide eyes were searching his face. Her smile, so polished earlier, looked slightly more strained now. "Demetrios."

He drew himself up straight. "Your Highness," he said stiffly.

"Anny," she corrected, her voice soft, the way it had been in bed.

He ground his teeth. "I don't think so." His voice was, he hoped, pure steel. He braced his back and elbows against the railing, and glared down at her.

"Anny," she insisted. "It's who I am."

"Certainly not all of who you are," he reminded her sharply. "You could have told me." He looked around for Gerard, expecting him to appear at her side. But her prince had moved away and on the other side of the deck, deep in conversation with Rollo and another studio executive Demetrios knew.

"I could have," she admitted. "I didn't want to. Why should I?" Her tone was indifferent, as if it could make her idiocy appear perfectly reasonable.

"Because I might have liked to know?" he snapped.

No one was close to them. The sextet had begun to play. A clarinet was warbling. Thank God, because this wasn't a conversation anyone should be overhearing.

"I asked you to tell me what I should know about you," he reminded her.

"You didn't need to know that."

"You asked me to sleep with you!"

Color flared in her cheeks. She glanced around quickly as if fearing people would hear.

A corner of his mouth twisted. "Something else you don't want anyone to know? Afraid your elderly widower will learn what you were up to?"

"My what?" She looked confused.

"Your fiancé," he bit out. "The man who is oh-so old and decrepit and who doesn't love you."

"I never said he was elderly or decrepit. Gerard is twenty-one years older than I am," she said through her teeth. "Which may not seem like much to you, but it is a different generation."

He grunted, acknowledging that. But it didn't explain the rest. "So why are you marrying him? Daddy forcing you? Are you making a governmental alliance?" He spat the words.

"Something like that."

He snorted. "Give me a break. This is the twenty-first century!"

"It can still happen," she maintained.

"You're saying your old man sold you off to the highest bidder?"

"Of course not! It was simply…arranged. It's good for both countries."

"Countries? That's what matters? Not people?"

She lifted her chin. "Gerard is a fine man."

"Whom you betrayed by sleeping with me," he pointed out sardonically.

She opened her mouth as if she would deny it, but then she

closed it again, her lips pressing into a thin line. The color was high in her cheeks. She looked indignant, furious, and incredibly beautiful.

"Obviously I made a mistake," she said tightly, hugging her arms across her chest. "I was out of line. I never should have suggested anything of the sort. It was…" She stopped, her voice not so much trailing off as dropping abruptly.

"What was it?" Demetrios asked her, trying to fathom what was going on in that beautiful head of hers.

She shook it. "Nothing. Never mind. Forget it."

"Will you?" he asked her.

"Yes." The word came out quickly. Then her gaze dropped. So did her voice. "No."

At her soft yet stark admission, his own eyes jerked up to search her face, to try to understand her. Once he'd caught on to Lissa's duplicitous behavior, he began to have an inkling what she was up to, though God knew he'd had no idea how far she would go.

But Anny didn't sound like she was lying now. Not this time.

"Did it solve anything?" he pressed her.

She didn't answer. Finally, when he thought she wasn't going to reply at all, she shrugged. "I don't know." She wasn't looking at him now. She'd come to stand next to the railing, too, and now stared across the water toward the lights of Cannes. Her shoulders were slumped.

Demetrios was still angry, though whether he was more annoyed at her or at himself, he couldn't have said. After Lissa, he damned well should have known better. And what the hell was Anny doing, letting herself be a pawn?

It was none of his business, he reminded himself. He should turn and walk away. But his feet didn't take the hint. They stayed right where they were. Behind them the sextet had segued into something lilting and jazzy.

Anny didn't seem to notice. Her gaze never wavered from the shore.

"Fascinating, is it?" he demanded when she still didn't look at him.

"It's beautiful," she replied simply.

He grunted. "All lit up like a fairy tale," he said mockingly, keeping his eyes straight ahead.

"Some would say that," she agreed quietly.

"Not you?" He pressed her. The breeze lifted her hair. It smelled of citrus and the sea. He wanted to touch it, to brush it away from her face, hook it behind her ear, touch her cheek. Touch her.

He knotted his fingers together instead.

"I'm not a big believer in fairy tales," she said in a soft monotone.

"Except for one night," he reminded her harshly.

"I'm sorry. You could have said no," she pointed out.

His jaw tightened. "Should have said no," he corrected.

The breeze caught her hair again and tossed tendrils of it against his cheek. More citrus scent assailed his nostrils. Demetrios turned his head away, but just as quickly turned back to breathe in the scent again, to feel the softness touch his face.

She took a careful breath. "I want to thank you for going back to see Franck."

"No thanks necessary. I didn't do it for you," he said flatly.

"I know that. But even so, it means a great deal. To him," she added. "And taking him sailing." She turned her head to smile at him. "Brilliant. I can't believe you got him to do it. But he loved every minute."

Demetrios didn't want her thanks. He didn't want her smiles. He shrugged irritably. "I was glad to do it. He's a good kid. Smart. He's got a lot of potential."

"Yes." Anny smiled slightly. "I agree. I'm afraid he doesn't."

"He's angry. Given what happened to him, why shouldn't he be?" Demetrios remembered all the times in the past three years when his own anger had stopped him cold, threatening to derail his dreams. There were too many to count. Now he took a slow careful breath. "He'll find his way," he said. They continued to stare at the seafront in silence for a long moment, then he added, "He'll get there with some support from friends like you."

"And you," Anny added.

Demetrios shook his head. "I'm leaving. Bright and early tomorrow morning. I'm taking my brother's boat to Santorini."

"But you won't forget Franck." She sounded certain.

How could she know him well enough to be sure of that when he felt like she didn't know him at all? Demetrios didn't know. But he had to admit she was right in this case. "No, I won't forget him. I'll stay in touch."

She smiled, satisfied. "He'll like that." She stared down at the water, unspeaking for a long moment, but she didn't walk away.

Neither did he. He didn't feel as angry now. He couldn't have said why, except that this Anny, princess or not, was the one he remembered.

She brushed a lock of hair away from her face. "I thought you'd be gone by now. You got what you came for—excellent distribution, a highly acclaimed film."

"Rollo's taking it on, yes. And the critics have been kind."

"I'm sure it's not just kindness."

"You didn't see it?" Surely princesses could see whatever they wanted. Royal prerogative or some such thing.

"No. I—I wanted to. But I didn't want you to think—" She stopped.

"Think what?" he demanded.

She shrugged awkwardly. "That I was…chasing you. I meant what I said, one night. I told you the truth, Demetrios. I just…didn't tell you all of it." She had turned and was looking at him intently now, as if she were begging him to believe her.

Did he? Or was she as good an actress as Lissa?

It didn't matter, he reminded himself. Princess or not, she wasn't part of his life. Not after tonight.

But he couldn't stop himself saying, "Look, Anny. You can't do this if you're not sure. Gerard might be a great guy. But marriage is—" He let out a harsh breath, knowing he was the last person on earth who should be offering advice on marriage. But then, who knew better the mistakes you could make even when you thought you were marrying for love?

"Marriage is what?" she asked when he didn't go on.

"Marriage is too damned hard to risk on flimsy hopes!" He blurted the words angrily, not at her, but at Lissa.

Of course Anny didn't know that. She stared at him, eyes wide at his outburst.

Demetrios stared back. It was none of his business. *None of his business.* The words echoed over and over in his head.

"Adriana!" Gerard's voice behind them made them both start.

"I have to go," Anny said quickly.

Demetrios straightened up at once, and gave her a polite distant nod. "Of course."

But still she didn't move away. She faced him and looked into his eyes for a long moment, a slight smile on her face. "Thank you."

He raised a brow. "For the memories?" he said sardonically.

She nodded. Their gazes locked.

"Adriana!" Gerard's voice came again, more insistent this time.

Anny turned to go. Demetrios caught her hand and held her until she looked back at him. "Don't regret your life, princess."

Demetrios kept away from her the rest of the evening.

Of course he did. Why wouldn't he? He thought she'd used him and lied by omission. It hadn't felt like a lie. It had felt like being able—for once—to share herself, the woman, not the princess, that she really was.

But she didn't suppose Demetrios saw it that way. He was probably avoiding her. Or maybe he had forgotten her already. She was the one who had vowed to remember. And dear God, she was. Every single second Anny knew exactly where he was. She saw who he talked to, who talked to him.

As Gerard's unofficial hostess she was required to focus on other things, on all his guests. And no one could have faulted her attention to her role. She chatted with his guests, gave them what she hoped appeared to be her undivided attention—even when it was being shared with the tall, lean man with wind-blown hair talking to this producer or that actress.

Gerard kept her close, smiling at her and nodding his approval. "Your papa is right. You are marvelous," he told her.

Yes, Papa would be proud. But Anny's heart wasn't in it. Her soul wasn't in it. Only later that evening when, shortly before midnight, she saw Demetrios board the launch back to the harbor, did her heart and soul let her know where they were. A hollow desperate ache opened up inside her.

He wasn't for her. She knew that.

She repeated it over and over in her head even as she continued smiling brightly at the couple telling her about their South Pacific cruise. She nodded, commented, laughed at a witty remark and didn't miss a beat.

But she didn't miss the sight of Demetrios standing alone on the deck of the launch looking back at the yacht, either.

As soon as she could, she made her excuses and slipped away to stand in the bow of the royal yacht to catch a last glimpse of the launch as it grew smaller and smaller and finally merged with the lights of the harbor, and he was gone.

They were ships that passed in the night, she told herself. One night.

"Adriana!" Gerard's voice called to her once more.

She swallowed, then called, "*Je viens*. I'm coming."

She heard Demetrios's words echo in her mind. *Don't regret your life, princess.*

She prayed desperately that she wouldn't.

CHAPTER FIVE

DEMETRIOS WAS up at dawn.

He wanted an early start. He hadn't slept well. Not true. He hadn't slept at all. He'd gone to bed determined not to spare a thought for Her Royal Highness Princess Adriana.

And he couldn't get her out of his mind.

Of all the irritating demanding things that he'd anticipated having to cope with during these past two weeks in Cannes, dealing with a princess—or any woman at all, for that matter— had never made the list.

After Lissa, he couldn't imagine one breaching his defenses.

He'd allowed himself the one night with Anny because it had been clearly *one night*. No strings. No obligations. No relationship.

It still wasn't, he tried to tell himself. But until last night he'd managed to convince himself that she'd known what she was doing.

Now he didn't believe it for a minute. And he couldn't get her out of his head!

Fine, he'd get an early start. The sooner he set sail, the sooner he'd put Cannes—and Her Royal Highness—behind him.

He flung the last of his clothes into his bag and checked out of the small hotel where he'd spent the past two weeks. Then, hefting his duffel bag, he headed for the harbor. The morning was still and quiet, almost soundless so far. Few cars moved through the streets. A lone cyclist rode past him.

When he crossed La Croisette, there was a bit of traffic, a few pedestrians walked briskly on morning constitutionals, a couple of joggers ran by and he saw a man walking a dog. Cannes getting back to normal.

Demetrios wanted to get back to normal, too. He quickened his pace, eager to board the boat and be at sea at last.

Near the Palais du Festival, work crews were beginning to gather to take down the hospitality tents. He skirted them, heading for the dock where Theo had left his sailboat.

It was a magnificent boat—a bit over forty feet, sleek and trim, with two small cabin spaces fore and aft, and a main cabin that could sleep an extra kid or two if required. It was fast and fun and yet it could still accommodate Theo's new lifestyle as a married man with kids. He and Martha had two now—Edward, who was five, and Caroline, not quite three.

Demetrios had always figured himself for the family man, while Theo would always be the family's nautical equivalent of the Lone Ranger. That wasn't the way it had turned out.

"Lucky you," Demetrios had said, feeling a small stab of envy at Theo's life.

"Yeah." Theo hadn't misunderstood. "I hate taking the time to sail to Santorini with Martha and the kids there already. From here by myself it'll take me almost two weeks."

"Tell them to come here. Make a holiday of it."

Theo shook his head. "Caro's getting over croup. Martha worries. She's got commissions to work on. And Eddie gets seasick."

"Your son gets seasick?" Demetrios's mind boggled.

"He'll grow out of it. But we hate seeing him miserable. It isn't fun. And you know how it can blow this time of year."

They both had experienced their share of gale-force winds in the Mediterranean during frequent visits to Greece to see their mother's parents when they were children. "It's worse other times," he said truthfully.

Theo shrugged. "Fine. You do it."

Demetrios had thought he was joking.

"Never been more serious in my life. You want to sail her to Santorini after the festival, she's all yours."

Demetrios hadn't hesitated. "You bet."

The last time he'd sailed any great distance, it had been not long after his wedding. He'd chartered a sailboat so he and Lissa could sail from Los Angeles to Cabo.

"It'll be fantastic," he'd promised Lissa.

It had been a disaster—one of many in their short marriage.

But this trip wouldn't be. It wouldn't be a piece of cake to do it solo, but he had plenty of experience and, after Cannes, a real desire to be on his own. It was the carrot he'd held out for himself for the past two weeks, every time the festival threatened to drive him crazy.

Now he reached the dock and could spot Theo's boat tied up in a slip at the far end. A couple of men from the crew of one of the nearer yachts were already making ready to sail. They gave him a wave as he passed. He waved back, but kept moving,

The red-orange rays of sunrise were turning the gleaming hulls bright pink against still cerulean water. It looked like a painting.

Until someone stood up and moved away from where they had been sitting on the stern of the boat.

Demetrios stopped dead, disbelieving his eyes. He frowned, gave his head a shake, then came closer to be sure.

And she—he could tell it was a female, could even tell *which* female—came toward him, too. Even though she looked totally different.

Gone was the midnight blue dress that glittered like starlight when she moved. Gone were the diamond necklace and dangling diamond earrings. Gone was the sophisticated upswept hairstyle with its few escaping tendrils. There wasn't a hint of Princess Adriana in evidence anywhere.

Nor was there a hint of the classy competent professional woman he'd met that day at the Carlton. No blazer, no linen skirt, no casual dress shoes.

This Anny was wearing jeans and running shoes, a light-colored T-shirt with a sweatshirt knotted around her hips. And her hair was pulled back in a ponytail. Tendrils still escaped, but they made her look about fifteen.

Hell's bells, he thought. All the roles she played, she could give Lissa a run for her money!

"What are you doing here?" He was equal parts suspicion and annoyance. He was tempted to just brush right past.

"I came to say thank you."

His gaze narrowed. "For what? Sleeping with you? My pleasure." He made sure it didn't sound like it. "But don't come around thinking it's going to happen again."

"I know that," she said, with as much impatience in her voice as he had in his. "I didn't come for that."

"What then?

She hesitated a split second, then looked right up into his eyes. "For courage."

Demetrios didn't like the sound of that. He gave her a short, hard look, grunted what he hoped was a sort of "that's nice, now go away" sound. Then he did brush past her, tossing his duffel bag onto the deck and jumping on after it.

He heard her feet land on the deck barely a second after his. He spun around and confronted her squarely, stopping her in her tracks. "What do you think you're doing?"

"Telling you what happened."

He scowled at her. He supposed it was useless telling her he didn't want to know what happened. He folded his arms across his chest and leaned back against the rail. "So tell me."

"I…talked to Gerard last night. After the party. I told him I couldn't marry him."

Demetrios stared at her, aghast. Of course he'd seen her turmoil. But that didn't mean she needed to burn her bridges!

"Why?" he demanded harshly, suspiciously.

At his tone, her eyes widened. "You know why! Because I don't love him. Because he doesn't love me."

"So? You knew that last week. Hell, you probably knew it last year! Didn't stop you then."

"I know, but—"

But Demetrios didn't want to hear. He spun away, grabbing his duffel and tossing it into the cockpit. Then he straightened and kneaded tight muscles at the back of his neck, thinking furiously. Finally he turned to nail her with a glare.

"This doesn't have anything to do with me," he told her as flatly and uncompromisingly as possible.

"You gave me the courage."

Not what he wanted to hear. He said a rude word. "Don't be stupid."

"You told me not to regret my life."

"I didn't expect you to turn it upside down!"

"Maybe I'm turning it right side up," she suggested.

He raked fingers through his hair. He supposed he had said some damn stupid thing like that. Giving her the benefit of his own regrettable experience, no doubt. And she, foolishly, interpreted it as him having some common sense.

"So everyone left and you just walked up to him and said, 'Oh, by the way, Gerry, I can't marry you'?"

She looked taken aback at his tone, not understanding what the problem was. Of course she didn't understand—because the problem was his, not hers.

"I wasn't quite that blunt," she said at last. "It just… happened." She gave him a sort of sad reflective smile. "He'd said he wanted to discuss things between us—about the wedding. He wanted to set a date—a specific time. And—" she shook her head helplessly "—I couldn't do it."

He stared at her for a long moment. Then he said again, "Not because of me."

A tiny line appeared between her brows for a moment. And then she seemed to realize what he was getting at. "You mean, did I suddenly realize I'd rather have you?" She laughed. "I'm not that presumptuous."

"Good," he said gruffly, embarrassed at having made the leap at the same time he was relieved it had been in error.

"Well, good for you," he said finally, at length. What was he supposed to say? He gave her a quick approving nod, then climbed down into the cockpit, unlocked the door to the companionway and kicked his duffel down into the cabin.

"It is good," she said, her voice brighter now. "It was the right thing to do." Behind him Demetrios heard her take an expansive breath. "In fact, it feels wonderful."

He grunted. He supposed it must. Like dodging a bullet. The way he'd feel if he'd never married Lissa. He glanced up at her. "Congratulations."

She grinned. "Thank you."

He cocked his head, considering how simple it had been. Maybe too simple? "And Gerard was okay with your breaking it off?"

"Well, not exactly," she admitted. She shoved a tendril of hair that had escaped her ponytail away from her ear. "He said all brides have jitters. That I should think things over. Take some time. Get to know my own mind." She snorted—a ladylike snort. "I do know my own mind."

Did she? Demetrios doubted it. She'd agreed to marry Gerard, hadn't she? She must have thought it was a good idea at one point. And Gerard obviously expected her to come to her senses.

"And your father?" Demetrios demanded. "What did he say?" When she didn't answer at once, he narrowed his gaze. "You did tell him?"

Anny tossed her ponytail. "I sent him an e-mail."

Demetrios gaped. "You sent your father—*the king*—an e-mail?"

She shrugged, then squared her shoulders and lifted her chin defiantly. "He might be everyone else's king, but he's my father. And I didn't want to talk to him."

"I'll bet you didn't."

"He'll understand. He loves me."

No doubt he did. But he was also king of a country. A man who was used to ruling, commanding, telling everyone—especially his daughter—what to do. And he had told her to marry Gerard.

"He'll get used to it." But Demetrios thought Anny's words were more to convince herself, not him. "It will just take a little time. He might be…upset…at first, but—" another shrug "—that's why I'm leaving."

He looked up at her. "What do you mean, leaving?"

Anny turned and hopped back down onto the deck, and for

the first time Demetrios noticed the backpack and the suitcase sitting on the far side of the dock.

As he watched, she shouldered the pack, then picked up the suitcase. "I'm going away for a while."

He came to rest his elbows on the back of the cockpit and stare at her. "You're leaving Cannes?"

She nodded grimly. "Papa will be on my doorstep as soon as he gets the e-mail, finds his pilot, and fuels the jet. I don't intend to be here when he comes." She shrugged. "He will need time to come to terms. So I'm off. I just—" she smiled at him "—didn't want to leave without telling you, saying thank you."

Frankly, he thought she was carrying the etiquette a bit too far. And *You're welcome* didn't seem much of an answer. Whatever advice he'd given her had been based on his messed-up marriage and might have nothing to do with hers. What the hell had he thought he was doing?

"Maybe you should give it some time," he said now. "Don't be too hasty. Think for a while, like Gerard said. Then decide."

She stared at him as if he'd lost his mind. "I'm not being hasty. And I *have* thought! We've been engaged three years. First I wanted to finish grad school. Then I wanted to finish my dissertation." She paused, then met his gaze squarely. "I did decide, Demetrios. I think I decided—in my gut—a long time ago, which is why I kept putting it off. You're just the one who gave me the courage to say it."

They stared at each other until finally, abruptly, Anny stepped back and gave him a small salute. She smiled. "'Bye, Demetrios. Thanks for the courage." The smile broadened. "And the memories."

Then she squared her slender shoulders, shifted the backpack slightly, picked up the suitcase, and marched back up the dock toward La Croisette.

Demetrios stared after her, unmoving, while his brain whirled with fifty thousand sane reasons to turn around and start getting the boat ready to sail.

But not one of them was proof against the fear of what could happen to her if he did.

Damn it!

"Anny!" He vaulted out of the cockpit, then scrambled off the boat onto the dock. "Where are you going?"

A small figure halfway down the dock turned back. She shrugged. "I don't know yet."

She didn't sound as if it mattered.

Demetrios knew it did. His stomach clenched. Scowling now, annoyed that she could be so blasé about something that important, he stalked down the dock after her. "What do you mean, you don't know?"

He knew the hard edge to his voice made her eyes widen, but she didn't shrink away from him.

She simply set the suitcase down and faced him. "Exactly what I said. I haven't a clue. I just need to go somewhere Papa won't expect me to be. He'll look in all the places, the likely places," she allowed. "So I'll just go someplace else. It's not like I made plans, you know."

He knew. And he didn't like it one bit. She was a young woman alone. Kind, trusting. Not to mention rich—and a princess, besides. She'd be prey for more unsavory characters than he wanted to think about.

"I thought I might hitchhike," she said blithely in the face of his ominous silence.

"*Hitchhike!*" He spat the word, furious.

She burst out laughing. "I'm not going to hitchhike, Demetrios," she assured him. "I was joking. You looked so intense. I'll be fine. Don't get so worked up."

"I'm not worked up!" He was very calmly going to strangle her.

She was still smiling. "Right. Okay. You're not worked up." She gave him a sideways assessing look. Then she tried more reassurance. "You don't need to worry. You *are* worrying," she pointed out in case he hadn't noticed.

"Because you're acting like an idiot! You don't just pack up and head out at the drop of a hat. You need plans. A place to go. Bodyguards!"

She blinked. "Bodyguards?"

"You're a princess!"

"I haven't had a bodyguard since I left university. I'm perfectly capable of taking care of myself." She smiled again. It was a regal smile. It made Demetrios's teeth ache they were grinding together so hard.

"But thank you for your concern," she added, in that proper bloody well-brought-up royal tone of voice she could put on when she wanted to. Then, as if he were some mere peasant she'd just dismissed, she picked up the suitcase and started away again.

Demetrios muttered something unprintable under his breath, then stalked after her and grabbed her by the arm, hauling her to a stop. "Then you're coming with me."

Her head whipped around. She stared at him, eyes wide, mouth agape. "With you? To Greece?"

"Why not?" he demanded. "You don't have a plan of your own. You can't just wander around Europe. It's not safe."

"I'm not a fool, Demetrios. I went to Oxford by myself. I went to Berkeley!"

"With watchdogs," he reminded her.

"I was young then. Almost a child. I'm not a child now."

"No. You're a raving beauty and any man with hormones can see that!"

"I meant I'm not going to be anyone's prey."

"Right. You're big and strong and tough. That's why I practically kidnapped you right in the middle of a hotel lobby!"

"You did not!"

"I walked off with you!"

"Because I *let* you. I knew who you were. I could have screamed," she told him haughtily.

He snorted. "Everyone would have thought you were an overexcited fan."

"I can take care of myself. I don't get into cars with strangers. I don't make foolish decisions."

"Really?" He gave her a sardonic look. "You were going to marry Gerard. You propositioned me. You went to bed with me."

She glared at him. "Up until now, I didn't consider that a foolish decision."

"Think again." He dragged a hand through his hair. "Look. You're a damned appealing woman, princess. You swept me off my feet, didn't you?" he said.

She made a face at him. "I promise you, you were the one and only. Besides, I've got my memories now."

He didn't let himself think about that. "What if someone else wants a few of his own? If anything happens to you out in the big bad world, it will be my fault!"

"Don't be ridiculous. You have an outrageous sense of your own importance. What I do is my responsibility, not yours."

"But you owe it to me," he reminded her. "You said you did. That's what you came down here for—*to thank me*!"

Anny folded her arms across her breasts and glowered at him. "Obviously a mistake. So much for etiquette."

"Next time don't be so damn polite." He picked up her suitcase, then hung on determinedly as she tried to grab it out of his hand. "This is going to look great on all the paparazzi shots," he reminded her silkily.

Abruptly, she let go and glanced around, looking hunted, then annoyed. "There are no photographers!"

He shrugged, unrepentant. "There could be. You want them following you all over Europe? Bet Papa can ask them where you're hiding." He gave her a mocking look over his shoulder and kept walking.

For a long moment he was afraid she'd just let him go off with her suitcase while she went in the other direction. But finally he heard her footsteps coming after him.

"This is insane," she told him. "You don't want me with you."

"More than I want you dead in the gutter." He heard the explosion of breath that meant she was gearing up for another round, so he turned and forestalled her. "Look, blame it on my mother. It wouldn't matter if it was really my fault or not, I'd think it was. *She'd* think it was."

"You'd tell her?"

"I wouldn't have to. She'd know."

Malena Savas had eyes in the back of her head and she knew what all of her children were thinking before they ever thought it. Demetrios knew his mother had a far greater understanding of what he'd been through these past three years than he'd ever told her. Or ever would tell her. She understood at least a part of what he'd gone through—and she didn't blame him, which he considered a miracle.

But if he left Anny alone now, she'd have his head.

"She doesn't know about me," Anny protested.

"Not yet."

Anny muttered under her breath. He just kept walking. Every step took them closer to the boat.

"I suppose it will be safer for you if I come along," she said at last.

"Safer?"

"The boat will be easier to sail if there are two of us. Although I'm sure you could do it on your own."

"I could. But, you're right," he added. If that convinced her, who was he to argue?

"Still, you said you wanted solitude," she reminded him.

"Maybe you won't talk all the time," he retorted in exasperation.

She smirked. "And maybe I will."

"Then I'll put you off on Elba."

"Like Napoleon?" Her lips twitched.

"Exactly." Their gazes met. Locked. Dueled.

"Napoleon escaped," Anny said loftily.

"You won't."

"How do you know?"

"When I leave you, I'll tell your father where you are."

They were joking. But they weren't joking at the same time. He meant it—and he could tell from the look on her face that Anny knew it. Stalemate.

At long last she let out a sigh. "You're serious, aren't you? You're going to stand here and argue with me for as long as it takes."

"Not that long. I might just throw you over my shoulder and dump you in the boat."

"You wouldn't."

"Want to try me?" He gave her his best Luke St. Angier hard-ass hero look.

She narrowed her gaze at him, then she said finally, "If I come, you won't think it's because I want to go to bed with you again?"

"What?" He stared at her.

"Because I don't want you thinking I'm stalking you."

"Wouldn't matter if you did," he told her flatly. "I'm immune."

"Yes, I could tell," she said drily.

He scowled. "I didn't say I didn't enjoy sex with a beautiful woman. I said, I don't want anything more than that."

That made her blink. "Ever?"

"Never." No compromise there.

Anny cocked her head and studied him carefully, as if her scrutiny might detect cracks in his armor. He could have told her there were no cracks. Not after Lissa.

He didn't. But he stood firm and unyielding under her gaze.

"You shouldn't say 'never' like that," she told him, her tone gentle, as if she intended to comfort him. "Never is a long time and you might meet someone you love as much. Differently," she added quickly. "But as much."

Demetrios stared, jolted. But he didn't correct her misunderstanding. She only knew what the press had printed, after all. She'd got the story of their marriage that Lissa had wanted read. And after Lissa's death, he'd had nothing to gain from airing their private problems.

Saying something wouldn't change things now, either. So he just waited, let her think what she liked.

"What *about* sex?" she said abruptly

His mouth fell open. He couldn't help it. "What?"

"I'm not asking you for sex," she assured him quickly. "I just want to know what's expected."

So do I, Demetrios felt like saying because God's own truth was, if he lived to be a hundred, he doubted he would be able to predict the next words out of Princess Adriana's mouth.

"It's up to you, princess," he told her gruffly. "I can't say I didn't enjoy it. I can't say I'm not willing. But I'm not falling in love with you. So don't get your hopes up."

Color flared in her cheeks. "As if!"

He grinned, then shrugged. "Just saying. You brought it up. Fine. If this is going to work, we need some plain speaking. I'm telling you right now I'm not getting involved. I'm bringing you along to keep you safe. Period."

"Whether I like it or not," she said in a mocking tone of her own.

"Whether you like it or not," he agreed. "As for sex—" he shrugged "—I have no expectations. Whatever happens on board, princess, is entirely up to you."

She blinked. Then she seemed to consider that. Her brow actually furrowed and she thought about it for long enough that Demetrios had time to wonder what the hell she could possibly be thinking.

But then she smiled, nodded and stuck out her hand. "Deal."

Out of the frying pan.

Into the fire.

Her life was turning into one big cliché.

Anny knew she should have said no. She should have turned and walked away and kept right on walking.

More to the point, she should never have come down to the harbor to find Demetrios in the first place.

She had because…because, she forced herself to admit, he was the only one she knew who would understand. He was, as she'd told him, the one who had given her the courage to do it.

He and Franck.

But she could hardly talk to Franck about this. She was supposed to be his support, not the other way around. She hadn't been expecting support, per se, from Demetrios, either. Well, nothing beyond a "good for you," which in fact he'd given her.

That was all she was hoping for. *All*! She had definitely not expected Demetrios to insist that she come with him.

She ventured a glance at him now as he prepared to leave the harbor. He was paying her no attention at all. He was stowing gear and checking charts and going over things that Anny knew were important and knew equally well she would be in the way of if she tried to help.

So she kept out of the way and waited until he gave her directions. She was by no means a solo sailor. But she'd been on boats since she was a child. And while Mont Chamion's royal yacht had a very competent crew, she had taken orders from her father when he and she and her mother had gone sailing. She was sure she could help Demetrios here.

That wasn't going to be the problem.

She wasn't a fool, Anny had been at pains to assure him. But what else could you call a woman who went from a three-year engagement to a man she didn't love to a two-week solo boat trip with a man who would never love her?

Not, Anny assured herself, that she was in love with him.

But she wasn't indifferent to him.

She…liked him. Had once had a crush on him. He had, as she'd told him in somewhat vague terms, been the dream of her youth.

And even now she respected him for his career. She admired him for coming back from the devastating personal tragedy that had been his wife's death. She certainly esteemed him for his kindness to Franck over the past couple of weeks, and—let's be honest—for his generosity to her. In and out of bed.

But she didn't love him. Not yet.

Not ever, Anny told herself sharply.

She was, despite what her dutiful engagement to Gerard might say about her, basically a sensible woman. She didn't dare fate or walk in front of buses.

Now she considered herself warned. It was more than a little humbling to hear him spell out his indifference in such blunt terms. As if there were no way on earth he might ever fall in love with the likes of her.

Fine. So be it.

Right now she was looking for a respite—some peace and quiet and a chance to learn the desires of her own heart.

So she would take what he offered: two weeks of solitude

during which her father would never be able to find her. Two weeks to formulate plans that would allow her to make her own way in her adult life.

Yes, marriage, she was sure, would be a part of it. But not marriage to Gerard. Despite his suggestion that she take some time and reconsider, Anny knew she'd made the right decision. She only regretted that it had taken her so long to come to her senses and realize she needed more than duty and responsibility to get her to the altar.

She'd suspected it, of course. But it had taken her night with Demetrios to show her that passion, too, had to play a part.

The passion, the desire, hadn't dissipated since that night.

How she was going to handle that for the next two weeks, she wasn't sure. Had he meant it when he said it was up to her?

Demetrios started the engine. The boat's motor made the deck vibrate beneath Anny's feet.

"Hey, princess, cast off." Demetrios was at the wheel, but he jerked his head toward the line still wrapped around the cleat at the stern.

Anny clambered off, unwound the line, and jumped back aboard.

He throttled the engine ahead. The boat began to move slowly out of the slip. Anny felt the cool morning breeze in her face, smelled the sea, felt a heady excitement that was so much better than the dread with which she'd awakened every morning for too long.

She knew how Franck had felt when he'd gone sailing—alive.

But she knew, too, that it was a risk.

Spending two weeks alone on a sailboat with Demetrios Savas could be the closest thing to heaven, or—if she fell in love with him—to hell that Anny could imagine.

CHAPTER SIX

MALENA SAVAS, Demetrios's mother, was fond of crisp character assessments of her children. Theo, the eldest, was "the loner," George, the physicist, was "the smart one." Yiannis was "our little naturalist" because he was forever bringing home snakes and owls with broken wings. Tallie was, of course, "baby girl."

And Demetrios, her gregarious, charming middle child?

"Impulsive," his mother would say fondly. "Kindhearted, honorable. But, dear me, yes, Demetrios tends to leap before he looks."

Apparently that hadn't changed, the middle child in question thought irritably now as he edged the boat out of the slip and headed her toward the open sea. You'd have thought that by the age of thirty-two he'd have got over it. His marriage to Lissa should have cured him of impetuosity once and for all.

But no. He'd actually gone after Anny—*Princess* Adriana—and insisted she spend the next two weeks on a damn sailboat alone with him!

What the hell had he been thinking?

Exactly what he'd told her—that sweet and kind and innocent, she was far too trusting to be let out on her own. And that it was his fault.

Not the sweet and kind and trusting bit—that was Anny. But the "out on her own bit" he felt responsible for. Hell, she'd *thanked* him for making it possible!

So he'd opened his mouth—and now here she was, standing

in the cockpit waiting for him to tell her what to do. She was smiling, looking absolutely glorious in the early morning light, the light breeze tangling her hair. He remembered its softness when his own fingers had tangled in it.

They'd happily tangle in it again. And more. But fool that he was, while he'd insisted she be on his boat for two weeks, he'd left the sleeping arrangements up to her!

Refusing to think about it, Demetrios concentrated on getting the boat out into open water. He tried not to look at her at all. But if he so much as turned his head, there she was.

"Maybe you should take your stuff below," he said, "in case anyone does recognize you while we're still in the harbor." Barely a creature was stirring on the docks or on any of the boats. But all it took was one nosy person… "I'll call you when I need your help with the sail."

She smiled. "Thanks." And picking up her suitcase, she started to carry it down the companionway steps. They were too steep. He started to offer to help, but Anny simply dropped it down the steps with a thud. Then she and her backpack disappeared after it.

Well, she was resourceful. He would give her that. And he breathed easier when she was below. It was almost possible—for a few seconds at a time—to pretend that he was still alone on the voyage.

But then as he moved beyond the harbor, he spotted the royal yacht of Val de Comesque on its mooring. And as he motored slowly past it, Demetrios could see the crew were already up and stirring.

Was Gerard up, too? Was he prowling the decks worrying about Anny?

Or did he simply think she'd gone home, gone to bed and would come to her senses in short order?

According to Anny, he'd said for her to think about it. Obviously he was confident she'd change her mind. She had sounded confident she would not.

But was that true or mere momentary bravado?

Demetrios wasn't surprised she'd balked. But he didn't

share her confidence when it came to being sure she wouldn't change her mind.

It was one thing to say you weren't going to marry a powerful wealthy, admittedly kind man like Prince Gerard and another thing to hold fast to the notion.

Maybe she really did just need time to think, to be sure.

Sure, yes? Or sure, no?

Not his problem, Demetrios told himself firmly. He believed she was right to take the time and consider her options. God knew he should have taken a couple of weeks to think about what he was doing when he'd married Lissa!

He might have come to his senses. Something else he wasn't going to think about. Too late now.

He drew a deep breath of fresh sea air and shut Lissa out of his mind. She was the past. He had a future ahead of him.

He had a new screenplay to work on. And two weeks of sea time to ponder it.

And, heaven help him, Anny.

"Anny!" He shouted her name now that they were well past the royal yacht.

Instantly she appeared in the companionway, looking at him expectantly.

"Still want to help?"

"Of course." She scrambled up into the cockpit.

He nodded at the wheel. "Steer this course while I hoist the sail."

Her eyes widened in surprise. "Steer?" She looked surprised, then delighted, stepping up to put her hands on the wheel. Her face was wreathed with a smile.

"You do know what you're doing?" he said a little warily.

"I think so," she said. "But usually no one wants me to do it. 'Can't let the princess get her hands dirty.' That sort of thing."

"For the next couple of weeks, you'll have dirty hands," he told her.

"Fine with me. I'm happy to help. Delighted," she said with emphasis. "I was just…surprised." She shot him a grin. "But thrilled."

Her grin was heart-stopping. Eager. Apparently genuine. It spoke of the sort of enthusiasm that he'd once dreamed Lissa would show toward their sailing trip to Mexico.

"Show me," she demanded.

So he showed her the course he was sailing and how to read it on the GPS. She asked questions, didn't yawn in his face and file her fingernails, and nodded when he was finished. "I can do that," she said confidently.

He hoped so. "Just keep an eye on the GPS," he told her, "and do what you need to do with the wheel. I can straighten it out if you have a problem."

"I won't," she swore.

He went forward to hoist the sail, pausing to shoot her a few quick apprehensive glances, hoping she really did know what she was doing.

She seemed to have no qualms about the task, keeping her eye on the GPS and her hand on the wheel. She had pulled on a visor of Theo's that hid most of her face from him, but as he watched, she tipped her head back and lifted her face so that the sun touched it. His breath caught at the sight.

Demetrios was accustomed to beautiful women. He'd worked with them, he'd directed them. He'd been married to one.

Flawless skin, good bones, perfect teeth all mattered. But facial features were only a part of real beauty. The superficial part. And Anny had them.

But more than that, she had a look of pure honest joy that lit her face from within. It was an uncommon beauty. *She* was an uncommon beauty.

She was also a princess who had just made a serious, life-changing decision if she decided it was the right one to make. She didn't know her own mind.

Demetrios knew his. However beautiful, sexy and appealing she was, he wasn't getting involved with her.

But he was already beginning to realize that unless Anny decided to share his bed it was going to be a very long two weeks.

* * *

Anny was exultant, loving every minute, beaming as the sun touched her face and the breeze whipped through her hair.

She felt free—blessedly unburdened by duty and responsibility for the moment at least. She had also forgotten how much she loved to get out on the water and really sail.

Her most recent experiences on boats had all been parties like the one on Gerard's yacht last night. They were so elegant and controlled that they might as well have been in hotel dining rooms. If she hadn't had to take the launch to get to the yacht and back, she would have forgotten she was even on a boat.

It certainly hadn't been going anywhere.

Now she was moving. The boat, once Demetrios had the mainsail and jib raised, was cutting through the water at a rate of knots, and Anny gripped the wheel, exhilarated. It was glorious.

When he dropped into the cockpit beside her she relinquished the wheel, but couldn't act as if it was no big deal.

"I feel alive!" she said over the wind in her ears. "Reborn!" And she arched her back, opened her arms wide and spun around and around, drinking in the experience. "Thank you! Thank you, thank you, thank you!"

He gave her a sceptical, wary look—one that reminded her of the way he'd looked at her the night she'd asked him to make love to her, that said he was seriously concerned that she'd lost her mind.

"Don't worry about me!" she said, beaming. "Truly!"

Demetrios still looked sceptical, but he didn't reply, just moved his gaze from the GPS to the horizon, then made adjustments as required.

Anny stood watching, drinking in the sight of him as eagerly as she did the whole experience. She'd seen him in a number of roles in films over the years. He'd done slick and sophisticated, hard-edged and dangerous, sexy and imbued with deadly charm. She'd seen him in a lot of places—big cities, high deserts, dense jungles, and bedrooms galore—but she'd never seen him at sea before.

It was a perfect fit. He looked competent in whatever role he played. But he wasn't playing a role now, and he seemed perfectly suited to the task.

"I didn't realize you were such a sailor," she said.

He shrugged, keeping his eyes on the horizon "Grew up sailing. We always have. It's bred in the bone, I guess." There was a slight defensive edge to his tone that surprised her.

She smiled. "I can see that," she said. "Lucky you."

Now he slanted a glance her way, his brows raised as if her comment surprised him. "It doesn't appeal to everyone. Some people find it boring."

It was her turn to be surprised at that. "I can't imagine," she said sincerely. "It seems liberating to me. Maybe it's because, being...who I am—" she could never bring herself to say "being a princess" "—when I was home as a child, I always felt hemmed in. But when my parents and I went sailing—even on one of the lakes—it was like we suddenly could be ourselves."

"Getting away from it all." He nodded.

"Yes. Exactly."

"I didn't think of it that way until I'd been 'famous'—" his mouth twisted on that word the way hers would have if she'd said "princess" "—for a while. But I know what you mean. I thought getting out and sailing was a way of getting back to who I was...." His voice rose slightly at the end of the statement as if he were going to say more. But he didn't. He just lifted his shoulders and looked away again.

"Did you have time to sail much?"

He shook his head. "Not often. Once." Something closed up in his expression. His jaw tightened. Then he fixed her with his green gaze. "Did you get everything sorted out below? Unpacked? Settled in? It's not a palace."

The change of subject was abrupt, as was the sudden rough edge to his tone. Anny wondered what caused it, and knew better than to ask.

"It's better than a palace," she told him sincerely. "I love it."

He grunted, not looking completely convinced.

"I took the back cabin—the aft cabin," she corrected herself. "It's a bit bigger, though, so if you want it, I'll be happy to switch. I just thought the forward cabin seemed more like it should be the captain's. Is that okay?"

"Fine. Whichever." He gave her a look that Anny couldn't interpret at all. Then he stared back at the horizon again, seeming lost in thoughts that had nothing to do with the situation at hand. Was he regretting having insisted she come along?

"I'll just go below for a while," she said. "If you need me again, shout."

Demetrios gave her a quick vague smile, but his mind still seemed far away. So she headed back down the companionway steps.

She had put her suitcase and laptop backpack in the aft cabin, but she hadn't unpacked them yet. Now she did, taking her time, settling in, discovering all the nooks and crannies that made living on board a boat so intriguing.

It was a gorgeous boat. Nothing like as opulent and huge as either the royal yacht of her country or of Gerard's, but it had a clean, compact elegance that made it appealing—and manageable. A good boat for a couple—or a young family like that of Demetrios's brother, Theo.

She felt a pang of envy not just for Theo's boat, but for his family. Some of her fondest early childhood memories were the afternoons spent sailing on the alpine lakes of Mont Chamion with her parents.

Now she found herself hoping that someday she and her own husband and children would do the same. Her mind, perversely but not unexpectedly, immediately cast Demetrios in the husband role. And there was wishful thinking for you, she thought.

She tried to ignore it, but her imagination was vivid and determined and would not be denied. So finally, she let it play on while she put things away.

Since she'd packed hastily in the middle of the night and had planned to escape Cannes by rail, she hadn't brought any of the right clothes. She'd assumed she would be losing herself in a big city like Paris or Barcelona or Madrid. So most of the things she'd brought were casual but sophisticated and dressy—linen and silk trousers, shell tops, jackets and skirts. Not your average everyday sailing attire.

The jeans and T-shirt she was wearing had been chosen so she could leave town looking like a student and not draw attention to herself. Unfortunately they were the only halfway suitable things she'd brought along, and in the heat of the Mediterranean summer she was nearly sweltering in them. She would need to go shopping soon.

She just hoped no one would recognize her when she did.

In the meantime she would cope. But somehow, for a woman who had spent her life learning what to do in every conceivable social situation, she had no very clear idea how to go on in this one.

Madame Lavoisier, one of her Swiss finishing school instructors, tapping her toe impatiently and repeating what she always called "Madame's rules of engagement."

"You are a guest," Madame would say. "So you must be all that is charming and polite. You may be helpful, but not intrusive. You must know how to put yourself forward when it is time to entertain, but step back—fade into the woodwork, if you will—when your hosts have other obligations. And you must never presume."

Those were the basics, anyway. You applied them to whatever situation presented itself.

And Anny could see the wisdom of it. But still it felt lacking now—because she didn't want to be a guest. She wanted to belong.

And how foolish was that?

Demetrios had told her clearly and emphatically that he wasn't interested in a relationship. He could not have made it plainer.

If she let herself get involved with him now, it would not be some fairy-tale night with a silver-screen hero. Nor would it be the adolescent fantasy of an idealistic teenager. It wouldn't have anything to do with duty and responsibility.

It would be a lifetime commitment of love to a real live flesh-and-blood man—a man who didn't want anything of the sort.

"So just have a nice two-week holiday and get on with your life," she told herself firmly.

She vowed she would. All she had to do was convince her heart.

* * *

About noon Anny brought him a sandwich and a beer.

"I figured you'd be getting hungry." She set the plate on the bench seat near where Demetrios stood, then went back down to return moments later with a sandwich of her own.

"I've been through the provisions," she told him. "Made a list of possible menus, and another of some things we should probably get when we go ashore."

He stared at her.

She finished chewing a bite of sandwich, then noticed the way he was looking at her, and said, "What? Did I overstep my bounds?"

He shook his head. "I'm just…surprised."

Anny didn't see why. "Maybe it was presumptuous," she went on after she'd swallowed, "but I'm a better cook than a sailor. And if I'm going to be here two weeks, I need to do my share. So I thought I'd do the meals."

"You cook?" That seemed to surprise him, too.

She flashed him a grin. "*Cordon Bleu,*" she told him, causing his brows to hike clear into the fringe of hair that had fallen across his forehead. "All part of my royal education. But don't expect that standard under these circumstances," she warned him.

He shook his head. "No fear. I'm happy with sandwiches. I wasn't planning on cooking."

"I noticed," she said drily. Besides bread, cheese and fruit, there was little in the pantry besides granola bars and protein bars and beer.

"I wasn't expecting company." His tone was gruff. The wind was ruffling his hair, making him look dangerous and piratical and very very appealing.

"I realize that. And I'm grateful. I—" she hesitated "—appreciate your offer to bring me along. Your insistence, actually," she corrected. "It is a better alternative than wandering around Europe trying to stay a step ahead of Papa."

He nodded, then looked at her expectantly because the note on which she ended made it clear she had something else to say.

Which she did. She just couldn't seem to find the right way

to say it. Finally she simply blurted it out. "But even so, I don't think we should make love together again."

Yet another look of surprise crossed his face, this one more obvious than the earlier two. His green eyes met hers. "You don't?"

Anny gave a quick shake of her head. "No."

Demetrios tilted his head to regard her curiously. "You didn't like it?"

Anny felt her cheeks begin to burn. "You know that's not true," she protested. "You know I liked it. Very much."

He scratched his head. "And yet you don't want to do it again."

"I didn't say I didn't want to do it again. I said I didn't think we should."

He stared at her. "Your logic eludes me."

"It would mean something if we did," she explained.

He blinked. "I thought it did mean something last time. All that stuff about your idealistic youthful self…"

"Yes, of course it meant something," she agreed. "But it would be different if we did it again. That time it was…like…making love with a fantasy." Now her cheeks really did burn. She felt like an idiot, didn't want to meet his eyes. But she could feel his on her, so finally she lifted her gaze. "When we did it then, I was with the you I—I had dreamed about. The 'fantasy' you. The one I imagined. If we did it again, it wouldn't be the same. *You* wouldn't be the same. You'd be—*you*!"

"Me? As opposed to…me?" He looked totally confused now.

Anny didn't blame him. She didn't want to spell it out, but obviously she was going to have to. "You'd be a real live flesh-and-blood man."

"I was before," he told her. "Last time."

"Not the same way. Not to me," she added after a moment.

He still looked baffled. "And you don't want a 'real live flesh-and-blood man'?"

What she wanted was to jump overboard and never come up. "It's dangerous," she said.

"No, it's not. Don't worry. I won't get you pregnant. I promise. I can take care of that."

"Not that kind of dangerous. Emotionally dangerous."

He looked blank. Of course he did. He was a man.

"I could fall in love with you," she said bluntly.

"Oh." He looked appalled. "No. You don't want to do that." He was shaking his head rapidly.

No, she didn't. Not if he wasn't going to fall in love with her in return, at least. And he'd made it clear that he had no intention of doing so. She supposed there was always the chance that she could change his mind, but from the look on his face, it didn't seem likely.

"Like I said, dangerous," Anny repeated. "For me." She shrugged when he just continued to stare at her. "You said it was up to me," she reminded him.

His mouth twisted. "So I did." He rubbed a hand through his hair. "That'll teach me," he muttered.

"I'm sorry."

He made a sound that was a half laugh and half something Anny couldn't have put a name to. "Me, too, princess," he told her. Then he gave her a wry smile. "Let me know if you change your mind."

"Sure," Anny said.

But it wasn't going to happen—she hoped.

She was the most baffling woman he'd ever met.

When she didn't know him, she wanted to make love with him. When she knew him, she didn't want to—but only because she might fall in love with him.

Where the hell was the logic in that?

Well, perversely, Demetrios supposed, squinting at the Italian shoreline as if it might provide some answers, there was some. But it wasn't doing his peace of mind much good.

It made all those glimpses of Anny he kept catching out of the corner of his eye all too distracting, though he supposed she intended nothing of the sort at all.

She wasn't coy and flirtatious the way Lissa had been, eager and enthusiastic one minute, pouting and moody the next. With Lissa he'd never known where he stood or what she wanted.

With Anny, she flat-out told him.

When she wanted to make love, she'd said so. Now she didn't, and she'd said that. No, he'd never met a woman even close to her.

After their discussion, she had finished her lunch, then taken both their plates below. He'd expected she would stay there to avoid him and his "dangerous" appeal. But she came back to put her feet up on one of the cockpit benches and leaned back to lift her face. She still wore Theo's visor, but for the moment her face was lit by the sun and the wind tangled her hair.

"Isn't this glorious?" she said, turning a smile in his direction. And there really was nothing flirtatious about the smile at all. Just pure enjoyment of the moment.

"Yeah," Demetrios agreed, because it was.

But also because it was pretty damned glorious to stand there and simply watch her take pleasure in the moment. For the longest time she didn't move a muscle, didn't say a word, just sat there silently, absorbing, savoring the experience.

She didn't glance at him to see if he was noticing. Lissa had always been aware of her audience.

He remembered when she'd badgered him to take her sailing. He had been in Paris at the time and she back in L.A., having just finished a film. And every time they talked on the phone she'd chattered about how wonderful it had been going sailing with a couple of big A-list stars.

"We could go sailing," she'd said to him.

It was the first time she'd shown the least interest in any such thing. When he'd taken her to his parents' place on Long Island right after they were married, she hadn't set foot on the family boat. She'd had little to do with anyone, and she'd been eager to leave almost as soon as they'd arrived.

He'd thought at the time it was because she'd wanted to spend some more time with him alone. Only later he began to realize a family vacation on Long Island wasn't fast-lane enough for her.

But when she'd made the remark about sailing, he'd taken her suggestion at face value and offered to charter a sailboat so they could go to Cabo San Lucas as soon as he got back home.

Lissa had been delighted.

"Ooh, fun," she'd squealed on the phone when he'd tossed out the idea to her.

They hadn't seen each other for more than two days at a time in the past two months. It seemed like a great way to spend some time alone with her. And he'd been delighted she was as eager for some uninterrupted time together.

"It will be wonderful!" Lissa had crowed. And he knew that tone of voice—it was the one that went with the impossibly sparkly blue eyes. She'd let out a sigh of ecstasy. "The wind. The water. The two of us. Oh, yes. Let's. I always feel as if I'm in communion with nature."

So two days after he got home, he'd chartered a boat, and they'd set sail to Cabo from Marina del Rey.

For the first five minutes Lissa had looked exactly as content as Anny did now. But an hour later the contentment had vanished.

The wind was too cold. The boat tilted too much. The ocean spray wasn't good for her complexion. She was afraid of sunburn.

Demetrios had tried to be sympathetic. Then he'd tried to joke her out of it. But Lissa didn't take teasing at all. She pouted. She wept. She slammed around and threw things when she was upset. They weren't two hours out of Marina del Rey and she had become seriously upset.

Demetrios did his best to placate her. "I've missed you, Lis. I've been waiting for this."

She looked at him, appalled and flung her arms in despair. "This? This? There's nothing here!"

"We're here. The two of us. Alone," he reminded her. "No press. No fans. No one at all. Just us. Relax and enjoy it."

But Lissa hadn't relaxed and she hadn't enjoyed it. She'd gone below, she'd come up to the cockpit. She'd flipped through a magazine, tried to read a possible script. There was no one to talk to. She was bored.

He'd offered to let her take the wheel. She'd declined. "I wouldn't know what to do."

"I'll teach you," he'd offered.

She hadn't wanted that, either.

As the hours passed, she'd become more agitated. She hadn't been able to sit still.

"When do we get there?" she'd begun asking when they'd barely left Catalina behind. She had looked around hopefully, as if their destination might materialize on the horizon. "It's only a couple of hours to Cabo."

Demetrios had stared at her. "Flying," he'd agreed. "Sailing it'll probably take us about a week."

"A week?" Lissa's voice was so loud and so shrill he thought they probably could have heard it in Des Moines.

"Well, depending on the winds, of course, but—"

But she hadn't let him get any more out than that. She'd lit into him with a fury he'd only seen before on the set when she'd played a drug addict deprived of her source. She'd got an Emmy nomination for the performance.

It turned out she hadn't been acting. It turned out Lissa had more than a small drug habit. She'd been intending to score some in Mexico, though Demetrios hadn't known it at the time. There was a whole lot about Lissa he hadn't known then—things that even now he wished he'd never known.

It would have made it easier to forgive her. To forgive himself.

That disastrous trip had occurred just six months into their marriage. Later he'd thought it was the beginning of the slide downhill. Even that wasn't true. The slide had begun before she'd even walked up the aisle to become his wife.

He'd been fooled. Conned. Duped into believing he'd found the woman of his dreams.

Because he'd wanted it so much that he'd convinced himself? Or because Lissa had played the role so well?

How much had been intentional misdirection and how much had simply been bad judgment? Demetrios had no idea still.

All he could remember is that she'd looked so perfect on their wedding day. So content. So happy,

Anny looked that way now—happy, her eyes closed, her face in repose.

But hers was not like Lissa's version of "happy."

Lissa's "happiness" had always had an effervescence to it. She had bubbled, emoted, reacted. She had *acted* happy.

Sitting here now basking in the sunshine, eyes shut, wind in her hair, Anny wasn't acting. She simply was.

There was no bubbliness, no bounce. No reaction. Her emotion was quiet, accepting, serene—and, heaven help him, enticing in its very stillness.

Dangerously enticing.

And Demetrios understood quite clearly now what Anny meant about making love with him being "dangerous" because it would involve her heart.

Indulging these thoughts about Anny—seeing in her the antithesis of Lissa—was dangerous in the extreme. It could undermine his resolve. It could make him vulnerable.

She didn't have to entice him intentionally. It was worse, in fact, that she wasn't. It made him want things he had promised himself he would never want again.

"You're going to get a sunburn if you keep doing that," he said gruffly.

Anny's eyes flicked open in surprise. She dipped her head so that Theo's sun visor shaded her face again and she sat up straight, then smiled up at him. "You're right," she said, flexing her shoulders and stretching like a cat in the sun. "But it feels wonderful."

To his ears, her voice almost sounded like a purr. He didn't answer. He didn't know what to say in the face of such inocent happiness.

He found himself wishing she were more like Lissa so she would be easier to resist.

At the same time he couldn't help being glad she was not.

CHAPTER SEVEN

CINDERELLA ONLY GOT a single evening to indulge her fantasy.

Anny had had her evening with Demetrios. But now, amazingly, it seemed as if she was going to get two whole weeks.

Two weeks to be simply herself—not a princess, not Gerard's fiancée. Just plain Anny. With no demands, no expectations at all.

Not even sex.

Not that she wouldn't have liked to enjoy sex with Demetrios. The one night she'd spent with him had been astonishing, revelatory, incomparable.

It had made her want more.

Too much more.

So much more that she had not dared to allow herself to think about it. Limiting it to one night and walking away had been possible. But indulging herself in the joy of spending two weeks of nights in his bed, in his arms, would not work.

She would want more than those two weeks.

She would want a lifetime of them. And not just of making love with Demetrios, but of being loved by him.

She wasn't there yet. But she would be if she allowed herself to give into the temptation. And so she'd said, "No sex."

She hadn't explained it well. She wasn't sure that she could ever explain it so that it made sense to him. He was a man. Men didn't think about sex the same way. And he clearly had no problem enjoying sex with her and then walking away without a backward glance.

He'd basically promised to do just that.

Well, more power to him, Anny thought wryly. She knew her own limitations. And she knew they precluded that. So she said she was sorry and she stuck to her guns.

Having made her statement, though, she went below to work on her dissertation for a while. It seemed a good idea to give Demetrios some space to get used to a platonic two weeks.

Apparently it didn't bother him at all because when she came back out on deck late that afternoon, he was perfectly cheerful and equable—as if it didn't matter to him a bit.

Which she supposed it didn't. Which served her right, Anny supposed, telling herself it was all for the best.

"When do you want to eat dinner?" she asked him.

"Up to you."

"Are you planning to sail through the evening or moor somewhere?"

He gestured toward the shoreline. "There's a small village with a protected harbor up ahead. We'll moor there. Too much work to sail overnight. And what's the point?"

She completely agreed. "Then I'll plan on dinner for after we're tied up."

"Sounds good." He slanted her a grin that made her heart beat a bit faster.

"Will you be going ashore?" she asked him.

He shook his head. "Not unless you want something."

She could use some clothes that were more appropriate for sailing. But she didn't want to go ashore to get them. Not in a small village not so very far from her own country. Too many people might recognize her around here. And they would certainly recognize Demetrios. He was famous the world over.

"No," she decided. "Call me if you need help," she said, knowing full well he wouldn't. Then she went back below and put together a salad and some bruschetta to go with the bread, then sliced some meat and cheese.

She was just setting the table when she heard him call her name.

Startled, Anny climbed quickly up the steps and saw that they were coming into the harbor.

"Come take the wheel while I bring down the sail," Demetrios commanded.

She blinked in surprise. But apparently he'd taken her offer at face value and was now looking at her expectantly. So she did what she was told.

"Theo would be a purist and skip the engine," Demetrios muttered as he started it up. Then he shrugged. "But I'm not as good at it as he is."

He seemed fine at it to Anny. His quick efficient competence as he hove to, then brought the mainsail down over the boom, seemed nothing short of miraculous to Anny. She hung on to the helm and tried to keep the boat where he wanted it as he finished furling the jib.

And she was just congratulating herself on doing her bit and handing the wheel back over to him, when he said, "Get up on the bow. I need you to signal me which side the buoy is on and then tie on to the mooring ball."

"Me?"

Something unreadable flickered in his gaze. Anny didn't even try to figure it out. She just said, "Right," and scrambled up to do what he asked.

Using her hand signals to guide him, Demetrios adjusted the course, backing down the motor as they closed in on the buoy. "Okay. Grab the mooring line," he instructed.

She grabbed it, then, continuing to follow his directions, she passed the bridle line through the eye, and quickly, trying not to fumble, wrapped the other end securely to the bow cleat. Then she sat back on her heels and waited for something dire to happen.

Nothing did. Or if it did, she was too inept to tell.

But then Demetrios called, "Great. That's it."

"It is?" she asked cautiously.

A quick glance at him and she saw a grin lighting his face. It was as if she'd been awarded some distinguished medal. At his thumbs-up, Anny took a deep breath and let it out again in a whoosh. She flexed her shoulders and grinned back at him. A warm elemental sense of satisfaction filled her.

The feeling was closest, she supposed, to the satisfaction she felt when she figured out a bit more of the culture and history of the cave painters she was writing her dissertation about. It was as if a significant piece of the puzzle fell into place.

She felt like that now.

But this was more. Now she felt a physical satisfaction as well. She hadn't done much of the sailing today. But she'd done more physical work than she ordinarily did. She was tired, her muscles had been challenged by the unaccustomed exertion. Her skin was a bit sunburned even in spite of the lotion she'd slathered on exposed body parts and the visor she wore. She felt alive, aware. Wonderful.

Free.

She opened her arms and spun around, embracing the whole world in the joy of it.

"That good, is it?" Anny heard Demetrios's amused voice behind her.

She felt faintly embarrassed by her childish exuberance, but not embarrassed enough to pretend complacency. She turned and smiled at him. "It's the best day I've had in years."

His brows lifted and he looked at her a long moment, as if he were trying to determine if she was sincere. She met his gaze squarely, unapologetically.

Finally, slowly, a heart-stoppingly gorgeous smile lit his face. "Then that is good," he said. "I'm glad."

He was glad he'd brought her along.

It was better than being alone.

All the time he'd been at Cannes, he'd longed for time alone. But he knew that if he'd been here alone, he'd have been restless. He would have sailed happily enough. But he would have spent most of the time in his head thinking about work, about the new screenplay, about the distribution deal he'd just done. He would not have appreciated the moment.

Now he couldn't help it.

It was hard not to with Anny embracing it every time he looked at her.

And he did look at her. A lot.

From the first day he'd met her, she had stirred something in him that he thought Lissa had killed. Not just his desire for sex—though admittedly Lissa had done a number on him there, too.

But Anny's whole outlook on life was so different.

Of course it would be, he could hear Lissa scoff in his mind. Princess Adriana had never had the disadvantage of growing up illegitimate in tiny, dusty Reach, North Dakota. Princess Adriana had always had everything her little heart desired. Why shouldn't she embrace life? It gave her everything she wanted.

Yes, he had known Lissa well enough to know exactly what she would have said about Anny. It was what she said about everyone. No one had ever had things as tough as Lissa. No one had overcome as much, had suffered more.

Admittedly his late wife had overcome her fair share of obstacles. But some of them, Demetrios knew, were of her own making. Some of them were the product of the chip on her shoulder she could never quite shake off.

"Why should I?" she'd said to him once. "It's made me who I am."

For better or worse, yes, it had. And what he knew above all was that it had never made her happy. She'd never felt joy like Anny had expressed tonight. She'd never opened her arms and embraced life.

"You're very pensive," Anny said to him now.

They were eating dinner on deck. She'd brought their salads, meat and cheese up to the cockpit because, as she'd said, "Why be down below when it's so glorious up here?"

They'd enjoyed the sunset while they'd eaten, and his mind had drifted back to the miserable nights he'd spent sailing to Cabo with Lissa, and how different it had been from this.

"Is something wrong?" Anny asked him. "They don't look like good thoughts."

He flexed his shoulders. "Just thinking how much better this is than the last time I went sailing."

"I thought you went with your brother and Franck," she said, frowning.

"I meant the last time I went a few years ago." But he smiled as he remembered the very last time. "When we went with Franck it was good."

"He thought so," she agreed. "I wish he could do more of it. Mostly he won't leave his room." She paused thoughtfully. "It's easier not to, I think."

"Yes." It was definitely easier not to risk. Safer, as well not to want what you couldn't have.

Demetrios drained his beer and stood up. "You cooked. I'll clean up."

"You worked hard all day," Anny said, standing, too. "I'll help." And carrying her plate, she followed him down into the galley.

She was no help. Not to his peace of mind, anyway. Oh, she washed plates and put away food. But the galley was small—too small for them not to bump into each other. Too small for him to avoid the whiff of flowery shampoo, the occasional brush of her hair as she dodged past him to get to the refrigerator, and—once—the outright collision that brought his chest and her breasts firmly against each other.

He remembered her softness. Wanted to feel it again.

The more time he spent with her, the more he wanted to spend. And, let's face it, the closer he wanted to spend it. He wanted to touch her fresh, soft skin. He wanted to thread his fingers through her hair. Wanted to carry her off to his bunk and know her even more thoroughly than he'd known her the one time he'd made love with her.

But it wasn't going to happen.

She'd said so. Had explained why. He understood. He just wished his hormones did.

He stepped back out of the galley and said abruptly, "Not going to work."

Anny blinked at him. "What's not?"

"This." He jerked his head toward her in the galley. "You can clean up or I will. Not both of us."

"But—"

If she were Lissa, all this brushing and bumping would have been a deliberate tease. Not with Anny. Now he just looked at her and waited for the penny to drop.

He could tell the moment that it did. Instead of looking at him coquettishly and giving him an impish smile as Lissa would have done, Anny looked mortified.

"You think I—" Her face flamed. She shook her head. "I never—! I'm sorry. I shouldn't have— Oh God!"

"It's all right," he said. "I can control myself. But I'd rather do the cleaning up myself."

Her cheeks were still bright red. "Of course," she mumbled, and she practically bolted up the companionway steps without a backward glance.

Demetrios watched her go. It was a tempting view.

He didn't need the temptation, God knew, but there were some things a man simply couldn't resist.

As the days went on it wasn't only the physical Anny that Demetrios found hard to resist. She was as appealing as ever physically.

But it was something more that attracted him. She was cheerful, bright, thoughtful, fun. And he never knew what she was going to do next.

One afternoon she decided she'd fish for their dinner. He scoffed at the notion. "You fish?"

"What? You think princesses can't fish?"

"Not in my experience."

"Known a lot of princesses, have you?"

"One or two," he told her. That one had been five and the other ninety-five didn't seem worth mentioning.

"Well, live and learn," she told him, putting the rod together and settling down on the deck. "We used to go fishing on Lake Isar in Mont Chamion. We had our own little hideaway there, a little rustic cabin my great-grandfather built."

"No castle?" he teased.

She shook her head, smiling, but her expression softened and she got a faraway look in her eyes. "About as far from a palace as you can get and still have indoor plumbing. Grandfather had that put in," she told him. "We loved it there— Mama, Papa and I—because we could be ourselves there. Not royal, you know?"

He didn't, of course. Not about the "royal" bit. But Demetrios nodded anyway because since he'd become famous he'd learned all about the need to get away.

"It was the perfect place," Anny went on. "Quiet. Solitary. Calm. I felt real there. Myself. My family. No distractions."

"Except the fish."

She grinned. "Except the fish."

"I presume you brought bait for the fish there—which is going to be something of a problem here." He nodded at the bare hook on the end of her line.

"Sometimes we did," she agreed. "Sometimes, though," she added saucily, "we used whatever was handy. Like now." And she dug into her pocket and pulled out a tin of sardines she'd found below.

Demetrios laughed. "If you catch a fish with that, princess, I'll cook it."

She laughed, too. Then she baited her hook and cast the line over the side. It was less than half an hour later that he heard her say, "I got one!"

It was a sea bass, Demetrios told her. *Spignola*. "Good eating," he said, taking if off the hook and heading down to the galley.

"I can cook it," Anny protested.

But he insisted. Once they moored the boat for the evening, she stayed on deck and kept fishing, he baked it with a bit of olive oil, lemon, tomatoes, and basil.

"Nothing fancy. Just something I learned at my mother's knee," he said when he brought the plates up on deck. He'd torn up greens for a salad and had two beer bottles tucked under his arm.

"Did you cook a lot?"

"No. But she made sure we all knew our way around a kitchen."

Anny thought she'd like to meet Demetrios's mother. She didn't say so. But she did ask about his mother and father and what it had been like growing up in a family of seven.

"A madhouse," he said. But the expression on his face told her the memories were good ones. "We were wild. Crazy. We rode bikes off roofs. We fell out of trees. We climbed up the sides of public buildings because we could. My mother said we'd all end up dead or in jail."

"Surely not!" Anny couldn't keep the shock out of her voice even as she envisioned a horde of obstreperous little boys.

Demetrios grinned. "She's given to hyperbole, my mother."

"Ah. Well, I think it must have been nice having all those built-in playmates."

He took a swallow of the beer and smiled wryly. "Sometimes. When we weren't trying to kill each other."

"You were lucky," she decided, even after he regaled her with half a dozen more stories that ended with either him or one of his brothers, usually George, in the emergency room.

"We pounded on each other quite a bit," he said with considerable relish.

"Like I said, you're lucky."

Then, for contrast, she told him about growing up in Mont Chamion, about what it was like to be "royal." There was no pounding. No emergency room visits—except once when she had an ingrown toenail. What there were were expectations.

"Duties," she said. "Responsibilities. Selflessness. Not that there's anything wrong with that," she added quickly. "But being a doctoral candidate is a lot easier. The hopes of a country don't ride on my dissertation."

"But they do when you're a princess." It wasn't a question.

But she pulled up her knees and wrapped her arms around them and answered it anyway. "Sometimes it seems like that."

"Like marrying Gerard."

"Yes." She nodded slowly, trying to find words to explain. "It's tricky, doing the right thing—for yourself and for your country. You have to learn to walk a very careful line. I'm still learning."

Demetrios was silent then in the face of her confession, and Anny didn't know what he was thinking. When she'd first tacked his poster up on her wall all those years ago, she'd imagined she knew him perfectly. She'd dared to believe, based on his acting roles and the few interviews she'd read, that she knew and understood him. She'd dreamed of a relationship with him.

Now she realized how little she had known him, how much better she knew him now. How much more she still wanted to know. "What about you?"

He flexed his shoulders. "What about me?" He sounded as if he didn't want to talk any more about himself, but she persisted.

"You got to choose your work. Is being a director what you always wanted to do?"

"You mean besides being a fireman or a cowboy?" The answer was pat—every little boy's dream—and so was the grin on his face. It was the grin from the poster boy.

Anny widened her eyes, considering him with mock seriousness. "I think you still could be," she told him gravely, "if you really want to."

He blinked, looking briefly nonplussed, then realized she was joking and laughed.

She laughed, too, but asked again, "No, really, Demetrios. What did you want?"

She thought he wasn't going to answer her he was so quiet again, and for a very long time. But then he let out a breath and said slowly, "I don't know. I guess I just sort of thought I'd do what they did—my grandfather and my dad. You know, grow up, get married, have kids." His tone changed, grew harder, and his expression turned suddenly bleak. He shrugged. "Nothing major," he ended gruffly.

Nothing major. Except everything he wanted had been ripped away with the death of his wife. Instinctively Anny reached out a hand to touch his.

But before she could, Demetrios stood up. "Good fish. If you're finished, I'll do the washing up."

Anny scrambled to her feet as well. "It's my turn," she protested. "You cooked." *We could do it together*, she wanted to say. Wanted to believe things had changed.

Their gazes met, locked.

Then Demetrios shrugged. "Fine. You do it."

It had been easier when he felt dead—when nothing mattered, when he didn't care.

Now as he sat on the deck and stared into the darkness, all the while aware of the sounds of dish washing going on below, Demetrios wished he could tap into that zombie-like indifference again.

He didn't want to think about how much he enjoyed Anny's company. Didn't want to experience the gnawing need to learn more about her, to know about her life when she was growing up or, damn it, what her hopes and dreams were now.

And he didn't want to want more. But he did.

When the sounds in the galley ceased and the light below flicked off, he breathed a sigh of relief, grateful that she'd decided an early night was a good idea.

It wasn't that he couldn't control his hormones when he was around her. He was attracted—no denying that—but could cope. It was that somehow she made him feel human again, made him care again.

He didn't want that, either. Not at all.

"What do you know about stars?"

He jerked, turning to see Anny's silhouette as she emerged from the companionway. She handed him a glass and poured each of them a glass of wine before asking again, "What do you know about stars?"

"Most of 'em are a pain in the butt." His fingers were strangling the stem of the glass. What the hell was she doing here now?

She laughed. "Not those kinds of stars. The ones in the sky."

His mind went briefly blank. And then he shrugged. "Nothing.

I don't know anything. Just a few constellations, the North Star, a few basics I learned as a boy for navigating in the way of Greek fishermen, without instruments. Why?"

She sat down across from him. Her profile was backlit by the sprinkling of lights from the small seaside village behind her. As he watched, she took a sip of the wine, then tipped her head back and stared up into the darkness.

"When I was little," she said, "I used to wish on them."

"Lots of little kids do," he said, aware that his voice sounded rusty. He set the glass down. He did not need wine to muddy his brain tonight.

"Did you?" she asked, her voice light. "Wish on stars?"

"No. I was a tough little kid. Tough little kids don't do sissy stuff like that."

She laughed. "Right. You were very fierce."

"I was. Had to be."

"I suppose." She spoke the words quietly. She lowered her head so that she wasn't staring at the stars anymore. It felt as if she was looking at him. Assessing him.

Demetrios shrugged his shoulders against the cockpit wall and stared back, though he couldn't make out her features at all. "You have a problem with that?"

He saw her shake her head. "No. I'm just trying to know you better."

He didn't like the sound of that. "Why?"

"I thought I knew you when all I had was your poster. I was wrong. Obviously. I'm trying to remedy my ignorance." It sounded almost logical.

He grunted, which was marginally more polite than saying, "Don't bother," which would have been wiser.

"I thought if you wished on stars, maybe you'd tell me what you'd wished for. And then I could tell you what I wished for. Conversation starters, you know? It was a whole section of Swiss finishing school 101—getting to know you," she said lightly.

Demetrios chewed on the inside of his cheek. He cracked his knuckles. He rolled his shoulders. He wasn't about to talk about what he'd wished for. But he didn't mind if she did. "What did you wish for?" he asked gruffly at last.

"A brother. I hated being an only child."

"You can have any of mine," he said promptly.

He heard her laugh softly. "Thanks, but I'm not wishing for them anymore. I've got them."

"And you're okay with that?" he asked, because wanting a sibling when you were five or eight wasn't the same as getting them when you were nearly twenty. He wouldn't have been surprised if she'd resented these little interlopers who were now closer to the throne than she was.

But she just said, "It's wonderful."

"So you're fond of them?"

"I love them," she said with quiet ferocity. "I hope I have kids just like them someday." She paused and glanced up to the heavens. "I *wish* for them."

Demetrios felt an unwelcome twinge at the thought of Anny as the mother of someone's children. Whose? he wondered, then deliberately shook the thought off.

"Yeah, well, I hope you get 'em then," he said.

They sat silently after that, the boat rocking beneath them. A minute passed. Two. Then Anny said wryly, "So much for conversation starters. Your turn."

"I didn't go to Swiss finishing school," he protested.

"You only need a bit of polite curiosity. Isn't there anything you want to know?"

There were a thousand things he wanted to know—none of which he was going to ask. So he asked the one thing that had occurred to him more than once ever since they'd set sail.

"Every day it's hotter than hell. Why do you keep wearing those damn jeans?"

"Because they're all I've got."

He straightened and stared at her through the black of the night. "*What?*"

She shrugged. "Everything else is city clothes—what I thought I'd be wearing. Blazers, linen trousers, silk blouses."

"And you didn't think to mention it?"

"I didn't want to go ashore. We were near Cannes. You're too well-known everywhere. People would notice. Papa would find out."

"You don't think Papa will find out if you die of heatstroke?"

"Oh, for heaven's sake! I wouldn't have let it come to that. I didn't realize it was bothering you."

"It wasn't bothering—"

"I'll cut the trousers into shorts tomorrow."

"You can go shopping tomorrow. We'll moor some place bigger and you can go ashore without me," he said firmly.

"I don't know—"

"Don't be an idiot, princess." He hauled himself up, stalked past her and clattered down the companionway steps. Moments later he came back and threw a T-shirt and a pair of his shorts at her. "In the meantime, wear those. You can use some rope to hold them up."

Anny clutched the clothes against her, staring up at him and he was close enough now that in the sliver of rising moonlight he could see a smile on her face. "Thank you," she said. "That's very kind of you."

"Yeah, that's me. Kindness personified."

"You are. You're—"

"Tired and I want to go to sleep," he cut her off brusquely. "So unless you have any more conversation starters that can't wait, I'd appreciate it if you'd vacate my nightly resting place."

There was a split second's silence in which he expected her to take offense. But she just got up, saying, "Of course."

She picked up the bottle and the glasses, wrapping them in his shirt and shorts. Then, just as he dared to breathe a sigh of relief as she headed for the companionway, she stepped directly in front of him, rose up on her toes and brushed a kiss across his lips.

"Good night, Demetrios. Sleep well."

CHAPTER EIGHT

SLEEP WELL? Yeah, right.

Demetrios was lucky he slept at all.

He lay awake half the night, staring at the stars, his mind full of visions of Anny making her damned wishes. He had no trouble at all imagining a wistful eight-year-old leaning on the window-sill, looking up at the stars, whispering wishes as if someone would hear them—and make them come true.

How childish and unrealistic was that? He ground his teeth, flipped over onto his side and punched the pillow he'd stuck under his head. Life didn't hand you your heart's desires on a plate. No one knew that better than he did.

But you couldn't tell Anny. She'd just look at you with her sweet gentle expression and then she would smile a commiserating smile, one that said she hurt for you, that she understood.

But she didn't understand. Never would.

But that wasn't his problem, he reminded himself. Anny was who she was, and nothing would change that.

Besides, for better or worse he'd done his bit—he'd listened to her talk about marrying Gerard and he'd opened his mouth about regrets. Now he had to give her space to figure things out for herself.

Even if he went quietly crazy in the process.

His mother would tell him it was his penance for sticking his oar in where it didn't belong in the first place. Undoubtedly she was right. She would tell him to get over it. She would be right about that, too. When he was a boy, banging around the house about the injustice of it all, she would grab him by the shoulders, point him toward the door, and say, "Get out of here. Go out and burn off some of that craziness."

Abruptly he sat up, yanked his T-shirt over his head, vaulted out of the cockpit, and dived into the sea.

Sometimes mothers really did know best.

It was sunny and bright when Anny awoke. For a moment she thought she was back in her room in the palace at Mont Chamion, the only place she lived where the sun streamed in across her bed.

But then the bed rocked and she sat up, blinking. Had she slept right through Demetrios starting the engine as they left the mooring?

The sound always prompted her to yank on her jeans, button up her shirt, and run a brush through her hair so she could get up on deck quickly to help when he was ready to raise the sail.

She looked around, bewildered. Then she threw back the sheet, put on the shorts and T-shirt he'd given her last night, and hurried up the steps, only to be confronted by the dead calm of the harbor where they'd moored last night—and the sight of Demetrios Savas sprawled sound asleep on one of the cockpit benches.

She stopped dead on the steps and stared, mesmerized by the sight.

He was lying on his back, wearing only a pair of shorts. One arm was out flung, the other clutched a T-shirt against his bare chest.

Cautiously she crept closer, barely breathing as she feasted her gaze on him. She'd been to bed with him, but she'd never slept with him. Had never seen him unguarded like this.

Awake his features were always animated. Perhaps it was the actor in him, but she'd never known a man who could say so much with a simple look or draw her eyes with the lift of a brow or the twist of his gorgeous mouth.

Even in repose, he was impossible to ignore. And given a chance she'd never expected, Anny simply stood there and took him in. Her eyes traced the line of his almost perfect nose, slightly askew, she knew, because his brother George had broken it for him when he was twelve. She marveled at his dark brows and thick lashes, which should have been wasted on a man, but weren't on him. They seemed ever so slightly to soften his sharp masculine cheekbones, rough stubbled jaw, and hard mouth.

He wasn't only a pretty face, though. He also had a gorgeous body—with broad shoulders, lean hips, sinewy arms, a strong chest, and muscled hair-roughened legs. She studied him slowly, leisurely, remembering what it had been like to touch him. And what it had felt like when he'd touched her.

He had gorgeous hands with strong square-tipped fingers and callused palms. Working man's hands, Anny thought. She loved watching them raise a sail or fillet a fish or tie knots. And lover's hands. Oh, yes.

He was thirty-two years old—a man in his prime, hard and tough and uncompromising. And when he was awake that was what you saw in him. But in his sleeping face, Anny could still see hints of the younger Demetrios—the idealistic young man whose poster she'd stared at for hours on end, dreaming, wishing…

It wasn't only stars she had wished on, Anny thought wryly.

Or maybe it was that she'd wished on Hollywood stars, too. One of them, anyway. Fool that she was.

Well, she was all grown up now and trying not to wish. Trying hard. It was just very difficult.

Demetrios came awake with a start when the sun hit his eyes. He squinted, disoriented, and it only got worse when the first thing he saw was Anny watching him.

His head pounded from lack of sleep. His skin felt crusty from the dried salt on it. His shorts were still clammy and damp. And he didn't know what the hell time it was, but clearly it was later than it should have been.

"What are you staring at?"

She smiled. No surprise there. Anny smiled more than anyone he'd ever met. Honestly smiled. Not like some Hollywood actress playing a part. "You."

He groaned and scrubbed his hands over his face. "Why?"

"I like to?"

At least she made it sound like a question. "You're not sure?"

"No, I'm sure," she said matter-of-factly. "I'm just wondering why I do. You're such a grouch."

Because it was easier being a grouch. Easier to keep her at a distance. Easier to remember that he didn't want to get involved with Princess Adriana.

He shrugged. "So don't." He stood up, stretched cramped muscles, then scratched his chest and rubbed a hand through salt-stiffened hair. He should have taken a shower after his middle-of-the-night swim, but the whole point had been to wear himself out and then collapse and go to sleep. That part had worked. Finally. But now he felt like something stuck to the bottom of a fish tank. "What time is it?"

"Eight-thirty."

"Why didn't you wake me?"

She shrugged. "We're not on a schedule." She stretched her long bare legs out in front of her and he noticed that her jeans were gone and she was wearing his shorts and NYU T-shirt. She should have looked scruffy, nondescript and unappealing in them. Good luck, he thought grimly. In fact she looked bright and fresh and far too enticing for a woman who wasn't going to sleep with him.

Anny stood up, too, the morning sun graciously outlining her curves for him. "I made coffee. Do you want some?"

It was undoubtedly the best offer he was going to get. "Yeah. Let me grab a shower. Then we can get going."

The morning sun gave way to clouds by midday, something might be blowing up and bringing a storm their way before nightfall. While he kept them on course, Anny got on the radio and checked the weather reports.

"Rain and squally winds," she reported back. "This evening or tomorrow morning."

"We'll tie up midafternoon then. Give you a chance to do your shopping."

"It's not necessary now that you've lent me these." She nodded down at the shirt and shorts.

He didn't argue. But that afternoon he chose a mooring near a place big enough to have shops. It wasn't a great harbor, though. He didn't really want to ride out a storm here. As soon as they'd tied up, he readied the inflatable for her.

She didn't argue, either. She clambered into the small inflatable. She was still wearing his shirt and shorts, as well as Theo's sun visor and a pair of wraparound sunglasses. She had pulled her hair into a ponytail, which poked through the back of the visor. As a disguise, he thought it worked.

"I've got the grocery list," she said, tucking it into the pocket of the shorts. He started the small engine for her and gave her instructions about how to start it for the return trip.

She listened, nodded, then said, "I'll manage." She settled in, and Demetrios stepped back onto the sailboat, then gave the inflatable a shove to send her on her way.

"Of course you will." But as he watched the small inflatable boat chug slowly away, he cracked his knuckles, thinking that this must be what it felt like to watch your child leave home on the first day of school.

He scrubbed the deck and polished the bright work and mended a tear in the jib while she was gone. All things that needed to be done. And if they kept him up on deck so he could see the moment she got back to the inflatable, it was only to be sure she didn't have any problems getting the engine started.

She didn't. And she was beaming when he held out a hand and hauled her on board. "I brought pizza!"

"So much for *Cordon Bleu*."

She laughed. "You'll love it." She also brought two bags with what he presumed were new clothes, and two more bags of groceries. "Come and see," she invited. Her delight in both the pizza and her shopping expedition was obvious. She was like a kid with new toys, he thought, not a princess who had everything.

Bemused, Demetrios followed, and discovered it was olives

and tomatoes and fresh bread that she was thrilled about. She seemed in no hurry to change out of his shirt and shorts.

"Here." She handed him plates. "Take them up top. We can eat on deck. I'll bring the wine."

It was hardly a feast. But Anny's simple joy made it seem like a party. She told him everything she had seen in town.

"I know it's only been a week, but I'd forgotten what it was like to be in shops and on streets. I almost got run over by a motorcyclist!"

"You need to be careful," he said, not smiling at the idea even though she was.

"I'm all right," she said cheerfully. "It was fun. And no one even looked at me twice."

He doubted that. Even deliberately cultivated anonymity would not make Anny disappear. She was too bright, too animated.

"I bought a bikini," she told him with delight, making him choke on his wine. "Let's go swimming after we finish."

"No."

She blinked. "No? But—"

"I want to sail on. We need a more sheltered harbor if it's going to storm." And he had no desire to see Anny in a bikini. His memory and his imagination were quite enough.

Anny didn't argue. She said, "Aye, aye, sir," and took the plates and dishes below to clean up.

He got them underway again and she appeared on deck to take the wheel while he raised the sail. The harbor he wanted to reach was another hour or two south, longer if they ended up sailing into the wind the whole way. He didn't know how long they had until the rains began.

The winds shifted and picked up before they had traveled much more than an hour. They were getting close when he felt the first drops of rain.

Anny appeared in the companionway. "Can I help?"

"I'll bring her in there," he said, jerking his head toward a sheltered harbor not far away. With luck, he thought he could bring the boat in before the rain began in earnest.

Lady Luck, however, had other ideas. He did manage to get around the spit of land, gain some shelter, drop the sail, and cut the engine. But he didn't make it to the mooring before the rain began pelting down.

Anny, who had gone below once he'd got the sail down and taken the helm again, appeared again, rain streaking down her face, plastering her hair to her head. The T-shirt was gone. So were the shorts. She was wearing two scraps of material and damn all else.

"What the hell are you doing?" he demanded.

She started to climb up toward the bow. "What I do every night." She gestured toward where she always stood and tied the mooring line.

"Like that? In a bikini?"

"The clothes were wet and hard to move in. And it's not cold, even though it's raining. Besides a bikini is easier to dry. So this is better."

The hell it was. "I don't want you out there. Too dangerous." The boat was tossing about on the waves. They were getting bigger every moment.

She turned and stared back at him. "So how are we going to anchor?"

"I'll do it."

"And it's not dangerous for you?"

"It's—"

But she didn't wait for his reply. She was scrambling toward the bow and he found himself staring at a very shapely, barely covered royal posterior. He felt an almost overwhelming desire to smack it.

"Damn it, Anny, clip on your harness line!" he shouted at her. Though God knew what she'd clip it to.

"I'm not stupid." Her words floated back to him on the rising wind. His heart caught in his throat as he watched her balancing as the boat tipped and jerked.

"*Anny!*"

Please, God. Ah, there. He breathed as he saw her fumble with the harness and clip on somehow. Then she started giving him hand signals.

His fingers strangling the wheel, Demetrios tried to bring the boat in as close as he could, as quickly as he could, as smoothly as he could, and get her back safe. The boat dipped and leaned. Anny slipped, dropped the line, and he felt his insides somersault as he watched her.

"Come on, Anny!" He wanted her back. Wanted her safe. She crouched, went down on her knees, reaching and—

"Got it!" Her words were thin on the wind.

But then she was up again, and slip-sliding back to him. Demetrios cut the engine and yanked her back into the cockpit. Into his arms.

His heart was slamming against the wall of his chest. "Don't. Ever. Do. That. Again." He clutched her hard, his arms wrapping around her, his knees still shaking at the memory of her out there, teetering, in harm's way. "Promise me."

She twisted to stare up at him, her eyes wide with surprise, rain still streaming down her cheeks. "I'm f-fine." But her voice sounded thready and insubstantial, though it could have been the wind causing it.

"I'm not," he said. "You scared the hell out of me." And he still didn't want to let go of her, though it wasn't only fear of disaster averted that had him holding her now. It was the feel of her in his arms, the rightness of it.

"I'm sorry. But I was fine. Really. Mission accomplished. And it wasn't so hard."

"No. The hard part would have been me telling your father his daughter had drowned." And knowing it was all his fault.

"I wasn't going to drown." She twisted again and he let her go this time because holding her was not a good idea.

She didn't even seem to notice. "I did exactly what I was supposed to do. It had to be done, and you needed to steer. But—" now she paused and beamed at him "—thank you for worrying about me."

"I was worried about *me*," he said gruffly. "Your old man would probably have had me guillotined. Or do it himself."

"Papa is very civilized."

"I wouldn't be," Demetrios muttered under his breath and knew it for the truth. He glared at her standing there in her bikini. The rain was getting colder now, and her nipples were standing up against the thin fabric. "And for God sake, go get dressed!"

Thank God she did, though not without arching her brows and looking at him thoughtfully for a long minute before she left. Thank God she didn't say anything else, either, but just let it ride.

Demetrios did not want to talk. He did not want to deal with the roil of emotions churning inside him. Did not to face the maelstrom of feelings or the woman who was causing them.

Of course he had to follow her below because he could think of no excuse for staying up on deck in the middle of a pounding rain. Fortunately she was in her cabin. He went to his. He would have stayed there all evening, but she tapped on his door an hour later.

"Dinner's ready."

He hauled himself off his bunk, where he'd been trying with no luck at all to focus on his screenplay, and opened the door a few inches. "We ate."

She shrugged. "Fine. If you're not hungry." She was still looking at him speculatively. "I made bruschetta." A pause. "I'm sorry if I scared you."

He muttered under his breath. "Just don't do it again." He came out and sat down at the table. The rain still pounded down, but the wind seemed to have slacked off a bit so the boat didn't heel over quite as much. It didn't bobble and tip constantly. It made the meal easier to serve and to eat. But he wasn't particularly hungry.

He was distracted by what he was thinking, by what he was feeling. By how badly he didn't want to be thinking and feeling any of it.

Anny was making an effort at conversation. He recognized a couple of her "conversation starters." Questions that invited participation, that welcomed a response. She used them when he wasn't cooperating. Next thing you knew she'd be reduced to asking him what he was thinking.

And there was no way he was telling her that.

She'd barely finished her last mouthful when he stood up. "I'll clean up. You go ahead and work."

Her eyes widened. "Work?"

"Aren't you writing a dissertation?"

The eyes widened a fraction more. Then they narrowed and she looked at him the way his mother had when he'd been a particularly fractious child. But unlike his mother, Anny didn't say anything. She dumped her plate in the sink and gave a small shrug. "Well, you know where to find me."

Anny went straight into her cabin and shut the door. Hard.

What was his problem? She could hear him banging plates and silverware in the galley. If he kept that up, he'd break something, she thought, wincing as she heard a particularly loud clank.

Well, if he did, he could buy Theo whatever it was he'd broken. She wasn't going to do it. Whatever was eating him, it wasn't her fault.

She tried not to care. Tried not to think about it. But like all the rest of her waking moments since he'd swept her away from the Ritz that first afternoon, these moments, too, were filled with Demetrios.

A lot of good not going to bed with him had done—because despite her better judgment and best efforts, she'd fallen in love with him. Not the young man from the poster, though he was part of it, too. But the man who'd taken time for the children at the clinic, the man who had told her not to make decisions that would cause her to regret her life, the man who had offered her refuge on his boat, who made her laugh and made her wistful, who had one night made beautiful love to her, who had been frightened for her. Who had held her in his arms.

Who hadn't kissed her, she reminded herself.

No, he'd held her tight, reassured himself that she was fine, then abruptly let her go. Because he cared. She couldn't say he didn't care. But he wasn't in love with her the way she was with him.

The clanking and clattering in the galley finally ceased. The cabinet door banged shut one last time. Then she heard the door to Demetrios's cabin open and close. And then silence—except for the wind and the rain.

Anny started to reach for her laptop, told herself she might as well work. He was right that she did have her dissertation to do. And it was a part of her future even if he wasn't.

And then she heard the door to his cabin again, then his feet on the companionway stairs heading to the cockpit. Probably checking everything one last time before he battened down for the night.

The splash surprised her.

The boat dipped and it sounded as if he'd thrown something overboard. But what? And why?

It was dark so Anny had to turn off the light to peer out the porthole. At first she couldn't see anything except the lights of the village beyond the harbor and the streaks of reflections across the water.

And then, suddenly, rising out of the water she saw the silhouette of a man's head.

She pressed her nose against the porthole, disbelieving. Then she turned, jerked open the door and pounded up the steps. "Demetrios!"

She reached the cockpit and scrambled over the side onto the deck. "*Demetrios!*"

She scanned the choppy dark sea desperately. What had possessed him to come up on deck? And what had he been doing to fall overboard? He'd been the one worried about her and now—

"Demetrios!" She spotted him now. He was a good twenty yards off the starboard bow and against the streaky reflections she could see his arms stroking in quick rhythm as he cut through the water.

Swimming! *Away* from the boat!

"Demetrios!" Princesses didn't yell. Anny had never bellowed so loudly in her life. "*Demetrios!*"

This time he heard. And slowly, almost reluctantly, it seemed, he turned toward her, treading water. He flicked his hair back off his forehead and slowing, lazily began stroking back toward the boat. "What?" There was a note of annoyance in his voice.

He was annoyed? She thought he'd fallen overboard! And he'd dived in on purpose?

She leaned her forearms on the railing and glared down at him, furious. "*What the hell are you doing*?"

He was beside the boat now, his hair plastered to his skull, droplets glistening against the stubble on his jaw. He looked up at her but he made no move to climb aboard. "Taking a swim," he said, as if it were the most logical thing in the world.

"Now? After dark? Alone? In this weather?" Her voice was shrill. She couldn't help it.

"I felt like some exercise."

"You should have said so," she said through her teeth. "I'd have come with you."

He muttered something she didn't hear.

"What if you'd drowned?" she demanded.

"I wouldn't have drowned." He sounded sure of it. "I've been swimming all my life."

"Then you should know that you shouldn't swim alone! Especially in the dark."

"I was fine."

"I was fine on the bow tonight," she reminded. "You got angry then." She narrowed her gaze down at him as he trod water beside the boat. "Is this payback?"

"What? No. Of course not." He looked indignant.

"Then what is it?"

He didn't answer. Instead he turned and started to swim parallel to the boat as if he were going to continue on past it.

"Swim away and I'm coming after you," Anny warned.

He turned back. "You jump in and I'll drown *you*." There was a level of fury in his tone that didn't make sense to her. The whole stupid episode didn't make sense. But he was a man—that probably explained everything.

"Fine," she said. "If you're so desperate to swim, go right ahead. I'll just sit right here and watch."

"What? And play lifeguard?" He gave her an exasperated look. "Going to hold the life preserver?"

She shrugged. "Why not? I won't say a thing, and I'll only throw it to you if you start to drown." She gave him a saccharine smile.

"Oh, for God's sake!" He took three strokes, reached the side of the boat, then hauled himself up and over the side. Water streamed off his bare legs and dripped from the hems of his shorts. He glared down at her, then shook himself like a dog, showering her with more water than the sky was presently providing.

"Happy now?" he snarled.

Anny stared at his hard muscled body and could barely find the spit to get a single word out of her mouth. "I—"

But Demetrios didn't wait to hear her answer. He vaulted over the side into the cockpit and pounded down the steps to the cabin without another word.

When she dared to follow him a few minutes later, he was already in his cabin. The door was shut. The shower running.

A while later she heard it shut off. There were a few more noises, a cabinet door banging.

Then silence.

Silence as long as she stood there, listening.

"Demetrios?" Her voice came, soft but firm, from the other side of the door. "We need to talk."

No, that was the last thing they needed to do. "Go to sleep," he called.

"I can't."

"Well, I'm going to sleep." He flipped off the light, rolled onto his face, and pulled the sheet over him.

She knocked again. And again.

"Damn it, princess!"

"Please."

The perennially polite royal. Damn it. Demetrios rolled over again, then scrubbed his hands against his hair. "Hang on."

He flicked on the light again, dragged on a pair of boxers and some shorts, pulled a T-shirt over his head, then sucked in a deep and, he hoped, sustaining breath, and cracked open the door.

"What?"

She was looking at him the way she'd looked that night on Gerard's yacht. Worried. Bewildered. Almost as if she was in pain. The last thing he wanted now was a woman in pain.

"I'm confused," she said with her best finishing school eloquence. "And I was hoping you'd enlighten me."

"I'm not very enlightening, princess," he said roughly. "And I don't have a clue what you're talking about. I wanted a swim. I needed some exercise. I'm safe and back on board. So could we maybe do this tomorrow and—" He started to shut the door.

She put her foot in it.

They both looked down at her bare toes. Nails painted a delicate peach color. After a moment, she wiggled them experimentally, then looked at him again. Waiting. Foot not moving.

Demetrios sighed heavily. Then he turned her around and put a hand against her back, moving her out into the main cabin where he pointed her to a chair and sat down opposite. "What do you want to know, princess? On what subject am I supposed to 'enlighten' you?"

She leaned toward him. "Why are you angry at me?"

"I'm not angry at you."

"You're angry at someone."

"No."

But she clearly wasn't buying that. "Not me, then. Yourself?" she ventured. "For letting me come along?"

"No. Yes. Hell, this isn't twenty questions."

"Until you start volunteering something, it will be. We were getting along very well. And now we're not. So what's wrong?"

He narrowed his gaze at her. "Why? Do you think you can fix it?"

"If you won't tell me, we won't know, will we?"

He scowled, then ground his teeth in the face of her gentle, curious, bloody innocent smile. He shoved himself out of his chair, paced the length of the galley, then spun around and snarled, "It's elementary biology, princess."

Her eyes widened. She stared. "It is not."

He blinked, momentarily nonplussed at her denial. "Of course it is. Men. Women. Desire. Surely you remember propositioning me the night we met."

"Yes, and you argued vehemently against it," she replied, color high in her cheeks.

"But apparently not hard enough," he said with a sardonic smile. "Because we had sex."

She opened her mouth, and he wondered if she was going to correct him, use the words she'd used at the time: make love. But she didn't. She said, "And it so thrilled you that you didn't care if we ever did it again."

Now it was his turn to stare. "What?"

"You said it was up to me," she reminded him.

"Because I wasn't making it a condition for you coming along. I said I'd be glad to do it anytime! Just say when, remember?" He arched a brow at her.

She shrugged, then stood up and met his gaze. "Fine," she said. "Let's do it."

He stopped dead still. Couldn't believe his ears. "What did you say?"

She lifted her royal chin. "I said, let's do it." Her gaze was unblinking, her stance defiant.

He felt instantly wary. "You said you needed to protect yourself," he told her, doing his best to reconstruct her argument.

She gave a negligent lift of one shoulder. "Didn't work."

He braced a hand on the galley cabinet. "What do you mean, it didn't work?"

"I fell in love with you, anyway."

He felt as if she'd punched him in the gut. His knees felt weak. Slowly, dazedly, he shook his head. "No, you haven't."

"Clairvoyant, are you?"

"Damn it, Anny. You can't."

"I tried not to," she agreed. "Didn't work. My problem. Not yours. So—" she held out a hand toward him "—shall we?"

He couldn't move. Felt as if he had a rock the size of

Gibraltar stuck in his throat. He took a deep breath. Then another. And another.

"No," he said.

They stared at each other then. Her blue eyes were wide and disbelieving. He didn't blame her. He wasn't sure he believed himself.

"You want me," she said, but she didn't sound entirely convinced.

"Wanting and doing something about it are two different things," he told her in no uncertain terms. He leaned back and folded his arms across his chest. He didn't say a word. He didn't have to.

Outside the rain continued to pelt down. But the wind had slackened. The boat barely rocked.

"I don't understand," she said after a long moment.

"It isn't going to happen."

"You're never going to have sex again?" She cocked her head. "Or you're never going to have sex with me?"

His teeth came together with a snap. Then he said bluntly, "Not with you."

Her lashes fluttered and she shook her head as if he made no sense. "Why?"

He began pacing again. "Simple. You want love. You want marriage. I don't."

"I'm not proposing, just propositioning you. But since you brought up the subject of marriage, why are you so against it?"

His fingers curled into fists. "It's none of your business."

She was quiet a long moment. And then she drew a breath slowly, let it out and said, "Because of Lissa."

He jerked, his gaze sharpening at her words.

"I understand," she said softly. "But you can't mourn her forever, Demetrios. You can't die just because she did. I know you loved her and she loved you. But someday you may love someone else and—"

"She didn't love me," he snapped.

Her fingers knotted in her lap. She looked at him with worried eyes.

"My marriage was a disaster," he told her baldly and saw her eyes widen in shock. "It was the worst thing that I ever did. I made the biggest mistake of my life. It gutted me. And I'm never doing it again. Ever."

She didn't move for an age, and then almost in slow motion she sat up straighter and looked at him, her eyes gentle, warm, compassionate. All the things he didn't need—or want.

"I thought… The magazines said," she corrected herself, "that it was wonderful. You were perfect for each other. She was beautiful."

He leaned a hip against the table and folded his arms across his chest. "I thought so, too. Once," he allowed. "It wasn't like that. She wasn't. Not inside. Not where it matters."

He didn't want to talk about it. Did not want to force himself to relive his marriage to Lissa. He'd already been through it on his own too many times—hundreds of them, maybe thousands, each time an attempt to identify where he could have done something, fixed something, said something to make a difference.

"She was driven. She wanted to be the best. To have the best. That's what mattered. The good films. The good roles. The right house. The right man." He grimaced. "It was all a role in the end. One she'd set her heart on since she was a kid. She had to prove herself."

"Like me," Anny said softly. "Needing to be someone besides a princess."

"Not at all like you," he protested. He flung himself down into the chair beside hers. "You're finding out who you are. But you're not stepping on anyone else in the process. You don't use up and spit out."

She pressed her lips together, but didn't speak. Just listened. And Demetrios, once started, couldn't seem to stop talking.

He told her about the whirlwind courtship, the sense of having found the perfect person to complement who he was. "She played a role. She was—for a time—who I wanted her to be, the love of my life, the woman who was going to bear my children." His jaw tightened. He felt Anny's knuckles rub his knee, was conscious of her touch and grateful for it.

"She used people to get what she wanted, where she wanted," he went on heavily. "I was a stepping-stone on the way. Even when I began to realize things weren't the way I thought they'd be, I believed I could change it. I thought I could make her happy. I thought if we had a family, she'd settle down, be happy." His mouth twisted in rueful recognition of his own self-delusion. "I don't know if anything ever would have made Lissa happy." And that was God's own truth.

"She might have learned," Anny said. "If you'd had children—"

"No," he said sharply. "She didn't want them. She said she did at first. Lied about it," he corrected himself. "Or hell, maybe she even believed it. I don't know where her roles ended and the lies began. But she didn't want kids. She wanted a career. And nothing or no one was going to stand in her way."

He leaned back in the chair, his legs sprawled, his gaze on the ceiling. He didn't say anything for a long moment. Then he went on tonelessly. "I was finishing a film in South Carolina. Acting. Not directing. She'd just finished one herself, and I wanted her to come with me. I thought once I finished there we could go some place together, try to work things out. Start again. Start a family." He stopped. Swallowed. Looked at Anny.

The corner of her mouth tipped gently. She waited.

"She got offered a role in Thailand. Fantastic part, she said. She couldn't turn it down." He recited it all calmly, trying for resigned detachment. Failing. "Wouldn't turn it down. She went to Thailand before I got home. I could have gone when I finished. But she said she was working too hard. She didn't need distractions. And I didn't hear again until I got the call from the director that she was in the hospital." He stopped.

"From a blood infection?" Anny said.

"Yes."

"How horrible. Such a freaky thing to get." She reached out and caught his hand in hers.

"She got it aborting our child," he heard himself tell her. He'd never told anyone that.

Anny stared at him, her eyes wide with shock and disbelief. She didn't say a word. Her fingers said it for her. They wrapped around his tightly—and hung on.

He chewed on the inside of his cheek as he felt the familiar ache in his throat, the sting behind his eyes. "I didn't even know she'd been pregnant. Not until I got there. Not until she told me it didn't…fit into her plans."

He couldn't mask the aching hollowness now. He could talk about Lissa with a certain amount of detachment. But he couldn't ever quite get past this part of her betrayal without feeling like she'd driven a knife into his guts.

As if to illustrate, a gust of wind shoved the boat sideways. It rocked and pitched. And Demetrios sat, depleted, disconnected—except for his fingers still caught in Anny's hand.

Finally he shrugged without looking at her and sighed. "So now you know."

She still didn't speak for a long moment. Then she said quietly, "Now I know." Neither of them moved. Neither of them spoke.

The silence went on. And on.

She kept on holding his hand, her thumb rubbing against the side of his finger giving closeness, contact, comfort.

But he couldn't take any more than that.

"That's why the answer is no, Anny. Because I'm not using you. I'm not taking. I don't know why you think you love me. And I hope to God you're wrong. When you make love again, you should get it in return. You deserve it. And I haven't got any left."

CHAPTER NINE

NOW YOU KNOW.

Anny kept hearing his voice saying those same three words over and over in her head. She didn't sleep a wink.

The determined detachment followed by the bitter pain in Demetrios's voice would have been enough to keep her awake. But imagining the nightmare that had been his marriage kept her tossing and turning the whole night.

She—like everyone else in the world—had thought Demetrios Savas's self-imposed exile had been to come to terms with the loss of the woman he so deeply loved, a woman he'd lost to a mysterious virulent infection of the blood.

It was tragic, certainly.

How dare the reality be so much worse?

She wanted desperately to go to him, to comfort him, to assuage all the pain and anger in him.

At the same time she knew that nothing she could offer would do that. There were some losses so deep that people were never the same after. There was always the aching speculation about what might have been, the hollowness that couldn't be filled.

But wasn't it possible to go on? She wondered. To relearn the ability to love? A man as deeply devoted to his family, as genuinely interested in others, as kind and caring as he'd been to her had to know what love meant.

The fact that he'd denied himself the pleasure of physical

release because "it wouldn't be fair to her" was, perversely, a kind of love in itself.

But she couldn't tell him that. She couldn't tell him, either, that she didn't need him to be the perfect man he'd seemed in her youthful fantasies. Or the perfect man he seemed to expect himself to be. She'd fallen in love with the man he was now, scars and all. And if those scars were deeper than she'd ever imagined, it didn't mean she loved him less.

If anything she loved him more for overcoming the pain, for fighting his way back to a productive life, a spectacular career, a compassion for others.

It wasn't that he didn't have love for other people, Anny decided. It was that he didn't have any for himself.

For the next four days Demetrios kept to himself. The weather turned fine so there was no reason not to focus on making the fastest time possible. He kept conversation to a minimum, said he didn't have time to go for a swim or while away the evenings talking under the stars.

He had a screenplay to write, he told her. And she had a dissertation. So when he wasn't actually sailing the boat or eating a meal, he shut himself in his cabin.

You'd think she'd get the point.

But Anny acted like he hadn't spilled his guts and told her what a mess his marriage had been. Her smiles still seemed genuine. Her questions about sailing, about fishing, about recipes his mother had made, for heaven's sake, didn't abate. She didn't give him pitying glances, thank God.

But she was still Anny. And she wore his NYU shirt and his shorts too damned much.

He should ask for them back. She had stuff she could wear now. She'd bought that damn bikini and a couple of shirts and other shorts and pants as well, hadn't she? But while she wore them, it seemed to him she wore his NYU shirt more.

As if she were silently declaring a bond between them. As if the shirt was hers. As if he was.

He wasn't, damn it! But the awareness that existed between them still hummed loudly, even though Demetrios assured himself it would go away.

It would, but Anny didn't.

He'd always thought Theo's yacht was a decent size. It had always felt spacious, roomy, enough for a whole family. He was wrong.

The boat was tiny. Cramped. Everywhere he went, there was Anny. Even when he was on deck, alone, there she was, below him somewhere, in the galley making dinner, or working on her dissertation in her cabin.

After four days he couldn't take any more. Nothing made any difference. She'd got under his skin. She made him want things he swore he'd never want again, prayed he'd never be tempted by again.

Not because she flirted or teased or promised anything special. She'd done it simply by being Anny.

So when they sailed into the harbor at the tiny Greek island of St. Isaakios the following afternoon, Demetrios felt as if he'd got an answer to his prayers.

Anny watched with growing amazement as hordes of people gathering on the waterfront of tiny St. Issakios. The tiny Greek island where they had put in for the night was celebrating its namesake's feast day.

She had thought Demetrios would give it a miss. But he seemed keen to go ashore. It was the first thing he'd seemed keen on since the night he'd turned her down. She supposed grimly that it was good that something appealed to him.

But she knew she wasn't being fair. He was a man in pain. But the truth was, she wasn't exactly thriving on all this rejection herself.

So when he'd suggested stopping, she said, "Why not?"

"You don't have to go ashore," he told her.

But she'd had enough of being on a boat with a man who looked away every time she came into view. She wanted noise and bright lights and hordes of people as much as he did.

"I can hardly wait," she told him recklessly and was gratified to see his dark eyebrows raise.

The transformation of what was surely the normally sleepy island home of a few hundred fishermen and their families was well underway by the time they climbed into the inflatable just past dusk. Waiting until dark was the one concession they made to the desire for anonymity.

When they finally got ashore, Anny found she didn't have her "land legs" yet and stumbled as she started up the dock. Luckily Demetrios caught her and set her back on her feet. But just as quickly, he let her go again.

"You don't have to stick with me if you'd rather not," Anny said.

Demetrios looked at the milling crowds of people, half of them already drunk and the other half well on their way in that direction. "Don't be an idiot," he said gruffly. "Come on."

The waterfront was jammed with people. Thousands of tiny fairy lights were strung along the streets near the harbor. The heavy bass from the beach concert made the ground shake under their feet. Hurrying to keep up with him, Anny stumbled again.

This time he caught her and hung on. The crowds were growing thicker and more boisterous as they moved away off the dock and onto the street facing the harbor. The noise was deafening and after all their days on the water, this sea of humanity was overpowering.

"It's insane!" she yelled, jostled by a group of boys running through the square. Hundreds, maybe thousands, of people were singing and dancing and shouting, drinking and yelling and throwing each other into the sea.

"You want to go back to the boat?" he shouted the words in her ear.

Someone on the beach was setting off fireworks. Someone else was shooting bottle rockets. Photographers' flashes were like sparklers, glittering and incessant. Anny shook her head. "No." There would only be solitude on the boat. She didn't want that. "It's amazing," she yelled back. "We don't have anything quite like this in Mont Chamion!"

"Lucky you! Let's find a place to eat."

They walked away from the waterfront and found the crowds and the noise dwindled a bit. When they did find a restaurant with an empty table, Demetrios was in no hurry for once.

He'd bolted his meals with her the past four days. But that was when they'd been alone. Now he seemed quite content to eat slowly and order another beer. He didn't talk about anything personal. She did her best with Madame's "conversation starters," but he was immune to all of them. When he did talk, he talked about ideas for his screenplay or about people he needed to talk to when the trip was over—as if he could hardly wait.

Anny listened. She took her time over her meal, too. She knew that they would be in Santorini tomorrow. This was the end of the road. And if this was all she was going to get of Demetrios Savas in her life, she would hang on to the evening for as long as she could.

She did her best. Even so it seemed no time at all—though it was probably at least a couple of hours—until Demetrios said, "We should get an early start in the morning. I talked to Theo today and he wanted to know what time we'd be in. I figure we can be there by late afternoon." He even smiled, as if he were counting the minutes until he got rid of her.

Anny just nodded and said, "I'm looking forward to meeting your brother."

Demetrios blinked, as if the notion hadn't occurred to him. Was he going to shuffle her off to a hotel before she could even meet Theo?

He didn't say. But abruptly he called for the check and paid for the meal, standing up as if she didn't still have a half a glass of wine in front of her. "We should get going," he said.

The crowds in the streets had dispersed somewhat now, some moving into *tavernas* to get down to some serious drinking, others onto the roofs of local houses where small parties continued.

The main party had moved from the beach to the *agora*—the small open-air market area—which faced the harbor. The loud rock band had dispersed—probably into the *tavernas* or away in boats—and a smaller group playing more traditional music was delighting the crowd. Couples were dancing, arms around each other, moving to the music, to each other. Anny slowed her pace, watching them, envying them.

"Come on." Demetrios caught her hand so they could skirt around the crowd.

But caught by a combination of music and desire, Anny dug in her heels. "Dance with me."

"*What*?" He stopped abruptly, a flicker of annoyance crossing his features. He gave her hand another tug.

Anny didn't move. "Just one dance." She looked at him beseechingly.

His jaw tightened. "Anny—"

But she wouldn't be gainsaid. Not now. "One dance, Demetrios. One."

The musicians weren't great. The music was tinny and sometimes out of tune. It didn't matter. Their trip was almost over. She knew Demetrios wasn't going to wake up and discover that she wasn't Lissa, or anything like her.

She couldn't argue him around to believing that. Just as she couldn't argue him around to loving her.

So she'd take what she could get: one dance.

She wanted to feel his arms around her one more time. Not making love. But loving. Loving him.

Tomorrow or the next day these memories would be all she'd have left to relish, to savor. She looked up at him, her eyes speaking to him.

His mouth twisted. He rubbed a hand over the stubble that was now a reasonably respectable two-week-old beard. If he danced with her she could turn her head, press her cheek to his jaw and feel that beard. She'd only felt it in her imagination until now.

If they danced, she'd have one more memory to sustain her.

"Just a dance, Demetrios. To remember."

He hesitated, then shrugged. "Oh hell. Why not?"

It was hell—and heaven—all rolled into one.

The minute he slipped his arms around Anny to dance with

her, the moment he felt her body fit itself to his, Demetrios knew he was done for.

He would have laughed bitterly at his own foolishness, if the desire for her weren't so intense, if the longing weren't so real. Anger and desperation he could fight.

He couldn't fight this.

It was like having his dreams come true. It was like being offered a taste of all he'd ever longed for. A single spoonful that would have to last him for the rest of his life.

"To remember," Anny had said, like it was a good thing.

How could it be good to have a hollow aching reminder of the joy he'd once believed was his due. It wasn't. He didn't believe in promises anymore. Yet, as much as he tried not to give in, he couldn't resist.

It was like trying to resist gravity. Like agreeing to step off a cliff—then refusing to let himself fall.

Impossible.

He drew her closer, looped his arms around her and rested his cheek against her hair. It was so soft, tendrils like butterfly wings tickled his nose. He breathed in the scent of her—a heady combination of citrus and the sea, and permeating everything something indefinably essentially Anny.

They barely moved as the music played on. They simply held each other, swaying, savoring, dreaming—

The camera flash came like a shot in the dark. Once. Twice. Half a dozen times. Blinding him as it moved in and around them in quick succession.

Not, he realized at once, just aimed at him. Aimed at Anny, too. And the rapid repeat fire speed of the shutter flashes told him it wasn't a tourist's camera. *Paparazzo.*

He swore under his breath as he felt her stiffen in his arms. He drew her close, shielded her. "Are you okay? I'm sorry. I'll get him. I'll stop him!"

But almost instantly she stepped back, looking as stunned as he was, but immediately laying a hand on his arm. "No. It's all right. It happens."

She sounded calm, collected. He was furious. "It'll be in every damn tabloid on the continent. Totally misconstrued."

Lissa had loved that sort of thing, delighted in the notoriety. But he was surprised that Anny wasn't more upset.

"I'll talk to him." She was already looking for the jerk.

"Talk?" Since when did you talk to paparazzi?

But Anny was hurrying after the photographer, calling out in perfect fluent Greek, "Please stop. Come talk to me."

Please? Demetrios rolled his eyes.

But the photographer stopped. Demetrios would have happily grabbed his camera and throttled the man on the spot.

Anny was all charm. "Isn't the festival wonderful?" She smiled at the photographer. "How long have you been here? Did you get lots of good shots? Have you had a good day?"

Her and her bloody "conversation starters"! But it worked. And while Demetrios watched, Anny used an arsenal of charm and camaraderie to disarm and enchant the man who had stolen their privacy.

She didn't take his camera and destroy his pictures. She gave him a story to go with them, explaining that she was getting her Ph.D. in archaeology and did he know about the nearby ruins? She'd always wanted to see them and her dear friend Demetrios, whom she'd chanced to meet up with at the festival in Cannes, had offered to bring her today.

Not a word of it was untrue. She never said they'd actually seen the ruins. She never said she'd spent close to two weeks on a sailboat with him. She said they'd had a wonderful time and a wonderful meal and who could resist dancing after such a wonderful day?

Then she said with an impish smile, "Will you dance with me?"

The photographer almost dropped his teeth.

"I'll hold the camera," Demetrios offered helpfully.

But the photographer was no fool. "Nice try," he laughed. "But even a dance with a princess isn't worth the price of these photos." And giving them a quick salute he hurried away.

"You would have crushed his camera," Anny said flatly.

"Damn straight."

She sighed, then shrugged. "Well, you have your way and I have mine."

"He'll print the pictures."

"Yes. But it won't embarrass my father when he sees them."

Demetrios sat silently with his hand on the tiller of the inflatable's small engine all the way back to Theo's boat. He had closed in on himself in a way that shouldn't have surprised her.

He'd been more and more reclusive since he'd told her about his marriage to Lissa. But this felt different. He didn't seem bitter so much as thoughtful. He was probably upset about the photos, thinking she had been a fool. She didn't think so. Her father had taught her never to be adversarial unless it was absolutely necessary. It hadn't been.

But she felt sad now. Happy she'd been able to defuse the situation with the photographer. But at what cost?

The end of her closeness with Demetrios. The flashes had come like the clock striking midnight in the middle of Cinderella's last dance. And now whenever she remembered their dance, the memory wouldn't be the one she wanted.

But they couldn't go back to the *agora* and recapture it. The photographer had departed happily enough, and she wasn't worried about what he would say in his story. But their anonymity had departed with him.

Now everyone stopped to look at them. To whisper. To stare. To nudge.

"A princess," they whispered. "With Demetrios Savas—he is Greek, you know."

So they'd gone to the dock and came straight back to the boat. She got a rock in her sandal and didn't even stop to shake it out until they were on the boat.

Now, after he'd tied the inflatable onto the stern of the sailboat, Demetrios helped her out, then hauled the inflatable aboard after them.

"Can I help you stow it?" Anny offered, knowing the answer before she even asked the question.

"I can manage." He made quick work of stowing it.

Anny, having lost her chance at the dance, still wouldn't give up on the moment. She sat down on the bench in the cockpit and took off her sandals while she watched Demetrios work.

The sound of the music carried across the water. Sweet hummable, danceable music that made Anny remember the way Demetrios's arms had felt around her, the way his beard had felt against her cheek. Her throat ached. She curled her toes, then relaxed them again, then rubbed the muscles on the sole of her foot.

"Let me."

She looked up, startled, to see Demetrios sit down next to her and pull her foot up onto his lap and begin massaging her instep. She wanted to whimper.

Maybe she did whimper. His fingers were so strong, so firm. So unexpected.

Then he reached down to pick up her other foot, and once more strong fingers kneaded her sole, stroked her toes.

"Better?"

She nodded. Her feet felt boneless. Her body was quivering. Her eyes flickered shut.

"Then dance with me."

Her eyes flew open. She stared. It was almost totally dark. His expression was unreadable. There was a rough edge to his voice.

"No flashbulbs here," he said. "But we can still hear the music." Then he lifted her feet off his lap and stood, holding out his hand to her.

Anny swallowed. Then she stood and went into his arms. She felt them close loosely around her, then tighten, fitting their bodies together. Her lips brushed his beard as she lifted her face. Then he rested his cheek against her hair.

She slid her hands up his back, and relished the feel of the soft cotton and hard muscle under her palms. Her fingers caressed the nape of his neck, kneaded and stroked, then traced the curve of his ear.

It was heaven. Eternity. She memorized every touch, every

movement, the pounding of his heart against hers. She didn't ask why. She only knew joy. Dared to believe.

And then the music stopped.

He didn't step away. He stayed there, stood there, holding her. Then a long while later, when the music began again—something light and lively this time—he lifted his head and she reached up and touched his bearded cheek, lay her palm against it and knew she would never forget the feel.

He took her hand and opened it to kiss the center of her palm.

Anny felt a shiver of longing run through her. "Please," she whispered.

Their gazes locked, held.

A sound caught in his throat. And then he took her and drew her toward the stairs.

Maybe it was because she didn't use the word *love*.

Maybe it was because he was at the end of his rope.

Maybe—and this was what she dared hope for most of all— he finally believed in the love she felt for him and was learning he loved her in return.

He never said. She didn't ask.

It was enough tonight to simply show him. No past, no future—only now.

They were kissing again before they got down the companionway steps. She nearly fell on top of him.

"Careful." He caught her and began undressing her.

They barely made it to her cabin. He scooped her up and laid her on her bunk, then came down beside her, his hands tugging her shirt over her head as hers did the same to his.

She raked her fingers over the soft, yet wiry, hair on his chest, even as he cupped her breasts and bent to kiss them through the lace of her bra. But it wasn't enough. His fingers fumbled for only a moment with the clasp, and then he had it off and was kissing her there again.

She grabbed his hair in her fists and tugged. He lifted his head to say, "You don't like that?"

"I like it. I—" She shifted, unable to say what she wanted, what she liked. "It makes me…want more."

And he promised, "There will be more."

He kissed her again, down the center of her chest, then each breast in turn. He laved them, teased them, made her nipples peak and her body move restlessly on the bunk.

And then he was skimming the rest of their clothes off and stroking her, starting at her feet, kissing her knees, letting his fingers wander up her thighs.

Anny bit her lip, trembling at the sensations he caused. But it wasn't only the sensations, it was the man. It was Demetrios she loved. And her own fingers reached to touch him, to trace their way down his belly, following the line of dark hair to the core of his masculinity.

She ran her fingers through the thatch of dark hair at the juncture of his thighs, trailed the tip of one finger along the length of him. He sucked in a sharp breath.

"Anny!"

"What?"

But then his fingers found her, too, dipped in and caressed her, and she didn't need to ask "what" anymore. She knew. She shivered and pressed against his fingers.

Then he nudged her knees apart and settled between them. He loomed over her, his eyes hooded, the skin taut across his cheek-bones, his face more beautiful now than she had ever seen it.

She touched him again, stroked him. Learned the shape and hot silken texture of him. She hadn't dared do this last time. She barely dared now. And as soon as she had, she wanted to do it again. And again.

A breath hissed between his teeth. "Anny."

"Yes," she said.

"Now," she said.

"Please," she said.

At that, a sudden laugh caught in his throat. And then he slid into her. Her own breath caught.

Perfect. Union.

His eyelids fluttered. His head tipped back, the chords of his neck stood out. For a long moment he held himself perfectly still. And then he began to move.

And Anny moved with him. Rocked him. Held him.

And the two of them shattered together. Their solitary beings broken, splintered by their climax.

But as she ran her fingers lightly down his sweat-slicked back, in her heart Anny made them whole together in her love.

CHAPTER TEN

THEY WERE ALREADY underway the next morning by the time Anny awoke.

That had never happened before. She'd always awakened the moment the engine started. Not this morning.

But she'd never before had a night like last night, either. She rolled over in Demetrios's bed, feeling more amazing than she'd ever felt in her life. He was gone, of course. The sheet was cool. So was the pillow. He hadn't stayed, but it didn't matter— because he loved her.

When you make love again, you should get it in return. You deserve it. He had said those words to her. He wouldn't have done it if he hadn't.

She reached for his pillow, picked it up and brought it against her face, drawing in a deep breath and, with it, the subtle scent of him—sea and salt, a faint hint of some sort of balsam shampoo, and something essentially Demetrios.

She hugged the pillow to her as she'd held him last night, wrapping her arms around it, clinging as if she would never let go. Of course she had. And he had gone.

But he loved her. She knew it.

She got up and took a shower, long and leisurely, discovering as she did so that her body felt different now. Muscles she had barely known she had were a little sore, a delicious reminder of her night of love with Demetrios.

She washed her hair, combed it long and straight, then dressed in a pair of her own new shorts, but chose to wear Demetrios's NYU T-shirt with it. It was hers.

And she was his.

She took her time, savoring the moments, making breakfast for the two of them before she took the eggs and ham up to him. She felt fresh and loved and yet oddly self-conscious as she climbed the stairs and smiled at him.

He saw her the instant she appeared. There was no answering smile.

He said, "I'm sorry."

Anny stiffened, felt as if she'd been slapped. "*Sorry*? You didn't like it?"

"Of course I liked it. It was…amazing. But…I'm sorry it happened. It shouldn't have."

Stung, tears springing to her eyes and blinking rapidly because she was damned if she was going to cry, she retorted. "Oh? And do you say that to all the girls?"

Demetrios's knuckles went white on the wheel. "No, damn it, I don't. Because ordinarily I don't make mistakes like that."

"You married Lissa."

He jerked as if she'd slapped him.

"I'm sorry," she said quickly. Then retracted the apology at once. "No, I'm not. I'm sorry you had a bad marriage. I'm sorry she hurt you. I'm sorry—beyond sorry—she aborted your child and destroyed your dreams. I'm sorry she's dead. But I am not Lissa!"

"No," he said roughly. "You aren't. You're worth a thousand of her. You're worth a thousand of me. You deserve a whole hell of a lot better than what happened between us last night."

"Thank you very much," she said tightly. "Not."

"Hell, Anny." He raked a hand through his hair. "See? That's why it was a mistake. You care!"

"So do you!"

"No."

"Liar. You said when I made love next I deserved to get it in return. I got it last night."

His jaw clenched. He looked away, shaking his head, then finally back at her. "I care about you, yes," he allowed.

"Big of you," she muttered.

"Which is exactly why it was wrong. I was wrong. I was…caught up in the moment. God, that sounds asinine. I wanted a memory, too! But I shouldn't have done it. I shouldn't have raised your expectations. I shouldn't have—"

"Oh, you raised my expectations, did you? Did you think I was coming up here to propose marriage this morning?"

A harsh line of red lit his cheekbones. "I hope not," he said flatly. "Because while it was wrong, it doesn't change anything."

It changed everything. He just didn't know it yet. But she didn't say it. This wasn't something she could convince him of by argument. He had to come to know it in his gut the same way she did.

He had further to go. She needed to give him time.

"I love you, Demetrios."

He flinched at her words. His teeth came together and he shook his head. "Don't."

She smiled through her pain. "Too late now."

"It's not," he insisted.

"Yes," she said firmly. "It is."

And that was the absolute truth.

They reached Santorini late that afternoon.

A man instantly identifiable as a Savas was waiting at the dock. She knew Demetrios had radioed Theo to say what time they would be arriving. It was obvious he hadn't bothered to say that he wasn't alone.

Theo's curiosity was instant and obvious. Demetrios was determinedly offhand. "This is Anny. Anny, my brother Theo. Anny lives in Cannes. She's a doctoral student, working on her dissertation. She needed a break for a couple of weeks, so she came along to crew for me."

Theo grinned. He took Anny's hand in his big callused one

and gave it a squeeze. "Doctoral student, huh? Impressive. Smart and beautiful. Little brother's taste is improving."

Demetrios looked up sharply from the line he was stowing. "She's not—"

Theo lifted a brow. "Not smart? Not beautiful? Not single?" he challenged.

Anny couldn't help but laugh.

Demetrios's teeth came together with a snap. He stood up abruptly. "Don't just stand there. Get my gear and I'll take Anny's. She'll be staying at Lucio's."

"Ma won't hear of it."

"*Ma* won't—" Demetrios stopped dead and turned his head to stare narrowly at his brother. "Ma's not here. Theo, tell me she's not here."

Theo shrugged helplessly "What can you do? It's their house."

Demetrios muttered something under his breath. For a moment Anny thought he might balk, leave her there and head straight back out to sea. He seemed to be considering his options. Theo gave Anny a conspiratorial look, but just waited patiently.

Finally Demetrios sighed and rubbed a hand over his face. "You knew," he accused his brother.

"I didn't, actually. Martha might have," he allowed. "Ma works in mysterious ways. And, let's face it, she wants to see you."

Demetrios appeared to grind his teeth. Then he nodded. "Right. Let's get it over with."

The Savas house, which had originally belonged to Theo's wife Martha's family, and was now shared by both extended families, had been expanded by their taking over houses on both sides.

"Room for everyone," Theo told her as he tossed their duffel bags into his car. He gestured up the steep hillside overlooking the town of Thira. "It's a great place. Best thing the old man ever won."

Anny gave him a quizzical look. "Won?"

So while he drove them up the narrow winding road, Theo regaled her with the tale of the sailboat race that he, in fact—not his father—had won against Aeolus Antonides. It was a tale of golf games and sailboat races and in the end it had garnered them a share of the lovely old house. "And my wife," Theo said. "And Tallie's husband."

Anny's eyes widened. She'd only heard of these people. Demetrios had talked about his family growing up. He'd not been very forthcoming about more recent years. But there was no time to ask now because as Theo finished, he was pulling to a stop in front of the walled steps leading up to the house.

"Come on, then, prodigal son," Theo said cheerfully, giving his brother a cuff on the shoulder before he opened the door.

Truer words were never spoken, Anny thought as she watched from the backseat. For the minute Theo opened his car door, the gate to the walled stairway banged open and a veritable horde of people of all sizes and ages hurtled out onto the pavement.

A pretty young dark-haired woman grabbed Demetrios before he could even get out of the car. An older man who must have been his father did pull him out, and he was immediately wrapped in the arms of a woman who could only be Demetrios's mother. She was talking and laughing and crying all at the same time.

Demetrios looked stunned. He moved stiffly at first, but then his arms came up and wrapped hard around his mother and his father as well. He bent his head, kissed them both. And then he was completely enveloped by all of them, then swept up the stairs, leaving her in silence.

Theo opened the car door for her and offered her a lopsided grin. "They do the prodigal thing pretty well, don't they?"

Anny swallowed the lump in her throat. "They do. And they should. It's wonderful to see how much you all love him."

"We do," Theo agreed. He banged the car door shut. "Though he's made it damn difficult these last few years." He opened the boot and got out their duffel bags. "The folks haven't seen him since Lissa's funeral," he told her. "No one in the family has except me. And I did because I turned up on his doorstep once without warning and he couldn't pretend he wasn't home." He dropped their luggage on the pavement, then slammed the lid. "She has a lot to answer for, that woman."

Anny was surprised. "You know about Lissa?" She didn't think from what Demetrios said, he'd told anyone.

Theo snorted and confirmed it. "Not from him. He wouldn't say a word. But I know my brother. I know what he's like—what he *was* like," he corrected himself. "She wasn't good for him. She changed him. I'm sorry she's dead," he said gruffly. "But I'm not sorry she's out of his life."

Which pretty much summed up her own feelings, Anny thought.

"It's a relief to see him with you, let me tell you." Theo held open the gate to the stairs for her and she passed gratefully from the blistering heat of the midday sun to the relative coolness of the trellised bougainvillea-shaded stairs that wound upwards toward the house.

"He's not— We're not…together," Anny felt compelled to say, however much she wished it weren't true.

Theo stopped and narrowed his gaze at her. "No? Who says? Him? Or you?"

Anny couldn't help smiling at how well Theo had assessed the situation. "Demetrios."

A grin slashed across Theo's tanned face. "Ah, well. As long as you don't say it."

Anny didn't say anything at all because they had reached the front door, which stood open to a wide entryway leading to an open living room full of the same jumble of people. She didn't see Demetrios.

"Ma will be feeding him," Theo said. "Come on and meet the family. There won't be a quiz at the end or anything, so relax. They don't bite."

He took her from group to group and introduced her to their sister Tallie, who turned out to be the young woman who had opened the car door, her husband Elias, and their children, another brother, Yiannis, who was arguing with a guy called Lukas who might have been Elias's brother, but Anny wasn't sure.

She met Martha, Theo's wife, who kissed both her cheeks and said, "Have we met? You look familiar?" She seemed to be studying Anny closely.

Quickly Anny shook her head. "No. I haven't met any of Demetrios's family."

Martha laughed. "Lucky you. But then, we're glad to have you. And if you survive all the Savases and the Antonideses, we'll know you deserve him. Good luck."

So it seemed that more than just Theo thought they were "together." Anny was pleased, though she didn't imagine Demetrios would be.

"He's a good man, Demetrios," Martha said. "Almost as good as this one," she said, slipping her arm around Theo's waist.

Anny envied them their obvious love, their easy closeness. She saw the same thing again between Tallie and Elias. He had one of their twins on his shoulders and the other hanging off one arm, but his free arm was around his wife as he talked to Yiannis and Lukas. The joy of connection—of a relationship based on true love and commitment—was so clear. So obvious.

Anny wanted it so badly. With Demetrios.

She wondered if her yearning showed on her face for Theo said suddenly, "Come on out to the kitchen. You need to meet the folks."

Malena and Socrates Savas welcomed her with open arms and profound apologies.

"We didn't realize Demetrios was bringing a guest," his mother said. "We are so happy to meet you. So glad he brought you. Where are you from? Who are your parents?"

"She's a friend, Ma," Demetrios cut in before she could reply. "She crewed for me. That's all."

Malena raised a brow, then said. "Of course, dear." But it didn't stop her from studying Anny closely, then nodding and patting her cheek. "You have done him good."

"Ma!"

Malena ignored him. "Come." She steered Anny to a chair in the kitchen. "Sit down. Eat."

The rest of the afternoon was a whirlwind of activity—of siblings and in-laws, nephews and nieces, all of them eager to welcome Demetrios home again.

"It's a madhouse," he muttered at one point when he came to stand beside her. "I'm sorry."

Anny wasn't. "I love it. You are so lucky to have them. All of them. Such a wonderful family. You are blessed."

He grunted a reply. But she knew he agreed. She'd heard that love those evenings when he'd talked to her about his family. He had missed them. He just needed to figure out how to fit back into the family group.

They made it easy for him. His parents were, of course, thrilled that he was finally home. His sister and brothers—they were all there except George—never mentioned the past three years. They just caught him up on what was going on. They drew him back into the fold as if he'd never been away. The in-laws were equally welcoming. The oldest nephews, Tallie's twins, Nick and Garrett, and Theo's Edward had seen videos of Luke St. Angier. They even remembered him as a favorite uncle from the pre-Lissa days. And it didn't take them long to warm up to him again, to climb all over him and drag him into their games. And while sometimes he looked briefly lost and hollow-eyed, they won him over.

They won Anny over, too. And she won them because she knew the games that little boys played. She told them all about Alex and Raoul and David and said how much her brothers would love to play with this roughhousing clan.

"Go get 'em," Edward suggested. "Bring 'em here."

Anny laughed. "I'd love to, but they live a long way away."

"Take a plane," Nick advised.

"Or a limo," Garrett said, making car noises.

"Limos don't go fast," his brother argued.

"Do so!"

"Do not!"

The discussion that followed didn't require any help from Anny at all.

Nothing much required her help for the rest of the day and evening. But she never felt left out. They made her feel a part of their family. And of course she wasn't allowed to go to Lucio's.

"It's crazy here, Ma. She doesn't need to put up with this," Demetrios argued.

Malena straightened up and gave a sharp look. "This is our home. We want her here. She is welcome here. You will stay, Anny?"

Demetrios wanted her to go, she could see it on his face. But Anny was determined to take what she could get.

"I would love to stay, Mrs. Savas."

Demetrios's mother beamed and wrapped her in a warm hug. "Malena, dear. You must call me Malena."

She spent the night in the room right across the hall from him. Shared it with his three-year-old niece, Caroline, for God's sake. She didn't seem to mind a bit when his mother suggested it.

"At Lucio's she'd have a room of her own," he'd pointed out.

But no one listened to anything he said. Just like old times, he thought.

But it was painful to watch her with them. She was so obviously delighted to be part of things. They were falling all over themselves to bring her into the fold, and nothing he could say or do seemed to have any effect at all.

The next morning she and Caroline appeared together in the doorway to the breakfast room, holding hands.

"Ah. Did you sleep well, my Anny?" his mother asked.

Her Anny! His teeth ground together. He took a gulp of coffee and nearly scalded his throat.

"Come." His mother was making a place for her at the table across from him, between Yiannis and one of the babies in a high chair. "Sit. We have yogurt, fresh fruit. Eggs, ham. Martha is making French toast. Do you like French toast?"

"I love it," Anny said and, as usual, offered to help.

Next thing he knew she was eating a yogurt with one hand, feeding the baby next to her, and talking to his sister, Tallie, about Viennese pastries at the same time. Her gaze lit on him regularly. He watched her while trying not to. But he was weak where she was concerned. He couldn't help it.

And seeing the woman he loved—yes, all right, he loved

her!—happily involved with his family was a scene he'd always dreamed of. He'd cast Lissa in that role and knew very quickly the mistake he'd made. He wasn't going to make another one. And he wasn't going to let Anny make one. But watching Anny take a cloth and wipe the baby's mouth, then offer her another spoonful of cereal, was a sight that made him ache.

Suddenly the door to the roof garden banged open and Edward hurtled into the room. "Daddy! There's a limo coming up the hill."

"It's stoppin' right out front!" Nick and Garrett came roaring in on his heels.

Abruptly, Theo, Yiannis, Lukas and Socrates hurried up the stairs to have a look. Demetrios didn't move. Anny went suddenly still.

His mother paused, putting eggs on a plate. "A limo? For you, Demetrios? Not already," she said.

He shook his head. "Not for me." But he knew who it was for. "It's for Anny."

Anny knew who the limo was for the moment Edward said the word.

The jig is up, she thought. *The fairy tale is over. The photos had reached the palace.*

And yet, at the same time, she didn't believe it. She was a princess wasn't she? Princesses got happy endings—especially if they risked for them. It was the essence of good storytelling.

Besides, Demetrios loved her.

Anny knew it. She could see it in his eyes when he watched her. And even when he pretended he wasn't watching, she knew better. Wherever he was in the room, she could feel his gaze on her.

Now she looked at him and smiled tentatively, but determinedly. Prayed that he would smile back. That he would own up to his feelings, accept them, act on them. Love her.

Of course there would have to be explanations. Anny knew that. His family would have to be told. She dabbed at the baby's sweet face once more, making sure it was clean, then pasted on her best public smile and prepared to make them.

But abruptly Demetrios said, "Anny's not just Anny, Ma. She's Her Royal Highness, Princess Adriana of Mont Chamion."

For a split second Malena Savas looked at her middle son as if he were speaking a foreign language. Uncomprehending. Then, as the truth dawned, her face registered shock. Then, abruptly, resolution. In the next instant, she was wiping her hands on a towel and saying briskly, "Go get your father, Tallie. And tell him to tuck his shirt in."

Anny wanted to say it didn't matter. Nothing mattered but this—she and Demetrios. Being part of his family. Forever.

She looked at Demetrios.

He straightened almost imperceptibly. "I'll get the door."

Her father hadn't sent his driver. He hadn't sent his minister.

When Demetrios came back a few moments later and opened the door to allow the newcomer to precede him, Anny discovered that her father had come himself.

He stood just inside the door, a man of medium height and average build. But you knew he was a king just by looking at him, Anny thought. He had the carriage of generations of royal upbringing. He stood straight under years of responsibility. He had an aura about him of presence, of command. He was in charge and no one doubted it.

Yet in his eyes she saw concern. New lines of worry seemed to crease his face. They softened now at the sight of her. "Adriana."

"Papa." Her voice wobbled for a moment, weighed down by the sudden guilt she felt from having caused those lines, that concern. "You didn't have to come all this way."

"Of course I had to come," he said. "You are my daughter."

"Yes, but—"

"I saw the photos," he said. "I knew who you were with. Where you had to be going. Certainly I had to come." He held out a hand to her then.

Vaguely aware that the room behind her was filling with amazed and intrigued family members, coming back down from the roof garden and tumbling out of the kitchen to stare, Anny crossed the few feet that separated them. She kissed her father on both cheeks and felt the gentle but firm press of his lips on hers as well.

She stepped back, but he didn't let go. He held her away from him and looked into her eyes for a long moment, seeking, searching. And once more she felt a stab of guilt at the same time she knew that she had done the right thing. She couldn't have stayed and married Gerard. She had to make her own way, be true to herself, to love as she would.

Instantly she looked around for Demetrios. He was standing by his father, his expression unreadable. She reached out a hand to him.

"This is Demetrios, Papa," she said.

He stepped forward, but he didn't come and take her hand. He nodded politely to her father. "Your Highness."

"Yes. We met when he answered the door." Her father's gaze settled on Demetrios, looking at him with that same searching look.

Now, Anny thought. *Say it now. Say you love me. Tell him.*

But Demetrios remained silent, meeting her father's gaze implacably.

And so Anny stepped into the breach. Madame would have been proud. "Papa, I'd like you to meet Demetrios's family."

She introduced them all. Malena offered him coffee and biscuits. Socrates inquired about his flight. Garrett, Nick and Edward hopped up and down and finally wanted to know if the limo driver would let them see the inside of it.

Demetrios didn't say a word.

Her father drank a cup of coffee and ate two biscuits. He listened politely when Anny talked about their journey and drew Theo into a discussion of the boat.

Demetrios didn't say a word.

Her father discussed private jets with Socrates, and boat-building with Elias, and he generously allowed the little boys to roam all over the limo and seemed amused when Lukas and Yiannis clattered down the steps to have a look with them. He looked at Demetrios.

Demetrios didn't say a word.

Anny willed him to speak. Willed him to come to her, to hold out a hand to her and admit his love. She didn't see or even feel his gaze upon her though she stared at him nearly every moment. He was in the room, but he seemed to have withdrawn completely.

Finally her father declined another cup of coffee, said, "No, thank you very much," politely to the offer of more biscuits, and stood up. Instantly every man and woman in the room stood up, too.

"If you will collect your things, my dear. We should go."

Go. Leave her dream. Go back to the real world. Anny held her breath, wishing on all the stars in the universe as she looked across the room at the man of her dreams, her heart in her eyes.

"I'll get her bags," Demetrios said.

CHAPTER ELEVEN

DEMETRIOS couldn't stand there and watch her go.

He got her bags from her room and carried them down to the car, aware of what seemed like hordes of his relatives pressing around Anny and her father, following them to the limo. He couldn't do that.

So he said goodbye the only way he could. He went up to the rooftop garden and looked down to watch her embrace his parents, his sister, his brothers, all the children. Then she looked around.

For him? He knew the answer to that. Of course she was looking for him—because she loved him. As, God help him, he loved her.

He had fallen in love a little bit when she'd let him sweep her off her feet. She'd been a good sport when he needed one. And when he'd seen her with Franck and the other kids at the clinic, giving of herself, doing what needed to be done, he'd fallen a bit more. He'd fallen a little deeper that night on Gerard's yacht, when he realized how far she'd been prepared to go—to marry for her country, not for herself. Loyalty and devotion were so much a part of who Anny was.

It was none of his business, of course, but he knew he couldn't let her do it. Though how he would have stopped her, he didn't know. Thoughts of breaking up a royal wedding to save her from herself were a bit over-the-top—but not by much.

But how could he let her tie herself to a loveless marriage?

He knew about loveless marriages. Knew the aching loneliness, the sense of failure. Gerard wasn't Lissa, of course. But Anny deserved so much more.

So when he was tempted to hurtle down the stairs and say, "Don't go," he didn't. His knuckles tightened on the waist-high white-washed wall, anchoring him right where he was.

Then the chauffeur helped her in. Her father joined her. And the limo pulled away. The glass was tinted. He couldn't see past it, couldn't see Anny now. But he didn't need to see her to know how she looked.

She was there on the inside of his eyelids when he closed them. She was there in his dreams when he slept. She was a part of every fiber of his being.

She'd said he loved her, and truer words were never spoken. But what did he have to offer a woman like Anny?

He had made it back from the disaster that had been his marriage to Lissa. But he wasn't the man he had been. He had nothing to give her except what he'd given her these past two weeks—the chance to be herself without the demands of her country and her title, the chance to discover what she wanted, who she was.

He knew who he was.

He also knew she didn't need a man like him. He had too much baggage. Too many bad memories. Too little belief in happy endings.

And more than anyone he knew, Anny deserved a happy ending.

At least he had memories, thanks to her. It was ironic, he supposed, that she'd been the one to ask him for a memory that first night. He'd never imagined how much it would matter to him that he had it, too. And he had memories of these past two weeks with her as well. Memories of her laughter, her joy, her hard work, her generosity, memories of the most lively, loving woman he would ever meet.

And last night. He would never forget last night—never forget making love to her one last time. He shouldn't have done it, should have resisted.

But how could anyone resist when Anny said, *please*?

Thank God she hadn't looked at him a few minutes ago and said, *Please. Please ask me to stay. Please don't let me go.*

If she had, there was no way he could have let her go back to her real life, to her kingdom, to whichever prince she would ultimately marry. To a future without him. He only managed to because he loved her. And because he'd come up here alone.

He couldn't have stood there among his family and watched her leave. Couldn't have smiled and said all those polite things Anny knew how to say. Couldn't have kissed her cheeks and wished her happy because he knew it was the right thing to do, because he knew she would be better off without him.

He might have three Emmy nominations, a Golden Globe and fifteen films under his belt, but he wasn't that good an actor.

They had barely left the Savas family behind when Papa spoke. "I have spoken to Gerard."

Anny jerked. "I'm not—" she began.

But her father shushed her and took her hand in his. "You are not marrying him," he said in his gentle but firm voice.

"Yes, I know."

"I'm sorry, Papa. I know you want me to. But I can't!"

"My Anny." Her father chafed her fingers with his, all the while regarding her gravely with his deep brown eyes. "I only ever wanted you to be happy." A rueful look flickered across his face. "And I hoped…" He shrugged. "Gerard is a good man. Older, yes, but not doddering like me."

"You're not doddering!"

"Perhaps not. But foolish I could be. The point is, I thought it would be a good marriage, a marriage like mine and your mother's. That you might grow to love each other as we did. Our marriage was arranged, too, you know."

"Yes," Anny said quietly. But she'd always believed her parents had been in love before their marriage. She'd blinked in surprise at her father's revelation. And then she'd said, "I'm glad it happened for you. But I can't!"

He nodded. "I know. I knew it when I saw the pictures."

The pictures.

He picked up a folder from the seat and opened it, handing her a stack of photos, and the tabloids that had printed them. And seeing them, Anny knew they were easily worth a thousand words apiece, those pictures the paparazzo had taken on St. Isaakios.

There were half a dozen at least of the two of them dancing. She and Demetrios had their arms locked around each other, their bodies in tune with each other. In one his cheek was against her hair. In another her lips brushed his ear. She looked up at him, her heart in her eyes. He looked down at her, brushed a hand through her hair.

"You might have been happy," her father allowed, "if you had had the time together to learn to love each other. But not, my Anny—" he touched her cheek, tucked a strand of her hair behind her ear "—when you are already in love with someone else."

She was in love with someone else. And she believed he loved her.

He would come to his senses, she told herself. He would see that they belonged together, that their lives were incomplete without her.

But if he did, she never heard about it.

Her father took her back to Mont Chamion and she spent a few days with him and her stepmother and her little half brothers. She thought he would come there, would sweep her off her feet, promise her undying love, ask her to marry him and live happily ever after.

That was what Prince Charming did, after all.

Pity she hadn't left a sandal behind, she thought grimly. Not that it would have done much good. Days passed.

Before a week was up she left Mont Chamion and went back to Cannes. Tante Isabelle had come home in the meantime, and she took one look at Anny and said, "My dear, you need a holiday and some rest."

Anny laughed. "I had a holiday," she said. "I just came back."

"Well, don't tell me where you went," Tante Isabelle said. "If it has made you this pale and miserable, I do not want to know."

Anny had left a message for Franck when she'd left Cannes after breaking her engagement. In it she'd told him he'd given her the courage to make a move, to take a risk. She was determined to smile and assure him it had been the right thing to do regardless of how miserable she felt.

But Franck wasn't there.

She felt a stab of panic at the sight of a complete stranger in Franck's bed until Sister Adelaide, the head nurse, reassured her. "He has gone to Paris. For surgery."

"Surgery?" Anny knew about the surgical option. Franck had mentioned it. It was experimental. A new technique that might relieve pressure if the nerves weren't dead. If it was successful and you worked like mad, exercised within an inch of your life, you might walk again. Might. Maybe. A little bit.

As far as she knew, he'd rejected the whole idea.

Sister Adelaide said, "He said you gave him the courage to do it."

Anny gaped. "Me?" Oh, yes, that was her, the poster child for taking risks.

"And Luke St. Angier," Sister Adelaide went on. "The actor. I forget his name. Very handsome."

"Demetrios Savas." Anny was proud of herself for being able to say his name as if her heart weren't breaking.

Sister Adelaide smiled. "*Oui.* Monsieur Savas. You know he came back several times during the festival?"

"Yes. They went sailing."

Sister beamed. "I think that was a big influence. And then the last day, before he left he came bringing Franck a whole folder of information about the surgery. He'd printed it out from articles he'd looked up online. He said it was important to be informed, but that was only a start. Ultimately you had to decide what mattered—what you were willing to risk. You had to ask yourself what you were afraid of—and decide if it was worth it.

Whatever Franck was afraid of, he'd made his decision.

"When is his surgery?"

"Next week."

"And then?"

Sister Adelaide smiled. "And then we will see. Franck will recover. He will exercise. He will work very very hard. If he walks, he will be very very happy. It is his dream."

Anny prayed that he would get his dream. She knew his fear and admired him for risking disappointment. It wasn't easy, she knew. And not all endings were happy. She knew that, too.

She didn't want for Franck the pain of hopes dashed, of dreams that never would come true.

After Lissa's death, Demetrios shut himself off from the world.

He was the grieving widower, after all, the tragic bereaved spouse who had just lost the most beloved person in his life.

It wasn't hard to act the role. It was easier, in fact, than being honest.

There was nothing to gain from being honest. No one really wanted to know the truth.

His parents and his siblings might have suspected that things weren't all they should be between him and Lissa. But he'd never told them. He hadn't wanted them to worry about him. And it was no one else's business.

Besides, after Lissa died, he had been grieving, just not for what everyone thought he was.

So he went off by himself. He spent six months at a beach house on the Oregon coast, running on the sand, swimming in the ocean, and trying to write out his pain and frustration. He'd grown fit and strong, and his pain and frustration had made a hell of a screen-play.

When it was done, he'd seen it as a way to get his life back.

So he'd taken it. He'd got financing, made his movie, found his place in the world again. He'd gone to Cannes telling himself he was whole again.

What a laugh.

He wasn't even close to whole. His life now was even more

of a fiction than his perfect marriage to Lissa had been—because he was lying to himself.

He had left his family in Santorini the day after Anny had left. He'd told them he had to get back to work. And he'd gone. He'd flown back to Hollywood, gone to script meetings, production meetings, design meetings, casting meetings. He'd pretended he was fine, that he could cope, that life would go on now just as it had after Lissa's death.

But he wasn't getting over Anny. He couldn't lie to himself about that.

He sat in the spacious opulent Southern California house he had shared with Lissa, staring at its multitude of walls and plate glass windows and felt a soul-wearying emptiness. In his mind's eye he saw the cramped quarters of the sailboat he'd shared with Anny and remembered laughter, happiness, joy.

He dived into his pool and swam countless meaningless laps. Inside he remembered the frustration that had driven him to dive into the roiling Mediterranean sea to try to get Anny out of his mind.

He lay in his wide solitary bed—a new one that he had never shared with Lissa—and remembered the two nights he'd spent making love with Anny.

He remembered her softness, her warmth, her smooth skin and shining hair, her hands that had learned him even as he had learned her. He remembered her wrapping herself around him, drawing him in, making the two of them whole together.

He would never be whole without Anny.

Never.

He padded from room to room, telling himself to stop thinking about the past, to focus on the future. But when he faced the truth he knew that the only future he wanted was with Anny.

Anny.

She'd taken a risk when she'd broken off her engagement with Gerard.

The boy Franck, Demetrios knew from a series of e-mails, had taken a risk by having the surgery.

They'd both credited him with giving them the courage.

"It's what you would do," Franck had written.

Was it? Demetrios wondered now. Or did he just talk a good fight?

Mont Chamion was a small country. But it was big enough to get lost in—if you wanted to—even if you were the crown princess.

Especially if you were a crown princess needing some time and space—a few days on her own—without her worried papa, her gentle stepmama, her rambunctious, inquisitive brothers.

Anny knew all the out-of-the-way rooms in the palace. She knew which bookcase to press to open the secret door to the turret. She knew how to find great-grandfather's folly in the woods and the best time to be alone in the summer house. But none of them would give her more than the respite of an hour or two.

Now that her brothers were older, there were fewer places she could go that they couldn't find her. They took great joy in it. And it had become something of a game in the last couple of years. A sort of royal hide-and-seek.

They'd played it often since she'd come home after her trip to Santorini. After Demetrios. Papa had wanted her here. She knew it even though he hadn't insisted. The boys had.

"You're gone too much," her middle brother, Raoul, had told her.

The youngest, four-year-old David, had climbed into her lap and said, "It's no fun without you, Anny."

And Alexandre, who, at nearly eight, was becoming aware of his responsibilities said, "Papa worries about you, Anny. You should stay here where we can take care of you."

And so she had stayed. For a while. To make them happy. To reassure her father. To spend time with her stepmother and her brothers. To feel loved because she was still raw from Demetrios's rejection.

But she'd been here nearly three weeks now. A long time. Too long. She should go back to Cannes again and get to work. But going back would mean facing every day remembering what had happened there. Remembering Demetrios.

As if she would ever forget.

She wouldn't. She knew that. But just as she and Papa had had to go on after her mother's death, she knew she had to go on now.

And so this morning she had asked her father for the key to the lake cabin.

"Are you sure, my Anny?" he asked. "There are memories there…."

"Good ones," Anny said firmly. "I am sure, Papa."

He had raised his brows silently and rolled his pen between the palms of his hands. "No one goes there now," he warned her. "It was our place. I never took Charlise and the boys. They have seen it, but the gardens are overgrown. It is old and dusty and run-down. Are you sure you will not be too lonely. Is it really a good idea?"

"Yes, it is. I'll clean it," Anny said. "Please, Papa. Just for a few days. I need some space. And," she added, " the boys won't find me there."

He smiled. But as he reached into his desk drawer and drew out the key, he said, "You hope."

The cabin was as old and dusty as he'd predicted. But to Anny it brought back wonderful memories. Some were sad. But she didn't regret them. And as she cleaned and scrubbed and swept and washed windows she felt herself settling down, coming to terms, putting things into perspective.

When her mother died, Papa had brought her here to remember. "We will look back," he had said. "We will remember. We will carry her with us as we go on."

She would do that now. Only this time she would remember Demetrios.

And then she would go on.

As night fell and the sky darkened, she went out onto the porch and, wrapped in a shawl in the cool mountain air, she sat down and stared up, watching as first one star and then another star winked into sight.

Wishing stars, Mama had called them.

Conversation starters, she thought with an ache in her throat, remembering the nights with Demetrios.

She started to shove the thought away, to think about the future. But then she stopped. She let the memories come. She had come here to remember. She didn't have to go on—not just yet.

She looked up at the stars and she wished.

She wished for Demetrios to find happiness. She wished he would know love. She wished that someday he would realize love wasn't only painful, that it could bring joy.

She wished it would bring her a little joy. Someday. Somehow.

Mostly she wished she would stop crying. She swallowed hard and scrubbed at her eyes.

And then she heard the footsteps. Light. Hesitant. Unsure of their way.

Oh, Papa! she thought despairingly, knowing what he had done. He'd worried about her being here by herself. He'd given the boys hints. Maybe not David, but Alexandre and Raoul were old enough that he would let them follow these paths. He knew she wouldn't turn them away.

She straightened and cleared her throat. "I hear you," she said. "You can stop sneaking around."

"Anny? Thank God."

She almost fell off the porch. Then, tripping over the shawl, she stumbled to her feet. "*Demetrios*?"

She stared in amazement into the darkness, wondering if she were hallucinating, as a tall lean man picked his way up the narrow overgrown path, then stopped at the foot of the steps and looked up at her.

She couldn't read his expression. From his stance he looked wary, uncertain. Pretty much the way she felt, Anny thought. Her knees were shaking. She clutched the porch rail to keep herself upright.

"What are you doing here?"

"Right now? Thanking God I found you," he said with a shaky laugh. "I almost don't believe it."

"Neither do I," Anny said, which had to be the understatement of the year. She wanted simply to stare at him, to drink in the sight of him—what little she could actually see in the darkness.

She wanted to pinch herself to be sure she wasn't dreaming. She didn't even know why he was here.

Finally she remembered her manners. "Would you like to come in?" she said politely. "I can make some coffee. I have some biscuits."

He made a sound that was half sob, half laugh. "Oh God, Anny, I've missed you. Yes," he said coming up the steps, so close now she could touch him. "I'd like to come in. I'd like coffee. I'd like biscuits. I love you."

She stared at him, stunned, disbelieving. He was right in front of her, his shirt brushing against her sweater, his breath warm against her face. Real. And saying the words earnestly, not grudgingly. She opened her mouth and closed it again.

He didn't move away. He touched her cheek, tipped her face so that she looked straight into his eyes. The only light she had to see them by was starlight. It was enough. "I mean it," he said urgently. "I love you, Anny. I have since—hell, I don't know when! But it isn't going away. I'm glad it isn't going away," he said fiercely. "You know I love you. You told me I did," he said, sounding a little desperate at her silence.

Anny nodded numbly. "Yes, but—"

"But I didn't want to hear it." He shook his head. "And I still don't know what to do about it. I have so little to offer you. I failed Lissa—"

She couldn't stay silent now. "You *didn't* fail Lissa!"

"I didn't help her. I couldn't reach her. I didn't even really know her."

"You knew me. You reached me. You gave me strength and courage and hope. And love," she told him. And she felt her throat tighten and feared she would start crying again, so she took his hand. "Come in."

She led him into the cabin and switched on the light, and felt her heart kick over at the sight of him.

He wore a long-sleeved, open-neck denim shirt, a rough canvas jacket and a pair of clean but faded jeans. He was clean-shaven now, and his thick dark hair had been neatly trimmed. He was every bit as gorgeous as she remembered. As far as she was concerned, there was no man on earth with a stronger, more masculine, yet more beautiful face.

But beautiful as they always were, his eyes were different tonight. On the boat they had watched her, but had always held her at a distance. Even when they'd made love and they'd warmed with desire and clouded with passion, they'd still held her off.

Tonight they invited her in.

And Anny didn't need any more explanation than that. She trusted his love. She trusted his being here. She framed his face with her hands and raised herself on her toes to touch her lips to his.

In an instant his arms wrapped around her. He crushed her against him, burying his face in her hair. She felt a tremor run through him, and she knew her own heart hammered with the joy of the hallelujah chorus in her chest.

"I love you," he said again. His words teased the tendrils of her hair, touched her ears. And her heart.

"I love you, too," she vowed.

He kissed her cheek, her temple, her hair, then down her jawline to her mouth. His tongue parted her lips, tasted her, and she tasted him in return. Her arms slid up to go around his neck. He wrapped her close, drew her against him, and she felt how well they fit—as if they belonged together. Because they did. He deepened the kiss. His fingers traced the line down her spine, cupped her buttocks and held her against him, let her feel the need that matched her own.

Then she pulled back. "Are you sure you want coffee and biscuits?"

He laughed. "I'd rather have you."

She took his hand to draw him toward the bedroom. "That can be arranged."

But he didn't move. "Not just tonight," he said, his hooded eyes dark. "Always." He ran his tongue over his lips. "I didn't know the protocol," he said. "But I asked your father if he'd agree to my asking you to marry me."

Anny's eyes widened. "You talked to my father?"

He nodded. "You weren't in Cannes. You weren't in Berkeley." At her surprise, he added, "Tante Isabelle said she didn't know where you were. You might be in Berkeley defending your dissertation."

"Not yet," Anny said, smiling, knowing Tante Isabelle well enough to know she'd been determined to make the man who'd broken her goddaughter's heart prove his mettle before he found her.

"So I discovered," Demetrios said. "So I went to the palace. Without an appointment. That's apparently not done."

But he'd done it. "Papa would have wanted to talk to you."

"Oh, yeah, he did. Gave me an earful. Wouldn't tell me where you were."

"And then relented when he saw you meant it?"

Demetrios shook his head. "No. He said I could damned well find you myself if I loved you." He squared his shoulders. "So I did."

She stared. "No one but Papa knew where I went."

"But your brothers at least knew you were in Mont Chamion. And your father said you didn't want distractions. That you didn't need to be bothered. So I knew where you'd gone."

She stared. "You did?"

"You told me about this place. Your refuge by the lake where you wished on the stars. Where you'd gone after your mother died. I guess I didn't know for sure," he admitted. "I hoped. So I asked your father for directions to the lake house. And that was when, I think, he realized you'd trusted me with something you didn't talk about to everyone. There was a faint crack in the royal facade."

She smiled. "Yes. We don't talk about the cabin to anyone."

"So he gave me the directions—along with an introduction to his sword collection and word about what a good fencer he is." Demetrios's mouth twisted wryly. "I am allowed to ask you to marry me. He said it was up to you—but if you said yes, I'd better never hurt you again."

Anny laughed. Her heart was near to bursting. "You won't." She knew that for a fact. If he'd faced his demons and come looking for her, she had nothing at all to fear. "So are…you asking me?"

"Will you marry me, Anny?" He didn't stop there. "You are everything I've ever wanted—a woman to share with, to talk with, to joke with, to sail with, to ride out a storm with." He swallowed. "To have a family with."

It was her turn to kiss him then. To run her fingers lightly over his scalp, to stroke his now short hair and nuzzle his smooth-shaven cheek and inhale—and cherish anew—the scent of him.

"You are everything I ever wanted, too," she told him. "Not just the man on the poster. The man I met in Cannes. The man I sailed with. The man I made love with—fell in love with. Yes, I'll marry you, Demetrios. And have a family with you," she whispered. "Yes. Oh yes, please."

Royal weddings took an inordinate amount of time to arrange. If, Charlise told her stepdaughter, you wanted to do them right.

"By right, I mean, with all proper pomp and circumstance, protocol and rigamarole." She paused. "But if what you want is the right man and the right woman and the right people there to celebrate with you, I think we can do it in six months."

Anny goggled. "Six months?"

"A year would be better. Or two."

Demetrios wasn't going to wait a year. Certainly not two. Six months would be a strain, Anny knew. For both of them. But they'd discussed it and she knew he was willing to deal with her royal obligations.

"It's who you are," he'd said. "I love you."

Now that he was saying it, he said it often. She never tired of hearing it. They both said it every night.

He was philosophical about the six months. "They can't expect me to wait on the same continent that long," he'd said. "I'll go to Mexico and work on my film."

But he'd called her every night. They'd talked. They'd laughed. They'd argued about how many children they'd have and what they'd name them. And every other week either she'd flown out to him or he'd come to Mont Chamion to spend a few days with her.

Even so, they were the longest six months of Anny's life. She had a thousand decisions to make, but as she told Charlise, "It's not really important. I've made the only decision that matters."

"You have," Charlise agreed. And so did Papa.

He had welcomed Demetrios into the family. Besides his introduction to the sword collection, Demetrios had been given a long lecture about his responsibilities to his new bride. But at the end, he'd shaken Demetrios's hand and wrapped him in a warm embrace.

"You love her. I can see that. And I know she loves you. The kingdom is of far less importance than my daughter's happiness. She will be your wife and you will love each other," he told Demetrios. "That's what matters. The rest—we will work it out."

Now, as she waited with her father to walk down the aisle on the morning of their wedding, Anny lifted her veil and leaned up to kiss him. "I love you, Papa. Thank you so much for being my father. For trusting me."

"You will smear your lipstick," he chided her, even as he kissed her cheek and brushed a tear from his eye. "Of course I trust you. How could I not? You are my daughter, the light of my life."

She would have cried then, but she couldn't. Not yet. No one wanted to watch her walk down the aisle with tears streaming down her face.

Just then the introductory organ music paused dramatically—and plunged into the formal wedding march.

Her father touched her hand. "It is time."

Demetrios's sister, Tallie, his sister-in-law, Martha, and Martha's sister, Cristina, and dear Tante Isabelle were her bridesmaids.

One by one they preceded her down the aisle.

And then it was her turn. Papa's fingers squeezed hers, and then together, slowly, they made their way down the aisle.

The church was filled to the rafters with people come to cheer on Mont Chamion's only princess and her handsome, clearly besotted groom.

For the past six months all the tabloids had been writing about the upcoming royal wedding. They'd written endlessly about Anny and revisited over and over the charmed life Demetrios Savas had lived. They wrote about his talent, his Hollywood career, his perfect short-lived first marriage, how he had mourned as a recluse the death of his first beloved wife. But now, they wrote, while it was tragic, it was a codicil to his nearly perfect life.

Demetrios never contradicted it. He said how delighted he was, how Anny's love made him the happiest man on earth. He never alluded to the past except when asked, and then as always, he was honorable. He was kind.

Because that's the sort of man he was, Anny knew. Only she knew the truth. She knew the man. She loved him more than life itself.

And as she walked down the aisle now, she could see him waiting, and in a row beside him, his brothers: Yiannis on the end, bemused and tapping his foot nervously, George, next to him, lean and watchful and seriously intent. Then Theo, tall and dark and smiling broadly.

And between Theo and Demetrios was the best man.

Anny stared, not quite able to believe her eyes, at a younger man, not as tall as the Savas brothers, dark-haired and very thin, grinning widely and standing tall, though he still leaned on two metal hand canes.

"Franck." Her step faltered. The tears began to fall.

Her father gave her a kiss and gave her hand to Demetrios. "Love her," he exhorted.

"I do," Demetrios vowed. "I always will."

And then, although it certainly wasn't protocol, he tipped the veil aside to peer in at her. "I thought you'd be crying." His expression was tender, his eyes were smiling as he shared her joy at Franck's presence, at his progress. At his dream come true.

"I can't believe he's here."

"He is. It was his goal as soon as I asked him," Demetrios told her. "But we'd better get this show on the road. He doesn't stand up for long."

The priest cleared his throat. "If you please."

Demetrios grinned and dropped her veil. He straightened and attempted to look serious. Anny squeezed his hand. He squeezed back.

"Dearly beloved," the priest intoned.

And Anny, looking around, knew how true that was. Everyone here—all their family, all their friends gathered to celebrate their wedding with them—was dear and beloved. All of them gave joy and meaning to her life.

But no one was more dear or beloved, no one gave her more joy or meaning than Demetrios.

Theo lent them the sailboat for their honeymoon.

They had to wait six weeks to take it because Demetrios had filming to finish. But Anny was philosophical.

"I'll get to watch you work," she said happily. "And," she added, "you can't work all the time."

No, he hadn't worked all the time. But he was looking forward to some time alone with Anny. Just the two of them. Back on the boat. Together.

"Don't wreck it while you're busy doing other things," Theo added gruffly.

"What other things?" Demetrios said with all the innocence he could muster.

Theo cuffed his shoulder and rolled his eyes, then he fixed Anny with a hard look. "He's got my boat to sail. Keep him in line," he said to Anny.

Anny laughed. "Not likely." And Demetrios grinned, too. She knew him all too well.

"Go away," he said to his brother now. "We'll be fine. Your boat will be fine. Stop bothering us."

Theo grinned. He made a few more adjustments. He made a few more comments. Mostly to annoy because that's what brothers did. But finally he left.

And so at last did they, Demetrios raising the sail as Anny steered her out away from Santorini's small harbor. They were sailing her to Cannes.

"The same, but different," Anny had said when he'd suggested it. Because they wouldn't be fighting their desire this time. They'd be spending their days sailing and their nights in each other's arms.

"Better," Demetrios vowed.

"Maybe," he said as he carried her over the threshold of their cabin that night, after a beautiful day of light winds and easy sailing, "we can get to work on those kids whose names we argue about."

He dropped her lightly on the bunk and dropped down to lie beside her, to undress her, to kiss her, to love her, to cherish her.

"I don't think so." Anny shook her head.

He stopped, stared at her.

She grinned and slid her arms around him, pulling him on top of her, wrapping him in her embrace. "We already have."

He stared, felt his heart kick over. "Anny?" He pulled back to look at her, to see if she was joking.

She smiled and gave a little wiggle beneath him. "It's true, Demetrios. In about seven and a half months Zorathustra will be here."

Demetrios stared. And then he grinned and kissed her. "You mean, Melchisedeck," he corrected.

Anny laughed. "Zorathustra."

"Melchisedeck."

Anny kissed him, laughing against his mouth. "Maybe I'll have twins."

Demetrios laughed, too, and rolled her in his arms. "Fine with me, princess." Everything was fine with him. Life was beautiful. Anny was beautiful. And, dear God, he loved her. "Maybe you will."

THE VIRGIN AND HIS MAJESTY

BY
ROBYN DONALD

Robyn Donald can't remember not being able to read, and will be eternally grateful to the local farmers who carefully avoided her on a dusty country road as she read her way to and from school, transported to places and times far away from her small village in Northland, New Zealand. Growing up fed her habit; as well as training as a teacher, marrying and raising two children, she discovered the delights of romances and read them voraciously, especially enjoying the ones written by New Zealand writers. So much so that one day she decided to write one herself. Writing soon grew to be as much of a delight as reading—although infinitely more challenging—and when eventually her first book was accepted by Mills & Boon she felt she'd arrived home. She still lives in a small town in Northland, with her family close by, and uses the landscape as a setting for much of her work. Her life is enriched by the friends she's made among writers and readers, and complicated by a determined Corgi called Buster, who is convinced that blackbirds are evil entities. Her greatest hobby is still reading, with travelling a very close second.

CHAPTER ONE

AS CORONATION balls went, Rosie Matthews thought, surveying the palace ballroom, this one in Carathia had to be about as good as it got.

Wherever she looked flowers glowed richly against the white and gold walls. Men in the austere black and white of formal evening clothes radiated power and privilege, and beautiful women dazzled in couture so *haute* the ballroom looked like a catwalk for society's most favoured designers. Light from the gilded ballroom chandeliers scintillated opulently from famous and priceless tiaras, earrings and necklaces.

And every other woman in the ballroom seemed tall and impossibly elegant, including the one beside her. Hani Crysander-Gillan, Duchess of Vamili and sister-in-law of the newly crowned Grand Duke Gerd, was another racehorse, and the tiara glittering against her dark hair featured the rare and beautiful fire diamonds from her homeland of Moraze.

'I envy you,' Rosie told her cheerfully. 'This will be the only coronation ball I'll ever attend, but to get a good view I really need to stand on one of those gilded chairs. Still, I've never seen so many fabulous jewels. And the clothes—wow!' She gave an elaborate sigh. 'I feel like the proverbial poor relation. And I'm not even a relation!'

Hani laughed. 'A likely story. You look stunning, and you know it. I don't know how you managed to find something the exact honey-amber of your hair.'

Rosie glanced down at her balldress. 'It was a stroke of luck; there's a really good vintage shop just around the corner from my flat. And this doesn't seem to have been worn much. It doesn't look ten years old.'

'Who cares how old it is? It's a classic.'

Certainly its body-skimming flow gave Rosie some much-needed extra height, assisted by a pair of killer heels that had cost her almost the last of her savings.

Hani raised her brows. 'It's not like you to be afflicted with self-doubt. What's the matter?'

'It's not self-doubt, it's the realisation that the jewellery alone must be worth more than most small countries,' Rosie returned airily.

She lied. Prince Gerd Crysander-Gillan, Grand Duke and ruler of Carathia—crowned only that day—happened to be dancing right in front of her with the woman expected to become his bride. Princess Serina was yet another willowy, impossibly beautiful creature, her dark hair sleeked into an elegant chignon that showed off the diamonds of her family tiara to perfection.

'And the fact that every other woman in this room is at least ten centimetres taller than I am and wearing a tiara,' Rosie went on mournfully, before flashing Hani a gamine grin. 'However, being short means no one can see me, and Gerd won't expect glitz from a cousin by marriage.'

Especially a cousin by marriage who'd just finished her degree, only to discover that the job market had dried up.

Lifting her small, round chin, she let her eyes roam across the dancers. Inevitably they found the man who'd invited her—and hundreds of others—to his rich little country to celebrate his coronation. As Rosie's gaze found his arrogantly handsome face Gerd smiled at the princess in his arms, then lifted his black head and looked across the ballroom, his boldly chiselled features radiating force and authority.

Flushing, Rosie lowered her eyes. Of course he wasn't looking at—far less *for*—her. He was just making sure everything was going according to plan. Gerd always had a plan, as well as the ruthless determination to carry it through, no matter what the obstacles.

A hungry longing ached through her. She'd been so certain the tenuous thread of hope that had kept her dangling for years would be severed once she saw him with the glamorous, entirely suitable Princess Serina.

Instead, coming to Carathia, seeing him again, had reignited a fire that had never died.

So who's being melodramatic? she mocked silently. How could a fire die when it had never really been lit? OK, so three years ago—on the other side of the world—she and Gerd had been thrown together for a whole magical summer.

Although they'd known each other all her life, things had changed during those long, hot weeks, but even at eighteen Rosie had been wary. Gerd was almost twelve years older, and probably a couple of centuries further advanced in sophistication. As well, her mother's lamentable history with men had coloured Rosie's outlook, so although she'd become giddy with excitement whenever he smiled at her, she'd masked it with the brash, cheerful façade she'd made her defence against the world.

Yet while they'd sailed, swum, ridden horses and talked at length about almost everything, her childhood affection for Gerd gradually developed into a deeper emotion, something that shimmered with a promise she didn't dare recognise—until the night before he went away.

When he had kissed her…

And Rosie had gone up in flames, all fears forgotten in a shocking, mesmerising rush of passion. He'd muttered her name and tried to pull away, but she'd clung, and as if he too was caught in the grip of some elemental summons he'd kissed her again, and then again, his arms tightening around her while every kiss took her deeper and deeper into unknown, thrilling territory.

How long they'd kissed she never knew, but each sensuous exploration stoked the fire that burned away her virginal inhibitions, and she was crushed against his lean, strong body in an ecstasy of surrender when he suddenly jerked free.

And said in a thick, impeded voice, 'I must be *mad*.'

Chilled, the intoxicating hunger rapidly vanishing, she'd dragged in a painful, jarring breath, unable to speak, unable to feel anything but an icy, bitter wash of humiliation at his rejection.

He'd straightened and stepped back further. In a controlled, coldly remote voice he said, 'Rosemary, I should not have done that. Forgive me. You still have a lot of growing up to do. Enjoy university, and try not to break too many hearts.'

A small, cynically rueful smile tugged at the corners of her mouth. The only heart that had been affected was hers. For the first—and only—time in her life Rosie had known the wild, intoxicating charge of desire.

Why hadn't it happened again? She'd met men almost as handsome as Gerd, men with reputations as superb lovers, and not one had stirred her emotions, not one had summoned that ravishment of her senses, as though she'd die if it wasn't satisfied...

Only Gerd.

Her eyes narrowed slightly when Gerd said something to his partner. The princess lifted her face and smiled, and they looked so utterly *right* together that Rosie winced at a stark return of the aching emptiness that had followed Gerd's departure that summer.

Whatever had happened during those enchanted weeks—the companionship, the closeness—had meant nothing to him. Not once had he contacted Rosie. News of him came through his brother, Kelt.

Don't be an idiot, she told herself robustly. Of course he hadn't contacted her. Once he'd left New Zealand his life had been packed with action and events.

Immediately after he'd arrived in Carathia his grandmother, the Grand Duchess, named him heir to her throne, and he'd had to deal with disaffection amongst the mountain people—disorder that became riots, and had then turned into a nasty little civil war.

No sooner had it been decisively won than Princess Ilona slipped into the lingering final illness that forced Gerd to become the de facto ruler of Carathia. A year of official mourning had followed her death.

Which had given her three years to break free of the spell of the hot, lazy days she'd spent falling in love.

It wasn't through lack of trying. She'd kissed enough would-be lovers to gain herself a reputation as a tease, but nothing—and no one—had matched the sensuous magic of Gerd's kisses. Flirting had become a defence; she used it as a glossy, sparkling shield against any sort of true intimacy.

How *pathetic* to be still a virgin!

Yet when she did make love she wanted it to mean something—and she wasn't going to succumb until her feelings matched the hungry passion Gerd had summoned so effortlessly in her.

Rosie focused her attention on the rest of the dancing throng, but inevitably her gaze crept back to Gerd and his partner.

He was looking over Princess Serina's head, straight at Rosie. For a heart-stopping second she thought she read anger in his topaz-gold survey before the woman in his arms said something, and he glanced back at her.

Rosie's heart thumped violently and a swift flare of colour burned up through her skin. Turning to Hani, she gave a quick nod in the general direction of the dance floor and forced her voice into its normal insouciant tone. 'They look good together, don't they?'

Hani was silent a moment before saying slowly, 'Yes. Yes, they do.'

Rosie would have liked very much to ask what was

behind the equivocal note in her voice, but the music stopped then, and Kelt, Gerd's younger brother and Hani's husband, came up. Hani's face broke into the smile she kept only for him.

Rosie sighed silently; even after several years of marriage and a gorgeous little son, Hani and Kelt still looked at each other like lovers. And, when the band struck up again after the interval, she watched them melt into each other's arms on the dance floor and fought back a shaming surge of envy, of wonder that they'd found such joy and satisfaction, when she...

When she'd let a memory rule her life. One summer of laughing, stimulating companionship and a few passionate kisses had fuelled a futile desire without any chance of fulfilment.

Enough's enough, she thought on a sudden spurt of defiance. She was tired of being moonstruck. From now on—from this moment, in fact—it was officially over. She'd find some nice man and discover what sex was all about, get rid of this humiliating, futile hangover from the past—

'Rosemary.'

The floor shifted under her feet and her stomach contracted as though bracing for a blow. She sucked in a sharp breath before slowly turning to look up into Gerd's face, its angular features imprinted with the intimidating heritage of a thousand years of rule.

Here it was again, that seductive, treacherous ache of longing, almost more potent than the physical hunger that accompanied it. Pride persuaded her to ignore the shivers tingling down her spine.

'Hello, Gerd,' she said, hoping her voice was as

steady and cool as his. 'Why can I never get you or my mother to call me Rosie?'

His wide shoulders lifted fractionally. 'I don't know. That, surely, is up to you?'

Rosie's snort was involuntary. 'Try telling Eva to shorten my name and see how far you get,' she told him briskly. 'And I seem to remember asking you quite often to call me Rosie. You never did.'

'You didn't ask—you commanded,' he said with a faint smile. 'I didn't take kindly to being ordered about by a tiny snip some twelve years younger.'

You are *not* in love with him, she reminded herself with desperate insistence. You never have been.

All she had to do was get him out of her bloodstream, out of her head, and see him as a man, not the compelling, powerful, unattainable lover of her fantasies.

'Dance with me.'

Her brave determination melted under a sudden surge of heat. To be in his arms again...

Resisting the seductive impact of that thought, she summoned a smile glinting with challenge. 'And *you* have the audacity to accuse *me* of ordering people about?'

'Perhaps I should rephrase my request,' he said on a note that held more than a hint of irony. 'Rosemary, would you like to dance with me?'

'That's much more like it,' she said sedately, hanging on to her composure by a thread. 'Yes, of course I'll dance with you.'

His mouth quirked at her formality, and something jabbed her heart. It took a determined effort of will to walk beside him onto the dance floor.

But when Gerd took her in his arms her natural sense

of rhythm almost deserted her. Concentrating fiercely, she followed his lead. In that dazzling, dazed summer they'd danced together several times and she'd never forgotten the sensation of being held against his big frame, the way she'd felt so deliciously overpowered by his size and latent strength.

Now, close to him again, every cell in her body sang a wanton song of desire.

You're not in love with him, she repeated fervently. Not a bit. Never have been…

This was merely physical, a matter of hormones and hero-worship. He'd imprinted her the way a mother goose imprinted her goslings.

The thought curved her mouth in an involuntary smile. How apt. She was behaving just like a goose!

Gerd broke a silence that threatened to drag on too long. 'How long is it since we've danced together?'

'I don't know.'

That was a stupid response, an instinctive attempt at defence. And he'd noticed. Defiantly Rosie cocked her head and met his unusual eyes, tawny and arrogant as an eagle's.

Hoping her tone projected amusement tinged with nostalgia, she continued, 'Oh, yes, of course I do. How could I forget? It was my first grown-up party, do you remember? You were on holiday in New Zealand that summer.'

'I remember.' His voice was lazy, as amused as hers, the dark lashes almost hiding his eyes.

'You gave me my very first grown-up kisses,' she told him, and laughed before adding, 'Ones that set an impossibly high standard.'

If she'd thought to startle him, she failed.

'There have been plenty to judge them by since then, I understand,' he said austerely.

Disconcerted, she demanded, 'How do you know that?'

Again he shrugged, the muscles flexing beneath her fingertips. 'Information travels fast in this family of ours,' he told her laconically.

Rosie pointed out, 'Except that I'm not proper family. The only connection is that my father's first wife was your cousin. A fairly distant cousin at that. So I'm actually flying false colours. Everyone seems to think I'm a Crysander-Gillan, instead of a very ordinary Matthews!'

'Nonsense,' he said negligently, adding with an oblique smile, 'There's nothing ordinary about you. Anyway, your half-brother *is* my blood relation as well as a good friend, and Alex would very properly have told me where to go if you hadn't been invited.'

Of course she'd been aware that only Gerd's iron-bound sense of duty had led to this invitation, but his laconic acknowledgement of it stung nevertheless.

Stifling her hurt, Rosie switched her gaze to the half-brother she'd never really known. Her parents' marriage had disintegrated before she was old enough to realise that the boy who appeared occasionally in her life was actually related to her.

Gerd's arm around her tightened; Alex forgotten, she followed the almost imperceptible command and matched her steps to her partner's. A sensuous thrill ran through her as they pivoted, their bodies meeting for an intimate moment.

Heat flamed through her at that subtle pressure; she dragged in a painful breath, only to find it imbued with the potent aphrodisiac of Gerd's faint body scent—pure, charged masculinity. She was becoming aroused, readying herself for a passion that would never be returned, never be appeased.

And then Gerd drew back and she felt the distance between them like a chasm.

Determined to break the sense of connection, the feverish hunger, she said bleakly, 'You know Alex better than I do. My mother banished him to boarding school before I was born, and we rarely saw him.'

'He told me you're having difficulty finding a job.'

Startled, she lifted her head, parrying his coolly questioning survey. 'For someone on the opposite side of the world from New Zealand you certainly keep your finger on the pulse,' she said forthrightly. 'Yes, the downturn in business has meant that inexperienced commerce graduates are in over-supply, but I'll find something.'

'Surely Alex could fit you into his organisation?'

'Any position I get will be on my own merits,' she told him abruptly.

'I'm flattered you allowed him to pay your way here. He said he had to almost force you to accept the offer.'

Her brother had dropped in on her the day she got the invitation, and when she'd told him she couldn't afford to go, he'd lifted one black brow and drawled, 'Consider it your next Christmas present.'

She'd laughed and refused, but a few days later his secretary had rung to ask if she had a passport, and given her instructions to meet his private jet at Auckland's airport. And her mother had applied pressure, no doubt hoping that a holiday among the rich and famous would make Rosie reconsider her next move—to find a job in a florist's shop.

'You might just as well be a hairdresser,' Eva Matthews had wailed. 'It was bad enough when you decided to take a commerce degree, but to turn yourself into a *florist*?' She'd startled Rosie with her virulence. 'Why, for heaven's sake? Everyone says you're clever as a cartload of monkeys, but you've done nothing— nothing at all!—with your brains. You were a constant disappointment to your father—what would he have thought of this latest hare-brained scheme?'

Rosie had shrugged. Starting with the fact that she'd been born the wrong sex, she'd never been able to please her parents.

'This is something *I* want to do,' she said firmly.

Her years at an expensive, exclusive boarding school had been for her mother. University had been for her father, although he'd made his disapproval clear when she'd chosen a commerce degree instead of something more academically challenging that would befit the daughter of a famed archaeologist.

Neither of her parents had known that she'd always planned to work with flowers. The degree had been her first step, and during her holidays she'd worked in a good florist's shop, honing her skills and a natural talent for design. A few months before the end of the university year the shop had closed down, a casualty of the recession, and, with the financial world on the brink of panic, now was not the time to set up. Even if she'd had the capital, which she didn't.

Rosie had discussed her situation with Kelt. He'd advised finding a job, saving like crazy and waiting for an upturn in the situation.

Good advice. Her expression unconsciously wistful, she turned her head and watched him dance with Hani. They looked so perfect together...

Just as Gerd and the Princess Serina had looked—a matching pair.

'They are very happy together,' Gerd said, an abrasive note in his words startling her.

'Oh, yes, so happy. But who wouldn't be, married to Kelt?'

Kelt didn't write her off as a lightweight or treat her as though she had the common sense of a meringue. A growing girl couldn't have had a better substitute brother, but his marriage to Hani had taken something from the special relationship he and Rosie shared; he had other loyalties, other responsibilities now.

Rosie had expected it to happen and she didn't resent it, but she missed their closeness.

Gerd asked laconically, 'So what is your plan?'

'Oh, take a look around, see what I can find,' she said airily. 'And what are your plans, now that you and the country have emerged from the year of mourning? What changes are you going to make in Carathia?'

'Only a few, and those slowly. I didn't realise you were interested in my country.'

She met his eyes with a swift, dazzling smile. 'Of course I am. Being related to the ruler of Carathia gave me immense prestige at school. I used to boast about it incessantly.'

He held her away from him, examining her face.

Bracing herself as a flame of awareness sizzled through her, Rosie met that intent eagle-amber gaze with cool challenge.

The grimness faded from his expression, although his smile was narrow as a blade. 'I don't believe that for a moment. Why did you decide to become an accountant?'

She wasn't going to tell him about her love affair with flowers. 'It just seemed a sensible thing to do. As I'm sure you're aware, my father was hopeless with money—he spent everything on his expeditions—and my mother isn't much better. I wanted to know how things worked in the financial world.'

Cynicism tinged his deep voice. 'Or did you just decide to shock your parents?'

She shook her head, stopping abruptly when her curls bobbed about in a childish fashion. 'I wanted to come away from university with something concrete, skills I could use.'

Something that made people see past her outward physical attributes. Most people took one look at her and wrote her off as a flirtatious little piece of fluff.

On a cool note she finished, 'And I don't regret it at all.'

Gerd looked sceptical. The music swelled, and he caught her closer to steer her around a slight traffic jam of dancers ahead. Resisting the quick, fierce temptation to let herself relax against him, Rosie followed his steps.

Above her head he said, 'You asked what changes I plan; in parts of Carathia change is treated with suspicion, so I'll be treading carefully, but I intend to extend the scope and the range of education, especially in the mountain districts.'

'Why education? What about health?'

Broad shoulders lifted in another swift shrug. 'My grandmother concentrated on health services. They're well-established, but not as fully used as they could be, especially in the mountains where superstition is still rampant and many people prefer to use the local wise women. When patients do finally present at hospitals, they often die there.'

Rosie nodded. 'So I suppose they try even harder not to go near them.'

'Exactly.'

'And you think education will help? How?'

'By giving children an understanding of science and some knowledge of the outer world. Life in the mountains is still very insular, very remote. Children in the alpine villages have to travel to the bigger towns for secondary education, so most miss out. I want to take higher education—*good* higher education—to each market town.'

'It seems logical,' she said thoughtfully. 'What's the school leaving age?'

'Thirteen. Far too young, but parents say they need them at home to help with farming, so any alteration will have to be managed with tact.'

Gerd felt her curls tickle his throat when she nodded.

Thoughtfully she said, 'To change attitudes you need to corral them at school while they're still open and receptive. How are you going to set up this system of a high school in every valley?' She glanced up at him, wide blue eyes intent and serious for once. 'I assume that's what you're planning?'

Gerd told her, sardonically amused because he was discussing his plans for Carathia with the precocious, light-hearted girl-child who'd jolted him with the passion in her kisses—and his own violent and unconsidered response to them.

That summer three years ago had revealed that behind her sexy, laughing face lurked a keen, quick brain. He'd enjoyed their discussions, but her ardent kisses on the final night when he'd yielded to the forbidden temptation of her sultry mouth had reminded him she was far too young and innocent to do what he'd wanted to do—carry her off to the nearest bed and make reckless, sensuous love to her.

Thank God he'd rejected her open invitation. Etched into his brain was the sight of her kissing Kelt the very morning after she'd turned to flames in his arms. He'd realised then that she'd been using him as a substitute for the man she really wanted.

Did she still long for his brother? If her expression when she watched Kelt dancing with Hani was anything to go by, it seemed more than likely.

Kelt had always been there for her when her father was away searching for ancient civilisations, when her mother was off with the latest boyfriend. A beautiful woman with everything going for her, Eva Matthews wasted her life chasing some sort of rainbow fantasy of the perfect love. Judging by the stream of men through her university years, her daughter was doing the same.

Searching for a security she'd never known? Possibly. Trouble in a delicious little package?

Undoubtedly. But she was no longer naïve and inexperienced.

Above her froth of amber curls he sketched a humourless smile. He was acutely aware of her small, elegantly curved form in that sinuous dress, its colour reminding him of the beaches on his brother's estate in New Zealand. Subtly glittering, the fabric made the most of her curves and narrow waist without clinging. In a room full of women clothed to impress, she stood out because she wore no jewellery at all, not even a ring on a slender finger.

A strand of hair snagged itself on his lapel, glittering in the light of the chandeliers. She jerked free and said, 'Sorry about that. I did try for dignity, but my curls are uncontrollable.'

'It would seem so.' His voice sounded odd in his ears, and he frowned, fighting back a swift, elemental appetite, a headstrong physical goad that knotted his gut and dried his mouth.

Half smiling, she gazed up at him, dark lashes wide around the intense, gold-flecked blue of her eyes. 'I straightened my hair once and it just hated it and went all lank and limp, so now I let the curls do their own thing.'

Gerd closed his mind against a swift, erotic image of her, sleek and golden and laughing against crisp white sheets, but the maddening questions refused to go away. Would she be as passionate as the promise of her soft, laughing mouth?

Hard on the heels of that came another question, even more insubordinate. Was she like this—provocative, tempting—with her lovers?

Of course she was. And now she was twenty-one and experienced, there was no need for restraint…

CHAPTER TWO

GERD dampened down a compelling surge of desire to say remotely, 'Although you affect to despise your hair, it's very pretty. As I'm sure you know.'

Rosie should have been gratified; apart from that final crack about her hair—delivered with aloof kindness, as though she were ten—he had at least treated her like an adult.

Unfortunately, since they'd moved onto the floor she'd reacquired a taste for the danger and zest of crossing swords with Gerd. Like fencing with a tiger, she'd decided dreamily three years ago.

Her pulse rate skyrocketed when her glance skimmed the strong, boldly chiselled features, intimidating yet profoundly sexy. Now she understood why she'd always been attracted to men with a slight cleft in their chin and hawkish profiles.

Rapidly discarding her first impetuous response, she told him briskly, 'I could say, just *you* try living with a head covered with red curls and see if anyone takes you seriously, but instead I'll ignore your remark. I'll bet you were born looking like a king.'

His smile was lazy, almost teasing. 'I'm not a king, and it was meant to be a compliment.'

'Then I'm afraid you'll have to try harder.'

His eyes narrowed, and for a second—perhaps less?—something flashed between them, a brittle tension that robbed her of words and breath.

To her relief the music died away, and he released her and offered his arm. She rested her hand on it, feeling insignificant as he escorted her to where Kelt, Hani and Alex waited for her.

They were almost there when he said formally, 'Thank you for coming, Rosemary.'

'I wouldn't have missed it for the world,' she returned, smiling pleasantly at a dowager wearing a serious dress in satin and more pearls than was decent. Taking refuge in flippancy from the aching emptiness that threatened her, Rosie decided the only thing missing was a lorgnette.

She went on, 'It's been a truly amazing week. And the coronation ceremony was…' She searched for the right words, finally settling on, 'Truly awe-inspiring. Hugely impressive.' And profoundly moving.

'I'm glad you found it so,' he said, his neutral tone revealing nothing. 'You're leaving the day after tomorrow, aren't you?'

'Yes.' She'd like to ask him what he'd planned for tomorrow night, but no doubt he had better things to do than entertain a nobody from New Zealand.

Kiss Princess Serina, perhaps?

When they reached the others they talked pleasantries for a few minutes until Gerd walked away, and at last Rosie could draw breath.

All she wanted to do was skulk up to her bedroom and hide there until she felt more…well, more *herself*.

But it was almost over. If she organised her life with care and some cunning she need never exchange words or glances with Gerd again. And when the wedding invitation arrived she'd produce a very good excuse for not attending—a broken leg should do.

Even if she had to break it herself.

From the corner of her eye she saw Gerd talking to the princess, and stiffened her spine. OK, so exorcising this unwanted hunger would take willpower and a rigorous refusal to indulge in daydreams, but she could manage that—she'd had a lot of practice.

The evening wore on. Resolutely keeping her gaze away from the person who held her attention, Rosie danced and laughed and talked and flirted with several interested men. By midnight her rigid self-control was beginning to take its toll and she allowed herself another longing thought of the bed waiting for her in the private apartments of the palace.

But when the ball ended, Alex told her casually, 'Gerd's asked us to his quarters for a nightcap. Just the family.'

No princess? Rosie banished a treacherous needle of excitement. 'How kind of him.'

He lifted a brow and after an uncertain look at his handsome face she began to chatter. She loved her brother, but they had never known each other well enough to develop the sort of relationship that made for confidences.

It was definitely a family gathering—although Gerd seemed to be related to a lot of European royalty.

But no Princess Serina. Stifling an ignoble relief, Rosie refused a glass of champagne and accepted one of mineral water, then glanced around. The private drawing room was big, furnished with more than a salute to Victorian taste. It wasn't all heavy furniture, however. Her gaze travelled to the large painting in a place of honour on one wall.

'Kelt's and my New Zealand grandfather,' Gerd said from behind her. 'Alex's great-great-uncle.'

'He's very handsome,' she said inanely. 'More like Kelt than you.'

'You're intimating that I'm not handsome?' he drawled lazily.

Colour burned along her cheekbones. Keeping her eyes on the portrait, she returned in her most limpid tone, 'I'm forever being told that it's only women who need constant reassurance about their attractiveness.'

His low laugh held a sardonic note. 'Well avoided.'

'All I meant was that your grandfather and Kelt have that northern-European look, whereas you show your Mediterranean heritage.' And a drop-dead gorgeous set of genes he'd inherited—a strong-boned face emphasised by those raptor's eyes and his powerful, long-legged physique.

'Like most ruling families, the Crysander-Gillans have a very mixed heritage. The original founder of my house was a Norseman who arrived here with a group of Vikings via Russia some time in the tenth century. They stayed, and imported princesses from almost every country in Europe and the occasional one from considerably further away.'

Well, Princess Serina wouldn't have far to come! Her

family lived in exile on the French Riviera. Rosie's heart contracted. 'I like this portrait,' she said swiftly. 'He looks…utterly dependable, yet dangerous.'

Gerd smiled and said something in a language Rosie recognised as being Carathian. 'That's an old Carathian proverb—*A man should be a tiger in bed, a lion in battle, and wise and cunning as a fox in counsel.* The Carathians believe that my grandfather met that standard.'

Rosie kept her attention religiously fixed on the painted face. 'He looks all that and more. How did the ancient Carathians know about tigers and lions?'

He drawled, 'There used to be lions in southern Europe, and people from the Mediterranean got around— remember, Alexander the Great marched as far as India. I imagine those who made it back arrived home with stories about tigers.'

'Was Carathia part of Greece originally?'

'No, although as a state it began with a band of Greek soldiers who lost a battle a thousand years or so before the Christian era and fled this way. They found this valley, and helped the local tribespeople against an attacking force sent to control the pass. For their endeavours they were rewarded with Carathian brides.'

'I hope the brides approved,' Rosie observed tartly.

'Who knows?' He sounded amused.

Rosie's heart did a ridiculous flip. If those ancient Greeks had been anything like Gerd their brides had probably been delirious with excitement.

Gerd went on, 'Over the years various of my ancestors acquired the coastal region and its offshore islands.'

'How?' she asked, intrigued by the long history of the small country.

'Usually by conquest, sometimes by marriage.'

She asked curiously, 'How many languages do you speak?'

'Kelt and I grew up speaking both English and Carathian as first languages. We've learned a couple more along the way.'

'I'm very impressed by the way people here switch from language to language without any effort. It makes me feel very much like a country cousin.'

'Languages can be learnt. Besides, you know the one everyone understands.'

Startled, she swivelled her head to survey his face.

His eyes were half-closed, his chiselled mouth curved in a smile that hit Rosie like a charge of electricity. 'Your smile speaks the most fundamental language—that of the heart.'

'Thank you for such a pretty compliment,' Rosie said hastily, furious because her hot cheeks revealed her astonishment. 'I don't think it's true, but I'd love it to be.'

Brows raised, Gerd said, 'You're embarrassed. Why? I can't believe no other man has told you that your smile is a most potent weapon.'

More than a little wary, she said, 'Actually, no.'

Men tended to concentrate on her more physical attributes.

Relief seeped through her when a manservant came up. Gerd looked down at him and the servant said something in a low voice. After Gerd's nod the man went across to the windows and drew back the heavy drapes to reveal the starry burst of a swarm of skyrockets.

Charmed, Rosie joined in the soft murmur of appreciation around the room.

'The Carathians enjoy firework displays and have organised this,' Gerd said as the wide French windows were opened.

Everyone trooped out into the warm night onto a stone terrace. 'Come here, Rosemary,' Gerd said, making a space for her so she could see easily.

Sheer pleasure seeped through Rosie as she took her place beside him. The private apartments in the palace looked over the walls that had sheltered the people of the old town for centuries. Across the vast valley outlines of mountains reared black against a sky glittering with stars she'd never seen before.

But the stars were put to shame when more fireworks flared into life high above them, a depiction of the Carathian crown she'd watched the archbishop place on Gerd's black head earlier that day. At that moment of crowning, of Gerd's commitment to his country, a roar had risen from the crowds outside the cathedral who were watching the ceremony on big screens.

Recalling the fierce, unexpected sound echoing around the ancient stone walls, she took a deep breath. Something fragile and strange expanded within her, filling her with an almost painful anticipation.

Other displays of fireworks burst across the night sky, drowning out the stars. The royal coat of arms formed a triumphant pattern, followed by the emblem of the country—a lion rampant and then a cupped flower, pure white and beautiful.

'The national flower of Carathia,' Gerd told her. 'It blooms in the snow. To the people it symbolises the courage and strength of Carathians.'

To Rosie's horror her throat closed. Torn by an emotion she didn't understand, she abandoned her usual flippant response. 'I suppose in the past they've often needed that symbolism.'

'Indeed they have,' Gerd said, his tone so noncommittal that Rosie looked up.

As though he sensed her regard he glanced down, his brows rising in a silent question when their eyes met. She suppressed a shiver and transferred her gaze to the flower, fading swiftly against the depthless darkness of the sky.

'You're cold,' he said quietly.

'No, not a bit.' She flashed him a swift smile. 'Just impressed all over again. This is an amazing place.'

'I'm glad you're enjoying it.'

Conventional words, meaning nothing. No fuel for dreams there, she told herself firmly, and pinned her attention to the display as once more the sky exploded into colour, this time a joyous, fiery free-for-all that eventually sank into darkness. A collective sigh seemed to whisper over the city, and in the silence someone not too far away started to play what sounded like a cornet or trumpet. The silvery, plaintive notes were unbearably moving in the quiet air.

'A folk tune,' Gerd said quietly, just for her. 'A song of lost love.'

To Rosie's utter horror, tears prickled at the backs of her eyes. She had to swallow to be able to say lightly, 'Aren't they all? The world's literature and music is built on broken hearts.'

The notes died away into a momentary silence that was followed by an eruption of cheers and the sound of horns and whistles.

Half an hour later Rosie surveyed her bedroom, decorated to pay tactful tribute to the age of the palace without sacrificing comfort, and thought of the time she'd spent in Carathia.

Watching Gerd, sophisticated and formidable amongst the world's elite, had emphasised as nothing else could the huge difference between them.

In New Zealand his heritage and position hadn't seemed so important. He'd always been dominant, that formidable inbuilt air of confidence more intimidating than arrogance could ever be. No one, least of all his New Zealand relatives, had been surprised when the business enterprise he'd set up with Kelt had turned into an empire with ramifications all over the world.

But seeing him in Carathia had added another dimension to his depth and compelling authority, giving him a mystique based on his people's affection and respect and trust.

Yes, she'd made the right—the only—decision. She wasn't going to waste her life longing for a man who could never be hers.

Shivering a little, she eased out of her dress, climbed into pyjamas and got into bed. Normally she read for a while, but nothing about the book she'd brought with her appealed, so she turned off the lamp and courted sleep.

An hour later, still wide awake, she got out of bed and padded across to her window, pulling back the drape to gaze down across the city. Although the lights had dimmed, the Carathians were still celebrating their ruler's coronation with gusto. She could hear singing, and recognised the sad beauty of the folk tune. Clearly it meant something important to the people of Carathia.

A sense of aloneness chilled her. Gerd belonged here in his palace above the city, and Kelt and Hani too, and Alex, although he possessed no royal blood, fitted easily into this gathering of the world's elite and powerful.

Rosie Matthews, unemployed, from New Zealand didn't.

Even the moon, she realised suddenly as she stared at it, was different—back to front from the one that beamed down on the other side of the world.

'So what?' she said into the night air, fragrant with scents she didn't recognise. 'Stop feeling sorry for yourself and at least get some rest.'

She must have slept for a few hours, because she dreamed—tangled images that had faded by the time she woke—but confronting her reflection the next morning made her inhale sharply and then apply cosmetics to banish the only too obvious signs of a restless night. Breakfast was served in her room, interrupted by a visit from Hani, who eyed her with concern.

Rosie pre-empted any query by saying firmly, 'I was too excited to sleep much last night—just like an over-wrought kid after a birthday party.'

'Tell me about it,' Hani said in the resigned tone of a mother who'd had to deal with just that situation. 'But it was a great day, wasn't it?'

'It's been a fabulous week,' Rosie said in her airiest voice. 'Like living in the Middle Ages, only with bath-rooms and electricity.'

Hani laughed, but the glance she gave Rosie was shrewd. 'You say that as though you'll be glad to get back home.'

'I will, but I'll never forget Carathia.' Or the man who now ruled it.

Hani said, 'I'd like to go straight to New Zealand, but Kelt has a meeting with the head honchos from Alex's firm in London, so we're going there first.' She gave a swift, lovely smile. 'I'll be interested to see how our little Rafi enjoys big cities.'

Hani was right—the sooner she got away from here the better, Rosie thought mordantly as she waved the family party off later that morning. Then she could stop being such an idiot.

Once back home she wouldn't spend wakeful nights wondering when Gerd was going to announce his engagement to Princess Serina.

By telling herself bracingly that it was completely stupid to feel as though her life was coming to an end, she managed to give Gerd a glittering smile when they met later that morning. In her most accusing voice, she said, 'Alex tells me you killed him while you were fencing before breakfast.'

Amused, he surveyed her. 'For a dead man he looked remarkably energetic afterwards.'

'He's disgustingly fit.' Rosie smiled, hoping it didn't look as painful as it felt. Damn it, she'd get rid of this crush no matter what it took. 'I didn't know he was a fencer.' In fact, she didn't know much about her half-brother at all.

Gerd understood, perhaps more than she liked. 'He learned at university, I believe. He's good. I believe you're using today to visit the museum.'

Rosie nodded. 'I'm looking forward to that, and afterwards I'm checking out the shopping area.'

'Just make sure you don't lose your guide—the central part of the city is like a rabbit warren and not many of the people speak English. If you got lost I'd probably have to mount a search party.'

His smile made Rosie's foolish heart flip in her chest. He isn't being *personal*, she told herself sternly.

He went on, 'I'd like to show you around myself, but my day is taken up. I'm meeting my First Minister and then farewelling guests.'

Including Princess Serina? Rosie concealed the humiliating question with her friendliest smile, the one that usually caused Kelt to view her with intense suspicion. 'Rather you than me,' she said cheerfully. 'I'm going to have a lovely day.'

She did, discovering that Carathia's national flower was actually a buttercup. New Zealand too had a mountain buttercup, and, strangely enough, it too was pristinely white.

How foolish to feel that the coincidence formed some sort of link between the two countries!

The shopping area displayed interesting boutiques and the usual big names; her guide, a pleasant woman in her thirties with an encyclopaedic knowledge of Carathia, did her best to encourage her to buy, but Rosie resisted, even the silk scarf exquisitely embroidered 'by hand', the shopkeeper told her, pointing out the fineness of the stitches. She held it up. 'And it suits you; you have the same delicate colouring, the soft clarity of spring.'

'It's lovely,' Rosie said on a sigh, 'and worth every penny, but I don't have those pennies, I'm afraid. Thank you for showing it to me, though.'

Her regret must have shown in her tone because the woman smiled and nodded and packed the beautiful, fragile thing away without demur.

Back at the palace she found a note waiting for her. Apart from his signature on birthday and Christmas cards it was the first time she'd seen Gerd's writing; bold and full of character, it made her heart thump unnecessarily fast as she scanned the paper.

He hoped she'd had a good day, and suggested that they have dinner together at a restaurant he knew, one where they wouldn't be hounded by photographers.

And where they wouldn't be alone, she thought with a wry quirk of her lips. Perhaps the princess objected to him dining with another woman in the privacy of his palace apartment, even when the other woman was related by marriage.

It was probably only his excellent manners that stopped him pleading a previous appointment and avoiding her altogether.

Temptation warred viciously with common sense. Should she go or do the sensible thing and say she was too tired? In the end her weaker part won. What harm could a dinner with him do, chaperoned as they'd be by the other diners, not to mention the waiters?

She rang the bell and gave the servant her answer.

Now, what to wear?

Anticipation built rapidly inside her; just for tonight—just this once—she'd let herself enjoy Gerd's company.

After all, there weren't going to be any repercussions. She was adult enough to deal with the situation. She'd forget her foolish crush and treat him like...oh, like the other men she'd gone out with. She'd be friendly, interested, sparkle for him, even flirt a little. It would be perfectly safe because Gerd was going to marry either Princess Serina, or someone very like her.

Someone *suitable*.

And when tonight was over Rosie would never see him again. Well, not in the flesh, she thought mordantly. He had a habit of turning up in the media— arrogantly handsome royalty was always good for a headline, especially when it came to love and marriage.

Eventually she chose a slender dress in a clear, warm colour the blue of her eyes, one of Hani's rare couture mistakes. It had been shortened, of course, but the proportions were good. And so what if she'd worn it twice since arriving in Carathia? Princess Serina might have been dressed in a completely different outfit each time she'd appeared, but Rosie couldn't compete.

Ready to go, she critically eyed herself in the huge mirror and gave a bleak nod; the soft material skimmed her body so her curves weren't too obvious and the neckline was discreetly flattering.

She'd aimed for discretion in make-up too, but her glowing reflection made her wonder uneasily if she shouldn't apply a little more foundation just to tone things down. Not that foundation would mask the sparkle in her eyes.

She hesitated, then shrugged. Who was she fooling? She was going out with Gerd because she craved a tiny interlude of privacy, of something special.

To build more dreams on?

'No,' she said aloud, startling herself. 'To convince

myself once and forever not to dream any more, because dreaming is a total, *useless* waste of my life and I'm over it. I'm free and twenty-one and unemployed, and I will put fairy tales behind me.'

CHAPTER THREE

STIFFENING her shoulders, Rosie turned away from her reflection, picked up a small blue evening bag and went out.

Her composure lasted exactly as long as it took for her to set eyes on Gerd.

The previous week should have accustomed her to his magnificence in austere, perfectly tailored black and white. Only it hadn't. A wild tumult beat through her blood and she had to stop herself from dragging in a shaken breath.

Don't you dare stutter like a besotted teenager, she commanded.

That horrible prospect gave her enough energy to steady her erratic breathing and say in a voice that almost sounded normal, 'You're an amazing family, you and Kelt and Alex. You're all gorgeous in your different ways even when you're in ordinary kit, but put you in evening clothes and you all take on a masculine glamour that should come with flashing signs to warn impressionable females. Most men look vaguely like penguins at formal occasions, but not you three. Have you ever been approached to model male cosmetics?'

'No.'

Just the one word, but she was left in no doubt about his feelings. Laughter bubbled up inside her. 'Alex has. He looked just like you did then.'

'I can imagine it,' Gerd said with a half-smile. 'If you think we men need warning signs, you should hand out sunglasses.'

Nonplussed, she stared at him. His face was unreadable, but she thought she saw a glint of amusement in his eyes, enough to give her voice an edge when she said, 'Thank you, I think. But it's not me, it's the dress—Hani gave it to me.'

His voice deepened. 'Nonsense, it's always been you. Hani calls you instant radiance.'

Shaken by both his words and their tone, she grabbed at her precarious poise. 'Radiance? I haven't noticed myself glowing in the dark, so I assume I'm safe.'

His eyes narrowed a fraction. 'Ah, yes, but what about those close to you?'

'I don't think you need worry,' she said kindly. 'Hani and Kelt let me play with their precious infant, and that's as good a safety recommendation as you can get.'

To her disappointment he glanced at his watch. 'We'd better go. One of the minor irritations of life here is that it's ruled by the clock.'

'Even when you're off-duty?' she asked on the way down.

'Basically I'm never off-duty.'

A car waited discreetly by one of the side doors of the palace. Two men sat in front—one in uniform, one without.

Gerd stood aside to let her in first and, once

settled, she said thoughtfully, 'I doubt if I could cope with that.'

'I've always known I was going to have to do it.' He clicked his seat belt in and glanced across at her already fastened one. 'When I was younger I was resentful of paparazzi, but I grew out of that.'

A grim note in the deep voice made her wonder how hard it had been for him to achieve that resignation. Something about the man sitting in front of her caught her eye. 'Gerd, the man in the passenger seat isn't wearing a seat belt.'

Straight brows drawing together, he told her, 'He's a bodyguard.'

'Oh.' Feeling foolish and slightly uneasy, she asked, 'Bodyguards don't?'

'No. They need to be able to react instantly.'

Perturbed at the thought of him in danger, she said, 'I didn't realise you'd need them here.'

Although she should have. Only a couple of years ago the Carathians had been fighting each other over his accession.

Quickly she asked, 'Is everything all right here now?'

He said in a tone that dismissed her concern, 'Yes, of course.'

But something his First Minister had said to him that morning echoed in Gerd's mind. 'Things are quiet now; the discovery that the ringleaders were in the pay of MegaCorp and that the purpose of the insurrection was to take over the carathite mines horrified every Carathian. And while the people are basking in the afterglow of the coronation and the harvest is on the way, no one is going to have time to call on ancient legends to back up any lingering dissatisfaction.'

Gerd trusted his judgement; the First Minister came from the mountains, where the legend that had bedevilled his ancestors for centuries had its strongest adherents.

Before Gerd could speak the older man had added, 'But with respect, sir, you need a wife. Further celebrations—a formal betrothal followed by a wedding and the birth of an heir as soon as possible—would almost certainly put an end to any plotting. Your plans for higher education should mean that the old legend will never have the hold over future generations that it has in the past.'

Gerd said grimly, 'At least we don't have to worry about further problems from MegaCorp.'

He'd seen to that, using his power in the financial world to clinically and without mercy ruin the men who'd so cynically played with other men's lives.

He glanced down at the woman beside him, lovely and eminently desirable, her wide blue eyes anxiously uplifted. Concern was in them and something else, something that disappeared so quickly he barely recognised it.

Deep inside him a fierce instinct stirred. She was so young, but it wasn't hero worship he'd caught in her gold-sprinkled eyes. If she *was* still longing for Kelt, it was a total waste of a life.

And he suspected he could do something about it…

Rosie could gather nothing from his impassive, gorgeous face. Repressing a quiver deep in the pit of her stomach, she demanded, 'What do you mean, *of course everything's all right*? I thought—'

'Once the ringleaders of the insurrection were shown to be the pawns of a foreign company who wanted to take over the mines,' he interrupted, 'the fighting stopped. No one in Carathia wanted that.'

'Of course they wouldn't.' The country's prosperity was based to a large degree on carathite, a mineral necessary in electronics. 'What happened to the people who started the rebellion?'

Gerd looked ahead. A gleam from the setting sun caught his black head, summoning a lick of blue fire. For a few seconds Rosie allowed herself to examine his profile, hungrily taking in the bold, angular outline. A potent little thrill burnt through her. His mouth should have softened his features; instead, that top lip was buttressed by a firm lower one and the cleft square of his chin.

He said calmly, 'They are no longer in any position to cause further trouble.'

This was Gerd as she'd never seen him before, his natural authority tinged with a ruthlessness that sent a chill scudding down her spine.

He turned his head, and she flushed. His brows lifted slightly, but he said in a level voice, 'Somehow I find it difficult to see you as an accountant.'

'Why?'

'As a child you adored flowers. I always assumed you'd do something with them.'

She gazed at him in astonishment. 'I'm surprised you remember.'

'I remember you being constantly scolded for picking flowers and arranging them,' he said drily.

'I grew out of that eventually. Well, I grew out of

swiping them from the nearest garden! But actually, I'm seriously thinking of setting up in business as a florist as soon as I can.'

He said thoughtfully, 'You'll need training, surely?'

Briefly she detailed the experience she had, finishing, 'I can run a shop. I have the financial knowledge, and I was left in sole charge often enough in my friend's shop to know I can do it. I helped her with weddings, formal arrangements for exclusive dinner parties, the whole works. I can make a success of it.'

'So how are you going to organise things financially?'

She kept her gaze resolutely fixed in front, but from the corner of her eye she sensed him examining her face. 'I'll manage,' she said coolly.

'Alex?'

'No.' She hesitated, then said, 'And before you ask, I'm not going to ask Kelt for backing, either.'

'I refuse to believe your mother is happy about this.'

He spoke neutrally, but she knew what he meant. 'She'll get used to it.'

He said quietly, 'You didn't have much luck with your parents, did you.' It wasn't a question. 'Your father didn't live in the modern world.'

'None of us had much luck,' she returned, forcing a note of worldliness. 'Yours died early—Alex's mother too—and mine just weren't interested in children. Still, we haven't turned out badly. Perhaps that happy home life children are supposed to need so much is just a myth.' She finished casually, 'Like perfect love.'

'Can you see Kelt and Hani together and believe either of those assumptions?'

'No,' she said instantly, ashamed of her cynicism. 'They are the real thing.'

Perhaps her envy showed in her voice because he asked rather distantly, 'Is that what you're looking for?'

'Aren't we all?' she parried, wary now. She loosened fingers that had tightened on each other in her lap, and gazed resolutely at the streetscape outside. Perfect, eternal, all-absorbing romance was the elusive chimera her mother searched for, restlessly flitting from lover to lover, but never succeeding.

Was Gerd hoping for that same eternal sense of fulfilment with Princess Serina?

She could ask him, but the words refused to come, and the moment passed as the car turned into a narrow alley in the older part of the city.

'Here we are,' he said without emphasis.

The vehicle drew up outside the heavy, ancient door of an equally ancient building. People turned to look when the security man, until then a silent presence beside the chauffeur, got out. A doorman moved across the pavement to open the car's rear door.

It was all done swiftly, discreetly, yet the smooth operation sent a chill down Rosie's spine as she and Gerd went through the door and into the building. Her own life was so free, compared to Gerd's.

On the other hand, she thought with an effort at flippancy, she wasn't rich enough to dine in places like this.

As though he could read her mind, Gerd said, 'This is the aristocratic quarter of town. In fact, right next door is the town house of the Dukes of Vamili.'

Her brow wrinkled. 'That's Kelt's title, isn't it?'

'Yes. It's used for the second son of the ruler now,

but before the title was taken over by our family the Duke of Vamili was the second-ranking man in the Grand Duchy, with almost regal power over about a third of Carathia. About two hundred years ago the then Duke led a rebellion against the Grand Duke, and died for his treachery. He had only one child, a daughter, who was married off to the second son of the Grand Duke. The Grand Duke then transferred the title and all the estates—to him.'

'Poor woman,' Rosie said crisply. 'It doesn't sound like a recipe for a happy marriage.'

His smile was brief. 'Strangely enough, it appears to have been. Of course, he might have been an excellent husband. And women, especially aristocratic women, of those days didn't have such high expectations of marriage.'

'Unlike modern women, who have the audacity to want happiness and fulfilment,' Rosie returned sweetly, pacing up a wide sweep of shallow stairs.

Gerd cocked an ironic brow. 'Some seem to believe that both should come without any effort on their part.'

Like my mother, Rosie thought sombrely. Chasing rainbows all her life…

They were shown into a room that opened out through an arcade onto a stone terrace overlooking the great valley of Carathia.

Rosie sighed in involuntary appreciation, walking across to grip the stone balustrade, still warm from the sun. 'This is so beautiful, like a bowl half-filled with light.'

Dusk was creeping across the valley, and in the growing pool of shadow all that could be seen were small golden pinpoints, brave challenges to the darkness. Eastwards she could pick out groves of trees, closely planted fields of some sort of grain, clusters of red-tiled villages, the shimmer of silver-gilt that was the river and every detail on the slopes of the mountains.

Rosie felt eager and aware, her senses stirred and stimulated by the man standing beside her as he surveyed this part of his realm.

Quietly she said, 'I know there's a lot more to Carathia than this valley, but it seems complete in itself.'

'One of my ancestors called it a fair land set above,' Gerd told her. 'And yes, Carathia's much bigger than the valley. The country wouldn't be nearly so prosperous without the coastal strip. It gives us easy access to the rest of the world, and makes us a very popular tourism destination. Then there are the agricultural lands further north, and the mines—all important.'

'But this is where the capital is, where the ruler lives; the heart of the country?'

'Its heart and its soul,' he said after a few moments. 'This is where those original Greek soldiers fought and settled and took wives, and it's always been the centre of power.'

'You're a real Carathian, aren't you?' she said quietly, wondering why this sudden realisation struck like a blow. 'Kelt might be a Duke here, but he's a Kiwi really—his heart belongs to New Zealand. You spent as much time in New Zealand as he did when you were younger, yet you're Carathian.'

'I knew from the time I was old enough to understand that this place was my destiny,' he pointed out. As though bored with the topic, he turned. 'Where would you like to sit? We can go inside, or they will set up a table for us out here.'

'Out here,' she said without hesitation. 'I want to enjoy every moment of this lovely place while I can. At home it's winter, and probably raining and a lot colder than this.'

'It rains here too,' he said, nodding to someone behind, 'quite often in summer. If you want a real summer you should go down to the coast. Or out to the islands. They're the true Mediterranean experience.'

Rosie said simply, 'I can't think of anything more lovely, or more Carathian, than this.'

She'd never see the fabled Adriatic coast of Carathia with its Greek and Roman ruins, the rows of vines across the white hills, the palms, the castles that defended each tiny sea-port, and the fishing boats with an eye painted on each bow for protection while they were out on the shimmering blue sea.

She'd never come back.

A waiter arrived bearing a silver tray and ice bucket; with ceremony he opened a bottle of champagne and poured out two glasses before presenting them.

Behind him Rosie could see people laying a table. It appeared she and Gerd were going to be the only people eating here. A swift frisson of excitement swept up through her and she had to resist the temptation to take a tiny, nervous sip of wine.

Gerd said, 'Are you cold? If you'd rather change your mind and eat inside we'll do that.'

'No, it's lovely here, perfect.' But just in case he got the wrong idea she said demurely, 'I've always wanted to dine in a mediaeval building with a handsome man and drink superb French champagne. It will be something to tell any grandchildren I might have. Will there be candles?'

His smile was narrow and sharp. 'Of course. Although it's a Renaissance building, to be accurate.' He held out his glass. 'Very well, then, a toast. We'll drink to your next visit here.'

Their glasses kissed, then separated. Rosie drank, trying to fully appreciate a wine that was clearly something special.

Common sense told her briskly that Gerd probably took French champagne as his due, and gave her the brash courage to say, 'I suppose Carathia's next big occasion will be the announcement of your engagement to Princess Serina.'

'You shouldn't believe everything you read in the media,' he said in a tone that told her she was trespassing.

Rosie's reckless heart contracted. For once unable to speak, she sent him a glance through her lashes.

Gerd's expression was unreadable, the handsome face aloof. 'She's only your age; far too young for me.'

The shameless flare of hope that had blazed fiercely for a few seconds died instantly. If the princess was too young for Gerd, so was she...

So much for her brave decision to stop yearning for him!

'Too young?' she demanded rashly. 'You're only twelve years older than I am. Does the princess think you're too old?'

His mouth thinned. 'We haven't discussed it.'

OK, stop right there! Although barely a muscle

moved in his handsome face, he couldn't have made it more plain that she'd overstepped the mark.

'So you don't think I'm too old for someone of your age?' Gerd asked, a steely note in his voice.

Embarrassed colour heated her skin. He couldn't know how painful this conversation was for her, and it was entirely her own fault.

Shrugging, she said, 'It depends entirely on the person, surely?'

'A very diplomatic answer,' he mocked. 'Restraint doesn't suit you.'

'I can be restrained when I want to,' she said loftily, only to flush at his mocking glance. Talk about a childish rejoinder!

'I'd noticed.' When she stared warily at him, he elaborated, 'Rosemary, you've always had beautiful manners and a kind heart. That's not the issue. Would you, for example, think twice about marrying a man twelve years older than you?'

'Not if I loved him.' He'd never know just how bitter the words were on her tongue. Desperate to change the subject, she said lamely, 'I'm sorry, I didn't intend to pry.' She paused, then admitted with a wry smile, 'Actually, of course I did. You and she have been photographed together a lot recently.'

'She and I know a lot of the same people. Gossip columnists are an over-excitable lot,' he said satirically. 'I'm surprised you read that rubbish. For your information, the family will be the first to know if and when I decide to announce my engagement.'

Clever Gerd. Although he hadn't confirmed any plans to marry, he hadn't denied them, either.

'Fair enough,' she said, pinning a smile to her lips. 'But you can't stop people from wondering. After all, you're probably the world's most eligible bachelor right now.'

'And the Press has to sell newspapers and magazines,' he said caustically, then carried the war into her territory. 'Kelt tells me that Aunt Eva is doing her best to marry you off.'

'Strangely enough when you consider the disaster her marriage was, that's exactly what she's up to, although it does seem her sole criterion for a good husband is the size of his bank balance.' She gave him a cool glance. 'So far I haven't been tempted by the men she's introduced to me.'

Gerd looked down at her. The fading sun set shimmering little fires in her hair and sprinkled her perfect skin with gold dust. There had been no cynicism in her tone, merely rueful resignation.

'So who is the current lover?' he probed.

As a child her face had been mobile, every emotion displayed for the world to read. Since then she'd learned control; the Rosemary he'd known, the girl he'd kissed, had been banished, her place taken by this glossy, self-assured woman.

Her brows rose. 'Mother's?'

'Yours. Anyone I know?'

'Nobody at the moment,' she said lightly, her expression giving nothing away.

Frustration tightened Gerd's lips. She was so young—far too young to be making any lifetime promises—but her soft, sensuously curved lips, the conscious awareness in her eyes, her sophistication, meant she was no stranger to passion.

So? He'd known that ever since he'd kissed her. And if her ardent response hadn't convinced him of it, seeing her in Kelt's arms the next morning would have. The memory of those kisses he'd witnessed still burned like acid. Growing up in the care of a woman whose chaotic search for love had invariably ended in disillusion must have given Rosemary a distorted view of what a relationship could be between a man and a woman.

Reining in a cold, baseless anger, Gerd wondered for possibly the thousandth time if it had been Kelt who'd taught her the full depths of her passion.

He'd never mentioned them to his brother, not even a few hours after their kiss, when Kelt had issued a veiled warning cloaked in friendly banter but making sure Gerd understood that he was watching out for Rosemary. Ashamed of the loss of control that had prompted his desire the previous night, Gerd had responded with an icy aloofness that had convinced Kelt he had no intention of breaking the girl's heart.

He'd seen very little of his brother since then. Partly, he admitted, because he hated the thought of Kelt being Rosemary's first lover.

If he had been, it hadn't lasted long. Shortly after Gerd had returned to Carathia Hani had appeared, and Kelt had gone under like a drowning man.

It would be bitterly ironic if he'd broken Rosemary's heart, setting her on her mother's path of short, futile relationships that had no chance of surviving.

Was she still longing for Kelt? There had definitely been something in her eyes, in her voice, when she'd watched Kelt dance with Hani.

His instinctive distaste was backed by another, much less civilised emotion. Jealousy...

Gerd looked over her head. 'The table's ready for us,' he said brusquely. 'Come and sit down.'

She gave him a curious glance, but responded with cool friendliness, just as she had all week, treating him like a much older brother. To his intense irritation she kept it up while they ordered and settled into a discussion about the parlous state of the planet. He admired her quick intelligence, but he missed the sparkling challenge he'd only glimpsed since she'd arrived in Carathia.

Gerd despised himself for being both intrigued and disturbed. Over the past few days he hadn't been able to stop himself noting the way other men had looked at her, responding to her subtle, understated sensuousness.

His sharp, involuntary reaction to those speculative glances had angered him. He'd had to stop himself from moving in to—to what?

Establish some sort of claim?

Reluctantly he admitted it. Of course his intervention hadn't been necessary; her experience showed in the way she'd skilfully parried any advances.

He'd wanted her at eighteen, but it was impossible. He was no debaucher of innocent girls.

But now...now she was no longer innocent.

While they'd been talking darkness had fallen—thick, all-encompassing, enclosing them in an intimate circle of candlelight, yet Rosie sensed a distance in him, an aloofness that chilled her. An upward glance revealed that he was looking at her, his eyes remote behind the thick screen of his lashes.

He was watching her mouth.

Tension shafted through her, bringing with it a fierce delight. She'd seen desire often enough to recognise it. In spite of his formidable restraint, Gerd was attracted to her.

Rosie's heart clamped in her breast.

So? she thought, trying to tamp down the unwanted tumult of excitement. Desire was common coin; it meant nothing beyond the swift heat of passion. She'd always been repulsed by men whose only interest in her was physical.

But this was different; this was Gerd...

Don't go there! Doing her best to be sophisticated, she warned herself that Gerd was very much a man, and so just as capable of feeling meaningless passion as her rejected would-be lovers.

That hateful thought prompted her to remark tartly, 'Pondering matters of state, Gerd? Or should I call you Your Royal Highness now?'

Their eyes clashed, his hard and more than a little intimidating. 'Only if you say it in Carathian. And even then, only if you're a Carathian citizen.'

'So what do people who are neither call you?'

'My family and friends call me Gerd.'

'Then I'll stick to that,' she said jauntily, adding with a wry smile, 'even though I'm neither family nor friend.'

She didn't know what she expected from him after that—a smoothly bland statement that she was both, perhaps. But he leaned back in his chair and regarded her steadily, his handsome face sardonic.

For some reason an erratic pulse beat high in Rosie's

throat; she had to clasp one hand around the stem of the champagne glass to stop herself from covering that betraying little hollow, but she could do nothing about the exhilarating rush of adrenalin that charged through her.

Lazily he said, 'We've had this conversation before. Since you're Alex's half-sister, I consider you to be very much part of the family even though there is no blood connection. As for being friends, do you think a man and a woman can be nothing more than friends?'

'Some men, some women,' she returned. 'It's not impossible.'

His brows lifted. 'Let's be specific, then. Do you think you and I could be friends?'

Was he flirting with her? Tantalised by the thought, Rosie struggled to achieve the right throwaway tone. 'It doesn't seem likely. Friendships need to be worked at, and how often have we seen each other in the past three years? I don't think we can call ourselves friends. Friendly acquaintances, possibly.'

There, that should show him she didn't want any sort of *flirtatious* relationship with him. Darn it, she was trying to get him out of her system! Encouraging this sort of half-bantering innuendo was not the way to do that.

'An innocuous description.' But a raw edge in his voice sent surreptitious little shivers the length of her spine, warned her it might not be wise to take his words at face value.

A waiter arrived with the first course, a cold soup, and while they drank it Gerd steered the conversation into much safer channels.

Relieved, Rosie followed his lead, keeping her gaze away from those darkly golden eyes, that fascinating mouth. Only to discover she couldn't stop looking at his hands—lean, long-fingered and smoothly assured.

Little quivers tightened inside her as she found herself wondering what they'd feel like on her skin. She swallowed hastily and told herself to be sensible. She knew exactly what they felt like; when he'd kissed her he'd slid his hands across her back, causing a shuddery delight to riot through her.

Stop thinking about it! She forced herself to be bright, to wait a second before she spoke, and to restrict herself to impersonal glances and manufactured smiles.

By the time dinner ended she was as taut and tightly coiled as an over-wound spring. There wasn't the usual business with credit cards, and she bit her lip to stop asking how such payments were managed. Did the restaurant send a bill to the palace?

The same car met them again, with the same anonymous security man beside the chauffeur. Rosie sank back into the seat, clipping her seat belt across to form a fragile barrier between her and Gerd.

Stupid, because of course he wouldn't pounce!

Gazing out of the window, she said the first thing that came into her head. 'I like modern buildings, but I have to admit these old houses with their carvings and oriel windows and studded doors have something that makes me wish New Zealand had a longer history.'

'The novelty, probably.' He sounded distant, glad that the evening had finished. 'You're used to houses built of timber. The fact that in Carathia stone has always been the cheapest and most common material might make the buildings here more romantic.'

Rosie ignored a little jab of pain. 'Could be,' she agreed, and lapsed into silence as they drove through the still-busy streets and up the hill to the palace, huge and dramatically lit on the hill.

'It's so big,' she ventured, gazing at the classical splendour of it. 'Did the ancestor who built this have a particularly large family?'

'A particularly large sense of his own importance,' Gerd told her astringently. 'One of his barons married a woman from southern Italy who found the family's ancient castle intolerably cold. She must have been very beautiful and he must have been besotted, because he razed it and used the stone to build a mansion. Not to be outdone, the then Grand Duke had the original castle here demolished so he could build a much bigger, more grand palace than his vassal.'

'To the great relief of everyone who followed him onto the throne, I'm sure,' she returned cheerfully. 'I love castles—they're grim and powerful and evocative of history and passion and treachery and chivalry, but I'll bet the reason they're mostly in ruins now is because they were so uncomfortable.'

The car drew up inside the palace courtyard. 'Comfort over romance, Rosemary?'

Uneasily aware of his brief smile as he spoke, she said, 'Absolutely.' And it wasn't entirely a lie.

As they walked towards the door Gerd said, 'A nightcap?'

CHAPTER FOUR

COMMON sense told Rosie to make her excuses and her escape as quickly as she could with dignity.

But if she'd listened to common sense when Gerd asked her to dinner she'd have missed out on the bittersweetness of the evening. From now on she'd only see Gerd in photographs. The knowledge ached through her, summoning a kind of desperation, a need to hug each precious moment to her breast.

Think of it as a final goodbye, she told herself with bleak realism. Without a tremor she said, 'Thank you, I'd enjoy that.'

In his private sitting room he poured drinks while she examined the room. This was not the bigger one where he'd entertained the family, but a smaller, more intimate affair, furnished quite casually. Her gaze ranged from the huge sofas that befitted a man of his height to some exquisite glassware in a cabinet, and she made a soft sound of pleasure.

'From Venice,' he said, following the direction of her gaze as he handed her the drink. 'The Venetians ruled most of this coast at one time.'

'Did they conquer Carathia?'

'No, but they demanded a yearly tribute—wine and silver from the mines.'

'The glass is beautiful, such glorious colours. I didn't know there were silver mines here.'

'They've been worked out for a couple of centuries, but they were what made Carathia prosperous in the Middle Ages.'

Rosie sipped the white wine he'd given her. A silky, subtly sweet liquor, it breathed the scent of flowers. 'This smells like spring. And tastes like it too. Is it from here?'

'Yes.' Grim-faced, he looked down at her, and in a voice she'd never heard before said, 'I chose it because you always remind me of spring.'

Rosie froze, silenced by a fierce rush of adrenalin. She looked up into glittering golden eyes as a heady recklessness clamoured through her, a torrent both languorous and without mercy, sweet as honey and dangerous. Through the drumbeat of her pulse she tightened her shaking fingers around the glass. The voluptuous appetite Gerd roused with his kisses all those years ago blazed into open need.

She began to tremble.

Narrowed eyes gleaming, he took the almost untouched wine from her and set the glass on a table. Rosie's heart gave a great leap and the breath stopped in her throat. Heat pounded through her, softening her bones, banishing any coherent thoughts in a widening surge of hunger.

Yet as Gerd lifted her hands to his lips, she managed to croak, 'This is not a good idea, Gerd.'

'Have you a better one?' he asked deeply.

Shivers chased themselves over her skin, through every wakening cell in her body. 'I don't know—I just don't really think…' she said in confusion, the words slurring when he kissed the jumping pulse in one wrist.

His mouth was hot and demanding, lingering over the fine skin. Rosie swallowed to ease her dry throat. There was something she had to say, but she couldn't remember what.

Still holding her gaze, he held her hands to his chest so that the open palms rested above his heart. Its rapid beat echoed her own turbulent pulse, thundering a primitive call.

Rosie closed her eyes, but that made things worse; without sight every other sense was sharpened. She could hear his breath, hard and fast as though he'd been running, and his faint, masculine scent teased her nostrils—evocative, compelling.

Desperate, she forced up her lashes and held his gaze, wincing at the arrogant jut of his jaw and the golden glints in his eyes, the eyes of a predator.

She should be terrified.

She wasn't.

But something had to be said.

'Princess Serina?' she muttered almost pleadingly.

He told her harshly, 'I've made no commitment to her or to any other woman. She is not expecting a proposal from me.'

Rosie struggled to articulate a further question, but he kissed the unformed words from her lips, and she surrendered to desire so intense her knees buckled. Gerd's arms tightened around her. She gasped when he picked her up and carried her, mouth on mouth, across the room, sinking onto one of the big sofas without releasing her.

The kisses turned shockingly erotic when he bent her head back across his shoulder and explored her sweet depths with a torrid passion. Dimly, vaguely, Rosie wondered if she should have run while she had the chance.

Too late now. His slow, drugging kisses summoned a wildly incandescent response from every cell in her body and she had never felt so safe.

Yet never been in such danger...

Gerd lifted his head and scrutinised her face, penetrating eyes gleaming between dark lashes, the angular framework of his handsome face suddenly far more prominent. 'If you don't want this tell me right now, before it's too late.'

Rosie dragged breath into her famished lungs. Disconnected thoughts tumbled in freefall around her brain, fleeting scraps so coloured by emotion she couldn't assemble them into any coherent order.

Finally she managed, 'Why?'

Closing his eyes, he said in a rough voice, 'Rosemary, I've wanted you since I first kissed you, but you were far too young.' Catching her unawares, he opened his eyes again, fixing her with a fierce, unguarded gaze that set more nerves jangling. 'And now you're grown-up, but it has to be what you want too.'

His words jerked Rosie upwards. Mouth tight, eyes blazing, she surveyed his ruthless face.

It was too cruel of him to kiss her like that, as though she was the most important thing in his life, as though he'd longed for her just as fiercely as she'd craved him, and then let his damned principles get in the way.

Furious, she exploded, 'Of *course* I want you—I've wanted you since I understood what wanting is.'

He said harshly, 'You deserve more than a one-night stand.'

For some strange reason his words strengthened her resolution. She met his gaze with boldness. 'So do you.'

His chest lifted and she saw wry laughter gleam in the golden eyes.

And something else, she realised, her heart picking up speed once more. Determination, as though he'd come to some turning point and now saw the way ahead.

'So perhaps we will forget about it being just one night,' he said. In a voice without any inflection he asked, 'What is your decision?'

'Why do *I* have to decide?' she demanded.

He gave her a taut, narrow smile. 'You know why.' He held out his hand. Slowly she put her hand into his keeping. Against the tanned strength of his, hers looked fragile, almost lost.

He wrapped his fingers around hers and said, 'Pull.'

'I don't have to.' Her stupid hand was shaking, and she fought back an unregenerate sizzle of excitement. 'I know you're stronger than I am.'

'That's why *you* decide,' he told her inflexibly.

Clearly, he wasn't going to change his mind. Without thinking she hauled back. Instantly his fingers closed around hers, holding them in a firm grip that didn't hurt.

And then he let her go. In a voice as uncompromising as that grip had been, he said, 'Make up your mind, Rosemary.'

Awash with a hunger that screamed for satisfaction, Rosie forced herself to think. Part of the hold he had on her had to be simple frustration because she'd never made love. In her dreams it was wonderful, transcendental, but she'd listened to enough friends to understand it needn't necessarily be like that.

So if she experienced sex with Gerd chances were she could rid herself of this fruitless desire.

Or it might make things worse—give life to a craving she couldn't control.

But that had already happened. Hell, because of this man she was still a virgin!

Be logical, she told herself almost beseechingly. A long-distance friendship was difficult enough to sustain; a long-distance love affair—one based only on sex—would be even more difficult.

Eventually it must burn out, and when it did she'd be free of the lingering hangover of her adolescent passion for him.

She said, 'I—all right, now that we know that this...this *need* is mutual, why not just follow it and see what happens?'

His mouth tightened. 'Be sophisticated and adult about it?'

'Is there anything wrong with that?' she demanded, challenging him directly. 'It's better than being foolish and juvenile, surely? We're both adults. We both know this can't go anywhere, so why not take what we can from it and enjoy it and when it dies remember it without regret?'

Gerd smiled, but his eyes were coolly watchful, and she had no idea what he felt when he said, 'If that's what you want, then that is the way it will happen.'

But he made no movement to kiss her again, and an icy chill of panic gripped her. Had she repelled him, even disgusted him?

And then he smiled and said softly, 'I suspect you're every man's dream mistress, Rosemary—no strings, no commitment, no future planned. Just the promise of sex whenever we want it, wherever we want it.' His voice deepened. 'However we want it.'

'Oh, there's going to be some sort of commitment,' she told him, hoping she sounded as confident as her words. But she needed to get something straight, although her heart constricted when she said, 'Until we call a halt I'll be faithful to you, and I'll expect the same from you.'

The dark head bent in an autocratic nod. 'Very well, then, it's a deal.'

The words were blunt, as blunt as hers had been, she reminded herself.

'It's a deal,' she whispered, and held out her hand.

His mouth was a thin line, strangely ruthless, as they shook hands. But it gentled when he lifted her hand to his mouth and kissed her fingertips.

The sensuous caress sent more wanton excitement tingling through Rosie. And then he bent his head and kissed her again, and his mouth took her into that realm where thought and logic no longer mattered, where the only reality was Gerd's passion and her abandoned response.

But even as she yielded she wondered how he might react if he realised she'd never done this before.

It didn't matter. His kisses stoked the fires that had been smouldering so long; for the second time in her life real desire slammed through her, a relentless, consuming source of pleasure and anticipation that banished any apprehension.

When Gerd found the hollow at the base of her throat and kissed the feverish pulse there, she stiffened and gave a soft, involuntary groan.

'You even smell of spring,' he said, his voice low and impeded. 'All flowers and sweetness and energy...'

Rosie pushed his shirt back and kissed his shoulder, her mouth open and seeking. He tasted like every dream she'd ever had—a sexy mix of challenge and charisma and power, an earthy flavour that was Gerd alone, made from his body, the true essence of the man.

To her astonished delight, she felt him tense, and then his mouth moved to the curve of her breast.

Breath locking in her throat, she waited for the revulsion she usually felt, the sense of being invaded that always before had had her calling an abrupt halt.

It didn't come. When he kissed her she understood the true meaning of longing; tautly expectant, her breasts ached with voluptuous hunger that only he could ease.

But he lifted his head. She had only a moment to endure the cold chill of rejection before he began to push aside the ties that held up her dress.

'Am I likely to wreck this pretty thing by doing this?'

Gerd's raw voice only added to the reckless clamour in her blood. 'No.'

She wondered at her voice, husky and slow, so that

the syllable flowed into the silence in the room like liquid honey.

'Hold up your arms.'

Silently, eyes enormous and smoky in her face, she obeyed, and he eased the material over her head, dropping it over the arm of the sofa.

The dress had a built-in bra and slip, so beneath it she wore nothing but narrow briefs. To her horror Rosie realised she was blushing, the colour burning up from her bared breasts.

Too shy to look at him, she averted her face, freezing when he curved his hand around her jaw. Her lashes drooped; fascinated, shocked, she hardly breathed while he surveyed what he'd uncovered. His expression didn't change, but she felt a subtle alteration in him, a kind of charged awareness that ratcheted up her tension so that hunger exploded like a pain inside her, demanding and elemental, a force that consumed her entirely.

'Your skin is like silk,' he said.

The words sounded rough, yet she didn't make the mistake of thinking he was angry. She'd never imagined that Gerd could look at her with such...such intensity, as though she was something infinitely rare and precious, something he didn't dare touch.

A reckless shiver shook her. And she'd never felt so exposed, lying almost naked across his lap while he was still fully clothed.

Now what? For a horrified moment she thought she'd actually said the words.

'I have to get undressed too.' He spoke with harsh precision, as though he'd had to concentrate on what he was saying, and began to undo his shirt.

Rosie stayed still, her eyes on the dark, long fingers against the white material. She forced herself to take a breath, listening as it came through her lips, hearing the beating of her heart heavy and fast in her ears, the taste of Gerd in her mouth.

Should she tell him this was all new to her?

No.

It didn't mean anything, or perhaps it meant too much. She didn't want to load him with the burden of her virginity. Blurting it out would somehow make the fact that she was untouched more important than this languid, golden tide of passion, so intense it closed her throat.

Mutely, her heart hammering in her breast, she watched as Gerd shrugged free of the shirt and tossed it over her dress.

Rosie hesitated, but desire persuaded her to stretch out a tentative hand and trace with splayed fingers the path of the scroll of hair across his powerful chest. Startled, she registered the tension of muscles beneath that lightest of exploratory touches, and for the first time a tinge of apprehension shadowed her headstrong physical longing.

Perhaps he sensed her involuntary fear. His kiss was tender and gentle, only deepening when he felt the wildfire response she could no longer control.

And by the time his mouth found the pleading tip of her breast she was again on fire for him, writhing restlessly as he showed her just how responsive her breasts were to his caress.

When eventually he said in a thickened, harsh voice, 'Not here, I think,' she stared at him in bewilderment, her eyes huge and dark in her face.

His smile hard and savage, an elemental claim of

possession, he eased her off him before getting to his feet and picking her up.

'You're just the right size for this,' he said, and snatched another kiss before striding across the room.

Dazedly Rosie registered that the room he took her to was his bedroom. Eyes fixed on Gerd's hard-hewn face, she felt the cool kiss of sheets on her bare back.

He bent to remove her sandals, his fingers stroking up her leg. Rosie's breath locked in her throat.

But he straightened, and efficiently stripped off the rest of his clothes. Instinctively Rosie's lashes fluttered down. It took all of her willpower to force them up again; this might be the only time she had with him, and she wanted to see, wanted to know...

Storing up memories is dangerous, the last sensible part of her brain told her. Resolutely, she dismissed the bleak prophecy, allowing her gaze to linger.

Because Gerd was magnificently male, enough to dazzle any woman, tall and powerfully muscled, the dim light from the other room glossing his bronze skin to reveal more than the darkness hid. Without volition she held out her hand.

He took it, but didn't obey her silent plea. Instead, he said, 'Who am I?'

A frown pleated her brows. 'You know who you are,' she said uncertainly.

'Then call me by my name.'

'Gerd,' she said unevenly.

'Is that all?'

She didn't know what he wanted from her, but she said huskily, 'Gerd is all that interests me. Your surname comes from the past; Gerd is now.'

He raised her hand to his mouth and kissed the palm, then let his teeth graze the mount of Venus beneath her thumb. 'Rosemary,' he said, making her name an act of possession.

The tiny caress was more erotic than any previous kiss; her lithe body twisted of its own accord and on a low, dark laugh he came down beside her and gathered her into his arms and pinned her against his lean, powerful body and kissed her breath—and every thought—out of existence.

But even then he let her go and turned away. 'Just a moment,' he said quietly.

Hot-cheeked, she realised what he was doing. It was a measure of the enchantment he'd cast over her that she'd forgotten completely about the possibility of pregnancy!

And when he turned back everything was all right again, because this was Gerd, and she wanted him beyond—oh, beyond hope, beyond fear, almost beyond desire.

He wooed her with kisses and caresses, and a knowledge that could only be the result, she'd realise later, of vast experience. So lost in her wild response that she didn't care, Rosie forgot her total lack of experience and followed his lead, caressing him as he did her, until finally her body twisted against him, hips thrusting as she sought something else—something more than this exquisite, desperate pleasure.

Voice gravelly and raw, he said, 'Time?'

'Yes,' she whispered, 'oh, yes, please…'

But he didn't immediately move over her; instead he stroked her skin from her throat to the juncture of her legs, his skilled, questing fingers firing her anticipation into a fever.

Only then did he take her, thrusting past the fragile barrier and claiming her in that most primal of all embraces.

Gasping with the shock, Rosie clamped muscles she hadn't known she possessed.

Gerd froze, his eyes glittering, his chest lifting while he fought for air. 'What the *hell*?'

Her hips jerked upwards. It was so near, so close— yet not close enough. She slid importunate hands across his sleek back, pulling him down so that she could move frantically against him.

Although she could feel his resistance it didn't last; almost immediately he responded, his big body fiercely attuned to hers as he sent her further and further along the path towards an elusive goal that retreated and advanced in slow, erotic waves.

A delirious yearning gripped her with silken talons, until at last the sensation became so intense she gave a gasping sob as it overwhelmed her, hurtling her beyond some invisible border into another dimension where all that counted was the perfect ecstasy that surged through her.

Almost immediately Gerd too found that place and yielded to its untamed rapture, head flung back, body taut with barely controlled energy until repletion overtook him.

Dazed by exhausted pleasure, Rosie looped her arms around him, pretending, oh, pretending such *foolish* things as their breaths harmonised and slowly, slowly they coasted down that long slope to reality.

Gerd turned on his side and hooked his finger under her chin, tilting her face so that he could scan it, raptor's eyes metallic, like frozen fire.

He said something—from its tone, an oath—in Carathian, and as her eyes widened rasped in English, 'Damn it, why didn't you tell me?'

Rosie couldn't think of anything sensible to say. How could she have been so, so *abandoned*, so lost in his arms she'd neglected the one thing her mother had impressed on her—to make sure there would be no possibility of a child?

After several moments of taut silence he asked coldly, 'Are you using any sort of protection at all?'

She refused to lie. 'No, and I didn't need to, did I? You did.'

'I might not have,' he ground out. 'What would you have done, then?'

'OK, so I behaved like an idiot,' she said, her lovely glow dissipating into desolation under the icy onslaught of his anger. 'Probably because I was certain you'd be more careful.'

He swore again and let her go as though she disgusted him. 'And why didn't you tell me you were a virgin?'

Sick at heart, Rosie angled her chin away from him. It took every ounce of courage she possessed to say in a steady voice, 'It wasn't important.'

For some reason that made him even more angry. 'Not *important*?' he snarled. 'Of course it was important; if you didn't think so you'd have leapt into bed with any one of the men you've been connected to.'

Again there didn't seem to be an answer. To tell him

the truth—that if she couldn't have him she wanted nobody—was out of the question, so she shrugged. 'For heaven's sake, it's not an issue. I've always done what I thought was right for me.'

He leaned back against the pillows. Rosie glanced sideways, saw his arrogant profile silhouetted against the light from the open door, and in spite of everything her pulse started to quicken again; he looked magnificent, big and handsome and furious.

Hastily she turned her face away again.

He enquired icily, 'How could making love with me be right for you?'

'I don't know,' she said without thinking, and because that made her seem a complete fool she went on quickly, 'Oh, stop being so—so *macho* about this. I just didn't think it was necessary to tell you.' Colour heated her skin and she finished in a smoky voice, 'Besides, I wasn't thinking clearly at all—not after that first kiss, anyway.'

His eyes narrowed. 'I'm delighted to hear that,' he said with chilling courtesy. 'But condoms are not foolproof.'

Well, of course that was what he was worried about. What else?

A sense of self-preservation forced her to hide her bleakness with an airy tone. 'I can easily see a doctor and get protection. But if you want to call things off, I'll understand.'

After all, he'd thought he'd be embarking on an affair with a woman of experience. Possibly he found her caresses incredibly gauche and dull.

Her words were followed by an edged silence before he turned his head and surveyed the length of her body.

Rosie's skin prickled at that slow, almost insulting scrutiny, but deep inside her a humiliating heat began to smoulder into life.

'No,' he said silkily. 'We made a deal, remember? That we'd see where this goes.'

'I—yes, but you thought you were dealing with someone who knew what she was doing. Your reaction tells me you're not happy—'

'Only because you didn't tell me,' he interrupted, running a deliberate finger around the ivory curve of one breast, the light, tantalising caress tightening her skin and stirring a swift, heated response. 'If you had I'd have been more gentle.'

On a swift indrawn breath she whispered, 'I didn't need gentle. Are you sure you don't mind?'

'Mind?' he said deeply. 'I was just startled. And delighted. Why should I complain about your charming lack of experience? As I said before, you're every man's dream. No responsibility, and the pleasure of transforming that sensuous innocence of yours into knowledge. I'm holding you to our deal.'

Something about him made her move uneasily even as her heartbeat began to race. On an indrawn breath, she muttered, 'Only if you're sure?'

The words strangled in her throat when he bent his black head to trace with his mouth the path his finger had taken.

Against her skin he said, 'I'm very sure. It will be my pleasure to teach you.'

That uneasy feeling deepened until he lifted his head and said blandly, 'But not tonight. You'll probably be too tender.'

Rosie opened her mouth to protest, only to be surprised by a yawn.

With an ironic smile Gerd got up and gently pulled her to her feet. 'Besides,' he said, 'there are things to be discussed, and tonight is obviously not the time to do that. When you're dressed I'll take you to your room.'

Scrambling into her clothes, Rosie tried very hard to emulate his casual acceptance of the situation. But when he left her at her door, his kiss started off chastely, only to transform within seconds into something much more potent.

However, he lifted his head and stepped back, his expression giving nothing away. Rosie looked mutely at him, so awash with longing she couldn't summon any words.

'Goodnight,' he said evenly, and left her.

Half an hour later, her evening regime completed, Rosie lay in the big bed and tried to make sense of what had happened. He'd probably thought she'd slept with dozens of men, she thought acidly, before a second, more bewildering thought occurred to her.

Uneasily she turned and punched the pillow. Things—her life—had changed so fundamentally she didn't know how to cope.

It felt as though a balance had shifted, and their lovemaking had somehow given Gerd a power over her he hadn't possessed before.

No, that was foolish. She was the same person; well, almost the same, apart from knowing a lot more about sex than she had only a few hours ago.

And it had been wonderful, she thought dreamily; no matter what happened, she'd always have that.

He'd been masterful and skilled, passionate and fiercely tender, and she'd thrilled to every minute of it...

Smiling, she drifted off to sleep.

And woke the next morning to a slightly achy body and a much more practical frame of mind, half-bewildered yet still excited by what had happened the night before.

She glanced at her watch and gave a muffled yelp. 'Packing,' she muttered, leaping out of bed.

Most of the morning had disappeared, leaving her with practically no time to pack. She hadn't even thought of it last night, but Gerd hadn't said anything about her staying, so presumably he expected her to leave as planned.

When she'd arrived her luggage had been unpacked by a maid, and she'd been told to ring if she needed anything. She hadn't, and she didn't know whether she should leave a tip, or how such things were organised in the palace.

She should have asked Hani.

It was less stressful to worry about that than face the fact that she had no idea what was going to happen with Gerd. Did he want her to stay? Would he suggest a date for their next meeting?

The past week had shown her that his life was organised well ahead. He hadn't suggested she stay in Carathia, but he'd talked about contraception—surely that meant he intended some sort of ongoing relationship?

A knock on her door whirled her about; she hesitated, then called out, 'Come in.'

It was Gerd, tall and stern and aloof. 'Come with me.'

Chilled, she accompanied him into the room she'd been in the previous night. A glance at the big sofa brought a swift bloom of heat to her skin, but that soon vanished when he spoke.

'I've cancelled your flight home.'

CHAPTER FIVE

SHEER astonishment silenced Rosie—but only for a second. 'You had no right,' she flashed.

Face impassive, Gerd shrugged. 'Did you want to go back to New Zealand?'

The one question she didn't want to answer. After a deep breath she stated emphatically, 'That was my decision to make, not yours. I'm not one of your subjects, to be told what to do.'

He shrugged as though her protest meant nothing. 'It's done now. Last night you spoke of seeing a doctor about contraception. She'll be here in half an hour.' He paused, then said, 'But if you want to return to New Zealand I'll organise a flight for you—a much more comfortable one than riding cattle class in a jumbo jet.'

He smiled, and her heart twisted, anger draining away under the sensuous impact. Defying its effect, she repeated, 'But the decision was mine to make, not yours.'

'Was it the wrong decision?'

'I…' She took a deep breath and admitted, 'No.'

His brows shot up, then his expression relaxed. 'Kelt

has called me an arrogant bastard fairly frequently—perhaps he's right. What do *you* want to do?'

Uncertainly she said, 'I don't know.' Her lips trembled; startled, she blinked at the hot sting of tears and swallowed hard. 'Oh, damn!'

She stiffened when Gerd covered the two paces between them, but when he took her in his arms she melted, resting her forehead against his disarmingly broad shoulder.

'I'm not used to anything like this,' she admitted into his shirt. 'And you are.'

'I've told you before, don't believe the gossip columnists,' he said crisply.

'Even if only half of what's been written is true it means you're a whole lot more experienced than I am,' she pointed out miserably.

He held her away from him, his face closed against her. 'I have had lovers, yes. Not very many, and none of them have been casual.'

That hurt too; she didn't dare let him see how much. 'Go on.'

'I shall not tell you about them—it would be a betrayal of trust. Last night you laid down conditions—conditions I accepted. As long as we are together you do not need to worry about any other women.'

When she said nothing he held her a little further away and scanned her face with astute, penetrating eyes. 'Do you believe me?'

'I—yes.' She hesitated, then went on, 'Yes, of course I believe you. It's just that I don't know anything about *being together*.'

He smiled, and drew her against him again, holding

her with wonderful gentleness. 'Perhaps I should have expected some uncertainty, but it surprises me that the Rosemary who has always been so outspoken and confident should show such wariness. So, am I forgiven for assuming that you would prefer to stay here than fly to New Zealand?'

Rosemary suspected that she'd forgive him anything. The thought shocked her; she had a feeling he might ride roughshod over her if she didn't lay down boundaries.

What really alarmed her was that she didn't want to.

'Rosemary?'

She admitted, 'Yes, provided it doesn't happen again. And I promise that you won't have to worry about any other men, either.'

His face hardened. 'So, we understand each other.'

And he kissed her, a fleeting kiss on her forehead that somehow appeased her more than a passionate one would have, and drew her arm through his as he walked her towards the door.

He said, 'I have several more days of official and ceremonial engagements, but after that I'm taking a month's holiday at a villa I own on an island off the coast. If you don't mind being by yourself for four days it would be best if you went ahead to the villa.'

Rosie's heart chilled. 'Why?'

His face was unreadable. 'If you appear in the media as my latest mistress the paparazzi will be around you like flies.'

Wincing at being so casually described—and at the thought of the media scrummage that might ensue—she said, 'I see.'

Gerd said, 'I remember how you loved staying at the bach at Kiwinui, so you should enjoy the villa.' He smiled and dropped a swift kiss on her mouth, straightening far too soon. 'And four days is not very long.'

But they were the longest days in Rosie's life. Oh, the island was a dream—the fabled coast she'd been so sure she'd never see. White houses cupped a small harbour where gaily painted fishing boats puttered in and out. Olives shimmered silver-green on the hillsides, and vines braided the slopes. The salt of the sea mingled with the perfumes of flowers blooming in the gardens.

And the villa—surely a misnomer for such a big house—dreamed away the summer days beneath a sky as blue and potent as the sea that mimicked it.

But Rosie was lonely, racked by an aching emptiness that frightened her. Always before she'd enjoyed her own company; now she spent the days waiting, longing for the call Gerd made every day on the secure telephone.

Not that he murmured love words to her; a smile quirked her lips as she sprayed herself with more sunscreen. She just couldn't imagine Gerd mouthing sweet nothings.

And there was no *love* in their relationship. Reduced to the shameful truth, it was just a mutual itch that had irritated them for years. Now was their chance to sate it.

Once that was done they'd go their separate ways.

Even as an adolescent she'd known that there could never be a future for them. Gerd's life had been mapped out for him from birth; eventually he'd marry a princess of the right age and temperament, and they'd have children to carry on the succession.

He'd made it obvious she was the wrong age, and she'd always known she had the wrong temperament— a conviction strengthened by watching Hani, with her gracious charm, and Princess Serina, who'd seemed to know everyone and find just the right word for them.

On the third day Rosie leaned back in the hammock and frowned up through the branches of the big tree that shaded it. Tomorrow evening Gerd would come.

'So you'd better face the facts,' she said aloud. However distasteful they were, she needed to have them clear in her mind before he arrived and scrambled it with his smile, his touch...

They'd have their month and then she'd go back to New Zealand and find herself a job, save like crazy and one day—with any luck in the not-too-distant future— she'd buy her florist's shop.

A faint buzzing lifted her head. Frowning, she scanned the sky, blinking into the sun. A helicopter— coming this way and descending.

Gerd? Today?

Wild excitement pulsed through her, and an over-whelming shyness. She almost fell out of the hammock and stood tensely waiting as the chopper dropped down onto the helipad behind the villa.

It seemed an age before he came striding out of the house, tall and dark and dominating. Her heart drummed feverishly, and she thought, *Oh, you idiot! This is not lust. There's nothing casual about this at all—you're in love with him. Real, now-and-forever love!*

How had it happened? Three lonely days shouldn't have altered everything.

Of course it hadn't. She'd been in love with him all along, at least ever since he'd kissed her those long, empty years ago. Even though she hadn't recognised it, no other man had been able to break through the shield that was her love for Gerd.

The balance of power had shifted even further in his favour. If he ever found out, what would he do?

'Rosemary.'

Just the one word, but her world brightened into a brilliance she'd never known as he came up to her and bent over her, enclosing her in a hard, almost painful hug.

He didn't kiss her. For long seconds he simply held her against his powerful body, embracing her as though this fierce closeness was something he'd been craving since he last saw her.

'Miss me?' His voice was rough, almost harsh.

'Like crazy.' Was that her, that breathless, hopeful tone? Hopeless! Infusing her voice with lazy laughter, she asked, 'How about you?'

'Every minute, every second, all day, every night.' It sounded like a vow. 'Which is why I'm here before time.'

He found her mouth in a kiss so hot and urgent her knees buckled. His arms tightened even further, and he lifted her and sank into the hammock, pulling her on top so that she felt the intimate hardness of him beneath her.

Sensation roared through her, a rich, unfulfilled flood. When they broke the kiss she explored his face with her lips until he groaned and muttered, 'Stop this right now before I unman myself. Maria is expecting us for lunch in five minutes.'

Rosie laughed and cuddled against him. 'You said it would be four days before you could get here.'

He shrugged. 'As I said, I got away earlier.'

Something in his voice alerted Rosie—a reserve that sent an uneasy quiver along her sensitised nerves. She asked quietly, 'Is everything OK?'

Stretched along his lean body, she felt an infinitesimal tightening. Concerned, she raised her head so she could look into his eyes.

But they were shuttered against her, although he said smoothly, 'Everything's fine—and much better now I'm here.'

'Good,' she said, and scrambled off him, wary once more.

He let her go and got out in a lithe movement, then held the side of the hammock steady as she wriggled free and stood up.

Although the realisation might be newborn, she realised now she'd loved Gerd as long as she could remember—an unrecognised, unwanted love, always there like a steady fire, as much a part of her as her eyes and her voice and her heart.

Gerd didn't love her. OK, so he hadn't actually come out and said so, but he'd been quite straightforward about the situation, and she—fool that she'd been, unable to recognise her true feelings—had accepted his terms.

She'd even been confident she could deal with the inevitably bitter ending. Dear heaven, she must have been crazy…

She should have taken the coward's way out and run all the way back to New Zealand, but it was too late now.

Hard on that thought came another. He must never know.

It would be dishonourable to do anything else, because he couldn't give her the love she longed for.

She could cope with anything rather than pity.

So she had to make sure he never glimpsed her love; she'd have to monitor every word, every action, to keep him from guessing her secret.

He reached out a lazy hand for her, then let it drop. As they walked into the cool dimness of the villa he said, 'How have you entertained yourself without me?'

'I've swum a lot,' she said, forcing a light tone. 'And I've finished several books. You have a brilliant library here, and Maria assured me I could use it.'

'Of course. Have you done any exploring of the island?'

'I went with Maria into the market to buy fish; that was great fun, but apart from that and the swimming I've been disgustingly lazy.'

'Well-rested?' A glint in his eyes told her what he was insinuating.

Heat swept through her, sweet as honey, potent as wine. 'Very,' she said, falsely demure.

He laughed and took her hand, threading her fingers through his. 'We'd better go and eat lunch.' And as they walked into the cool house he added wickedly, 'First.'

Rosie's laughter was slightly forced, but it did help to ease her tension. All through lunch excitement built within her. The housekeeper had set the meal out on a small side terrace shaded by vines, the bunches of grapes already colouring up. A radiant sky glimmered through the leaves, its cobalt intensity matching the sweep of the sea, and the white sand sparkled.

'This is a wonderful place,' Rosie murmured as Gerd poured wine for her.

'It started off as a Roman villa,' Gerd told her, handing her the glass. 'When that fell into decay the islanders sensibly used the stone for centuries to build and repair their own houses. Then in Victorian times sea bathing was thought to be health-giving, so one of my ancestors used the foundations to build this house for his delicate wife. And what do you think of our beaches?'

Rosie said blithely, 'Without conceding that New Zealand beaches—especially those around Kiwinui— can be beaten in any way, I have to admit that these are gorgeous.' Her eyes glinted as she shook her head. 'Although the island would be vastly improved by a screen of pohutukawa trees behind each beach.'

He laughed. 'You Kiwis! You're incorrigibly in love with your country.'

'Did the sea bathing help the delicate wife?'

He served her fish, cooked with sea salt and lemon slices. 'No, she died young.'

'That's sad.'

Gerd's smile was touched by cynicism. 'He mourned her for two years, and then married a robust and enthusiastic German princess who presented him with five healthy children. They all used to come here for their holidays. I believe it was an extremely happy marriage.'

She glanced at his face. Unreadable, as usual.

Something tightened inside Rosie, warning her not to go in this direction. She knew what he wanted from her—an uncomplicated affair with no angst, nothing but shared passion. And a clean end to it when the time came.

Well, she could give him all of that.

With a theatrical sigh she attacked her fish. 'So much for a tragic love affair.'

'If they wanted to keep their integrity and their throne my ancestors had to be practical.'

Was he warning her not to develop any romantic hopes? She said, 'I hope the five children enjoyed their holidays here.'

'There are photographs showing that they did,' he told her.

The meal was superb; Maria used the foods of the island—fish, vegetables, olives and cheese and wine, pine nuts and basil—to produce magnificent, earthy dishes that echoed the Mediterranean.

Rosie watched in awe while Gerd ate with a healthy appetite, and was touched by Maria's delight when he demanded some of her yoghurt with honey and peaches at the end of the meal.

It was a pleasant return to the Gerd she remembered from those holidays in New Zealand when he'd just been Kelt's older brother and no one had thought anything of his position.

When she'd been a kid, and life had been simple.

'What are you thinking?' Gerd put down the spoon with which he'd demolished the dessert.

'About the holidays we used to have at Kiwinui,' she

told him. 'And what fun they were. Remember when you decided to teach me how to ride?'

His smile was a little set. 'Indeed I do. You fell off every time you got onto the pony, but each time you picked yourself up, dusted yourself down and got onto her back with gritted teeth and determination.'

'She was a sweet-tempered little pony.'

'Do you still ride?'

'When I can.' The words sounded distant, and she wished she hadn't started reminiscing. Her breath caught in her throat when he smiled at her.

As though he'd read her mind, Gerd picked up her hand from beside the plate and got to his feet, pulling her with him so that they faced each other.

'Has Maria managed to persuade you to take a siesta?' he asked, his voice deepening.

Rosie's heartbeat began to speed up erratically. 'She's tried, but I usually read.'

'A waste of a good siesta,' he stated autocratically, lashes drooping as he surveyed her face.

Quick excitement bubbled through her. 'Oh, really?' she said demurely. 'What other things can one do in siesta time? Besides sleeping, of course.'

'Things like this.'

Amusement fled, leaving behind only the passion, and she arched flagrantly into him as he bent his head and kissed her. All through lunch she'd been trying not to anticipate this moment. Now she surrendered to the erotic power of his mouth taking hers in a kiss so flagrantly sexual it robbed her of breath and set her pulses hammering heavily in her ears.

She felt herself being lifted and said dreamily, 'This is getting to be a habit.'

'A habit I enjoy,' he said, shouldering his way through a wide doorway.

'Because it makes you feel big and macho?'

His smile was a flash of white. 'Possibly because the only time I have some control over you is when your feet aren't on the floor.'

'I don't believe that. You deliberately changed my travel plans and lured me into abject surrender,' she drawled, folding one hand into a serviceable fist and hitting him firmly just above a rib.

'Ow!' she said when her fist met iron-hard resistance. She pulled back her hand and examined the reddened knuckles with rueful amusement.

'Never signal your intentions,' he said calmly. 'I had time to tighten the muscles.'

He must have chosen the room she was using, because even as she opened her mouth to tell him where it was he turned into the doorway. Strangely enough that gave her a warm feeling of being cared for.

Eyes glinting, he slid her down the length of his body, letting her feel just how she affected him, and by the time she was standing once more all sensible thought had fled and when she said his name it was in an urgent, harsh whisper.

'Yes,' he said, his voice raw and tense. 'But before—I assume you were prescribed contraception before you came down here?'

Some of her lovely anticipation leached away. 'Yes.'

'How long is it before it takes effect?'

She knew exactly. 'Another four days.'

He nodded, and kissed her with a lingering passion that rekindled the fire within. When he lifted his head his lashes were lowered so that all she could see beneath them was a line of gold.

'Then we know where we are,' he said thickly. 'We'll just have to be careful until then.'

Separation had honed their hunger to extremes; the first time they'd made love it had been slow and intensely sensuous, but now they fell onto the bed and came together with such a ferocious appetite that Rosie climaxed almost immediately, gasping something— Gerd's name, she realised later—in a sort of chant while sensation overwhelmed her in a maelstrom of passionate need.

Shuddering, clinging, she rode the storm wherever it took her. As she began to come down again she watched him, his handsome face stark and angular in the shuttered dimness, his head flung back and his eyes closed.

Minutes—hours?—later, he scooped her to lie across him in a tangle of limbs. 'There,' he drawled, his voice lazy and amused. 'Wasn't that better than reading? Or sleeping?'

Better than anything she'd ever experienced before...

But the words remained unspoken. He was keeping things very pragmatic, his uncompromising will containing that untamed passion so that he was always in control.

Well, she had to pretend to be just as cool, just as emotionally uninvolved.

'Mmm,' she murmured, withdrawing into herself.

'However, sleep has its place.' He tucked her head into his shoulder.

She had never felt so…safe, she thought dreamily as exhaustion claimed her.

But when she woke she was alone, and it was twilight.

No, she thought after a shaken glance at her watch, it was dawn! She'd slept the whole evening and night through. Shivering, she huddled under the light covering he must have put over her before he left and forced herself to look at the end of their affair.

They'd spend a month on this enchanted island together—a month in which she'd fall further and further in love with Gerd—and at the end they'd say a civilised farewell. Then she'd return to New Zealand, and he'd go back to his palace and the real, important part of his life.

She should leave for New Zealand now, while she was still…what? Heart-whole?

A laugh that sounded too close to a sob broke from her. Her heart already belonged to Gerd.

No, it was more courageous to stay, to search for the real, fallible man behind the façade he presented to the world. Surely, discovering that he had faults and idiosyncrasies like every other man would replace the hero worship of her childhood and adolescence with a mature adult understanding?

Or was she just weak and needy, grasping at any straw so she could enjoy the only time she'd ever have with him?

'And if I am?' she said half out loud.

She'd never get what she wanted from Gerd. It was time to face that and accept it, however much it hurt.

Slowly she got up and walked across to the windows, adjusting the blades of the shutters so she could see the beach. The crystalline sand blinded her and she closed her eyes against it and turned away.

All her life she'd been in hiding. Few of those who knew her had any idea that her bright personality was a façade to shield the child who'd known herself unloved by her parents. Kelt, perhaps, understood— and possibly Hani...

These next four weeks were all she'd ever have of Gerd, so she'd show grace and courage and style; when she left him she wanted him to see her as a woman he could admire, as well as the lover he'd enjoyed physically.

Did she have the courage to do that—to love unreservedly, knowing she'd have to walk away from him without a backward glance?

She dragged in a ragged breath.

Yes. Loving him would give her the strength to say farewell—and mean it in both senses of the word. She wished him nothing but good in his future.

Surely, if she could do that, she'd be able to leave him behind emotionally as well as physically.

Because people did recover from shattered hearts and unrequited love. They picked themselves up and went on, and eventually they were happy again.

Mind made up, she got ready for a month of bittersweet joy.

The next couple of days passed in a haze of pleasure. As each golden evening slid into the passionate darkness of night Rosie discovered how happiness tasted, how it coloured her world, what a difference loving Gerd and knowing that he wanted her made. Most of the time she could ignore the nagging knowledge of future grief and gave herself over to pleasure, to a deep, intense delight in his presence that she'd never allowed herself before.

She'd never imagined a person could be so happy, she mused dreamily, waking up on the third morning. The only flaw was that so far she'd slept alone; Gerd made love to her and then left her.

In some way his refusal to share a bed with her seemed to symbolise the distance between them—a distance that not even their passion could bridge.

Once up she straightened her shoulders. No whining; she'd accept the bitter with the sweet. And nothing was sweeter than making love with Gerd...

A cool shower revived her and she had just dressed in shorts and a T-shirt when someone knocked on the bedroom door.

Excitement funnelled through her, catching her breath and imparting an extra radiance to her smile. 'Come in,' she called.

Her heart swelled when she saw him. 'Gerd—New Zealand style,' she teased, eyeing his long, tanned legs and the casual cotton shirt—although, knowing Gerd, she suspected both had been made to fit his rangy, lean body.

'I could say the same.' His smile tightened as he let his gaze roam from her sunny curls to her bare feet. 'In Regency England they'd have called you a pocket Venus, and a diamond of the first water.'

She gave a theatrical sigh and came towards him. 'Typical,' she said. 'Trust me to be born into a time when the fashion is for narrow hips and no waist.' She laughed up at him. 'How do you know so much about Regency England?'

'It's a period I find interesting—the infiltration of the old aristocracy by up-and-coming industrialists. Not many countries dealt with the resultant power shift so creatively as the British.'

She said thoughtfully, 'Does it have relevance for Carathia?'

'I think it does.' He changed the subject. 'Would you like to go sailing?'

'Now?'

He smiled down at her. 'Why not? There's food on the yacht—Maria has stocked it with enough to feed an army. Along the coast there's a bay with the ruins of a Greek temple to Aphrodite overlooking it. It's in remarkably good repair, probably because the Romans took it over, and then in the Christian era the islanders simply dedicated the temple to the Virgin.'

Intrigued, she asked, 'So it's a church now?'

'It was never used for actual worship—or not in modern times, anyway. Maria says that lovers still make pilgrimages to it with offerings of flowers in the hope that the goddess will guarantee them a happy romance.'

A sacrifice to love. Perhaps she should try that.

'I'd like to see it,' she told him.

He held out his hand. 'Come on, then.'

The yacht was quite small, easily handled by two. Remembering the burly man who'd ridden with them the night they went out to dinner, Rosie said, 'You obviously don't need security here.'

He gave her a keen glance, but his answer was delivered in a non-committal voice. 'Not here, no.'

'I'm glad,' she said, and then wished she hadn't said that. If Gerd realised how much she loved him he might call a halt to their relationship. So she added airily, 'I felt rude talking to you and ignoring both him and the chauffeur.'

'They wouldn't have been able to hear,' he said, loosening the mainsheet.

'I know, but although my mother is a stickler for manners she didn't actually instruct me in the correct way to treat bodyguards.'

'It's quite simple—you let them do their jobs without interference. Can you get my sunglasses? They're on a shelf in the saloon.'

Not particularly luxurious, the saloon sported a table beside the neat, efficient galley area, and some very comfortable seating. A door led to another cabin further forward that probably held a bed.

It intrigued her that Gerd, who'd forged a worldwide business before his thirtieth birthday, chose this yacht instead of something huge and opulent.

Handing the sunglasses over, she said as much, and he shrugged, donning them so she couldn't discern his expression.

'I enjoy sailing,' he said as though that explained everything.

Rosie decided his words and actions were explanation enough. Clearly he relished the physical effort of hauling on ropes and sails, and the mental contest with the wind and the waves around the rocky coastline.

'I can do that,' she said at one stage, scrambling to haul in a jib sheet after they went about.

He watched her pull it in until the sail stopped flapping. 'Thanks. Although you don't need to—it's set up for single-handed sailing.'

Which meant he sailed it by himself.

Or that the other women he brought here to visit the love goddess's temple weren't sailors, she thought realistically.

That hurt, but she ignored it. *Live for the moment* was her new mantra, and she intended to follow it without obsessing about what had gone before, or regretting what would come after.

Even though living for the moment meant living dangerously.

But she'd lived safely for years, and it had got her nothing but emptiness.

CHAPTER SIX

THE temple took Rosie's breath away. Still creamy-white after more than two thousand years on the headland, its perfect proportions and clean lines were as elegant as they had been when it was first built.

'It's—truly sublime,' she breathed.

Gerd gave a final tug to the anchor chain, and turned. She hadn't actually been talking to him; the words had come unconsciously. She was perched on the cockpit seat so that her legs were displayed to their best advantage, and a surge of lust gripped him so that he had to turn away to hide his physical response.

Although the top of her head barely reached his shoulder, she was strong; every cell in his body recalled the clamp of those legs around his hips, and he wanted her with a fierceness that clenched his hands by his sides. As elegantly curved as Aphrodite herself, her skin gleaming ivory-gold in the sunlight, she could have posed for a statue of the goddess.

Hell, he wanted to take her there and then. Perhaps the goddess was having a sly joke at his expense?

Leashing his unslaked appetite, he told her abruptly,

'They built her temple here because Aphrodite was born of the sea.'

Her upwards glance held a certain restraint that echoed in her tone. 'She's certainly got a great view of it from there. Can we climb up from the beach?'

'If you don't mind scrambling in the heat.'

'Will my shoes be suitable?'

Gerd checked her slender feet, sensibly enclosed in boat shoes. 'They'll be fine.'

The path wound up from the bay, steep but mostly shaded by the silvery leaves of ancient olives. Before they started Gerd said, 'If you think it will be too steep we can come here in the car one day.'

'No,' she said, looking amused. 'I'm sure I can cope, but if I can't then you can carry me. Although perhaps it would be a bit much to expect.'

He laughed, eyes gleaming as he said, 'If you can't get there I'll be more than happy to carry you.'

Her look sizzled with invitation, but she went on, 'I forgot to bring my camera, and I'd like to photograph this, so yes, it would be great to come again.'

And cope she did, scrambling up in front of him so that he was tormented by the sight of golden legs and the seductive sway of her hips.

'You're fit,' he observed.

She cast him a sly, laughing glance over her shoulder. 'So you don't need to stay behind me in case I fall or fade. My landlady has a dog—a fairly large mutt. Mrs Harley is elderly and although she takes him for a nice, gentle walk to the shops every day he needs more than that, so I do a morning and evening shift, and we walk up One Tree Hill and back down again.'

He recalled the extinct volcano, one of many that dotted Auckland. High and grass-covered, its terraced slopes revealing its past as a Maori fortress—it reared above the city, an excellent workout for both dog and handler.

Gerd asked casually, 'Do you ever think of leaving Auckland?'

She sent him a startled glance. 'If I had a good enough reason I would,' she said after a moment. 'Not that I dislike Auckland. I love Kiwinui. That's always been my ideal.'

Because Kelt lived there? The thought goaded Gerd into silence. Once at the top he watched as she turned to examine the building with wide, awed eyes, and answered her questions as best he could, intrigued by her quick curiosity and interest in everything.

Why had he asked her to come to his coronation? Oh, he'd told her it was because he saw her as family. It hadn't been exactly a lie—more a convenient half-truth.

Admitting that he felt there was unfinished business between them would have given her invitation too much importance.

She interrupted his reluctant admission by pointing towards a distant hillside village. 'I presume the grassed-over track from there used to be the route to the temple.'

'Yes, the ancient processional way. When we come by car I'll leave the vehicle in the village and we'll walk up that path.'

'I'm amazed it's still visible after all these centuries,' she said reflectively, her tone quiet and solemn.

'It was probably used quite regularly until fairly recently.'

'What are the bushes growing in that gully?'

Amusement tinged his words. 'Actually, a very distant relative of the pohutukawa that grows by your beaches. It's a myrtle and is sacred to Aphrodite. It's flowering now, in fact—they're creamy-white, and sweetly scented.'

An underlying note in his voice lifted the hair on the back of Rosie's neck. She didn't know how to deal with this, she thought despairingly. They weren't touching, but she was so aware of him her skin felt taut and stretched, as though he had the power to affect her physically from a distance.

It was too much—sensory overload. Turning abruptly, she gazed at the temple again, a monument to the power and strength of physical love, and thought how incredibly appropriate that was.

Did Gerd make a habit of bringing his lovers here…?

'Is it safe to explore inside?' she asked brightly, pushing the ugly query into the back of her mind and refusing to allow it to hurt.

'It's in good condition. There have been tactful repairs made these past few years.'

She cast him a swift look. 'Did you have anything to do with that?'

'I've set up a foundation to care for the ancient monuments of Carathia,' he said, and began to tell her of the statue that had been found near by, a magnificent thing of creamy Parian marble lost so long ago its existence had become a myth, only half-believed until it was found by a peasant in his olive grove. 'It had been buried so carefully that it was remarkably intact.'

'Where is it?' she asked, looking around the empty expanse of the temple.

'In a museum in the biggest town over on the mainland coast,' he told her, and answered the query in her glance. 'For security. It was almost stolen.'

She said, 'I suppose that's a constant fear.'

'It is,' he said grimly. 'There are extremely rich men who'd enjoy nothing more than to gloat over something as beautiful and rare.'

Rosie nodded. 'I've read about that, but to me it sounds sick.'

'You could say it shows a commendable love of beauty.'

'But you don't believe that,' she said swiftly.

'No.' The flat, lethal tone of his voice revealed more than his dispassionate words. 'Like you, I think it shows a sick desire to own something no one else can enjoy.' He gestured at a marble podium. 'She stood there.'

Rosie said, 'Oh—look.'

On the ancient stone someone had put flowers—a white-ribboned posy made up of the golden daisies that dotted the processional way and the fringed, delicately perfumed flowers that had to be myrtle.

'An offering,' Gerd told her. 'Someone wants something from the goddess.'

'Or is thanking her.'

'That possibly,' he agreed. 'Come and see the view from the front.'

It was astonishingly beautiful, a great spread of violet-blue sea dotted by islands, all overlooked by a sky as brilliant and clear. While the soft wind swirled and played amongst the golden flowers Gerd named each island, and showed her the darkness to the north that was the mainland of Europe.

'Greece and Asia lie to the east,' he said, 'and Italy to the west.'

She said soberly, 'For some strange reason it makes me horribly homesick.'

He surveyed her quizzically. 'Both have sea,' he agreed, 'and an island shelters the Kiwinui coastline. Apart from that I don't see much resemblance. Kiwinui is lush and green, every gully thick with bush and flax, and it looks out on to thousands of miles of open ocean. And although the myrtle is a vague connection to pohutukawa, it really doesn't look like it.'

'I think that's the problem—it's so completely different.' She gave an ironic smile and shrugged. 'But this is glorious. I can see why you like to come here for holidays.'

He took her hand and laced her fingers in his, his eyes direct and cool and too perceptive. 'I think you need something to drink. We'll go back to the boat and have lunch.'

'Thank you,' she said automatically, her breath catching in her throat as she met his eyes. Anticipation heated her blood, and she looked away again, feeling the slow pulse of desire throb through her body.

On the yacht he insisted on organising the meal, moving deftly around the area that served as a kitchen, and while she drank the glass of champagne he'd given her he downed a beer, and told her stories of the island that made her laugh and occasionally sigh.

After lunch he waited until she drained the coffee he'd made for her before asking, 'Do you want to go ashore again?'

'I—no,' she said quietly.

'Good, because I don't either,' he said, and bent his head and kissed the place where her neck and shoulder met.

His lips were warm and seeking, and slow, hungry tremors coursed through her when he bit the skin there lightly. Rosie made an inarticulate little noise and turned her head into his shoulder.

'What is it?' His voice was harsh.

She looked up and saw passion darken his eyes, but although he wanted her she knew it wasn't in the all-consuming way she longed for him. 'Nothing,' she whispered.

And yielded to his practised caresses and her own urgent passion. This time it was languid, yet intense; he kissed her with his desire held well in check until she was gasping and aching, her body on fire and her voice gone.

The other cabin did contain a bed, and there, rocked by the tiny wavelets, they reached the agonised rapture of delight.

This time the climax was so sweet and prolonged Rosie had to close her eyes to hide the tears, but perhaps he noticed. As she started the slow downwards glide he began again, driving her mercilessly on into an ecstasy that left her shaking and mindless, her whole world narrowed to this man, to Gerd, to this moment in his arms, linked to him in the only way he would allow.

And when they finally slid into sleep, he was still with her, still keeping everything but joy at bay.

When she woke she was still in his grip, her body moulded to his, the regular rise and fall of his chest telling her he hadn't wakened.

This was the first time he'd stayed with her, the first—and probably the only—time she'd ever wake in his arms...

Forcing up heavy eyelids, she took the rare chance to scan his beloved face without the fear of him catching her at it. Such perfect features, she thought, eyeing the arrogant blade of his nose, his strong jaw, the masculine beauty and strength that was his mouth...

Memories of what his mouth could do to her made her shiver deliciously.

Silently she adored his skin's golden sheen, the long, powerful lines of his body—the body that could take her on an erotic journey to paradise, that rapturous nirvana where her very sense of self was cut loose and she could only surrender to the dark enchantment of Gerd's magnetism.

Her heart started to pick up speed and her breasts bloomed, the nipples tight buds of excitement—waiting for his mouth, for his touch...

Without thinking she stretched out tentative fingers and skimmed his flat, muscled midriff, only to snatch back her hand at his movement. She froze, but almost immediately he sank back into sleep.

Slowly her gaze drifted down, past lean hips...

Her breath came faster when she realised he was aroused. Heat smouldered into life within her, moistening the passage that longed for him, contracting internal muscles she'd barely learned how to use.

Barely able to breathe in a mixture of shyness and reckless hunger, she touched him, her fingers lingering as she explored. Silky and hot, yet hard and—getting harder, she realised.

She glanced up, but his eyes were still closed, and she realised that, although his breathing had quickened, he was still asleep.

Curious, excited, she tightened her hand gently around him.

He moved like lightning, so quickly she only had time to gasp when he plunged into her, his big, lithe body taut as a bowstring. Drowning in erotic pleasure, Rosie arched against him, and he flung his head back and spilled into her as she climaxed around him, her body taut and seeking, her heart thundering wildly in her breast.

Gerd said something—her name—and then swore violently in Carathian, his face dark with anger as he tore himself free from her to sit on the edge of the bed, his spine dead straight and the broad, glistening shoulders set.

Still shaking from the elemental passion of that urgent coupling, Rosie sat up too, pushing her wet curls back from her face, shocked at the swift ferocity of their joining. She looked up at his back, so squarely presented to her, and closed her eyes at the red marks her fingernails had clawed across the broad expanse.

'Oh, *God*,' she whispered, appalled. 'We just made love—'

He got to his feet and turned, towering over the bed like some grim deity from ancient times. 'We did,' he agreed, his voice lethal. 'With no protection. How long does it take for the Pill to work?'

'Seven days,' she said in a muted voice.

'So we're not quite in the safe zone yet?' he asked on a note that brought her head up with a jerk.

We, he'd said. The automatic coupling of them as a unit gave her a little comfort.

'No,' she said, and her breath clogged her throat as she remembered—too late—that he'd knocked on her door before she'd taken one of the tablets she'd been religiously swallowing these past few mornings.

'What is it?' he demanded, his eyes suddenly intent.

Sickly, she told him. 'I didn't even think of it,' she whispered.

Because she'd been spellbound by the prospect of a whole day alone with him. 'Gerd, I'm so sorry.' Her voice shook and she couldn't say any more.

She didn't know what to expect. Anything—accusation, denunciation, ordinary old fury—would be appropriate, she thought half-hysterically.

After one glance at his face she looked away. The angular features were stark and honed, formidable, but, oddly enough, not angry. He probably looked like this when he was faced with a constitutional problem.

Her breath hurt in her starved lungs when she took a rapid breath.

In a voice so aloof it made her shiver, he said, 'Do you have the tablets with you?'

'No,' she said miserably. 'They're in the bathroom at the villa.' She hadn't gone back in there after he'd come for her, and she hadn't thought of taking one because she was so ridiculously, *stupidly* happy at the prospect of a whole day with him…

'So there's a reasonably good chance that you're completely unprotected.'

'I don't know, but there's a warning about using other protection if you miss one…' Her voice trailed away as he stood up and walked across to the porthole, staring out as though—as though he couldn't bear to look at her.

Then and there, Rosie made up her mind that if she was pregnant she would love their baby enough for two.

'It's just five days since I took the first one,' she said bleakly. 'I didn't—I didn't know that—'

'You didn't realise men could make love while they were asleep,' he said in a level voice that told her nothing.

She pushed her wildly curling hair back from her hot face. His earlier words echoed in her mind like doom-bringers. *No protection.*

'No,' she admitted in a muted voice.

'So now you do know. Anyway, it wasn't your fault.'

But it was. She'd touched him, caressed him…

He said, 'There is something—the morning-after Pill.'

No!

Appalled, she gazed at his arrogant features, so controlled she couldn't read anything but an inflexible decisiveness when he went on harshly, 'I would prefer not to go that way, but I realise the decision is yours to make.'

'I don't…I know it seems silly, but I can't help but feel it's…' Rosie floundered, then said on a jagged indrawn breath, 'I don't want to do that. Do your pharmacies here sell test kits?'

'I'll get one sent from the capital,' he said curtly. 'It will be more discreet.'

'I'm so sorry.'

'Why?' He gave her a tight smile. 'For giving me the best sex I've ever had?'

Pink-cheeked, she accused, 'You said you were asleep!'

'Not for long,' he said drily, his face relaxing as he surveyed her. 'But I could no more have stopped than I can fly. We'd better get dressed.'

Once back at the villa he said, 'Go and take that pill now.'

Heart sinking, she hurried inside and swallowed the wretched thing, closing her eyes to the warning on the packet. For long seconds she stood in the bathroom, one hand pressed to her heart, and then she straightened her shoulders and walked back to help Gerd tidy the yacht. While he coiled ropes she made the bed, biting her lip when all evidence of their wild mating had been erased.

They walked back together, tension tightening between them like invisible cords.

Keep it light, she warned herself. But no, her wilful heart had to wildly complicate an already tangled situation. And now this…

He broke into her sombre thoughts. 'Would you like to go out to dinner?'

No, she wanted to go into her bedroom and howl like a banshee. Instead, she nodded and said sedately, 'That would be lovely, thank you.'

But that night they didn't make love. Rosie understood; she too didn't want to risk anything until she knew the result of her madness. Yet she found herself dreaming of babies, of losing something precious and irretrievable, waking a couple of times in the darkness with tears running down her cheeks.

The parcel from the pharmacist was scheduled to arrive after lunch the next day—a day with a sullen sun behind a bank of cloud, followed by rain scudding in across the sea.

Over a late breakfast Gerd said, 'I have papers to deal with. Will you be all right?'

Rosie lifted her brows. 'Of course I will,' she said solemnly. 'I need to give myself a manicure.'

'And that will take all morning?'

Rosie smiled. 'No,' she admitted. 'Gerd, don't worry about me—I'm able to entertain myself.'

To her surprise he picked up her hands and examined them. 'They look perfect as they are,' he said, adding with a narrow smile, 'and on my skin they feel…exquisite. And so very creative.'

He laughed at the fiery colour across her cheekbones, and carried her hands to his mouth, kissing each palm. 'I hope you don't plan to paint your nails black.'

'Black doesn't suit me,' she said promptly. Her need for him was a sharp pain, and his kisses sent the familiar quiver of delight through her. She went on, 'Besides, my mother always says that when you're on holiday clear polish is the only appropriate shade.'

In the end she did give herself a manicure. She'd just reassured herself that the polish had dried when her cellphone rang.

Startled, she lifted it. 'Hello?'

As though her words that morning had conjured her mother, Eva said tartly, 'You might have let me know where you were.'

'You have my number.' What had caused this unusual call?

'Yes, well, I've been busy, and there's been no need.' Eva paused to give weight to her next words. 'Until I picked up the paper this morning. Do you realise you're all over the newspapers of most of the world?'

'*What?*'

'You heard,' Eva told her. 'Surely you didn't think you could go off with Gerd and not have the paparazzi come along too? They've been waiting with bated breath for him to announce his engagement to Princess Serina, so photos of you together are particularly juicy.'

Rosie realised she was shaking, her fingers clenched around the telephone. 'But there haven't been any photographers—'

'Oh, yes, there have,' her mother interrupted. 'At least one's got a photo of you gazing dreamily up at Gerd—and sold it to every newspaper in New Zealand, it seems. According to a friend in London, the papers there are on to it too. Oh, they're careful to say you're a cousin of Gerd's, but that photo is pretty damning.'

Sick apprehension chilled Rosie. 'Damn,' she whispered.

Her mother said acidly, 'I hope you're not pinning any hopes on marrying him.'

'Of course I'm not.'

'Well, that's something, I suppose.' Eva paused, but when Rosie didn't speak she went on in irritation, 'Honestly, Rosemary, what are you *thinking*? I know you've always had a yen for him, but he's more or less engaged to that princess, and she's not going to be happy that he's spending a dirty week with you before their betrothal goes official.'

Rosie bit her lip. She wasn't going to tell her mother

that Gerd had promised her there was no relationship between him and the oh-so-suitable princess. 'Thanks for telling me,' she said levelly. 'I'd better go now.'

And let Gerd know. She felt sick, besmirched as she left the room to do just that. But she met him halfway to the room he called the study and realised he'd already found out. His brows were drawn together in a forbidding frown, and his beautiful mouth was a thin, straight line.

When she opened her mouth he held up a hand. 'We need to talk.'

'My mother's just rung,' she said quietly.

His face darkened further. 'What did she have to say?'

Briefly she enlightened him.

He bit off words in Carathian, and said, 'I've heard from my chief minister.'

'Is it so bad? I mean—you've had relationships before and you're not…'

Her voice trailed away as her mother's words echoed in her ears. *Just been about to announce his engagement…*

Had he lied to her? No, she thought, torn by anger and despair. Surely not.

Not Gerd.

But he said curtly, 'There's more to this than headlines.' He looked around the wide hall. 'Come into the study; it's going to take some explaining.'

In his office—a large room, half-office, half-sitting room, with a massive sofa in front of a fireplace at one end—he showed her the photograph on his computer screen. Frowning, she peered at it.

Clearly taken from some distance with a telephoto lens, it showed her and Gerd standing together. He had his arm around her shoulders, and she was laughing up at him. Thank heavens her shorts and shirt were discreet and not at all sexy, she thought, relieved for a second until that sick apprehension kicked back in.

Because she was looking at Gerd with her heart in her eyes.

'Where—? Oh, of course,' she said, realising it had been taken at the temple of Aphrodite.

'He—or she—must have been in the clump of trees on the next headland,' Gerd said without inflection.

Biting her lip, she straightened up. 'It's not too bad. I mean, I'm just laughing, and that's just a casual hug…' Her voice trailed away.

His brows lifted. 'No one looking at that could fail to see that we're lovers.'

Rosie took a deep breath. We *are* lovers, he'd said. Well, it was true—or had been until she'd lost her head on the yacht.

'All right, but I'm still missing something here. Why is this a disaster?'

'It's not a disaster,' he returned, so coolly detached she could have hit him. 'It's a complication. Come and sit down.'

Once on that wide sofa, she looked at him, her heart clamping. He leaned against the stones of the fireplace and said without preamble, 'Do you know anything about Carathia's legend of the second son?'

'Yes.' Astonished, she stared at him. What on earth had an ancient legend got to do with that photograph? 'Well, not much, really, only enough to know that there is a legend that caused you problems. It surfaced when your grandmother confirmed you as her heir—some idiots wanted Kelt instead because the legend says that if there are disasters and hardship it's because the wrong son is ruling the country, and the only thing to do is depose the current Grand Duke and put his sibling on the throne.'

His mouth thinned. 'And several hundred people died because of it.'

Rosie nodded. 'Yes, I remember. It was horrible, but what does it have to do with us?'

'Bear with me,' he told her austerely. 'A thousand years ago Carathia was ruled by my ancestor.'

'The Greek mercenary—the one who saved Carathia from being overrun?'

He shook his head. 'No, the Norseman who arrived here via Russia. His oldest son inherited the throne; unfortunately for him plague struck, and then they were invaded by a horde from Asia. They were still fighting them off when this area was hit by a tidal wave caused by an earthquake in the eastern Mediterranean. The ruler was deemed unlucky, and the people rebelled, forcing him from the throne and installing his younger brother in his place.'

'And that's what this legend is based on?'

'Not entirely. As soon as the brother ascended the throne the horde withdrew, the plague died away and no further tidal waves have ever hit this coast. However, after his death the son who ascended to the throne had to face another war.'

'So they got rid of him and installed his younger brother?' Rosie guessed.

'Exactly. Who fought a triumphant war against the invaders and beat them decisively, and had a long and glorious reign. That's when the legend took root, mainly amongst the people in the mountains, who'd suffered greatly from war and plague. As you can imagine, this has caused endless turmoil down through the centuries; only rulers with no siblings felt safe on the throne. Even my grandmother had to fight a rebellion fomented by her younger sister.'

'Is that why Kelt's always lived in New Zealand?'

He looked at her almost approvingly. 'Yes. Of course, he's a born and bred Kiwi, and the last thing he wants is to rule Carathia.'

'So that's all right, then.' But it wasn't, she could tell from his expression. He looked—forbidding. 'I don't see what any of this has to do with me.'

With us...

Except that there was no *us*.

'Ever since then there has been a considerable amount of pressure on me to marry and provide heirs for the throne. I've been advised that it's probably the best way to make sure of a peaceful reign.'

Rosie fought to breathe, to be able to speak sensibly. She looked out of the window and realised that while she'd been in the study the clouds had been whisked away and the sun was shining outside. It seemed cruelly fateful.

'Go on,' Rosie said, bracing herself. He was going to tell her he'd lied, that he planned to marry the princess and produce those heirs to satisfy his people.

His smile was humourless. 'Those photographs have caused a furore in Carathia. No, they haven't been published there, but people have seen them on television beamed in from the surrounding countries.'

'But—you've had—I mean, there have been other relationships,' she said uncertainly. Nothing about the princess, but her relief was brief and followed by even more doubt.

He shrugged. 'Carathians are conservative—they didn't see my other women as fit candidates for Grand Duchess.'

And neither was she. Rosie's emotions see-sawed again into bitter darkness.

It had to be the princess…

'I'll leave Carathia today, then—that should stop any gossip.' Intent only on getting out of there with some pitiful scraps of pride intact, she got to her feet.

Ignoring her statement, he said uncompromisingly, 'The situation is complicated by the fact that you and I are connected, if not directly related. The Carathians have a history of cousin marriage.'

'But we're not really cousins!' She stopped, because something wasn't right. Searching his face, she could discern nothing beyond a formidably inflexible determination.

Uncertainly she said, 'Gerd, exactly what is this all about?'

Still showing no emotion, he said, 'I'm asking you to marry me.' His mouth twisted into something that could have been cynical amusement, but his gaze never left her face. 'Unfortunately, I'm making a complete and total hash of it.'

CHAPTER SEVEN

STUNNED, Rosie stared at Gerd's angular face, now expressionless and uncompromising. His predatory stillness shocked and alarmed her. She sensed an inevitable fate closing around her, something she both longed for and dreaded.

When she answered her voice trembled with both fear and an undercurrent of shameful yearning. 'Why?'

His eyes narrowed. 'You can ask that after what's happened between us?'

She longed for some indication of how he felt, of why he was doing this. Instead, in his handsome features she could read only a ruthlessness that cut her more severely than any knife ever could.

So painful to have her every hope answered in this way—to see her most ardent desire within reach and know she didn't dare accept it.

'Would it be so hard, Rosemary?' he asked, and came towards her.

'Don't you dare,' she choked.

'Don't dare what? Don't dare to touch you? When I know how much you like it?'

His voice was controlled, yet beneath the cool, almost ironic tone she heard another note—raw and elemental. Nerves twanging, she stared at him, defying him without words.

Although a smile curved his beautiful mouth it didn't temper the unyielding intention Rosie sensed in him. Coldly deliberate, he was using the searing attraction that scorched the air between them to persuade her into surrender.

'When we both know how much you like *this*,' he emphasised, not taking that final step between them. Instead he reached out and traced the outline of her lips with a sensuous forefinger, so gently she hardly felt his touch.

That was all. His hand dropped to his side and he said, 'Rosemary.'

Just one word, but he didn't need to say anything more. That faint, intensely evocative scent that was his alone—the essential essence of the man—teased her nostrils.

He was aroused—as aroused as she was. The hunger he summoned so easily throbbed through her, eroding her determination, her knowledge that what he was proposing—and how cynical that was!—could only lead to anguish and grief.

Although every instinct urged her to get the hell out of there, she stayed, head high and her lips held in such a firm line they no longer trembled. At all costs she had to appeal to his icily rational brain before he kissed her. Once he did that she'd be lost.

If only Gerd hadn't been so honest—the honesty she'd demanded of him, she reminded herself savagely.

If he'd not told her of his position—the need for a wife, for children—she'd probably have been weak enough to agree to marry him. She loved him so much...

Dry-mouthed, hoping he couldn't see the naked longing behind the screen of her lashes, she said bitterly, 'What we have is just sex—not a sensible basis for marriage.'

'*Just* sex?' The mocking note in his voice made her flush furiously, but before she could answer he went on more grimly, 'There is also the fact that by joining you here I have tarnished your reputation.'

'Oh, that's so old-fashioned.' She shivered at the sound of her heart cracking. 'Besides, being your lover should only enhance my reputation.'

'Amongst a certain sort of person,' he agreed with distaste.

Desperately Rosie surged on. 'Anyway, I don't have a reputation to tarnish—you were shocked when you discovered—' She jerked to a stop, disconcerted by the sudden glint in his eyes.

'That you were a virgin?' he supplied smoothly. 'Yes, startled, certainly—but delighted.'

'Why? Because it made me more *suitable*?'

She realised the instant she spoke that she should have stayed silent. Marriage had been the last thing on his mind when they'd made love at the palace!

Before he could answer she blurted, 'I'm not going to marry you because we've been lovers, or for reasons of state.' Beads of sweat gathered at her temples.

'Then how about the fact that you might be carrying my child?' he told her brusquely.

Cornered, she stared at his implacable face. How could she love him so—so violently, yet be so angry with him?

Steadying her breathing and her voice with an effort that clenched her fists, she said, 'You don't need to worry about that. No woman nowadays has to have a child they don't want.'

He didn't move, but she sensed a reaction so intense she took an involuntary step backwards.

'Is that what you would do?' His voice was level and without emotion.

Rosie couldn't lie to him. 'I—no,' she admitted wearily. 'But—however great your need for an heir, you don't have to go to the extreme of marrying me.'

'I will not turn my back on my child,' he said with icy precision. 'Or you.'

Oh, that tempted her—and hurt. Rosie unclenched her hands long enough to spread them out in front of her. 'Gerd, we don't know yet—'

'I would also prefer not to have the world know if my child was conceived out of wedlock.'

'Would it matter so much?' The words tumbled out before she realised what she'd said. She couldn't let him believe she was even considering any possibility of marriage, but before she had a chance to qualify her statement he spoke.

'Not to me personally, but it would to quite a large number of Carathians. They are a religious, moral people, and rather proud of being so.'

'Then they shouldn't try to force you to do things you don't want to.' Like marrying someone entirely unsuitable. Hurriedly, she added, 'If I am pregnant I'll go back to New Zealand and no one will ever know who the father is.' Another thought struck her. 'And...you wouldn't be turning your back on the—on any child because I'd agree to access whenever you wanted.'

'Don't be an idiot,' he said stonily. 'Rosemary, if there is a child I want it to be an essential part of my life, not kept hidden away in New Zealand like a guilty secret. And you too—you deserve much more than that.'

She could have wept at that. He was being so intransigent—and for all the right reasons except the most important of all. 'You should marry Princess Serina—or someone like her. That way you'd satisfy your people and have a wife who knows how to behave as a Grand Duchess should.'

'I don't *want* to marry Serina.' The arrogant tone didn't abate at all when he added, 'And I imagine she'd be appalled if I asked her.'

Perhaps Serina had realised he didn't love her.

Rosie sternly quenched a foolish, irresponsible hope. That didn't mean he loved anyone else. He'd been forced into this position, and, being a man of honour he was determined to do his best for her and his possible baby.

His expression relaxed. 'I realise this has come as a shock to you,' he said more temperately. 'However, it is something I have been thinking about ever since you came here.'

Was there the slightest hesitation before the second half of that sentence, as though he'd substituted 'since you came here' for something else—something like 'since we made love without protection'?

'Why?' she asked baldly.

His smile was a masterful blend of irony and ruthless charm. 'You know the reason,' he said, his tone sending tiny, sensuous shivers through her. 'It has been there ever since we kissed three years ago.'

If only he would let her see his true emotions—but Rosie could read nothing in his face. She said tautly, 'I'm not going to agree to marry you because you need a wife and an heir to ratify your position, or because your people would be shocked if the baby was conceived out of wedlock.'

'Then how about because you want me?'

Her breath locked in her throat. 'Wanting's easy.' She tried to speak scathingly—boldly—but it came out sounding sorrowful. 'And commonplace,' she added, hoping the sting in her words would repel him.

'I forget that you know very little about sex and desire,' he observed. 'One of these days you must tell me why you were such an obstinate virgin. But trust me, Rosemary, that what we share is neither easy nor commonplace. Such communion is a rare treasure, one I've never experienced before, and one I'm reluctant to give up. Especially since there is no reason for such a vain sacrifice.'

White-faced, she watched him advance towards her, his intention plain.

How long could she hold out if he touched her—if he kissed her?

She stepped back, holding up her hands in a useless attempt to keep him away. He smiled, and bent his head and kissed her mouth.

One lonely night had sharpened her hunger into a

craving that corroded her precarious self-control. Although Rosie fought the weakness, the promise of his kiss smashed down her fragile barricades in a surge of sensory overload of such intense sweetness she could no longer resist.

His arms came around her as she kissed him back, and he lifted his head to say against her lips, 'There's no need for such determined resistance, my sweet one. I will be a good husband to you.'

Rosie had no doubt of that. He'd be an ideal husband in every respect except one. On a half-sob she said, 'I wonder if this is how my mother feels every time she takes a new lover?'

His eyes narrowed. 'I don't think so,' he said, his voice cool. 'I doubt if she ever put up such a determined resistance to any man. And what she seeks from her lovers—unconditional love—is not to be found any-where amongst humankind.'

Even as she accepted the validity of his logic, Rosie closed her eyes against it. Perhaps she was more like her mother than she'd realised.

Numbly she said, 'All right, if there's a baby I'll marry you.'

'You will marry me whether or not there is a child,' he stated, and at last kissed her properly, his arms closing around her as he carried her across to the big sofa.

And it wasn't one-sided; Rosie felt his body harden against her and shivered, exultant because he wanted her as much as she wanted him. Their mouths met again with such passion she felt herself melt, unable to think—unable to do anything but feel and want.

Against her lips Gerd muttered something before saying starkly, 'I need you. Here. Now.'

His raw tone shattered the last shards of her resistance. 'Yes,' she breathed into his ear, and found the opening of his shirt.

She ran a finger down it, relishing the smooth grain of his skin, the soft abrasion of the hair there. She knew exactly the pattern of that hair, the way it scrolled from one side of his chest to the other before arrowing down to disappear beneath his belt. She had followed that arrow...

Excitement pumped hot blood through her, a fierce sexual drive that transformed her into another person, a woman wanton with love, with desire.

She said harshly, 'I hope you have protection here.'

Eyes glittering, he rasped, 'I now have protection in every damned room in this villa.'

The muscles in his lithe body flexed with fluid power when he lifted her for another kiss. It felt like a brand, she thought dazedly, a seal on a contract...

It felt like heaven.

He set her down on the vast sofa, smoothly removing her T-shirt so that she was left in only her bra and trousers.

Her breasts tightened, and his eyes narrowed even further. 'I like that you can't hide your reaction to me,' he said. 'It makes me feel just a little less obvious.'

She expected him to take off the bra, a silky slither of flesh-coloured fabric. Instead he dropped to his knees beside the sofa and kissed her throat, then bent and took an importunate nipple into the moist heat of his mouth.

Instant fire. Instant, mindless need.

Desire so untrammelled the first waves of response shuddered through her. The pressure of his hand at the junction of her legs jerked her hips from the sofa in a thrust of animal hunger.

Gerd surveyed her, sprawled in helpless, voluptuous abandon before him. His face was drawn, set in lines of hunger and need that resonated shockingly through her as he took off her remaining clothes, making the process a drawn-out seduction that eventually had her almost sobbing in a potent mix of frustration and un-fulfilled appetite.

But he stood and wrenched off his own clothes as though he couldn't bear to wait, and when they came together he fuelled that desperate pleasure, goading her further and further towards ecstasy until every muscle in her body screamed for release, for the ultimate pas-sionate fulfilment that his big body and his consummate expertise would give her.

It came in an overwhelming wave of sensation that shook her heart, resounded in every cell, marked her for life. She was still buffeted by passion when Gerd reached his climax, head flung back as he poured himself into her. Locked in his arms, Rosie looked into the future and accepted a bitter truth she'd been afraid to face.

She'd learned to love Gerd when she was barely more than a child, and no other man would be able to take his place.

If she refused to marry him there would be no husband for her, no children…

Oh, she could make a good life, a worthwhile, even

satisfying life, but there'd always be an emptiness at its core.

Tears gathered, an ache behind her eyes, and clogged her throat as she fought temptation. Why not stop yearning for the moon?

Why not marry him, take what joy she could from living with him and bearing his children?

Because it would kill something in her to know he didn't love her—would *never* love her the way she loved him. She only had to think of her mother, dedicating her life to a rash, fruitless search for that unconditional love Gerd had been so scathing about.

But there would be compensations, the siren voice whispered. And didn't the alternative seem bleak and unsatisfying?

Oh, yes, her heart mourned. Standing firm sounded staunch and positive, as did walking gallantly into a future without him. But when she thought of watching from a distance while he married someone else and sired those children his people needed…

Gerd stirred and said thoughtfully, 'I'm too big for this sort of thing.'

On an unwilling snort of laughter, she let herself be pulled up into his arms as he rose.

'If you're planning to make a habit of this, perhaps you should buy larger sofas,' she murmured.

He knew, she realised. Those hawk eyes saw too much, understood her too well.

'So, what is your decision?' His words were as uncompromising as his expression.

'I thought you'd already made it for me,' she returned acidly.

He shrugged. 'I hoped you'd see sense. But if not...' His gaze fell to her mouth, then moved to the soft mounds of her breasts. Amused yet relentless, he finished, 'If not, you have given me the perfect weapons to use against you.'

'Why are you pushing for this now—why not wait until after we know whether there is a baby or not?'

He said calmly, 'Because you would always feel that it was the child who caused my decision, and that is too great a burden for any child—and any marriage—to bear.'

If only he weren't so—honourable. And so right...

She said through her teeth, 'Tell me one thing— why do you think I'd make you a suitable wife?'

His mouth curving in an ironic smile, he said, 'I don't like the word suitable, but just this once I'll use your term. I know you, Rosemary. You're tough and vulnerable, straightforward and outgoing and intelligent and compassionate, and you make love like a very sexy angel. I've seen you with Kelt and Hani's little boy, and I like what I've seen. And I know you want me. I think together we can make a satisfying life and bring up happy children.'

Rosie felt his frankness like a blow to the heart. He didn't love her, and he wasn't trying to pretend that he did.

She said quietly, 'Thank you, but what makes you think that marrying you would be good for me?'

'I wonder if any other man in this world has to undergo such a catechism when he asks a woman to marry him.' He went on with formidable assurance, 'You will marry me, sweet girl. Because you want to. And because you know I want you to.'

And there, she thought wearily, he had her, because her love gripped her like a vice, locking her into a desperation so intense she could taste it.

With the heat of burning bridges on her back, she said starkly, 'All right, I'll marry you, but on one condition—two, actually.'

His face was unreadable. 'So—tell me these conditions.'

'That you're faithful.' How would he take this? She angled her chin at him and met his steady dark gaze without flinching, determined to make him understand. 'And that you'll always continue to be honest with me.'

'Of course.' He held her eyes, his own keen and searching. 'And I ask the same of you.'

'Yes,' she said simply.

Because too many emotions were roiling inside her, threatening to erupt in wildly humiliating disarray, she looked down at the clothes scattered on the floor and started to laugh.

A disconcerting note too close to hysteria alarmed her into abrupt silence. 'We'd better get dressed,' she managed to say, relieved when her voice sounded normal.

A distant clatter made her gasp and fling herself off the sofa, sheer terror clutching at her as she hauled on her clothes, gabbling, 'That must be—but it's too soon—it's not—'

'Calm down,' he said quietly. And when she went white, he held her shoulders and said, 'Don't look so horrified. Whatever happens now, I will be with you and beside you.'

Half an hour later she came out of her bathroom,

to find him standing inside her bedroom door, his face expressionless.

'I'm not pregnant. The test kit showed a negative,' she said tonelessly, 'so we don't need to—'

'Stop right there,' Gerd said between his teeth. 'You made me a promise.'

'But there's no need to go on with it now,' she cried, hiding her misery with a show of anger.

'It's too late,' he said. 'I've already contacted my Press secretary, and he's alerted the media for an announcement later today. I've drafted one out, but I need you to verify a few facts.'

Rosie stared at him incredulously, fighting back rage and a horrible feeling of helplessness. 'Why have you done this?'

'Because I suspected that if you weren't presented with a fait accompli you'd waste a considerable amount of time trying to persuade me to change my mind.'

His look should have put her in her place, but she was too angry to be subdued by any intimidating and utterly infuriating air of authority.

Hands clenching at her sides, she fought for words, finally coming up with an inane, 'You had no *right* to go ahead.'

'You agreed to marry me,' he said dispassionately. 'Naturally I warned my secretary, as it will be his job to deal with the media.'

'But—so soon…' Her voice trailed away, because of course she knew why he'd done it—to stop any further restlessness amongst his people.

From now on her life would be dedicated to Carathia, its welfare paramount. Rosie realised that secretly she'd hoped—oh, for a miracle, for Gerd to put her first.

It wasn't going to happen.

His voice cool, he asked, 'Why should we delay? By now probably everyone in Carathia knows you are here with me, so it is better that they realise who you are and why you are here.'

She could think of nothing to say that. After a few seconds she said, 'I'd better ring my mother, I suppose.'

'I have just rung her,' he said smoothly. 'Kelt and Hani also, and of course Alex. None of them seemed surprised. They all send their love and best wishes. Your mother will arrive in two days' time.' He waited for a couple of beats, then added too blandly, 'On her own.'

Thank heaven for that. Rosie asked, 'Is she coming here?'

For some reason she didn't want her mother in this lovely place where for such a short time she'd been so happy.

'We'll meet her in the capital.' He gave her a keen, too-perceptive glance and said, 'You haven't had lunch, Rosemary, and Maria is cross with us for not letting her know ahead of time so that she could prepare something special.'

She put aside her shocking, unexpected grief when she'd gazed at the pregnancy indicator and realised she wasn't carrying Gerd's baby. 'We'd better go and eat whatever she has prepared. But in future you should remember that I don't like surprises.'

His brows drew together. 'Then I shall endeavour not to present you with any more. Come now, and as there is no child you can drink some of the champagne I've chosen.'

Although Maria might have been cross, not a sign of it showed. Beaming at them both, she launched into a stream of rapid Carathian, pausing only long enough for Gerd to translate, 'She is wishing us a long and happy life with many brave, handsome sons and beautiful daughters.'

Rosie pulled herself together to smile, to assume what she hoped was the happy air of a newly betrothed woman. 'Thank her, and tell her I'm not so sure about *many* sons, but if the ones we have are as brave and handsome as you I'll be content.'

And was surprised to see a tinge of colour along his arrogant cheekbones as he relayed this to the housekeeper, who laughed and bustled away, still chuckling. He pulled out a chair for her, and waited until she sat down.

'I didn't expect you to go ahead and announce everything without talking to me about it,' she said quietly.

He sat down, the sunlight sifting through the flowers to give his black hair a dark ruby sheen. The warm light played over his classic Mediterranean features, their beauty reinforced by uncompromising strength. Eyes so close to gold shouldn't be cold, but Gerd's were right then.

Rosie's heart clamped painfully. *What had she done?*

Too late now to ask herself that question. She'd made a decision and now she had plenty of time—all her life—to repent it.

Or make the most of it…

A note of exasperation coloured his voice. 'I am sorry if the speed of the announcement bothers you. Perhaps I should have offered you time to become accustomed to the idea of marrying me, but I thought you understood that we might not have that luxury.'

Well, she'd left herself open to that. Biting her lip, Rosie nodded. He *had* made it plain. And she had agreed.

It was time to stop behaving like someone who wanted to be loved. If she kept this up he might suspect that she was longing—*aching*—for his love, and pride was all she had now.

'I did.' Her voice trembled a little, and she had to take a breath to steady it before she could go on. 'I didn't realise that a day or so would make any difference.'

'It might not have,' he admitted, pouring two glasses of champagne.

He'd seen her in so many ways—exquisite in her balldress, elegant in the softly pastel silk suit she'd worn to his coronation, casual in shorts and a suntop on the yacht.

Naked in his arms...

Every muscle in his body contracted in swift, violent desire. She only had to look at him to rouse that unsparing hunger.

But today she seemed...subdued, her glow dimmed, her face shadowed as though she'd lost some essential part of herself.

He said, 'I should have told you what I was planning to do. I'm sorry.'

Why had he not? He wasn't prepared to ask himself that question, nor to explore exactly why he felt uneasy.

He had no difficulty in reading the moods of most people, but Rosemary was different; although she seemed bright and open on the surface, it was hard to know exactly what was going on behind that sunny face.

And that was all the apology she was likely to get, Rosie decided wryly as she accepted the glass and put it down on the table. Gerd had been born an autocrat, and his upbringing and position had simply grafted more formidable layers onto a nature already dominant and decisive.

He reached out a hand, palm uppermost. 'Am I forgiven?'

She put hers into it, watching as it was swallowed up in his tanned fingers. 'Marriage is—or should be—a partnership, even if by marrying you I automatically become your subject. And partners discuss things with each other.'

'I stand corrected.' He lifted her hand to his mouth and kissed it. Little rills of sensation ran up her arm, and her breath came shortly through her lips.

When he released her he said levelly, 'My private secretary will be arriving in a couple of hours. We'll be discussing how to organise the wedding, so of course you will sit in on the session.'

Rosie's heart dropped. His words made the future seem suddenly much closer. However, she'd been the one who wanted to know things. 'How long will it take for the wedding to be organised?'

'About a year,' he said casually. 'But first there will have to be an official betrothal ceremony. That will be a family occasion in the palace chapel, but it will mark the official start of our life together.'

An opinion that was echoed by the private secretary, a thin, middle-aged man who greeted her with a smile and a shrewd, although respectful survey. He'd probably expected someone six inches taller and elegant, she thought gloomily, someone whose family tree was clotted with titles.

The private secretary went on in his careful English, 'That will give us time to organise it in a suitable manner, and it will also give you, Ms Matthews, time to become known to the people of Carathia, to learn the language and become accustomed to us.' He smiled benignly at her. 'It will be a busy year for you, so it will travel fast.'

Clearly he thought she was panting to marry Gerd.

When the interview was over and the secretary had gone to another room to draft the final announcement, Gerd said, 'We need to make quite a few decisions before your mother arrives.'

'Like what?' she asked warily.

His smile lacked humour. 'Like a date.'

Faced so brutally with the impact of her agreement, she said, 'It won't really matter to me. I don't organise my diary a year ahead, and as far as I know Mother doesn't either.'

He nodded. 'Then there is the question of where you will live for this next year. I suggest that you move into Kelt's house in the capital. He has already agreed, but of course the decision must be yours. I will supply you with a household.'

Colour drained from her face. She closed her eyes for a moment and took a breath before opening them again. 'Gerd, this is not going to work. A *household*? I wouldn't know what to do with a household except the housework.'

'Calm down,' he advised. 'What has happened to that backbone of yours? I've always admired your courage and your resilience.'

Rosie flicked him a mutinous glance. 'Anyone can be courageous and resilient when it's not a matter of their entire future.'

But the compliment warmed her heart sufficiently for her to listen when he said calmly, 'I refuse to believe that the bold, gallant girl I know was just a sham. And this is not negotiable. This morning you made me a promise; I accepted your word and acted on it.'

If he said this once more she'd—she'd *bite* him! She must have been mad and she certainly wasn't going to tell him that this morning, still fogged with sex, she'd have promised him *anything*.

When she said nothing he went on, 'So it is decided. You'll need a social secretary who knows court etiquette. I have someone in mind for that, but the ultimate decision must be yours.'

'How hard is Carathian to learn?'

'It's difficult,' he admitted, 'but not impossible. You'll have lessons, and of course you'll hear it spoken all the time; you'll probably be surprised at how quickly you absorb it.'

'I can deal with learning the language,' she said trenchantly. 'But why did you feel obliged to force the issue? Do you need a wife—*any* wife—that much? And if you do, why on earth—when there must be a hundred or so women out there, much better equipped to deal with the sort of life you lead—did you pick on me?'

He sent her a look that should have quelled the tumbling words, but perhaps he recognised the hurt beneath them because his voice was almost gentle when he said, 'You know why.'

'Because we're good together in bed? How very shallow of you, Gerd!'

CHAPTER EIGHT

THE scorn in Rosie's voice should have flicked Gerd's imperturbable control, but his steady regard didn't waver. 'That is not the sole reason,' he stated, a cynical smile curling his mouth. 'I think you will make an excellent Grand Duchess once you've got used to the idea.'

He sank a hand into her curls, gently pulling her head back to expose the length of her throat, vulnerable and creamy. 'And we are more than *good* together,' he said in a low, abrasive voice that sent ripples of sensation through her, 'we are bloody sensational.'

Rosie closed her eyes against his intense, devouring gaze. 'Don't you dare use sex against me,' she said, but her tone lacked conviction, and she wasn't surprised by his rough purr of a laugh.

'Why not? It works so well,' he parried, and kissed the corner of her mouth, the lightest of kisses, so soft she barely felt it. 'And I give you licence to use it against me whenever you feel like it. I'd enjoy that.'

No doubt, because he wasn't a slave to his emotions. He didn't love her...

Her skin tightened at the drift of his particular scent, that faint, evanescent fragrance that somehow had the power to overwhelm her common sense. The ripples of excitement became torrents, converging, building, heating every cell into molten anticipation. Hunger was like a drug, a reckless need that stopped her brain from working and changed her into some infinitely wanton stranger.

She opened her eyes, miserably aware that the fire he summoned had burnt away the proud rejection she wanted to make. This was Gerd, and she loved him. More than that, she trusted him. He'd promised fidelity; she was sure he wouldn't break that vow.

And she couldn't think of anything she wanted more than to be his wife, to bear his children...

So she'd follow her heart. In time he might learn to love her as wholly, as completely as she loved him—arrogance and all, she thought wryly. But she'd have to learn to be content with what he could give her, and if that was his respect and his affection and his lovemaking—well, many women had settled for less and forged happy lives.

Neither of them had had a normal childhood; Gerd's parents had died young, and, although his grandmother had loved him, she'd been a distant figure, intent on matters of state. Rosie had grown up lacking the loving support most children took for granted. But she knew now that Gerd would be a good father, and together they'd make sure their children didn't lack the love and security that came when parents were in a committed, stable relationship.

He said quietly, 'I think it will be better if we don't

make love until you are sure there will be no chance of pregnancy.'

'I—yes.' Her voice shook and she said fiercely, 'Why is everything so complicated?'

Without hesitation he answered, 'Life is complex, and made more so because we humans are a difficult lot, passionate and unreasonable and wanting things we know we shouldn't have.'

And Gerd was more complex than most.

Rosie glanced up to see him studying her face, his mouth disciplined into a straight, decisive line, eyes half-hidden by long lashes—yet not so impossible to read that she couldn't discern the speculation in them.

Did he suspect that she loved him?

The thought brought hot blood to her skin, so embarrassing that she turned her head away and walked across to the window to stare unseeingly out at the blue, blue sea.

What would she do if he could never match her feelings?

If she'd learned anything about him these past few days, it was that his duty to his country would always come first.

Looked at pragmatically, a wife who loved him would be perfect; that he didn't love her would give him the emotional freedom to concentrate on Carathia and its people and their welfare.

The thought of that was unbearably painful.

But hell, she thought cynically, the sex was good. No, it was more than good; as he'd said, it was fantastic. And she wasn't her mother, seeking an unattainable, fairy-tale love.

Or perhaps she was...

She turned her head and looked at him. He met her gaze, his eyes steady and direct.

Did she have the strength to walk away?

'I'll try not to disappoint you,' he said quietly.

Half a loaf is better than no bread.

The pragmatic, sensible thought popped into her brain from nowhere. How many times had she railed at it, demanding the whole loaf?

Now she realised she was going to accept what Gerd could offer.

Mind made up once and for all, she nodded. 'And I'll do my best not to disappoint you.'

Vows of eternal love weren't applicable, she thought ironically, yet this simple exchange went a little way to ease the hungry yearning inside her.

'So what happens now?' she asked.

'We go back to the capital.'

'Must we?' The words escaped before she had a chance to consider them.

'Much as I'd like to stay here, we have to.' Gerd's tone left no room for objections, but he softened slightly when he said, 'We need to have official portraits taken as soon as possible—tomorrow morning, in fact. My private secretary has organised a selection of clothes for you to choose from. I'd like you to wear something from a local designer.'

He paused as though expecting further objections, but Rosie nodded. That made sense. What didn't was the shiver of apprehension that chilled through her.

Gerd went on, 'In three days' time, once your mother and Alex and Hani and Kelt have arrived, there will be the official betrothal ceremony.' His expression indicated this was not negotiable. 'It's a traditional ceremony for family and friends, but you'll need to choose something to wear for that too—something formal.'

Startled, Rosie looked at his uncompromising face. 'As in long?'

'No. Formal day clothes—hat, gloves et cetera. I'm sure you know what sort of thing. If not, then the designer will advise you on the correct attire.'

Butterflies tumbled around in her stomach. 'It sounds as though this is a rehearsal for a wedding.'

'It's a long-standing tradition in the country, and a lot of people would feel the marriage was scarcely legal if it wasn't held.'

Reacting to his dismissive tone, Rosie asked tersely, 'Are there any other traditional occasions I need to know about?'

'Not immediately. After a week or so of festivities which we'll be expected to attend, things will settle down and you can move into Kelt's house.' He paused, then added, 'I suggest you ask your mother to stay with you for a month or so.'

'My *mother*?'

'She *is* your mother,' he reminded her coolly. 'Your only living relative apart from Alex.'

'Presumably this whole jolly family party thing is because it's important that my family—what there is of it—and yours are seen to accept the engagement?'

She couldn't bring herself to say 'our engagement'.

'That's part of it.' Gerd's voice didn't encourage her to go on, but she persisted.

'And the other part?'

He shrugged. 'After those damned photographs I want to put as official a slant on our holiday as it's possible to do.'

Rosie could see his point. In that photo they hadn't looked like a betrothed couple. They'd looked as though they couldn't wait to get into bed together.

Although her nerves were strung tight and twanging, she gave a sparkling, mischievous grin. 'Oh,' she breathed, 'I can just see it now—this is going to be such fun! Mother can't resist provoking Alex in every way possible, but when he lifts that eyebrow of his and cuts her down to size with a few scathing words she loses her temper. And then—pouf! Fireworks to match that display we saw from your windows.'

'Don't worry. Alex will be fine.'

'It's not Alex I'm thinking of,' she told him prosaically.

Gerd's expression hardened. 'Your mother will be fine too,' he stated.

And she was. Oh, the tension was there—it always would be, Rosie suspected—but Eva was on her best behaviour, saving her comments for when she and Rosie were alone.

'I hope you know what you're doing,' she said, looking around the suite allotted to her.

Rosie said aloofly, 'Don't worry about that.'

Eva glanced at her. 'I know what it's like to marry the wrong man. I'd just as soon not watch you do it.'

Rosie felt uncomfortable. Her mother was a beauty, one of those rare women who defied the years, but her expression had settled into lines of petulance. She'd never spoken before of her husband and the marriage that had only lasted for a few years.

And Rosie didn't want to discuss it. Her father had been fond of her in his absent way; it seemed disloyal to listen to him being denigrated when he wasn't alive to defend himself.

'You won't be doing that,' she said with far more confidence than she felt.

Her mother shrugged. 'At least you're older—just— than I was when I married your father. But you have to realise that if you marry Gerd there'll be no divorce. The Carathians haven't progressed much since the Middle Ages. Their attitudes—especially in the mountain people—are still rock-solid conservative. If it doesn't work out you'll have to stick it out.'

When it doesn't work out, her tone implied. Before Rosie could say anything Eva went on, 'And, although there's huge prestige and glamour in being almost a queen, there must also be a lot of boredom.'

Struggling to control the tension that gripped her, Rosie said with a slight snap, 'I don't bore as easily as you do. And I didn't realise you knew so much about the Carathians.'

'Your father came here several times when he was married to Alex's mother.' Eva turned away to concentrate on the view out over the city and the mountains. 'He found them an interesting study. Until they discovered that stuff they mine for computers they were stuck in a kind of time warp—poverty-stricken and mediaeval. I can't see that thirty years of prosperity will have changed them that much.'

Possibly not, but Gerd's plans to educate them would

help. Rosie said crisply, 'I'd already worked that out, although I doubt if they're quite as mediaeval as Father thought them.'

Her mother lifted her shoulders again. 'Very well, I've said all I had to say. Now fill me in on what's going to happen.'

Briefly Rosie told her of the formal betrothal ceremony that would cement the engagement in the eyes of Gerd's subjects, and the events that would follow when she and Gerd would be on show.

'Quite a programme,' her mother said with a lift of her brows. 'Is Alex here?'

'He's landing in an hour or so.'

Her mother flashed her a taut smile. 'Don't look so concerned. I do know how to behave, even with Alex.'

Back in her own suite Rosie stood for a long moment with closed eyes, trying to control the turmoil of her emotions. What had she expected? That her mother would suddenly turn into someone able to offer advice and support?

It was never going to happen, and she'd accepted that long before she'd even understood what she needed from Eva.

She would, she thought with a quiver of apprehension, always be on her own.

But there would be children…

A tap on the door heralded Gerd, who after a moment's hard scrutiny demanded, 'What's the matter?'

'Nothing,' she said automatically, and to prove it flashed him a glance that was all challenge.

His brows rose, but he said blandly, 'Can you come

along to my office and look over some rings I've had sent up?'

At her startled glance he added with a smile, 'Even in the wilderness of Carathia we have engagement rings.'

'Oh,' she said, and managed to produce a laugh that sounded unconvincing. 'I hadn't thought of rings.'

His gaze was uncomfortably keen. 'Then think of it now.'

'And Carathia isn't a wilderness,' she said briskly, still resenting her mother's comments.

Gerd held out his hand. 'Come here,' he said, his eyelashes drooping in a way that made her heart thud erratically.

Flushing, she went into his arms. He seemed to understand she needed comfort more than the erotic flashfire of passion, because he just held her, his cheek on the top of her head. Sighing, Rosie relaxed against him, taking immense comfort from his solid male strength and the warmth of his arms around her.

Eventually he said, 'Better?'

Feeling a little foolish, she murmured, 'Yes, I'm fine.'

He let her go, but retained her hand as they left the room.

In his office a tray of rings glittered against the black velvet of their case. Stunned, Rosie drew in a deep breath.

Gerd said, 'Although diamonds are the convention, I thought golden ones would suit you better than ones with blue fire. But if you don't like them the stones can be replaced.'

'I love them,' she said quietly, and then laughed as she scanned them. 'All of them! What an impossible choice!'

'Well, we can sort them out. A stone too big will weigh that elegant finger down, so these can go.'

He indicated three large solitaires.

Colour burned along Rosie's cheekbones. The last time he'd referred to her hands it had been about their effect on him when they made love.

'You agree?' Gerd asked.

'Yes.' How she wished she were tall and graceful and gorgeous, like the two women she knew had been Gerd's lovers. Neither of them had uncontrollable red curls; both had worn smooth dark hair pulled back from superb features, and they'd breathed a sophisticated intelligence.

Clearly he was accustomed to choosing jewellery. So what had he chosen for those women—rings? Probably not, she thought acidly. Rings might be taken to mean commitment. Necklaces? Or bracelets?

Whatever, anything he'd given his lovers had been chosen because he'd wanted them, and not for reasons of state. Hot jealousy—and a bitter spurt of envy—tightened her nerves.

'Something special,' Gerd said. He indicated one in particular. 'Do you like this?'

How had he known that of them all, this was the one she'd have chosen for herself? The stone wasn't huge, but it shone like the heart of summer, an intense honeyed glow that made the others pale.

'It's beautiful,' Rosie said. But a ring as exquisite as that should be a token of love.

He plucked it from the velvet and held it out. 'Try it on,' he invited.

Rosie hesitated, then held out her hand and watched numbly as he slid it onto her ring finger.

Gerd thought that it looked as though it had been made for her, the colour of the stone echoing the sunlit vibrancy of her skin and curls, the glints of gold that usually danced in her eyes.

He watched her face as the ring slid home, saw her mouth tighten and then relax, and wondered again just what was going on in her brain.

She was, he thought grimly, driving him mad. Previously he'd enjoyed civilised affairs; he'd liked his lovers and made sure they understood the limits he set on relationships. They'd been passionate enough to keep him interested, but not so intense that hunger took over his mind and got between him and his work.

Rosemary was different. From the start she'd defied all his rules, starting with that long holiday three years previously when he'd really got to know her. Slowly, insidiously his affection for the girl-child he'd known all her life had metamorphosed into a forbidden desire, one he was determined not to act on.

He'd restrained himself until the night before he'd left for Carathia, but something snapped then, and he'd taken an irrevocable step. It had been meant to be one kiss, and a very light one, but her sensuous response had knocked him sideways. The dangerous surge of desire it summoned had eaten away at his self-control; it had taken every particle of willpower he possessed to lift his head and lower his arms and step away from her, and afterwards he'd spent a sleepless night trying to deal with his reaction.

When he'd seen her kissing Kelt just as ardently it had been like a savage betrayal, one he'd vowed never to forget.

Discovering that she'd stayed a virgin had surprised him. More dangerously, the knowledge had satisfied something unregenerate and primal in him, stripping away his defences so that all he could think of was his craving for her.

In his arms she was wildfire and wine and erotic fulfilment, and he couldn't get enough of her.

Rosie looked up and caught the hunger in Gerd's gaze, a lick of fire that flared at her instant response. The hairs lifted on the back of her neck while adrenalin surged through her, and her eyes darkened.

He smiled, a tight, fierce movement of his lips, and said softly, 'Perfect.'

And raised her hand and kissed the ring, and then her palm. Exciting little shivers scudded the length of her spine.

More than anything Rosie wanted him to kiss her properly, but he resisted the vibration that sizzled between them and released her hand. Her pleasure evaporating, she looked down at the ring weighing her finger down like a badge of office.

Exactly what it was, she thought.

He said, 'So that's the betrothal ring. What sort of wedding band do you think would go with that?'

'I—don't know.' She looked down at the small sun glittering on her finger. 'I've barely had time to appreciate this gorgeous thing, and now you want me to choose a wedding ring?'

'It's traditional.'

'I thought that in Europe they didn't have the same traditions we do.'

'There has always been a wedding ring, and when my grandfather gave my grandmother an engagement ring, the first one in Carathia, every woman in the country wanted one as well,' he said drily.

Rosie thought a moment, her eyes fixed on the golden diamond. 'How about a ring with an inlaid silver pattern?' she suggested.

'Perhaps you could discuss it with the designer. He is waiting for us. You will need other jewels, of course.' His voice altered fractionally. 'Will you object to wearing some of the royal collection?'

'No.' Her voice whispered into the room. Burdened as she was by the reality of marrying Gerd, the royal collection of jewels somehow seemed a symbol of all that would be different in her life from now on.

Well, she'd agreed. So she swallowed and said more audibly, 'No, of course I won't.'

'There is an abundance to choose from,' he told her negligently. 'I'll make a selection of pieces you might like, and you can decide which ones you really like. Some are distinctly old-fashioned, so possibly they'll need resetting.'

The designer, a solid middle-aged man, bowed when he was introduced and wished them every happiness. He approved her choice of ring, and when asked about a wedding band whipped out a pencil and a pad and sketched something for her.

'I'm not sure about the roses,' she said, examining it. 'My name is Rosemary, not Rose.'

The designer looked chagrined. 'I'm sorry—'

Gerd intervened. 'Myrtle.' He smiled down at Rosie, his acting so good she could almost believe for a moment that he loved her. 'You liked it, didn't you, and because it and New Zealand's pohutukawa are very distant cousins, it will provide a link with your homeland?'

Of course, roses stood for love, whereas myrtle was sacred to Aphrodite, the goddess of passion and desire...

Rosie's answering smile was restrained. 'Oh, yes, how suitable.'

Gerd gave her a sharp glance, but the designer nodded. 'A charming idea.' Rapidly he sketched another design, then regarded it with a smile before handing it over to Gerd. 'Yes—the simpler the design the more effective.'

After he'd left Rosie said, 'That was an inspired suggestion.'

'You appeared to enjoy the scent of the sprigs of myrtle you picked,' Gerd said dismissively. Then he smiled down at her. 'Besides, we made some very pleasant memories there the day you first saw it.'

Her heart expanding, Rosie smiled back. 'So we did,' she said.

Surely, he couldn't look at her like that if he didn't feel something for her!

Buoyed by that idea, she almost enjoyed posing for the set of official photographs, even though it took almost half a day before the photographer was satisfied.

'I don't do dignity well,' Rosie sighed to Gerd when it was over. She glanced down at her clothes—a dress from a local designer that managed to be both formal and summery. 'But I love this and the other clothes that have come. Only…who is paying for them?'

'I am,' he told her calmly. 'And I think you do dignity very well. Dignity—but with warmth and interest.'

Right then she couldn't appreciate the compliment. 'I don't think you should be paying for my clothes,' she objected.

He looked at her, his expression uncompromising. 'I've already had this conversation with your brother,' he said inflexibly. 'I don't intend to go through it again with you.'

'I don't want either of you—'

'Rosemary, just leave it, will you?' His eyes were as crystalline and cold as the diamond she wore. 'You are in this position because I asked you to be, and so it is up to me to see that you have everything you need.'

'Gerd, we are not going to get along at all well if you tell me to leave things instead of discussing them sensibly,' she said through her teeth. 'If I'm old enough to marry you, damn it, I'm old enough to be consulted about things that might seem trifles to you but are important to me. It's disrespectful and unfair and patronising if we can only discuss things that are important to you!'

He looked down at her as though he'd been bitten by a kitten, then unexpectedly gave a wry smile. 'You are, of course, correct. Very well, then, explain to me how it will make you feel better if neither Alex nor I pay for the clothes you need for formal occasions.'

He had a point. But so did she. Rosie drew in a breath and said, 'I'm not in the same league financially as you or Alex, but I do have a little money in the bank. I can at least use that.'

'I would like you to keep it so that you don't feel entirely dependent on me.'

Neither yielding, they measured glances. Rosie was torn by indecision. In the end she said, 'I realise it seems quixotic, but—'

'It's a statement of independence?'

Actually, it probably was—a symbolic answer to the ring on her finger and all it represented. 'It's more that you just made the assumption that you'd pay without even talking it over with me.'

He nodded. 'I won't make that mistake again. But there is something we need to discuss right now. You will need an allowance.'

Rosie opened her mouth but before she could speak he said lazily, 'I shall feel compelled to kiss any further objections away, and you know where that will lead.'

Heat coloured her skin, but her eyes stayed steady. 'That is sexist. And two can play at that game.'

His eyes narrowed. 'Feel free, any time,' he invited silkily.

CHAPTER NINE

ROSIE glared at him, then closed her eyes in surrender. 'You don't play fair.'

'Neither do you.' Gerd's voice was low and amused and very, very sexy.

Her eyes opened and she warded him off with upraised hands. 'As it happens, I wasn't going to object to an allowance,' she said forthrightly. 'But I'll use my own money until it's gone.'

Gerd shrugged. 'You're not going to budge on this, are you?'

'No.'

'And you don't want me to try and persuade you…?' He let the suggestion hang in the air.

'I do not,' she told him as crisply as she could.

Which was not very effective. Her voice had softened, and the lazy, languorous note in it constituted a far from subtle invitation.

He knew, of course, that if he touched her, kissed her, she'd melt, and then she'd be lost. But he had to accept that he couldn't just make decisions for her and expect her to obey them without question.

So she repeated coolly, 'I can see the point of an allowance, so I'll accept that. But until my money runs out I'll buy my own clothes.'

'Your personal clothes,' he conceded. 'Anything you need to buy for official occasions will come from your household expenses.'

'Very well,' she said reluctantly.

He frowned. 'Are you always going to be like this?'

'I suspect I am.' A little acidly she went on, 'Feel like changing your mind?'

His face hardened. 'No.'

The evening before the betrothal ceremony he gave a dinner at the palace, where he introduced Rosie to his personal friends. It was a relaxed occasion, without formal speeches or toasts, but Rosie realised she was being assessed.

Afterwards Gerd dropped a light kiss on her forehead at her bedroom door. 'Sleep well,' he said.

'I'm scared,' she blurted, regretting the words as soon as they escaped. 'What if nobody likes me?'

He gave her a hug, but immediately freed her and stepped back. 'Has anyone ever disliked you?' he asked rhetorically.

Her mother, for one. 'Jo Green in Year Three hated me,' Rosie told him. 'She used to pinch me and call me Ginge.'

He laughed. 'Nobody will do that here.'

More seriously she said, 'I suppose what's really concerning me is that I simply might not be able to do the job with the sort of—well, gravitas that it needs. I don't want to fail you or your people.'

'I didn't realise that beneath that self-assured manner you're lacking in confidence.'

She shrugged. 'It is an unusual situation, and one I haven't been trained for.' Unlike Princess Serina, who probably wouldn't dream of dumping her insecurities on her chosen spouse, no matter who he was.

Gerd said calmly, 'I have complete faith in your ability to deal with anything.'

Rosie looked up, her heart thumping erratically. *So why don't you kiss me?* But he wasn't going to use that simplest of ways to comfort her. He seemed to have pulled up some emotional drawbridge, leaving her alone and forlorn on the other side.

Gerd said, 'Tomorrow morning after the ceremony a crowd might gather in front of the palace.'

'Why?' she asked blankly.

'To wish us joy. We will come out as a family and wave from the balcony off the grand drawing room.' He smiled at her startled look. 'So perhaps you will need even higher heels than usual so they can see you over the balustrade.'

'I'm not that short,' she said indignantly.

'Just as high as my heart,' he quoted.

Rosie smiled and closed the door on him, but her smile faded quickly into wistfulness. She wished—oh, how she wished—he wouldn't say things like that.

Not when he didn't really mean them…

Her dress for the official betrothal was already hanging in her dressing room, a silk in a champagne colour that just skimmed her body and made her feel elegant and tall. And fortunately her sandals had very high heels. The hat was cut so that everyone could see her face.

A knock on the door brought heat to her cheeks and

an aching hunger to her heart—a feverish anticipation that was dashed when her mother came in.

'Is anything wrong?' she asked.

'No.' Her mother noted the dress hanging ready to be worn, and said, 'Very appropriate. You get your taste from me. Your father didn't care about clothes.'

Rosie told her what Gerd had said about a crowd collecting, and her mother nodded. 'Oh, yes, I've been forewarned about it.'

'I doubt if it's going to happen. Why would they?'

'Curiosity,' her mother said dismissively. She paused, then said deliberately, 'I wouldn't take it personally. You could have two heads and they'd be delighted. What they want is children from you—preferably boys.'

Rosie lifted her brows. 'I suppose they do,' she said quietly, determined not to let her mother see how much that hurt. 'The succession has to be important.'

'It's hugely important in any monarchy, but for Gerd it's vital.'

'I know.' And because she didn't want to go into the reasons Gerd needed heirs, she said, 'Mother, Gerd and I discussed the situation before I agreed to marry him. And even if we hadn't, as you said a couple of days ago, it's too late to back out now.'

Eva said in dismay, 'Don't tell me he's convinced you that he's in love with you!'

At Rosie's steady gaze her mother looked slightly shamefaced, but she kept on with a bitter twist to her lips. 'And even knowing that he's going to use you as a baby machine, you still decided to marry him? Are you pregnant?'

Rosie kept her head high. 'No.'

'And there I always thought you were a runaway romantic,' her mother said with heavy irony.

Rosie's smile was twisted. 'No, you're the runaway romantic.'

'Forget about me. Don't try to persuade me that you're marrying him for the prestige and the money. I know you've been infatuated with him since you were eighteen.'

Please go right now. But Rosie couldn't say the words.

Her mother looked at her with an expression she'd never seen before.

'I've made a mess of my life,' she said abruptly. 'I married your father too young—I thought he loved me, but all he wanted was to go off on his various expeditions without having to bother about organising child care for Alex. He never got over losing his first wife. Oh, he was quite pleased when I had you, although he'd have preferred another boy, but we weren't important to him—his research was. Even Alex came a pretty poor second to that.'

'I'm sorry,' Rosie said quietly. 'But it's not like that with Gerd and me.'

'Gerd is...well, everything a woman could want, but he's going to be married to Carathia.'

'I know.'

'I hope you do,' her mother said bleakly. 'Otherwise you'll eat your heart out wanting something that's never going to happen.'

But that was exactly what she was going to do, Rosie realised in the sleepless hours that followed her mother's awkward departure. Thoughts raced through her head, jumbled and anguished, filled with emotions so painful she couldn't bear them.

Eventually she got up and walked across to the window. It would be simpler—and easier—if she didn't love Gerd.

She looked down on the darkened, silent city, the street lamps lonely beacons, starshine glimmering on a jumble of tiled roofs and the slick of wet concrete.

Why had her mother's words unsettled her so much? Easy—they'd struck home only because Rosie was more accustomed to exasperation than concern from her mother.

And away from Gerd's compelling presence, without the gloss of sexual passion clouding her brain, Gerd's proposal and her response seemed a cold, bleakly practical reaction to the situation they'd found themselves in.

Her hand drifted across to touch her waist. What if she couldn't have children?

Too late to worry about that now…

The words echoed in her head as she got back into bed and drifted off to a restless sleep.

Church bells woke her—a joyous cacophony that soared up from the city's churches. She sat straight up in bed, head aching slightly, then got up and inched the heavy curtains open a fraction. Although it was barely past dawn—in fact, over the mountains she saw the last star wink out—already people were moving in the streets below.

Heading towards the palace.

'Oh, lord,' she muttered, yanking the drapes closed in case anyone saw her peeking.

A knock on her door whirled her around. The maid who looked after her clothes came in, beaming when Rosie greeted her. With a little bob she said carefully, 'A beautiful day for us all in Carathia. I wish you great happiness, my lady.'

Rosie's nerves tightened painfully, her sense of doom increasing as the morning wound on. Although a betrothal ceremony was usually restricted to family and closest friends, because of Gerd's position there would be politicians and important people there too. All dressed to the nines, she realised when she was escorted into the front pew with Eva, who was slim and soignée in one of the vibrant colours she wore so well.

At least Kelt and Hani and their little Rafi sat with them, with Alex, saturnine as usual. And the service was short; it involved a blessing, the ceremonial bestowal of the ring by Gerd, dark and unsmiling as he slid it onto her finger, and the exchange of a kiss before the altar—both the kiss and Gerd's attitude being studiously impersonal. A brief homily from the priest, delivered in Carathian, was clearly an exposition of what was expected of them. Unable to understand, aware of Gerd's withdrawal beside her, Rosie had never felt so alone.

But walking back down the aisle with him beside her, part of a procession featuring candles and crosses, and choirboys who sang like angels, it warmed her to meet the smiles of those who'd been at last night's dinner.

And at the reception that followed, Gerd's approving nod and murmured words of appreciation, his hand in the small of her back, restored her confidence. It helped that most of the people used their store of English to converse with her. As a child Gerd and Kelt had taught her the conventional greetings and farewells in Carathian, but beyond those she understood nothing of the language as yet.

Language lessons, and soon, she decided sturdily.

Eventually the family was marshalled into order in the drawing room. Stomach flipping, she shivered at the murmur of the crowd in the huge square below.

'It sounds as though everyone in the city is out there,' she said to Gerd.

'Just about,' he said. 'Come on, it's time to go.' He looked down and his serious expression lightened. 'How do you manage to walk in those heels?'

'It's a technique small girls study from the first time they try on their mother's shoes,' she said, repressing another, quite different shiver at the glint in his gaze. 'By the time they reach adolescence it's completely automatic.'

And then it was time to move out onto the balcony. The hairs on the back of her neck lifted at the sight of the people packed into the square and the wild roar that greeted them as they moved across to the balustrade. Everyone in that huge, seething mass of people seemed to be waving something—brightly coloured streamers, flowers and handkerchiefs.

And the noise was indescribable—breathtaking and almost terrifying, except that everyone seemed to be smiling.

Gerd looked down at her. 'Smile, Rosemary. This is for you.'

But it wasn't. His people loved and respected him; they trusted him to marry a person who would fit into their world, and they believed she was that person.

Then and there, Rosie decided that such trust deserved to be honoured. She would become the person the Carathians believed her to be.

'Nonsense—they don't know me at all. This is all for you,' she said, and pinned a smile to her lips as she waved back.

Gerd said coolly, 'The Chief Minister has suggested that we travel into the mountains next week. The people there have a tendency to feel neglected.'

And that, of course, was where the last rebellion had been fomented. Rosie's stomach clenched, but she nodded and smiled brightly up at him, only dimly hearing the renewed burst of cheering that provoked.

Gerd said, 'We'll visit the largest town there, and it would be politic to go down to the coast.'

'That sounds great,' she said, waving again at the excited, happy mass of people who seemed determined to let their ruler know they shared his happiness.

His *supposed* happiness, Rosie corrected herself.

The crowd cheered anew and began throwing their flowers and ribbons in a shower of colour into the sparkling, sunlit air until eventually Gerd said, 'Time to go.'

With a final wave the family turned and filed back inside, adjourning to Gerd's private apartments, where they were served lunch.

Kelt gave Rosie a hug, saying, 'Thank you.'

'For what?'

He grinned. 'For taking Gerd on. I didn't realise it, but he needs someone like you—he's far too autocratic, and you'll keep him on his toes. And the Carathians will love you.'

Rosie laughed, but his words made her feel oddly disconnected, as though by marrying Gerd she'd turn into a different person.

She glanced across the room and saw Gerd watching them, his face impassive. Something tight and hard contracted inside her. He looked bleak and almost angry.

But only for a second. When he caught her eye he lifted his brows and came towards them and, as always, her breath shortened and she felt that secret heat stirring in her body.

Kelt gave him a brotherly cuff on the shoulder. 'About time,' he said obscurely.

Gerd's brows climbed again. 'I think Hani wants you,' he said.

Both Rosie and Gerd watched Kelt set off purposefully across the huge, gilt-decorated drawing room to his wife, who was perched on the edge of an ornate sofa. Hani's face lit up when her husband approached.

Pierced by a depressing envy and a feeling of intruding on something special between Kelt and his wife, Rosie turned away. 'It looked as though most of the city was there this morning.'

Gerd's voice was coolly non-committal. 'Quite a few,' he agreed. 'How do you feel?'

'Fine,' she said, surprising herself with the realisation. 'The betrothal ceremony made me realise that I need to start learning the language straight away, but you don't need words to wave from a balcony!' She thought for a moment, then said, 'I feel welcomed.

Which sounds silly, because that crowd gathered for you, not me, but everyone there looked warm-hearted and pleased for us both.'

'Carathians enjoy a good party.' Although he smiled down at her, his eyes were still remote. 'And you were welcomed, and are welcome. You did very well.'

His words should have warmed her, but the more legalities bound them together, she thought unhappily, the more distant Gerd became. She wondered if they would ever regain the laughter and burgeoning closeness, the thrilling hope, of those few crazy, passion-filled days on the island.

So far away they seemed now, so impossible to retrieve...

The next day Kelt and Hani took her to the town house, and for a little while she could relax in their undemanding company, playing with their little boy before being shown over the old, beautifully appointed building.

'I hope you enjoy living here,' Hani said, looking around. 'Kelt said it was still firmly Victorian until he inherited it; he had all the plumbing and wiring redone, and when we got married I organised the most hideous of the furniture into storage. We don't stay here much because of that legend, but it's very comfortable. And the Carathians are very kind.'

'Hani, it's lovely. Both you and Kelt have done a great job on it. But even nicer is that I can feel your presence here.'

Hani smiled mistily at her. 'Dear Rosie,' she said. 'We're all going to miss you like crazy, but I think the Carathians already know how lucky they are to have you.'

To Rosie's horror she felt tears sting her eyes. 'Thank you,' she said on a gulp. 'Oh, hell, I never cry—this is ridiculous. I'll miss you too, even though I expect to see lots of you and Kelt and little Rafi.'

She waved them off the next morning, with her mother, as they were all travelling back to New Zealand together. 'I have to tidy things up at home,' Eva said briskly, 'and then I'll be back.'

Rosie said, 'I know it will be a sacrifice for you. Thank you.'

Eva looked a little startled. With a hint of sarcasm she said, 'I didn't make any sacrifices for you as a child, so it's probably only fair that I should now.'

They looked at each other for a moment. Eva shrugged and went on, 'We should be able to live together for a couple of months without coming to blows.'

'I can't see why not. We're both adults,' Rosie said firmly.

'Think of it as training for all the sacrifices you're going to make for Carathia,' her mother advised.

In spite of that, Eva's attitude gave Rosie hope that perhaps she and her mother could form some sort of relationship.

'Not a real mother-daughter relationship,' she said to Gerd as they travelled back from the airport. 'But some sort of friendly association. She's changed.'

'How?' he asked, his tone disbelieving.

'She's a little softer—just as cynical, but somehow not so bitter. And there's no man in tow, yet she doesn't seem to care.'

Gerd leaned back in the car. 'Let's hope it lasts. Are you ready for our quick tour of the mountains?'

'Yes. Will the white lily be blooming?' She wanted very much to see Carathia's national flower.

'It's usually over by now, but there might be some pockets of it left.'

There were, and after an excited and friendly reception from the people who'd flocked into the biggest town in the mountain region, they flew by helicopter up to the edge of the winter snowline.

'There, my lady,' the guide said, indicating a plant nestled in against a rock.

Rosie gave an excited squeak and crouched down. Fragile and fleeting, white petals airily danced above the grim rocks and the matted tangle of its leaves.

'They're tough, aren't they?' Rosie said, crouching beside it. Carefully she stroked the flower, wondering at the resilience of such a lovely thing in this hard landscape.

The botanist and the mountaineer who'd accompanied them both nodded, the botanist saying in her limited English, 'Strong and beautiful—like the mountains.'

'Like Carathians,' the mountain guide said proudly. He glanced at Gerd, and said something in their language.

Gerd translated as Rosie stood up. 'He's recited a local proverb that compares a beautiful woman to the summer sun, warming the eyes and the heart.' His smile was swift. 'He means you.'

Rosie flushed. 'Thank you very much,' she said to the guide, who made a little bow.

She and Gerd could afford only a short time there in the cool, crisp air, and too soon they were back in the helicopter. As they swooped down into the valley, Rosie hugged the memory of the flowers and the look in Gerd's eyes when he relayed the guide's compliment.

Whatever his reason for keeping such a distance between them, it was not because he didn't want her. For a precious second she had seen a flare of passionate need turn his eyes to gold.

That night they attended a formal dinner with the local dignitaries before returning to the hotel, a large, tourist-oriented building, where they occupied the whole top floor. Dismissing her maid, Rosie got ready for bed, only to be surprised by a knock on the door.

Gerd?

And it *was* him. Her heart pumping into overdrive, she opened the door wider. 'Come in,' she said, hoping, hoping…and then hoping her eyes didn't betray her disappointment when he shook his head.

'Kelt's on the telephone,' he said. 'He's being put through to your phone, but I thought I'd warn you.'

'Warn me?' Instantly her confusion and hope were banished by fear. 'Is anything wrong?'

'No, but he has news for you.'

Bewildered, Rosie closed the door behind him and went back to the telephone, anxiously waiting for it to ring. When the sound burred into the quiet air she snatched up the receiver and said urgently, 'Kelt?'

'Rosie. I just thought I'd ring to tell you that Hani and I are expecting another baby.'

So relieved her knees felt weak, she collapsed onto the sofa. 'Oh, Kelt, that's wonderful! I did wonder while she was here—a couple of times she looked a bit peaky, but I thought maybe she was just tired. So when's the baby due?'

'In six months' time,' he said cheerfully.

'And you're still determined not to know what sex it is?'

'Absolutely. Hani says the desire to find out is the only thing that keeps her going through labour and the birth.'

The tenderness beneath the laughter in his voice made Rosie blink back tears, but she retorted, 'I don't believe that for a moment. Kelt, that's fantastic news! I'm so glad for you and for Hani. Can I say hello to her?'

'Actually she's in bed—no, she's all right, it's just that this one does seem to make her more tired than Rafi did. She's fine, and once you're back in the capital she'll ring and you can have a nice, long, feminine gossip.'

Rosie was laughing as she put the telephone back into the cradle, but her laughter faded, and unbidden, painful tears scalded her eyes and clogged her throat.

A familiar loneliness seeped through her, draining her of strength. She fought it with everything she could, but the tears came just the same, slowly falling. It was horrible to cry because Hani was going to have a baby.

She said aloud, 'No, it's not the baby.'

Her stupid tears were because Hani's children were the product of a union completely different from the marriage she had agreed to. When she was with Kelt and Hani it was impossible not to feel that unworthy envy of their profound and enduring love for each other. Their children were not symbols, not conceived to hold together a country.

For the first time Rosie wondered about the children

she and Gerd would have—would they hate living in the royal fishbowl, wish they'd been ordinary children born to ordinary parents and an ordinary life, able to work out their own destiny instead of being chained by tradition and the needs and expectations of millions of people?

The door opened and she turned, gulping back her tears, but it was too late. Gerd stood there, looking at her, his expression unreadable.

He walked into the room, closed the door behind him, and asked curtly, 'I knocked, but you didn't hear me. What's happened?'

'Nothing. I m-must be tired, I think,' she said, and wiped her eyes with one hand, looking around vainly for tissues.

Gerd came across and dropped an unused handkerchief into her lap. 'Use this,' he commanded, and walked over to the window.

She eyed his silhouette, big and lithe and forbiddingly distant, and her heart ached painfully in her breast. She loved him so much, yet it wasn't enough. If only she knew what it was that had made him decide to pull further and further away from her.

Without looking at her he said, 'Kelt told you his news?'

'Yes. It's lovely for them both, isn't it.'

'Is that why you were crying?'

Rosie flinched, then looked up anxiously. He'd turned and was watching her, but she could gain nothing from his expression. 'No,' she said too quickly. 'No, of course it's not. I'm thrilled for them. Hani's always said she wanted four children.'

She very much wanted to get to her feet, to draw herself up to her full height, but she didn't trust her legs to sustain her.

Anyway, she thought wearily, who was she kidding? Her full height was far from impressive.

Gerd said, 'I thought you'd got over Kelt.'

CHAPTER TEN

AT FIRST Gerd's words didn't register. Oh, Rosie heard them, but their meaning escaped her. 'What?'

He shrugged. 'It was always obvious you had a terrific crush on him.'

Rosie went white. It was so ludicrous an idea, so distant from what he must—surely—know already?

He went on, 'I admired the fact that you took his marriage to Hani so well. Was it because you knew you had to if you were going to be able to stay as close to him?'

Stunned, she said, 'No!'

His brows lifted. Dispassionately he went on, 'Because you must know by now that it's no use. He and Hani are not just husband and wife, they're lovers and soulmates.'

'I know that.' Afraid that she sounded defensive rather than convincing, she hurried on, 'But you're utterly wrong—couldn't be *more* wrong. I've never been in love with Kelt.'

He said tersely, 'Don't lie to me, Rosemary. I can cope with almost anything but lies, and we made a promise to be honest with each other, remember?'

A kind of wild hope mingled with enough anger to revive Rosie. Scrambling up, she said in a rough voice, 'I am being totally and completely honest with you! Of course I love Kelt—he's the big brother I didn't have, almost the *father* I didn't have! He's always been there for me. But *in love* with him? Where on earth did you get that idea?'

'I always knew you had a crush on him, but what clinched the fact was that the morning after we kissed—you and I—I came out onto the terrace at the homestead and saw you and Kelt walking up from the horse paddock.' His voice was chilling and detached. 'You hurled yourself into his arms and kissed him passionately.'

The colour drained from her skin, then flooded back. 'Oh, hell,' she said, and then started to laugh. It came too close to turning into a sob, but she managed to choke it back and meet his eyes defiantly. 'I was conducting a scientific experiment.'

He said blankly, 'What?'

'You heard.' She dragged in a breath and explained, 'You'd kissed me the night before, and—well, I was eighteen, but I'd never experienced anything like it before.' She spread her hands helplessly. 'Bells rang and skyrockets soared and stars exploded, and I was—I was *transported*. But I didn't know anything about grown-up kisses, and after worrying about it all night I decided to kiss Kelt and see if it happened all over again.'

Gerd's face was a mixture of emotions, none of which she could read. When he spoke his voice was hard and demanding. 'And what did happen?'

'Nothing,' she said simply. 'Nothing at all. It was

creepy, actually. And he was shocked until I told him
what I was doing it for, and then he laughed, but he told
me not to let myself get too interested in you because
I was far too young for you.'

'And he warned me off,' Gerd said harshly. 'We were
talking at cross purposes, of course, and I thought he
was interested in you.'

'He met Hani just after that, so you must have
realised then he wasn't,' she pointed out, a cautious
hope warming her heart.

'And you weren't in love with him?'

'No,' she said explosively. 'Of course I wasn't—
never have been! OK, I can understand how that
incident the night after we kissed must have looked—
I'll bet you thought I was a little tramp—but you must
have known that for me Kelt has only ever been my substitute brother.'

'It just seemed…logical. As you say, he looked out
for you. It would have been unusual if you didn't see
him as your particular hero. And you've always been
openly affectionate with him.'

'Well, yes, but it never meant anything! Surely—'

'When he and Hani left after the coronation you
were upset.'

'Of course, I was sad to see them go.' She was
talking too fast, the words tumbling over each other.
Afraid to allow herself to hope, she willed him to
believe her. 'I've been almost part of their family—a
sort of feckless younger sister, really.'

She scanned his handsome face for any sign of softening.

Not a thing. Still in that cool, judicial voice, he said,

'So why were you crying? I know Kelt rang you especially to tell you Hani is pregnant.'

Torn, Rosie almost put her emotions into words, but instinct warned her that it would be too dangerous to reveal her love for him, her abject reliance on him...

Lamely she said, 'There are happy tears as well as sad ones.'

'You can go,' he said abruptly.

Her heart turned to lead. She stared disbelievingly at him, overwhelmed with such anguish she could barely form the words. 'What...where?'

'Go home.' His words were delivered precisely, as icy as the metallic gold in his eyes.

'But I can't.' The foolish words barely registered in her mind. Pain sliced through her, numbing her brain, freezing her soul.

'You can. I'll organise a flight for you out of the country tomorrow.' And when she didn't move he said stonily, 'It's not going to work, so it's better to cut our losses now—before it's too late.'

Unable to respond, she stared at his ruthless, inflexible face.

He lifted one clenched fist and slammed it down on the windowsill. 'Go,' he said between his teeth. 'Go now, before—'

The flicker of hope encouraged her enough to say unevenly, 'Before what?'

'It doesn't matter. I'll ring your maid—'

She fanned that tiny glimmer of courage. This was too important for her not to fight for what she wanted. 'I need to know,' she said. 'Before what?'

'Before we end up hating each other.'

He wasn't looking at her, but his stance, his coiled strength, revealed a man with every muscle on the alert. 'Gerd,' she said, risking everything, 'tell me one thing— and remember our promise of honesty to each other. What do you feel for me?'

White-lipped, he stared at her. Rosie's breath stopped in her throat but she didn't dare back down. This was too important.

'You really want your pound of flesh, don't you?' he ground out eventually. 'Very well, then, you deserve to know. I love you.'

Rosie's incandescent blaze of joy was dowsed when he went on grimly, 'I love you desperately enough to have abandoned all my principles and more or less forced you into an engagement you didn't want, and a life I knew you hated the thought of. I told myself you couldn't respond so passionately to me if you didn't feel something more than lust. I knew it was less than love, but I was prepared to accept what I could get from you.'

How blind he was! Unsteadily she asked, 'So if you love me, why are you sending me away?'

CHAPTER ELEVEN

GERD'S head came up. In his most arrogant tone he said, 'I love you too much—I can't bear to see you unhappy. Your tears rip my heart out.'

Sheer ecstasy burst through Rosie like a nova, the glory of his words wiping out everything else. Unable to speak, she stared at him with dilating eyes.

Even more harshly he went on, 'I find in myself a certain distaste for pleading. But I have an even greater distaste of forcing you into a situation that causes you such misery.' He paused, then went on in the same level tone, 'Therefore I release you from your promise, and I wish you every happiness in the future.'

Gazing at his face—still pale beneath the tan, its framework boldly angular and forceful—she realised she'd managed to hide her feelings so well he had no idea of them. Somehow she had to convince him that his love, given with such reluctance, was matched and returned by her.

'Gerd, you *idiot*!' she said when she could control her voice. 'I was crying because Hani is pregnant, and I wasn't.'

He looked at her as though she were mad. 'What has that to do with anything?'

'I envy them like crazy, and I was wishing it was the same for us—that no-holds-barred kind of love and trust and respect.' Freed from anguish now, she said, 'I love you! How could you not know that? And if you send me away, I'll probably end up like my mother.'

'What the hell do you mean by that?' he demanded. 'You're nothing like your mother.'

She took a deep breath. 'Maybe not, but she did love my father in the beginning.'

'So she says,' he said caustically, and then, 'And what on earth has she to do with us?'

'I believe her,' Rosie told him. 'He couldn't return her love, so she left him. If you send me away I won't set off on a useless search for a love to replace the one I can't have. But I'll never marry anyone else, never love anyone as I love you. So if you don't want me to be your wife and have your children—'

'Don't *want* you?' he demanded in a voice she'd never heard before. 'I want you so much it's eating my heart out.' He made a quick, unconsidered gesture and said something low and angry before striding across the room towards her.

Not knowing what to expect, Rosie quivered, but she held her head high and met his eyes without flinching. Everything, she thought, hinged on these moments. Her whole life…

He stopped a pace away. In a raw, undisciplined voice he said, 'I don't dare believe you.'

'I'm feeling the same way.' She reached out a hand and laid it on his chest, welcoming the solid thunder of his life-force beneath her palm with a relief so intense it made her giddy.

From some final reserve of strength she summoned a smile. 'If you love me, why on earth have you kept away from me ever since we became engaged?'

His hand came up to cover hers and hold it clamped beneath his. She saw belief light his eyes to fire, relax the stark lines of his face, and joy lifted her so high she felt she was flying.

Although Gerd didn't smile, there was a note of humour in his voice when he said, 'Because I'm an idiot! Right at the start, you were so determined to keep our affair without strings that I was sure you couldn't love me.'

'I didn't want you to know I loved you. It seemed so—so *needy*! Especially,' she accused with spirit, 'when you so clearly didn't love me!'

He laughed deeply and began to pull her towards him, his eyes narrowing in the way she'd come to recognise. Her pulse beat heavily, erratically, in her ears.

When they were so close she could feel the warmth of his body, he said, 'But I did—and do—love you. And I want you to be needy where I'm concerned. Because I need you more than the breath in my body, more than anything I have ever coveted.'

'I wish you'd told me,' she said huskily.

His smile was brief and sardonic. 'I wish I'd had the courage,' he admitted. 'Blame it on my pride. I hoped that passion would be enough to break your reliance on Kelt. And that once you had learned to trust me you might learn to love me.'

She shook her head, no longer embarrassed by the

bob of her curls around her face. 'Even after seeing me kiss him, I don't know how you could mistake my feelings for Kelt for anything more serious than affection!'

'I was jealous,' he admitted with a wry glance. 'Jealous people don't reason terribly well, and when I'm thinking about you logic and common sense seem to fly out the window. Even when my plan seemed to be working, there was always that stab of jealousy, although I was happy on the island, and you seemed to be too.'

'Oh, yes,' she sighed, colouring. 'Until I got too bold,' she said ruefully.

His swift smile was sexy and reminiscent. 'I liked what you did very much. One day—or night—you'll have to repeat it.' He sobered then, and went on, 'And then I blew it. When I saw the chance to make you mine I couldn't resist. For the first time ever I didn't even care about Carathia; I just used it ruthlessly to persuade you. But you fought the idea with everything you had, and I realised that I'd been fooling myself about your feelings. You truly didn't want to marry me.'

'Oh, no,' she said, her voice trembling. 'I desperately want to marry you. I just didn't want it to be the *sensible* thing to do—a marriage for reasons of state was so cold, so impersonal.'

He gave a snort. 'Impersonal?'

Rosie frowned up at him. 'Well, you made it seem so,' she said forthrightly. 'I wanted to marry you because we loved each other enough to spend the rest of our lives together. It hurt to think it was for convenience.'

'Convenience?' he said incredulously. 'You've thrown my life into disarray, come between me and everything I've been brought up to believe were the most important things in my life, and you call it *convenient*?' He brushed an errant curl back from her face. 'I've never come across a *less* convenient woman. If I could take you to bed right now I'd show you exactly how I feel, but I don't dare do anything—in fact, I shouldn't even be touching you—because in ten minutes or so I'm due to take a call from the Chief Minister about the latest news on the economic fallout, and if I do more than kiss the tip of your nose I won't make it.'

'Far be it from me to keep you away from affairs of state,' she said demurely and stepped back.

'But after that,' he threatened, eyes hot with promise, 'all bets are off.'

Laughing, Rosie watched him go, then hugged herself with incandescent joy. It was too much to take in. After all the pain, the resolution had been so simple, so miraculously inevitable.

She went across to the window and looked out at the mountains. This place would always be precious to her because Gerd had confessed his love for her here.

Somewhere up on those high peaks the white lily bloomed—a link with New Zealand's high country. And on the island in the sunny Adriatic, myrtle bloomed around Aphrodite's temple—another link.

Appropriate that they should be flowers. Her desire for a flower shop seemed a distant, rapidly fading dream now, one she didn't regret. Loving Gerd was enough. And as his wife she'd look for a chance to do something in her favoured field.

She let the drape fall and settled down to write to Hani. If she hadn't loved her before, she thought as she sent the email, she'd love her now for being the—albeit unwitting—cause of this delicious happiness.

Two hours later Gerd came back to a supper table set for two with candles and flowers. He examined the table then said calmly, 'When is this being served?'

'In half an hour,' Rosie said. 'I thought we should drink some champagne first, so I told the butler to find the very best vintage in the cellar.'

Gerd checked the bottle. 'Ah, yes, that's perfect,' he said, and allowed his eyes to linger on her. She was dressed in a silky little shift, her hair pulled back into a ridiculous bobble of curls at the back to reveal the tender, innocent nape of her neck.

He said suddenly, 'Twelve years seemed such a hell of a difference when you were eighteen and I was thirty. It didn't seem so much a couple of hours ago, but right now you look like youth and joy and delight, and that makes me feel old and jaded and rakish.'

'You're none of those things,' she said indignantly. 'Shall we make another promise to each other? Shall we decide never to talk about the difference in ages again? I don't care about it and I don't see why you should.' She laughed up at him, the sunshiny girl he'd fallen in love with so many years before, and said, 'I plan to keep you young, anyway.'

Gerd's doubts fled, leaving him with a deep, intense joy he'd never thought to experience, a feeling of utter rightness. 'I'm more than happy to drink to that,' he said, and popped the cork on the champagne bottle. As he handed her one of the flutes he said, 'I think I must have fallen in love with you when I first kissed you.'

Rosie took a tiny sip. 'If you did, you wasted an awful lot of time before you did anything about it, and even then you had to be seduced into it.'

'*I* seduced *you*,' he said promptly, the hawk eyes gleaming gold. 'As for wasting time—no, I don't think so. You were a child. The years between us put me very definitely in the too-old category. Now they don't matter so much.'

'They don't matter at all,' she said quietly. 'The only thing in the world that does matter is that you love me and I love you. And I will love you forever.'

In the raw, stripped voice of deepest emotion, Gerd said, 'We're well matched, then, because that's exactly how long I plan to love you.'

Later, much later, when they were lying in bed entwined in the delicious, languorous aftermath of passion, Rosie smoothed a hand over his shoulder. 'I'm sorry I bit you. I didn't mean to.'

'Honourable scars,' he said complacently. 'You can bite me any time you want to. Just don't break the skin.'

After she'd kissed the marks better she asked, 'Why have you been so aloof and cold?'

He hugged her closer, and she felt his body tense against her. 'Because I was trying—too late and rather foolishly—to keep what was left of my mind clear during the year it's going to take us to get married.' His chest lifted as he laughed quietly. 'For all the good it did me. And partly to give you room—you were not happy, and I knew I'd forced you into this. I thought you needed time.'

'I needed *you*,' she told him trenchantly. 'Are we going to have to be discreet until we're married?'

'I'm afraid so.'

Rosie shivered as he ran a far from discreet hand over her. 'It's going to be hard,' she said thoughtfully.

'We'll manage.'

She held his hand still. 'When you proposed to me you said I'd be a good wife for you and good for Carathia too. What made you think that?'

After a pause he said, 'I love you, so I knew you'd be a good wife for me. As for Carathia—that's a bit more subtle, but people instinctively like you and enjoy your company. And you're intelligent and beautiful and kind and sensible. What country could ask for more?'

'I hope I can do it,' she said seriously. 'I don't know anything about being a Grand Duchess. I don't want to let you—or the Carathians—down.'

'You won't.' He held her against him, his voice so positive she allowed herself to relax and believe him. 'My grandfather was a New Zealander; he had no idea how to be the husband of the Grand Duchess, but the Carathians adored him. They're more than ready to adore another Kiwi. And you'll have my complete and utter support.'

Rosie said goodbye to the last of her fears. 'So when did you actually decide to marry me?' she asked, wriggling into a more comfortable position against him.

'You're not going to like this,' he said drily.

'Tell me just the same.'

'When I realised you'd been a virgin. It was obviously something you had believed important enough to preserve. Yet you had given it to me.'

Brows wrinkled, Rosie thought about that. 'So your proposal was a—some sort of recompense?'

'I'm getting myself further and further into quick-sand,' he said half-humorously. 'No. I hoped the gift of your virginity meant you felt more for me than casual lust.'

'*Casual?*' she asked on a choked laugh. 'If you thought that was casual…'

He smiled. 'And I suppose I should confess I couldn't bear the thought of anyone else making love to you. The thought of anyone else taking what had been mine filled me with a very uncomfortable posses-siveness.' He cupped her chin, tilting her head so that he could see her face. 'You don't seem shocked.'

No, because he was Gerd, Grand Duke of Carathia, and although he lived in the twenty-first century he hadn't entirely shaken off the high-handed attitudes of his ancestors. 'Only a little bit,' she teased.

'And now it's my turn to ask a question. Why were you so convinced I didn't—would never—love you?'

Rosie had rarely revealed her feelings, not even to her friends. She hesitated then looked up at him. This was Gerd, and he loved her.

She said, 'I think it must be that I grew up believing I wasn't lovable. My mother left me, and my father was away so often it sometimes felt as though he'd just abandoned me to the housekeeper. Not that I suffered— Mrs Jameson was always good to me. Alex was away at school for most of the time and the age gap was too big for us to be friends. When I got older, I lived for those holidays at Kiwinui. Kelt became a sort of surro-gate brother or father; I felt valued by him.'

Gerd said in a voice that made her cold, 'Apart from Kelt, we were selfish bastards, all of us.'

'No, you weren't,' she objected. 'I was much younger, and a girl—why would any of you want me tagging along? You were all kind; Kelt taught me to swim, you taught me to ride and Alex showed me how to play chess. And your grandmother was lovely. Even my father loved me in his own way, I think.' Her smile was tinged with sadness. 'He just loved other things more.'

Gerd said, 'I should have understood your basic insecurity.'

Heart overflowing, Rosie looked at him. 'How could you? I didn't even understand it myself. My mother's history of affairs gone wrong taught me that passion didn't mean love. But without realising it I must have decided that love was too hard, probably impossible— that I had no right to expect it. So I didn't.'

Gerd lay back on the pillows, his expression sombre. 'I kept thinking—she must know I love her. It has to be so obvious. Kelt knew, Alex knew, Hani knew—how could you not realise it? Yet there was always a barrier, a wall I couldn't breach however often and passionately we made love. And I knew damned well you only wanted an affair.'

She flushed. 'I thought I was being sensible,' she admitted, adding swiftly, 'At least I accepted that it would hurt when it was over!'

Gerd showed his teeth in a smile without humour. 'I suppose it was my damned pride that kept me silent. Two complete idiots,' he said. 'We deserve each other. I knew I was in deep trouble when the prospect of a child gave me an excuse for bulldozing you into agreeing to marry me.'

Rosie's snort was followed by a reluctant admission. 'So while I was angsting over whether or not to marry you and suffering because you didn't love me, you were gloating.'

'Hell, no. I was delighted when you agreed—until I realised exactly what I was doing to you. Because even before we went back to the capital, you started to retreat.'

'*I* retreated?' she exclaimed, startling them both by thumping him in the solar plexus. 'You never came near me—after I said I'd marry you, every night you kissed me on the forehead and left me at my bedroom door. What was I supposed to think?'

He jackknifed up, his face aggressive. Reaching for her, he said grimly, 'I was giving you time to get used to everything—to me as your future husband and Carathia as the place you were going to live—without passion clogging your brain.'

She held herself stiffly away. 'Did it clog yours?'

'Yes,' he said savagely, and kissed her. Then he let her go and got up off the bed, his shoulders set.

Rosie sat up and stared at him. 'I'm glad,' she said abruptly.

Without turning he said, 'It worried the hell out of me because it had never happened before. I told myself I was doing the right thing for Carathia, but I hated it that whenever I looked at you, touched you—hell, even thought of you—it drove any thoughts of duty to my country clear out of my mind.'

'Good.' His words satisfied her last shred of reservation.

He turned to look at her, sleekly golden-ivory in his bed, embedded in his heart. 'It no longer matters,' he said starkly. 'I know now that all I want, all I need, is you. Carathia will always be important to me, but you—you are at my heart's core, the one, infinitely loved constant in my life.'

Tall and tanned and leanly lithe, he filled her vision. Tears flooded her eyes, and she said in a shaken voice, 'And you are mine. Forever.'

'Forever,' he said like a vow. 'So now, would you like some more of that champagne?'

'No, I'd like something from a much better vintage,' she said sweetly, and laughed, holding out her arms as he tumbled her back onto the bed.

In his eyes she could see love and trust and passion, and she knew that for them this was the first day of their marriage, even though their vows had been informal and for their ears only.

They would have their big wedding to satisfy the good people of Carathia, but from now on they were joined in life and love.

After the wild carnival of bells that had rung her ears for days, Rosie greeted the silence of the villa with relief. Maria had met them at the door, beamed on them both and wished them every happiness, informed them at length of the food she'd left for them, and then departed, leaving them alone.

'Tired?' Gerd asked, slipping his arm around her shoulders.

'A bit,' she acknowledged, then gave a gasping little laugh when he picked her up. 'You won't be able to do this for much longer,' she murmured, gazing up into his face.

'Oh, I think I'll be able to manage three of you for some months yet,' he said, carefully negotiating the way to the bedroom.

'Twins,' she murmured, still dazed at the news the gynaecologist had given them only three days previously. She looked up at him, her gaze direct. 'We'll be careful of them, won't we? We'll make sure they have the kind of childhood neither of us had—a loving, happy, secure childhood, so they grow up confident and certain of themselves.'

Gerd's arms tightened around her as though she was infinitely precious. 'We will,' he said like a vow. 'I'm seriously thinking of banning all information about the birth so that no one will ever know—apart from you, me and the doctor who delivers them—which one arrives first. That should fool anyone who tries to resurrect that old legend.'

Rosie laughed. 'It should give Carathia breathing time, anyway,' she said. 'But I think your plans for education will do the trick better. By the time any question of the succession comes up—in fifty years from now, say—no one will remember the legend.'

He set her carefully down on the bed and looked at her, slim and glowing, her gold-flecked eyes warm with the love he no longer doubted.

That morning she'd walked towards him in a wedding gown, happiness radiating from her. This time they'd made their vows in public, and Carathia had celebrated the joy and commitment of their Grand Duke and his Duchess with festivities that would outlast the night, but here, in this house, in this room, they were man and woman, two lovers.

Husband and wife.

Gripped by emotion so intense he almost buckled under it, he sat down on the edge of the bed and bent to kiss her throat. Her perfume—soft, all woman—enveloped him, and her arms came around him and hugged him hard.

'How tired are you?' he asked, fighting down a fierce hunger.

Her laugh was slow and sensuous. 'Not too tired,' she whispered into his ear.

Rosie felt his body harden against her and, as they began the slow, deliciously sensual journey towards that passionate place reserved solely for them, she knew that, whatever the future brought, they would face it together. She and Gerd held each other's hearts in safe-keeping.

UNTOUCHED UNTIL MARRIAGE

BY
CHANTELLE SHAW

Chantelle Shaw lives on the Kent coast, five minutes from the sea, and does much of her thinking about the characters in her books while walking on the beach. She's been an avid reader from an early age. Her schoolfriends used to hide their books when she visited—but Chantelle would retreat into her own world, and still writes stories in her head all the time. Chantelle has been blissfully married to her own tall, dark and very patient hero for over twenty years, and has six children. She began to read Mills & Boon® novels as a teenager, and throughout the years of being a stay-at-home mum to her brood found romantic fiction helped her to stay sane! She enjoys reading and writing about strong-willed, feisty women, and even stronger-willed sexy heroes. Chantelle is at her happiest when writing. She is particularly inspired while cooking dinner, which unfortunately results in a lot of culinary disasters! She also loves gardening, walking, and eating chocolate (followed by more walking!). Catch up with Chantelle's latest news on her website: www.chantelleshaw.com.

CHAPTER ONE

ACCORDING to the private investigator he had hired, he would find his father's mistress here. Raul Carducci stepped out of his limousine and glanced along the quayside of the Cornish fishing village. Nature's Way—Health Foods and Herbal Remedies sat between an ice-cream parlour and a gift shop, both of which were shut and, from their abandoned air, would not open again until the start of the summer season.

Drizzle fell relentlessly from the leaden sky and he grimaced as he turned up his coat collar. The sooner he could return to Italy, where the spring sunshine was already warming the sparkling blue waters of Lake Bracciano, the better, he thought grimly. But he had come to Pennmar to follow the instructions set out in Pietro Carducci's will, and without further pause he strode towards the one shop in the parade that was open for custom.

Libby was so engrossed in studying the end-of-year financial report for Nature's Way that it took a few seconds for the sound of the windchimes which hung above the shop door to impinge on her brain. The chimes had not been a regular sound throughout the winter, she acknowledged ruefully as she lifted her eyes from the column of red figures in the accounts book. Customers had been few and far between after visitors to Pennmar had returned home at the end of the previous summer, and now the business was on the verge of bankruptcy.

Opening a health food shop in a remote Cornish village had been another of her mother's hare-brained schemes, Libby thought ruefully. The small inheritance from Libby's grandmother had quickly been swallowed up in refurbishing the shop, but her mother, with typical blind optimism, had been certain the business would be a success.

Thinking about Liz caused the familiar dull ache in Libby's chest, but a customer was waiting to be served, and she hurriedly pushed aside the beaded curtain that separated the back office from the shop. The man had his back to her, so that she was faced with formidably broad shoulders cloaked in a pale suede car coat. He was prowling restlessly around the shop, so tall that his head brushed against the roof beams, and Libby sensed the inherent strength of his big, powerful body.

'Can I help you?' she began brightly, but her smile faltered when the stranger swung round and trapped her with his piercing dark stare. He was not your average tourist, she realised. Indeed, there was nothing remotely average about this man. Hair as sleek and dark as a raven's wing was swept back from his brow. His chiselled features, razor-sharp cheekbones and a square chin were softened slightly by the sensual curve of his mouth, and his olive-gold skin gleamed like satin beneath the bright shop light. He was, beyond doubt, the most stunningly handsome man Libby had ever seen. She could not tear her gaze from him, and blushed when his eyes narrowed speculatively on her face.

Raul trailed his eyes over the shop-girl's purple patterned skirt and acid green top and shuddered. Bohemian chic might have featured on the Paris catwalks recently, but he preferred women to look elegant and groomed in haute couture. The tie-dyed hippy look did nothing for him.

But she was startlingly pretty, he conceded as he studied her oval face with its high cheekbones, surrounded by a mane of bright red curls that tumbled halfway down her back. Her vivid hair contrasted with her alabaster complexion, and even from a distance of a few feet away he could see the sprinkling of golden freckles across her nose and cheeks. Eyes the deep blue-green of the sea on a stormy day surveyed him from beneath long gold lashes, and from somewhere the unbidden idea slid into his head that her soft pink lips were infinitely kissable.

Frowning at this unwelcome train of thought, he lowered his gaze and winced at her lime-green tights and purple boots before his eyes were drawn back to her face. Her mouth was a fraction too wide, but that only seemed to enhance her appeal. Dressed in a designer gown rather than her garish outfit she would be exceptionally beautiful, Raul acknowledged, irritated by the unexpected tug of sexual interest that coiled in his gut.

His jaw tightened. His business was with his father's mistress, not this girl, and he suppressed the inappropriate urge to cover her lush mouth with his lips. 'I'm looking for Elizabeth Maynard,' he said abruptly.

The man's voice was deep-timbred, as rich and sensual as molten chocolate, and his pronounced accent was innately sexy. Italian, Libby hazarded a guess as she studied his golden skin and obsidian eyes. It was not every day that a drop-dead sexy man walked into the shop. He was, in fact, the only person to have entered Nature's Way all morning, she thought ruefully. Good manners dictated that she should answer him, but she had had an unconventional childhood, where hiding from loan sharks or speaking through the letterbox to the bailiffs while her mother escaped out of the bathroom window had been a frequent occurrence, and she was instinctively wary of strangers.

Another thought slipped into her head that caused her stomach to tie itself in a knot. True, the man did not look like a social worker—and she'd met plenty of those as a child—but what if he was here about Gino?

'Who are you?' she asked sharply.

Raul frowned. He had spent most of his life surrounded by servants whose sole duty was to please him and jump to his bidding without question. He saw no reason why he should explain himself to a shop-girl, and his eyes narrowed as he fought to control his impatience. 'My name is Raul Carducci.'

The girl drew a sharp breath and her eyes widened until they seemed to dominate her face. 'Pietro Carducci's son?' she faltered.

Raul stiffened with outrage. Had his father's mistress discussed the Carducci family with her staff? he wondered furiously. Had she boasted of her affair with a rich Italian aristocrat to the whole damned village?

He glared at the curtained doorway, trying to see if the owner of the shop was lurking behind it, but his view was obscured by the strings of gaudy plastic beads.

He gave an impatient shrug. '*Si*, Pietro Carducci was my father. But my business is with Ms Maynard—so if you would please inform her that I am here.' He could no longer contain the bitterness that had eaten away at him like a corrosive poison since he had been informed of the terms of his father's will, and he bit out savagely, 'No doubt she will be delighted when she learns that giving birth to my father's illegitimate son has ensured her a meal-ticket for life. She will no longer have to scrape a living from running *this* place,' he added, casting a disparaging glance at the array of health foods and potions, the stacks of decorative candles, and the smouldering joss-sticks that gave off a peculiar sickly scent as they burned. 'I fear, *signorina*, that you will soon have to look for another job.'

Libby stared at Raul Carducci in dumbstruck silence. Her mother had mentioned that Pietro had a son, but Liz's affair with her Italian lover had been no more than a brief holiday fling, and she had learned few details about his family. Her mum hadn't even realised that Pietro was the head of the world-famous Carducci Cosmetics company until she'd read an article in a magazine about him while she'd been waiting for an antenatal appointment, Libby thought bitterly. Liz had agonised over whether to tell her lover she was pregnant, but when she had finally written to him to inform him she had given birth to his child Pietro had not bothered to reply.

But although Pietro Carducci had not acknowledged his child, he must have told his older son about Gino,

Libby realised shakily. Raul's harsh words, *'my father's illegitimate son'*, filled her with a deep sense of unease. He sounded far from delighted about the existence of his half-brother. She did not know what to say, and while she hesitated the silence was broken by the jangling sound of the windchimes above the door.

Raul glanced round to see a woman manoeuvre a pushchair into the shop. 'Here we are, Gino, back in the warm,' the woman said cheerfully, her voice barely audible over the yells coming from beneath the buggy hood. She lifted the waterproof plastic cover, revealing the screwed up face of a screaming baby boy. 'All right, my lovely. I'll get you out in a second.'

Raul's eyes were drawn to the pushchair, and some indefinable emotion gripped him as he focused on the baby's olive skin and tight black curls. The woman had called the child Gino, and even though he was less than a year old there could be no mistaking his resemblance to his father. *Dio!* Raul thought numbly. He had been determined to demand a DNA test to prove the child's paternity, but there was no need. Indisputably this was Pietro Carducci's son.

He turned his attention to the woman, noting her ruddy cheeks, coarse brown hair and the lumpy figure shrouded in a beige coat. It seemed astounding that Pietro, whose love of classical beauty had led him to build a priceless art collection, had chosen this dowdy woman as his mistress—and it was even more impossible to imagine the woman working in a lap-dancing club!

Raul's mouth tightened as he recalled his meeting eight months ago with the lawyer his father had appointed as executor of his will.

"'This is the last will and testament of Pietro Gregorio Carducci,' Signor Orsini had read aloud. "'It is my wish that control of my company, Carducci Cosmetics, be shared equally between my adopted son, Raul Carducci, and my infant son and only blood heir Gino Maynard.'"

Seeing that Raul had been struck dumb by the revelation that Pietro had a secret child, the lawyer had continued reading. "'I leave to my two sons, Raul and Gino, equal share of the Villa Giulietta. It is my wish that Gino should grow up in the family home. His share of the company and the villa are to be held in trust for him until he is eighteen, and until he is of age it is my wish that his mother, Elizabeth Maynard, will live at the villa with him, and will have control of Gino's share of CC.'"

At that point Raul had sworn savagely, shocked beyond words at the news that he would not have sole control of the company he had been groomed for most of his life to run. He had found the expression 'blood heir' deeply wounding. He had been seven years old when Pietro and Eleonora Carducci had collected him from an orphanage in Naples and taken him to live at the Villa Giulietta. Pietro had always insisted that his adopted son was his rightful heir, who would one day inherit Carducci Cosmetics. Father and son had been close, and the bond between them had deepened after Eleonora's death ten years ago.

That was why it was so utterly unbelievable that Pietro had had a secret life, Raul thought bitterly. The man he had called Papa, the man he had wept for at

Pietro's funeral, was suddenly a stranger who had deliberately withheld the fact that he had a mistress and a baby son.

'There is a clause in your father's will that I think you will find interesting,' Signor Orsini had murmured. 'Pietro has stated that if Ms Maynard should marry before Gino is eighteen, control of the child's share of CC would pass to you until he is of age. I imagine Pietro made this stipulation to protect the company should Ms Maynard make an unsuitable marriage,' the lawyer had added.

'Carducci Cosmetics will need all the protection it can get if I am forced to share the running of it with a lap-dancer,' Raul had growled savagely. 'My father must have been out of his mind.'

At that, Bernardo Orsini had shaken his head. 'Despite the fact that Pietro had been diagnosed with an aggressive brain tumour, I am absolutely certain that he was of sound mind when he made his will. His main concern was for his infant son.'

Raul dragged his mind back to the present and stared at the woman who had entered the shop. According to the lawyer, Elizabeth Maynard had worked as a lap-dancer at a club called the Purple Pussy Cat, but six months ago she had disappeared from her South London flat, owing her landlord several thousand pounds in rent arrears. Raul had visualised his father's mistress as a bleached blonde tart, but even though the drab woman who was lifting the baby out of the pushchair looked nothing like he had imagined, he still balked at the idea of her moving into the Villa Guilietta, while the prospect of sharing control of Carducci Cosmetics with her would be frankly amusing if he had not been consumed by rage and resentment at his father's dying wishes.

'I knew he'd stop crying the minute he saw his mummy,' the woman said cheerfully, and handed the child over to the young shop assistant.

Shock ricocheted through Raul. He stared—at first uncomprehendingly, and then with a growing sense of rage—as the flame-haired girl kissed away the tears from the baby's cheeks and settled him comfortably on her hip. His brain finally accepted what his eyes had seen.

'*You* are Elizabeth Maynard?' he demanded harshly.

The girl lifted her head and met his gaze. 'I am— although most people call me Libby.'

Raul did not give a damn what most people called her. He was still struggling to comprehend that this stunningly pretty girl had been his father's mistress. She could not be more than in her early twenties, and Pietro had been in his mid-sixties. Revulsion swept through him, and with it another emotion that filled him with self-disgust when he recognised it as jealousy. *Dio!* No wonder his father had kept quiet about this flame-haired siren. He had no problem picturing *her* working in a lap-dancing club, Raul thought as his eyes focused on the rounded contours of her breasts outlined beneath her stretchy top. An image flashed in his mind of her dancing in a skimpy costume, tossing her mane of fiery hair over her shoulders as she unfastened her bra and slowly let it drop…

He bit back an oath, infuriated by his body's involuntary reaction to his wayward thoughts. '*You* are Gino's mother?' He sought clarification, aware that he had initially jumped to the conclusion that the older woman had been his father's lover.

Libby hesitated. Margaret was making a show of hunting through her handbag for something, but she was conscious of the older woman's avid curiosity. Her neighbour was a kindly woman, who often babysat Gino, but Margaret was an inveterate gossip. If she overheard that Libby was not Gino's mother, as everyone in Pennmar believed, but his sister, the news would be all around the village within the hour.

She recalled those first few terrible days after her mum had died. They had been living in London, packing for the move to Cornwall and the new life they had planned, when Liz had collapsed and never regained consciousness. Gino had only been three months old, and Libby had struggled to cope with her shock and grief while caring for her orphaned baby brother. Her friend Alice, a trainee lawyer, had been an invaluable help, but she had also warned Libby of the potential problems caused by Liz's death.

'If your mum didn't make a will and appoint you as Gino's guardian, then technically he becomes the responsibility of the State, and Social Services will decide who should care for him,' Alice had explained. 'Just because you are Gino's half-sister it doesn't mean they will automatically choose you.'

'But I've helped to care for him since the day he was born,' Libby had argued, 'especially when Mum was so tired after his birth.'

Liz's long labour had left her exhausted. At the busy hospital where Gino had been born no one had mentioned the potential dangers of deep vein thrombosis, and when Liz had felt unusually breathless Libby had been unaware that it was a sign her mother had developed a blood clot which had lodged in one of her lungs.

Liz had died before the ambulance had arrived. There had been no time for mother and daughter to say goodbye, no chance for Liz to stipulate who should care for Gino, but Libby was utterly determined to bring up her baby brother and love him as her mother would have done. She had moved to Pennmar a week after Liz's funeral, to the shop they had set up with the money left by Libby's grandmother. Everyone in the village assumed that Gino was her baby. After Alice's warning that Social Services might take him from her, Libby had encouraged that misapprehension, and now she was reluctant to reveal the truth in front of Margaret.

She would explain the situation to Raul Carducci later, she decided, her sense of unease intensifying when she glanced at his hard face and saw no glimmer of warmth in his dark eyes. 'Yes, I'm Gino's mother,' she said quietly, a shiver running down her spine when his expression changed from cool disdain to savage contempt.

He flicked his eyes over her, and Libby felt acutely conscious that she had bought her top in a charity shop and had made her skirt from an old curtain. 'You are much younger than I had expected,' he said bluntly. He paused and then drawled softly, 'I'm curious to know what first attracted you to my sixty-five-year old billionaire father, Ms Maynard?'

His inference was plain. Raul thought she was a gold-digger who had had an affair with a wealthy older man for his money, Libby realised, colour storming into her cheeks. But she could not defend herself when Margaret had given up all pretence of searching in her handbag and was unashamedly listening to the conversation. Raul Carducci was an arrogant jerk, she thought angrily, her hot temper instantly flaring. 'Forgive me, but I don't think my relationship with your father is any of your business,' she told him tightly, her eyes flashing fire.

She could sense that Margaret was practically bursting with curiosity, and she forced a casual smile as she turned to the older woman. 'Thanks for taking Gino out. The doctor says that the sea air will help his chest.'

'You know I'll have him any time.' Margaret paused and glanced from Libby to her foreign-looking visitor. 'I could stay and mind him now, if you and the gentleman have things to discuss?'

Yes, and Margaret would waste no time sharing what she'd overheard with the rest of the village, Libby thought dryly. 'Thanks, but I must give Gino his lunch, and I don't want to take up any more of your time,' she said brightly. 'Could you put the '"Closed" sign on the door on your way out?'

Libby contained her impatience while a disgruntled looking Margaret ambled out of the shop, but the moment the older woman had shut the door she glared at Raul. 'I assume there is a reason for your visit, Mr Carducci, and you are not here merely to make disgusting innuendos?'

The unfamiliar sharpness of her voice unsettled Gino. He gave her a startled look and his lower lip trembled. Libby joggled him on her hip and patted his back, still furious with the man who was looking down his arrogant nose at her as if she were something unpleasant on the bottom of his shoe.

'Before you say anything else, I'd better explain—'
She broke off as Gino let out a wail and began to squirm
in her arms. At ten months old he was surprisingly
strong, and she struggled to hold him, dismay filling her
when his cries turned into the familiar hacking cough
that shook his frame. Immediately Libby's attention was
focused exclusively on the baby, and she glanced dis-
tractedly at Raul. 'I must get him a drink. Excuse me,'
she muttered, and hurried through the beaded curtain
into the back part of the shop.

She took a beaker of juice the fridge, but Gino was
crying and coughing too much for him to be able to
drink. He was still wearing his thick outdoor suit, and
his face was turning steadily redder as he overheated.
Frantically Libby tried to unzip the suit with one hand
and hold a hysterical, wriggling Gino in the other, conscious that Raul had followed her into the room and was
watching her efforts.

'Here—let me hold him while you undress him,' he
said abruptly, stepping forward and lifting the baby out
of her arms before she could protest.

Gino was so startled that his cries subsided, but he
was going through a particularly clingy stage at the
moment and disliked strangers. Libby quickly tugged
down the zip of his suit, waiting for him to renew his
yells, but to her amazement he gave a little snuffle and
stared fixedly at Raul's face.

'You must have a magic touch. Normally he screams
blue murder if someone he doesn't know tries to hold
him,' she muttered, feeling faintly chagrined as she
freed Gino from the suit and he did not even glance at
her. 'But Gino is a Gemini, and people born under that
star sign are often very intuitive,' she added earnestly.

'Perhaps he instinctively recognises that there is a connection between the two of you. You are his brother—
well, half-brother,' she amended, when Raul's dark
brows rose sardonically.

'There is no blood link between us,' he informed her
dismissively. 'Pietro was my adoptive father.' He saw
the flash of surprise in Libby's eyes and wondered why
he had felt the need to reveal that he had no biological
link to the father of her child. The idea that she and
Pietro had shared a bed... He snapped a door shut on
that particular image, infuriated that his eyes seemed
to have a magnetic attraction to her breasts.

Elizabeth Maynard had been his father's mistress and
had borne him a child; it was inconceivable that he could
be attracted to her. He forced his gaze up from her lush
curves, moulded so enticingly beneath her clingy top,
and stared at her face, his body stirring as he focused
on the perfect cupid's bow of her mouth. Irritation with
himself made his voice terse as he said abruptly, 'It's
more likely the child was crying because he was scared
you might drop him.'

'Of course I wasn't going to drop him,' Libby snapped
furiously. She snatched Gino back into her arms and held
the beaker of juice to his lips, frowning when she heard
the horrible rasping sound in his chest as he breathed.
'I need to take him upstairs and give him his next dose
of antibiotic,' she said edgily.

She glared at Raul who was leaning against her desk,
unashamedly reading the financial report for Nature's
Way. He dominated the small room, tall, dark and so
disturbingly sexy that looking at him made her heart
race uncomfortably fast. She hated the way he unsettled
her and she wanted him to leave.

She crossed the room and slammed the accounts book shut. 'Why are you here?' she demanded bluntly. 'I read in the papers that Pietro had died. But that was more than six months ago, and in all that time no one from the Carducci family has ever been in contact.'

Raul gave her a look of haughty disdain. 'That is hardly my fault. You did a runner from your last address without paying the rent, and it has taken this long to find you. I am not here through choice, I assure you, Ms Maynard,' he told her scathingly. 'But my father stipulated in his will that he wanted his son to be brought up at the family home in Lazio—and so I have come to take Gino to Italy.'

CHAPTER TWO

FOR a few seconds Libby was too stunned to speak. Her friend Alice's warning reverberated in her head. 'Your mother didn't appoint you as Gino's guardian, and although you are his half-sister, legally you have no rights regarding his upbringing.'

If Liz had known she was going to die, of *course* she would have appointed her daughter as Gino's guardian, Libby thought desperately. But, as Alice had pointed out, she had no proof of her mother's wishes. It was ironic that Pietro Carducci, who had not even acknowledged his son's birth, should have made provision for Gino in his will. If the matter went to court, it seemed likely that Pietro's wishes would be taken into account, and possible that Raul would be granted custody of Gino and be allowed to take him to Italy.

Her heart was pounding with panic but one crucial thought stood out in Libby's mind. Raul believed that Gino was *her* baby. Clearly he had no idea that there had been two Elizabeth Maynards, or that the woman who had conceived Pietro Carducci's child as a result of their brief affair had died only a month after Pietro had passed away. She recalled the expression of disgust on Raul's face when he had asked her what had attracted her to his older, wealthy father. He believed she was a gold-digger, but it was better he thought that than discovered that she was Gino's half-sister and had no legal claim on him, she thought wildly.

She frowned, suddenly remembering something Raul had said. 'Why did you accuse me of owing rent on the flat where we—I,' she hastily amended, knowing she must hide the fact that she had lived in London with her mother, 'lived before I moved to Cornwall? Of course I paid the rent.'

Raul's eyes narrowed at Libby's belligerent tone. He was not used to being spoken to in that manner by anyone, and certainly not by a woman. His staff, both at the Villa Giulietta and at Carducci Cosmetics, treated him with the utmost respect, and the women he mixed with socially tended to hang on his every word. To his mind, a woman's role was to make light conversation, to provide soothing company after a day of hard bargaining in the boardroom and to grace his bed so that he could enjoy mutually satisfying sex without the complications of emotional involvement.

Elizabeth Maynard—or Libby, as she called herself, would be a far from soothing companion, he thought as he stared at her mass of wild red curls and stormy eyes. Her mouth was set in an angry line that challenged him to kiss her until her lips softened and parted and allowed him to slide his tongue between them. He inhaled sharply, and it took all of his formidable will-power to ignore the dictates of his body and listen to the cool logic of his brain. She was Pietro's tart, who had had no compunction about seducing a much older man with her nubile young body, and no way was the son going to repeat the mistakes of his father, Raul assured himself grimly.

'Your landlord said that you were frequently behind with the rent, and when you moved away suddenly you left owing him several thousand pounds,' he said coldly. 'Why would he lie?'

'To get back at me because I refused to sleep with him, most likely,' Libby muttered bitterly. 'He was a horrible old man. I used to take him the rent money regularly every month and he never missed an opportunity to try and grope me. He made it clear that he would reduce the rent if I "paid" him in another way.'

'Are you saying you weren't tempted?' Raul queried derisively. 'I assume you make a habit of sleeping with older men for financial gain. You certainly struck gold with my father,' he continued, ignoring her furious gasp. 'Having his child was a clever move, which I guess you thought would ensure you a meal ticket for life. You thought right; it has,' he said contemptuously. 'Pietro has granted you the right to bring up your son at the Carducci family villa, and take control of fifty percent of Carducci Cosmetics until Gino is eighteen.'

Raul gave a harsh laugh when Libby stared at him open-mouthed. He reached inside his coat and retrieved a sheaf of papers. 'Congratulations. You've hit the jackpot,' he drawled sarcastically as he thrust the documents at Libby.

She stared dazedly at the first page and saw that it was headed 'The last will and testament of Pietro Gregorio Carducci.' Conscious that Raul was watching her, she ran her eyes down the page until she came to a paragraph which stated that Gino's mother, Elizabeth

Maynard, should live at the Villa Giulietta, with all her expenses and living costs paid for out of the estate, until her son came of age.

It was astounding. She could barely comprehend it. But before she could read any further Gino made a grab for the documents. He was clearly fascinated by the white paper, and, remembering how he had shredded an important letter from the bank the previous day, Libby hastily handed the will back to Raul.

'So you mean you want me to live in Italy with Gino?' she said slowly, relief flooding through her that Raul hadn't sought her out to take the baby away from her. Not that she would have allowed him to, she thought fiercely. Gino was the only person she had left in the world, and she was prepared to do anything to keep him—even if that meant pretending that he was her son.

'I can't think of anything I'd like less,' Raul said, in a coldly arrogant tone that made her feel about two feet high. 'But unfortunately I have no say in the matter. My father clearly stated his wish that Gino and his mother should live at the Villa Giulietta.'

Libby glanced at her baby brother and felt her heart melt when he stared solemnly back at her with his big brown eyes. His light olive skin and mass of dark curls spoke of his Italian heritage, but he had her mother's smile, she thought, swallowing the sudden lump in her throat. Liz had adored her baby for the few short months she had spent with him. It seemed so desperately cruel that Gino had been robbed of his mother before he'd ever had a chance to know her, but she would take Liz's place, Libby vowed silently. Her little brother was her only link with her mum. She loved him just as deeply as if he was her own child, and she was determined to do what was best for him.

But would taking him to live in Italy, with Raul, who clearly resented his half-brother, really be in Gino's best interest? she brooded. Her doubts increased when she glanced at the autocratic features of the handsome Italian. 'We have things to talk about,' she said hesitantly. 'Perhaps we could meet in a day or two...'

Raul frowned impatiently. 'I don't have a day or two to waste hanging around here. And anyway, what is there to discuss? My father named Gino as his heir, and I can't believe you would turn down the chance to get your hands on his inheritance. Presumably you deliberately fell pregnant in the first place so that you could demand a massive payout in child maintenance?'

'I did no such thing,' Libby retorted angrily. Although he did not know it, Raul was insulting her mother, not her, and if she hadn't been holding Gino she would have slapped that arrogant smirk off his face. Far from deliberately falling pregnant, Liz had been utterly shocked when she had discovered that she had conceived a baby as a result of her holiday romance with a charming Italian.

'Gino was unplanned, it's true, but he was very wanted,' she told Raul huskily, remembering how Liz's shock had turned to delight that she was going to be a mother again. 'My mo—' She stopped in her tracks and continued hurriedly, 'Your father was informed of Gino's birth, but he never acknowledged his son and I never expected anything from him.'

Raul gave a disbelieving snort. 'My father was an honourable man who would never have turned his back on his child.' He frowned as a thought occurred to him. 'When was Gino born?'

'The seventh of June. He's ten months old now.'

'Pietro was very ill by June of last year, and he died in August,' Raul told her flatly. 'An inoperable brain tumour had been diagnosed the previous October and it grew rapidly. Did you know about his illness?' he asked Libby sharply.

She shook her head. Pietro must have fallen ill soon after her mother had returned from the Mediterranean cruise she had won. The cruise on which Liz had fallen in love with a gorgeous Italian, she had confessed to Libby, with a faintly embarrassed smile after all she had said over the years about the unreliability of men and the foolishness of losing your heart to one.

Liz had been devastated when she had heard nothing more from Pietro after the cruise—especially when she'd discovered that she had conceived his child. 'I've done it again, Libby,' she'd said tearfully, when she had emerged from the bathroom clutching a pregnancy test. 'I trusted a man and now I'm left with his baby— the same as happened with your bloody father. You'd think I'd have learned that all men are selfish bastards, wouldn't you?'

Libby had hated Pietro for hurting her mum, but according to Raul his father had returned to Italy from the cruise to learn that he was terminally ill. Perhaps he hadn't felt able to confide such devastating news to Liz, she thought, her heart aching for her mother and the man she had loved. When Liz had written to her lover to tell him of Gino's birth Pietro had been weeks from death, and maybe hadn't had the strength to reply. But surely the fact that he had included Liz and Gino in his will meant that he had cared for her mum after all?

Gino had been sitting quietly in her arms, but now he began to cough again, his chest heaving with the effort. 'I thought you said he was due some medication?' Raul commented, his frown deepening. He had as much experience of children as he had with aliens from another planet, but this baby sounded seriously unwell.

'He is.' Concern for Gino overrode Libby's reluctance to invite Raul up to the flat. 'You'd better come up,' she muttered.

'What's wrong with him?' Raul demanded when they reached the first floor landing.

Libby paused with her hand on the living room door. 'He had an illness called bronchiolitis, which is fairly common in babies, but he developed pneumonia and was very unwell. He was in hospital for a few weeks and now he can't seem to shake off this cough. The doctor said that the living conditions here don't help,' she confessed, recalling how the GP in the village had warned her that the mildew growing on the damp walls of the flat produced spores which Gino inhaled and were the worst thing for his lungs.

She pushed open the door, and stifled a groan at the scene of chaos that met her. Raul Carducci's unexpected visit had made her forget the disaster that had occurred the previous evening, when the bulge in her bedroom ceiling had given way and rain water had gushed through. Luckily, her friend Tony had been there. They had been sharing a bottle of wine while Libby had talked over her financial worries and the likelihood that she would have to close Nature's Way, and together they had grabbed her belongings and carried them into the sitting room, out of the deluge that had flooded her room. Tony had managed to block the hole to stop any more water pouring through, but he'd got soaked to the skin and had had to change into the sports gear that he kept in his car.

Her canvases were stacked against the sofa and her clothes heaped on the floor. Her underwear was on top of the pile, Libby noticed, flushing with embarrassment when she saw Raul's eyes rest on the numerous pairs of brightly coloured knickers. He glanced slowly around the room and she knew he was taking in the peeling wallpaper and the blue mould which had appeared on the wall again, despite the fact that she constantly scrubbed the area with fungal remover.

There had been so sign of damp when she and Liz had viewed the shop and flat the previous spring. Then, the place had seemed bright and airy, newly decorated, and with the windows flung open to allow the sea breeze to drift in. It was only during the wet winter that Libby had realised the rooms had been wallpapered to hide the patches of mildew.

She was irritated by the expression of distaste on Raul's face. It was clear from the superb quality of his clothes that he was very wealthy, and no doubt his home in Italy was a palace compared to the flat, but it was all she could afford—and actually even that was doubtful, she realised dismally when she remembered the letter from the bank that had informed her they would not increase her overdraft.

'Sorry about the mess,' she muttered. 'My bedroom was flooded last night and we piled all my things in here.'

'We?' Raul looked pointedly at the baby in Libby's arms.

'My friend Tony was here.' She followed Raul's gaze to the three empty wine bottles and two glasses on the coffee table, and watched his expression change from distaste to disapproval.

'Looks like you had quite a party,' he drawled.

Surely he didn't think they had got through three bottles of wine in one evening? 'Tony works in a bar and he brings me old wine bottles. I decorate them with decoupage and sell them at craft markets,' she explained. 'I'm an artist, and so is Tony,' she added, when Raul said nothing, just studied her with cool disdain in his eyes. Rebellion flared inside her. Why on earth did she feel she had to explain herself to this arrogant stranger?

Gino was wriggling to be set down. Libby's arms felt as though they were about to drop off from holding him and, distracted by Raul's brooding presence, she lowered the baby onto the floor and hurried into the tiny adjoining kitchen to fetch his medicine.

Gino immediately crawled over to the coffee table and reached towards one of the wine bottles. Raul grabbed him seconds before he pulled the glass bottle down on his head. The flat was a death-trap, he thought disgustedly as he swept the baby into his arms and stepped over the piles of junk on the floor to stand by the window. And there was an unpleasant musty smell in the room— caused, he guessed, by the fungus that was sprouting on the walls.

What was Elizabeth Maynard thinking of, bringing up her son in such appalling conditions? A pair of men's jeans was hanging over a chair, and he wondered if they belonged to the barman-cum-artist Tony, who had been here the previous night. Was he her lover? And, if so, what role did he have in Gino's life? Was he a stepfather to the child, or did Gino have a variety of 'uncles'?

Raul frowned, deeply disturbed by the idea. He knew what kind of woman Libby was: a lap-dancer and apparently an artist—or perhaps she meant *artiste*, he mused derisively. One thing was for sure. The sort of men who frequented strip-clubs were not likely to be suitable father figures for her baby. He pushed away the thought that his father had presumably met Libby at a club. He didn't want to think of Pietro like that. It sullied his memory. But, like it or not, his father had had an affair with Libby and she had borne him a child.

He looked down at Gino and was once more startled by the strong resemblance the baby had to Pietro. Gino's hair was a mass of tight curls, as his father's had been, and his big brown eyes had the same amber flecks. Pietro would have adored his baby son, Raul acknowledged. But Pietro had been dying when Gino had been born, and he had never seen his child. Raul could not understand why Pietro had not confided in him. All he could think was that his father had been ashamed of his relationship with a lap-dancer who was forty years younger than him. Perhaps he had suspected that Libby was a gold-digger, and that was why, in an effort to protect Gino, Pietro had stipulated that his infant son must spend his childhood at the Carducci family home.

It was a pity Pietro had included the child's mother in his will, Raul thought darkly. Libby clearly didn't have a clue about how to care for a baby. Gino had been staring out of the window, but he suddenly turned his head and gave Raul a gummy smile that revealed two little white teeth. The baby was cute, no doubt about that, Raul conceded. His mouth curved into an answering smile and he felt a sudden overwhelming feeling of protectiveness for Pietro's son. In that moment he knew that he wanted to care for Gino, and would love him—just as Pietro had cared for and loved *him*. This was his chance to repay his adoptive father for everything he had done for him. Pietro had made financial provision for his baby, but *he* would be a father figure to Gino, Raul vowed, and he was determined to make a damn sight better job of parenting than the boy's mother!

Libby hurried back from the kitchen. 'Would you mind holding him while I give him his medicine? He's not keen on it,' she added ruefully, thinking of the tussles she'd had, trying to persuade Gino to swallow the antibiotic.

She shook the bottle, poured the thick liquid into a spoon—and suddenly realised that in order to tip the medicine into Gino's mouth she would have to lean close to Raul. She tensed with the effort of trying not to touch him, but it was impossible to avoid him. Her senses flared, and she was conscious of the warmth emanating from his big body, the tactile softness of his suede coat and the drift of sandalwood cologne mingled with the fresh, clean smell of soap. She had never been so intensely aware of a man in her life. She was terrified he would somehow guess the effect he had on her, and she gave a silent prayer of thanks when Gino opened his mouth like a little bird and swallowed the medicine without a murmur.

'Good boy,' she said softly as she lifted him back into her arms and sat him in his highchair.

Raul tore his eyes from the sight of Libby's nipples jutting provocatively beneath her tight-fitting top, incensed by the damnable ache of desire in his gut. 'When can you be ready to leave for Italy?' he demanded tersely.

Libby gave him a panic-stricken glance, startled by his arrogant assumption that she would agree to take Gino to live in another country just because he had demanded it. And it wasn't just the move, she fretted. There was no getting away from the fact that she would be going to Italy under false pretences. She wasn't Gino's mother, and she did not know how she was going to live a lie. But what choice did she have? she wondered as she stared at Raul Carducci's cold eyes.

'I'm not sure,' she murmured evasively. 'I'll have to give my landlord notice that I'm closing the shop, and then I'll have to try and sell off the stock. And of course I'll have to pack.' Not that it would take long to pack up her possessions, Libby knew. Her wardrobe was sparse, to say the least, but she wanted to take all her art materials and her canvases, and the few mementoes she had of her mother. 'I could probably be ready to bring Gino to Italy at the end of the month.'

'I was thinking in terms of days, not weeks,' Raul said coolly. 'My staff will organise clearing the shop and transporting your possessions to Italy. All you need to do is pack a few clothes for you and Gino. That shouldn't take more than an hour.' He drew back his cuff to glance at the gold watch on his wrist. 'I see no reason why we shouldn't leave this afternoon.'

'This afternoon!' Libby's jaw dropped in astonishment. 'Surely you must realise that's impossible? I've a million things to do before I'll be ready to take Gino to another country to start a new life.' The words 'another country' and 'new life' thudded in her head, and fear unfurled inside her. She wasn't sure she wanted a new life. Her life in Pennmar was not easy—especially at the moment, when the shop was doing so badly—but at least it *was* her life, lived on her own terms, rather than a life of pretending to be someone else under Raul Carducci's haughty gaze. 'Anyway, what's the hurry?' she asked him, pushing her tangled red curls over her shoulder. 'What does it matter to you when we come?'

Against the backdrop of the dreary room and the sullen grey sky outside the window Libby's hair seemed as bright and alive as the dancing flames of a fire. In her garish clothes she was a splash of vibrant colour in a black and white world, Raul mused, as startlingly vivid as the numerous colourful canvases which were stacked around the room.

He chose not to answer her question. 'Are these your work?' he asked, glancing around at the bold pictures of land and seascapes that seemed almost to leap off the canvases.

'Yes. My favourite mediums are oils and char-coals.'

Raul studied a painting of a terraced garden with pots of brilliantly coloured flowers. The picture was loud and brash, with dashes of red, orange and purple seemingly flung at the canvas, yet somehow it worked, and he felt as though he could reach out and touch the flowers. 'Do you sell many?'

Libby detected scepticism in his voice and bristled. 'A few—quite a lot, actually. Although that was mainly in the summer, when the tourists were here. I display them in the shop, but trade is quiet at the moment,' she admitted dismally.

'You won't have to concern yourself with making a living once you move into the Villa Giulietta,' Raul informed her coolly. 'There will certainly be no need for you to work as a lap-dancer,' he added, his lip curling contemptuously.

'Well, that's lucky, because I've never worked as a lap-dancer,' Libby snapped, feeling hot all over when he trailed his eyes insolently down her body and lingered quite blatantly on her breasts.

'The Purple Pussy Cat Club?' he drawled.

Libby's face burned even hotter. Evidently Raul had learned about the seedy club where she and Liz had once worked, and now he thought that she had been a lap-dancer. The pitfalls of pretending to be Gino's mother were already becoming apparent. 'I...I wasn't a lap-dancer,' she mumbled, unable to meet his sardonic gaze. 'I worked behind the bar, that's all.'

Her dream of going to art college had been crushed by the reality of having to earn a living. Having left school with few qualifications, she had found her career choices limited, and she had worked as a cleaner and at a fast food outlet before her mum had helped her get a job serving behind the bar at the nightclub where Liz had already worked as a lap-dancer.

It had been the only job her mum could get when they had arrived back in England after spending several years living in Ibiza. Liz had hated it—but, as she had re-minded Libby, they needed the money, and anything was better than signing on for unemployment benefit. Her mum had been unconventional, and often irresponsible, but she had also been fiercely proud.

Raul was still staring at her, and something in his eyes sent a ripple of sensation through Libby. She couldn't look away from him. It was as though he had cast a spell over her which rooted her to the spot as he strolled nearer, those midnight-dark eyes boring into her as if he were looking into her soul.

He halted inches from her, and almost as if he could not help himself he reached out and wrapped a silky red curl around his finger. 'So, you're not a stripper?'

'*No!*' Her face felt like a furnace, but she was trapped by his magnetism and seemed incapable of moving away from him.

His brows rose and he looked down his arrogant nose at her. 'Pity,' he murmured. 'I might have considered paying you for a private performance.'

'Well, you would have wasted your money,' Libby snapped, her will-power finally reasserting itself so that she jerked away from him. She lifted Gino out of his highchair and hugged him to her. 'I don't think this is going to work. I'm not sure I want to bring Gino to Italy to live at the Carducci villa—certainly not if you're going to make comments like that. Anyway,' she added, desperately clutching at reasons why they should not go with Raul, 'I can't come with you now. Gino has an appointment with a paediatrician next week because my GP is concerned about his respiratory problems.'

Raul had moved back to the window and was staring at the rain, which was now lashing the glass. 'Of course you'll come. You're not going to turn down the opportunity to live a life of luxury,' he drawled confidently. He glanced back at Libby and tried to ignore the burning ache in his groin. Clearly he'd been too long without a lover if he could be attracted to his father's tart, he derided himself. It was a situation he would remedy once he returned home. He could take his pick from numerous beautiful, sophisticated women who understood that all he wanted was a casual sexual relationship with no strings attached.

But first it was imperative that he persuaded Elizabeth Maynard to return to Italy with him immediately. Much as he resented the fact, she controlled fifty percent of Carducci Cosmetics, and he could not run the company without her. 'Once we are in Italy I will arrange for the baby to see a private specialist,' he assured her. 'Gino is a Carducci, and I know his father would have wanted him to have the best of everything.'

The best of everything—the words echoed in Libby's head. Wasn't that what her mother would have wanted for Gino, too? She stared around the flat, at the threadbare carpet and the patches of damp on the walls, and bit her lip, conscious that Raul was watching her.

'How can you deny Gino his birthright?' he demanded. 'Already the spring sunshine in Lazio is warming the lake beside the Villa Giulietta, and the warm climate will be good for him. As he grows older he will have the run of the house and grounds. He can play in the orange groves and learn to sail on the lake.' He would teach his father's son, just as Pietro had taught *him* to sail when he had been a boy, Raul vowed silently.

A thought suddenly struck him that might mean an annoying delay to his plans to take his father's son to Italy as soon as possible. 'I don't suppose Gino has a passport?'

'Actually, he does,' Libby replied slowly. Her mother had applied for one soon after Gino had been born. It had been most unlike Liz to be so organised, but Libby guessed that her mum had hoped Pietro would send for her and his baby son. Liz would have wanted Gino to live in Italy, in a grand house rather than this flat, she knew.

To her surprise Raul did not sound as though he re-sented his baby half-brother, as she had first feared, and actually seemed to *want* Gino to live at the Carducci villa.

She thought of the bank's refusal to increase her over-draft, and the worry that had kept her awake for the past few nights of how she was going to pay the next month's rent on the shop and flat. The truth was that she was at rock-bottom, and there was a very real danger that she and Gino would be homeless. Pietro Cardicci's will was nothing short of a miracle which assured Gino's financial security for life. As Raul had pointed out, she did not have the right to deny Gino his birthright. And Raul had promised he would arrange for Gino to see a private specialist about his dreadful cough…

'All right,' she said abruptly, her heart thumping. She felt as though she was about to jump over the edge of a precipice into the unknown, but Gino had been offered the chance of a better life than the one she could give him in Pennmar, and for his sake she *had* to take it. 'We'll come with you today.'

'Good.' Satisfaction laced Raul's voice. He had never doubted that the lure of the Carducci fortune would persuade Libby to move to Italy. He strolled across the room and lifted Gino out of her arms. 'I'll hold him while you pack. My private jet is on stand-by at Newquay airport. I'll tell the pilot to be ready to take off two hours from now.'

CHAPTER THREE

'WE SHOULD arrive at the Villa Giulietta in a few minutes,' Raul announced abruptly.

Libby had been staring out of the car window, watching the Italian countryside flash past, but at the sound of his rich-as-clotted-cream voice she turned her head and felt a peculiar tightening sensation in the pit of her stomach when she glanced at his handsome face. He possessed a simmering sexual magnetism that fascinated her, and she could not prevent herself from staring at his mouth, imagining the feel of it on hers. Raul's kiss would be no gentle seduction. The thought slid into her head, and she was shocked to feel a hot, melting sensation between her legs.

Her face burned with embarrassment and she prayed he could not read her mind. How could she feel such a fierce attraction to a man she disliked intensely? But it was no good reminding herself that Raul was the most arrogant man she had ever met. Her body seemed to have a mind of its own, and his closeness, the subtle tang of his cologne, made each of her nerve-endings thrum with urgent life.

Her reaction was probably caused by shock that he had finally deigned to speak to her after he had ignored her throughout the flight to Italy, she decided irritably. Back in her flat in Pennmar she had hastily packed Gino's clothes and her own few belongings. When she had walked back into the living room Raul had compressed his lips at the sight of her bright orange coat, and his disdainful comment, 'You seem to be wearing just about every colour of the rainbow,' had made her wish that she owned elegant, sophisticated clothes rather than oddments she'd picked up from charity shops.

He was so stuffy, she thought rebelliously. He couldn't be more than in his mid-thirties, but he had a way of looking down his nose at her, just as Mr Mills—the headmaster of the secondary school she had attended intermittently—had done when he had told her that she would never amount to much.

Maybe all upper-class men acted like stuffed shirts? Miles certainly had, she brooded, recalling her brief relationship with Miles Sefton, which had come to an abrupt end when she had overheard him assuring his father, Earl Sefton, that of *course* his relationship with a waitress from the golf club wasn't serious; she was just a bit of totty.

The memory of that humiliating episode made Libby squirm. Why on earth had she agreed to come to Italy with Raul? she wondered, casting a furtive glance at his chiselled features. He made Earl Sefton seem like Father Christmas. Tears stung her eyes as she remembered how Miles's father had stated that she was little Miss Nobody from Nowhere. Now Miss Nobody was going to live in a grand villa with a man who despised her, and, although she would rather die than show it, she was scared stiff at the prospect.

Lost in her thoughts, Libby had not noticed that the car had slowed, but now it turned and purred up a sweeping driveway lined with tall cypress trees. Through the dark green foliage she glimpsed tantalising flashes of pink and cream stone, while in the distance she caught the sparkle of sunshine on blue water. She remembered Raul had said the villa was near a lake, and suddenly the line of trees stopped, the driveway opened out onto a wide courtyard—and her jaw dropped in astonishment as she stared at the most beautiful house she had ever seen.

'Wow...' she said faintly. The Villa Giulietta looked like a fairytale castle, with its four rounded turrets and myriad arched windows glinting gold in the evening sunlight. The pink and cream striped brickwork reminded Libby of a candy-stick, while the ornate stonework at the top of the turrets was exquisitely detailed.

The courtyard ran round to the front of the house, which overlooked an enormous sapphire-blue lake. A series of stone steps led up to the front door, and cream and pink roses grew in profusion over the elegant stone pillars of the porch.

'It's...incredible,' she murmured, utterly overwhelmed by the house's splendour.

'I agree.' For a moment Raul forgot the anger and frustration that had simmered inside him since he had read Pietro's will, forgot that the woman at his side had been his father's mistress who now had the right to live at the villa. This was his home and he loved it.

His ex-wife had accused him of caring more about the house than he had about her—particularly when he had refused to move permanently to New York. By then his marriage to Dana had been in its death throes and he hadn't denied it. When they had separated he'd offered her the Manhattan apartment, believing that she would not make a claim on the villa.

How wrong he had been, Raul thought bitterly. Dana had proved to be an avaricious gold-digger. Their divorce had made legal history when she had won a record alimony settlement after only a year of marriage. But although it had cost him a fortune he had at least forced her to relinquish her claim on the Villa Giulietta, and the experience had taught him that marriage was a fool's game which he had no intention of ever repeating.

As the car drew to a halt, a woman appeared at the top of the steps and watched them alight. Libby guessed her to be in her mid-sixties; whippet-thin and elegantly dressed, she did not move forward to greet them but waited imperiously for Raul to come to her.

'My aunt Carmina,' Raul murmured to Libby, before he strode up the steps.

'*Zia* Carmina.' He stifled his impatience as he took his aunt's hand and lifted it briefly to his lips. She was his mother's sister, he reminded himself. His father had been fond of her and had often invited her to stay at the villa. Raul knew that Carmina had had been deeply upset by Pietro's death, but she seemed determined to ignore his gentle hints that she might like to return to her house in Rome, and his sympathy was wearing thin.

Gino had woken when the car had stopped moving, and he gave Libby a gummy grin when she lifted him out of his seat. Feeling overawed by the magnificent house, she hovered uncertainly at the bottom of the steps, her heart sinking when Raul's aunt subjected her to a haughty stare that grew gradually more incredulous.

'Who is this woman?' Carmina demanded in Italian.

Raul gestured for Libby to join him. 'This is Elizabeth Maynard,' he replied in English. 'She was my father's...' He hesitated, conscious of the scandalised expression on *Zia* Carmina's face as she raked her eyes over Libby's wild red curls and garishly coloured clothes. For some reason he was reluctant to refer to Libby as Pietro's mistress, but his aunt had transferred her gaze to Gino and she threw up her hands in a gesture of disgust.

'This *girl* was my brother-in-law's mistress?' Again she spoke in voluble Italian. 'She looks so common. What was Pietro thinking? He must have been out of his mind to have invited his *puttana* to live at the Villa Giulietta.'

Raul had felt exactly the same sentiments, but now he felt a shaft of annoyance with his aunt for her rudeness, and was glad that Libby could not understand what she had said. 'My father was entitled to do as he wished, and he made it clear that he wished for his...companion and his infant son to live here,' he reminded the older woman coolly.

'Pah!' Carmina made no attempt to greet Libby, and after giving her another disdainful glance swung round and swept back into the house.

Libby watched her go and hugged Gino to her, startled to find that her hands were shaking. She hadn't followed any of the lightning-fast exchange between Raul and his aunt, but the older woman's sentiments had been plain. *Puttana* probably meant something vile, she brooded as she recalled how Carina had practically spat the word at her.

Once again she questioned her sanity in pretending to be Gino's mother. Perhaps the Carducci family would be more prepared to accept her if she explained that Pietro had not been her sugar-daddy? But if Raul learned that she had no right to remain at the villa he might order his chauffeur to drive her straight back to the airport.

He could not physically snatch Gino from her, she assured herself, automatically tightening her hold on the baby. But this was a man who travelled by private jet and lived in a villa that looked like a palace. His wealth and the power he commanded were undeniable, and she was sure that if he decided to fight for custody of Gino he would win.

The baby was heavy, and she transferred him to her other hip. 'Here—let me take him,' Raul offered, holding out his hands.

'No!' She gripped Gino convulsively, blushing when Raul frowned. 'Thanks, but he doesn't really know you, and I don't want to unsettle him while he's getting used to a strange house,' she muttered.

Raul stared at her speculatively. 'I'm sure he'll soon get used to me—and the house.'

He wondered why Libby seemed so nervous. Most women he knew would be unable to conceal their delight at the prospect of living at the villa with all expenses paid, but she looked as though she had been sentenced to a term in jail. She made an incongruous sight in her purple boots and skirt, green tights and orange coat, but nothing could detract from the loveliness of her face. His eyes focused on her soft mouth, and he could not banish the image of covering her lips with his own in a long, leisurely tasting.

Dio, she was a witch, he thought furiously as he moved abruptly away from her. 'Follow me. I'll show you to your rooms,' he ordered curtly.

Wordlessly Libby trailed after him, her misgivings increasing as she stepped into the hall and stared around at the marble floors and pillars and the exquisite murals which adorned the walls and ceiling. Rays of early evening sunlight slanted through the windows and danced across the stunning crystal chandelier suspended from the centre of the room. She would have liked to linger and study the beautiful bronze sculptures dotted around the hallway, but Raul was striding ahead and she had to race to keep up with him.

He led the way along endless corridors, past elegant, airy rooms filled with antique furniture. She could easily spend the rest of her life lost in these corridors, Libby fretted as she followed him up yet another flight of stairs. Raul suddenly stopped and pushed open a door, before standing back to usher her into a suite of rooms that comprised a sitting room, small dining area and an adjoining bedroom.

'I have arranged for this room to be the nursery,' he told Libby, opening another door into a smaller room which had been decorated in soft yellow. The stripped-pine cot and nursery furniture were attractive, and the pale blue striped curtains and matching rug on the floor added to the ambience of the room.

Libby set Gino down on the floor and he immediately crawled over to the box of brightly coloured toys in the corner. Raul watched him for a few moments before commenting, 'He doesn't seem too unsettled, does he? The nanny has the room next door to this one, by the way,' he added casually.

Libby stared at him. 'What nanny?'

'The one I have hired to help take care of Gino. She comes from the best agency in Italy and is highly recommended.'

'I don't care if she's Mother Teresa.' Fear sharpened Libby's voice. She did not want anyone to take her place in Gino's life. 'You can just *un*-hire her,' she snapped. 'I'm perfectly capable of looking after him myself.'

Raul's brows rose in an expression of haughty disdain. 'From what I saw of your flat in Pennmar, I disagree. It was a filthy hovel.'

Outraged by his description of her former home, Libby felt her temper explode. 'It was *not* filthy. I was always cleaning, and scrubbing the mildew off the walls. It's not my fault the flat was so damp.'

'The living room looked like a pigsty,' Raul insisted coldly.

'That was only because I'd had to move all my things out of my bedroom when it flooded—' Libby broke off at the sound of a knock on the door and stared suspiciously at the dark-haired woman who entered the room.

'Ah, Silvana.' Raul stepped forward to greet the woman. 'I'd like to introduce you to your new charge.' He scooped Gino into his arms, and to Libby's annoyance the baby chuckled happily and explored Raul's face with his hand. 'This is Gino.' Raul paused, and then as an obvious afterthought added, 'Oh—and his mother, Ms Maynard.'

Silvana gave Libby a cheerful smile and immediately turned her attention to Gino. 'What a gorgeous little boy,' she said in perfect English, and then in Italian, '*Sei un bel bambino*, Gino.'

'He doesn't understand Italian,' Libby said tightly, wishing that Gino had yelled when the nanny had spoken to him. But he seemed quite content in Raul's arms, and was giving Silvana his most winsome smile—the smile he usually only gave *her*, Libby thought dismally.

'Silvana is fluent in English and Italian, and she will talk to Gino in both languages so that he will grow up bilingual,' Raul informed Libby coolly. 'Italy is his home now, and obviously he will need to be fluent in his native tongue—don't you agree?'

'I suppose so,' Libby muttered. Of course Gino would need to be able to speak Italian, she just hadn't thought of it, and she was irritated that Raul was one step ahead. 'I'll have to learn too. I picked up Spanish fairly easily, so I guess Italian won't be too hard.'

'Did you learn Spanish at school?' Raul asked curiously.

'No…' Libby did not want to admit that she'd received no formal schooling until she and her mum had left Ibiza and returned to live in London, or that her attendance at the local comprehensive had been sketchy and she had learned very little. 'I spent part of my childhood in Ibiza and learned to speak Spanish there.'

She frowned when Raul gave Gino to the nanny, surprised that the baby did not remonstrate at being handed to a stranger. He was obviously growing out of his clingy stage, and it was selfish to wish that he only wanted her, she told herself firmly.

'Would you like me to give Gino his tea and a bath?' Silvana asked.

Libby opened her mouth to argue, but thought better of it when she noticed Raul's steely expression. When he opened the door and ushered her into the adjoining room she stalked past him, and as soon as they were out of earshot of Silvana she rounded on him.

'I can't stop you employing a nanny, but you're wasting your money—because *I* am Gino's mother and *I* will be his full-time carer, just as I have always been.'

Raul was surprised by her fierceness. He had convinced himself that Libby had deliberately conceived Pietro's child in the hope of claiming a huge maintenance allowance, and had assumed that she would be more than happy to hand over responsibility for her baby. But during the flight to Italy he had been struck by her devotion to Gino and her obvious love for him. 'You can't have cared for him entirely on your own in England when you had the shop to run,' he pointed out. 'You say you are an artist, but looking after a baby can't have given you much time to paint.'

Libby shrugged. 'I used to take him down to the shop with me. And I painted whenever Gino had a nap. But I've pretty much given up my artwork since…' She had been about to say since *Mum had Gino*, but quickly changed that to, 'Since Gino was born.'

Raul thought of the bold, beautiful paintings he had seen at her flat. 'That must have been hard—to give up something you love?'

Libby slipped off her coat and brushed her tangled red curls back from her face. 'Not really. Gino comes first. I love him more than anything,' she said fiercely.

Raul compressed his lips and walked over to the window, needing to look anywhere but at Libby. Now that she had removed her coat his eyes once again seemed to have a magnetic attraction to her breasts. He was bitterly aware that his body had been in a state of arousal ever since her soft curves had squashed up against him in the car. She was so intense; he brooded, so colourful and fizzing with energy. Had it been her energy and her fiery passion that had attracted his father to her? He pushed the thought away. He could not bear to think about her and Pietro as lovers... Not when he wanted her himself, whispered a sly little voice in his head.

Incensed by his own weakness, he swung round to face her. 'Like it or not, there will be occasions when you will have to leave Gino with Silvana. You cannot take him to board meetings,' he pointed out when she looked mutinous.

Libby frowned. 'I won't be going to any board meetings...will I?' she asked uncertainly.

'As I have explained, my father has left a fifty percent share of Carducci Cosmetics to Gino. But until he is eighteen *you* have control of his share of the company, and it will be necessary for you to attend meetings with the board of directors.'

'I see.' Libby chewed on her bottom lip, horrified at the prospect of discussing business matters with the board members of Carducci Cosmetics, who would no doubt look down their noses at her just as Raul was doing now. 'I don't really know a lot about running a company,' she admitted.

'That much was obvious from the precarious financial state of your shop,' Raul said scathingly. 'Do not fear. You won't have to do anything apart from sign your name where I tell you to.'

Libby glared at him resentfully, infuriated by his implication that she had mismanaged the shop when she had worked so hard to make Nature's Way a success.

'I suppose I'll have to leave Gino with the nanny while I attend meetings,' she conceded grudgingly. 'At least Silvana seems pleasant—unlike your aunt.' She grimaced as she recalled Raul's aunt's haughty disdain. Her careless tongue ran away with her and she added, 'She's a miserable old bat.'

Privately, Raul shared Libby's opinion of his aunt. But Carmina was a member of his family, his beloved mother's sister, while Libby had been his father's mistress—a cheap little gold-digger. 'I will not tolerate you speaking about any member of my family so disrespectfully,' he snapped. 'You are here because my father wished it, but I suggest you remember your place.'

His arrogance ignited Libby's temper like a match to dry tinder. 'What exactly *is* my place?' she demanded, throwing back her head so that her flame-coloured curls danced around her face. 'Your precious aunt looked at me as if I had crawled out of the gutter. And what does *puttana* mean, by the way? Maybe I'll ask Silvana to translate for me.'

Raul glared at her furiously. Never in his life had anyone challenged his authority or spoken to him in such a way as Libby had. He was tempted to grab hold of her and bring his mouth down on hers in a punishing kiss that would shut her up. His nostrils flared as he struggled to control his temper, but his eyes were as cold as chips of granite as he met her gaze. 'It means whore,' he said grimly.

'Oh.' Libby's temper deflated like a popped balloon and she felt sick inside. She had been under no illusion that she would be welcomed at the Villa Giulietta. Raul must have been shocked to learn that he was not his father's sole heir, and he clearly resented her, believing as he did that she had been Pietro's mistress. He had accused her of being a gold-digger who had targeted a much older, wealthy man—but a whore! 'That's horrible,' she muttered, tears filling her eyes.

Dio! Libby was a brilliant actress, Raul brooded, infuriated by the pang of guilt that gripped him when he saw her lower lip tremble. She looked so hurt and so achingly vulnerable, but in his experience most women were manipulative, and he was convinced that she was no different.

'*Zia* Carmina was my mother's sister. After Eleanora's death she remained close to my father,' he explained harshly. 'You must understand that my aunt was deeply shocked to learn that her brother-in-law, whom she loved and respected, had had a secret mistress and a child.' He frowned. 'You are so young. *Dio*, Pietro was old enough to have been your grandfather. It is not surprising that Carmina finds your presence here difficult when she is still grieving for my father.'

'Grief doesn't give a person licence to be nasty,' Libby said, rounding on him. 'I'm grieving too.' The pain of losing her mum was still raw. During the day she had to be strong for Gino, but most nights she still cried for Liz. 'These past few months have been the worst of my life,' she told Raul thickly.

Surely Libby was faking the emotion that throbbed in her voice? She could not really be as devastated by his father's death as she appeared? Raul stared at her in frustration, not knowing what to make of her. Before he had met her he had pigeonholed her as a brash tart devoid of any scruples. But Libby was nothing like he had imagined. If she were to be believed, it seemed that she had genuinely cared for Pietro. But why had such a beautiful young woman been attracted to a man forty years older than her if it hadn't been for his money? he asked himself angrily.

Raul tore his gaze from Libby, feeling a sudden need to get away from her. It would have been so much easier if she had been a hard-as-nails bimbo, he thought savagely. He wanted to despise her, but every time he looked at her he was consumed with a burning sexual hunger that shamed him.

He crossed the room and flipped open a briefcase sitting on the coffee table. 'It has been a long day, and I am sure you want to settle in. Your bag has been brought up from the car and the rest of your things at the flat will be packed up and sent on in a few days.' He lifted a sheaf of documents from the case and glanced at her. 'I need you to sign a few papers.'

'What are they?' Libby stared warily at the pile of printed documents, her heart sinking when she realised that Raul intended to wait while she read them.

'They relate to various decisions I have made regarding Carducci Cosmetics.' Raul flicked casually through the papers. 'This file gives details of a merger with a Swedish skincare company that I want to proceed with as soon as possible, and this document is to authorise the transfer of funds to one of CC's subsidiary companies in the US. I simply require you to sign your name—you don't have to read them.'

Libby frowned. 'How can I sign them when I don't know what I'm signing?

Irritation swept through Raul when she sat down, switched on the table-lamp, and picked up the first document from the pile. 'This is pointless,' he said grittily, noting how the lamplight turned her hair to spun gold.

'You said yourself you know nothing about running a company. I have no idea why my father stipulated that *you* should have control of Gino's shares,' he burst out, his frustration tangible. 'When Pietro died I expected to take full control of Carducci Cosmetics, but for the past eight months CC has been in a state of limbo. I couldn't find you, and because you control fifty percent of the company I have been unable to do more than keep the company ticking over.' He took a deep breath, calming himself. 'I'm not asking you to take a crash course in business management,' he informed Libby curtly. 'You can save us both a lot of time if you just add your signature to the bottom of each document.'

Libby stared at him, watching how the lamplight flickered over the hard planes of his face. A hard knot of anger was slowly forming inside her at the realisation that he hadn't insisted on rushing her and Gino to Italy because he was concerned about the baby living in the damp flat in Pennmar. No, all Raul cared about was Carducci Cosmetics—which, to his obvious anger, he now had to share control of with her until Gino was eighteen.

'I wonder why Pietro didn't give *you* control of Gino's shares?' she said slowly. 'Maybe he didn't trust that you would look after Gino's interests properly?'

Rage coursed through Raul's veins like red-hot lava flow, obliterating every other thought but the burning need to force an apology from Libby for her outrageous statement. 'You *dare* suggest my father did not trust me?' he snarled, hating her at that moment for echoing the doubts he had secretly harboured since he had read Pietro's will. Maybe she was right; maybe his adoptive father *hadn't* trusted him enough to award him control of Gino's share of the company. The thought tore at his heart, and anger was the only way he could deal with the pain. His nostrils flared with the effort of containing his fury—not just with Libby, but with himself and his shameful, shocking desire for her.

She had gone too far, Libby realised when she risked a glance at Raul's face and saw that his dark eyes were as cold and hard as polished jet. But she wanted the truth. 'Pietro must have had his reasons for stipulating that Gino's mother should control his share of Carducci Cosmetics,' she insisted. And if Pietro had had his doubts about his adopted son's trustworthiness, then so did she.

Raul jerked his head back as if she had slapped him. '*Dio*, someone needs to teach you to control your insolent tongue,' he growled, goaded beyond bearing.

He moved towards her with the speed of a panther homing in for the kill. Too late Libby realised that he intended the 'someone' to be him, but he had already tangled his fingers in her hair and tugged her head back, and her startled cry was lost beneath the pressure of his mouth as he captured her lips in a savage kiss.

CHAPTER FOUR

LIBBY stiffened; her body taut with rejection as Raul gripped her shoulder and dragged her against him. Shock quickly turned to outrage, and she pressed her lips tightly together and tried to turn her head away. But his strength easily outmatched hers and he tugged her hair, forcing her head back so that he could continue his sensual assault.

For the slide of his lips over hers *was* wickedly sensual, she acknowledged dazedly. It did not matter that she disliked him, or that he clearly despised her. She had fantasised about him kissing her from the moment he had strode into Nature's Way, and the reality of his hot, hungry mouth moving erotically over hers was so intoxicating that she was powerless to deny her response. His tongue probed the firm line of her lips, demanding access, until with a little gasp she opened her mouth and felt a thrill of wild excitement when he slid deep into her moist warmth and explored her with a thoroughness that made her tremble.

Each of her senses was acutely alive, and the taste of him, the scent of him—a tantalising mixture of his cologne and male pheromones—sent fire coursing through her veins. The urge to flee from him was replaced by another instinct: to submit to his superior strength and respond to his hungry demands with a passion she had not known herself capable of. She had never felt like this before—not even with Miles, whom she'd had such a crush on. With one kiss Raul had awoken her sensuality, and now she was eager to experience everything he offered.

She had placed her palms flat on his chest in an effort to push him away, but now she slid her hands up to his shoulders, allowing him to draw her closer. She could feel every sinew and muscle of his thighs and abdomen, and heat pooled between her legs when she felt the hard ridge of his arousal nudge against her pelvis.

His free hand roamed up and down her back, slid over her shoulder and traced the fragile line of her collarbone before moving lower to cup her breast. A quiver of pleasure shot through Libby. Her breasts felt heavy, and her nipples were taut and tingling, straining against the restriction of her lacy bra. She wished he would push his hand beneath the material and stroke her naked flesh. Colour scorched her cheeks at the wantonness of her thoughts, but he was still kissing her with the mastery of a sorcerer, evoking a need in her that caused her to move her body sinuously against his in a blatant invitation.

And then, with shocking abruptness, he ended the kiss and lifted his head to stare down at her for several taut seconds before he jerked away from her, breathing hard. Libby swayed slightly, shaking with reaction and feeling bereft now that his big, hard body was no longer melded to her softer curves.

'That should *not* have happened,' he said harshly.

His voice was laced with self-loathing, and Libby was sure she would see contempt for her in his midnight-dark gaze. Instead his eyes glittered with a feverish hunger that stunned her with its intensity. Raul wanted her. He might hate himself, but for a few unguarded seconds he had been unable to disguise his desire for her.

He had gathered up the sheaf of documents and shoved them back in the briefcase, and was now striding across the room. If he moved any faster he would be running out of the door, she thought, staring in astonishment at the dull colour that highlighted his magnificent cheekbones. She blushed as she recalled how eagerly she had responded to him. Maybe he was afraid she was going to jump on him and drag him back? She remembered the hungry gleam she had seen in his eyes before his thick black lashes had swept down and concealed his thoughts, and it struck her that maybe he was afraid of himself.

Raul grabbed the door handle and jerked the door open with such force that it groaned on its hinges. He was furious with himself—disgusted. *Inferno!* Libby had been his father's mistress and he did not understand how he could want her. He had kissed her in anger, wanting to punish her for suggesting that Pietro had not trusted him. But the punishment had backfired, because from the moment his mouth had claimed her soft, moist lips he had been consumed with a burning need to possess her.

He halted on his way out of the door and glanced back at her, heat searing his insides when he saw that her lips were red and swollen and unutterably tempting. She was a witch, he thought broodingly. A beautiful milky-skinned, doe-eyed sorceress who had ensnared his father—but from now on he would guard himself against her magic.

'I have a prior engagement tonight,' he said coldly, 'and as my aunt has informed me that she is feeling unwell and will not be joining you for dinner I have arranged for your evening meal to be served to you up here in your suite.' He paused, and when she made no reply continued, 'I have called a meeting of all Carducci Cosmetics' senior executives for midday tomorrow. We'll leave for Rome soon after breakfast as I have a number of things to attend to in the office before the meeting. Silvana will look after Gino.'

Libby bit her lip. 'How long will we be away? I don't want to leave him for too long.'

'I imagine the meeting will last for most of the afternoon. There are numerous urgent matters to discuss,' Raul told her with barely concealed impatience, thinking of the months that CC had stagnated while he had searched for his father's mistress. 'We have also been invited to a business dinner in the evening.' He shrugged when Libby frowned. 'Attending these sorts of events is a necessary part of running a company. Social networking is a vital avenue of business.'

He paused and then said smoothly, 'Of course there *is* a way that you could devote all your time to Gino, and perhaps have time to take up your painting again.'

Libby gave him a puzzled look. 'How?'

'You could sign over control of Gino's shares to me.' Raul spoke savagely when Libby immediately shook her head. '*Dio!* I have spent most of my life preparing to take my father's place as head of CC. Pietro erred on the side of caution, but I have plans for the company that will make it a world leader in the twenty-first century.'

'Maybe your father wished you were *more* cautious,' Libby said slowly. 'Maybe he was worried that you would take too many risks with Carducci Cosmetics, and that's why he stipulated that Gino's mother should have control of his shares until he is an adult. I might not know much about running a company,' she admitted, 'but I'm not stupid. I understand that high risk can mean high returns, but I'm not prepared to gamble with Gino's birthright, and I won't agree to any business ventures that I feel are too risky.'

Black rage swept through Raul. So the battle lines were drawn, he thought bitterly. The only subject he and his father had ever disagreed on was the future of Carducci Cosmetics. Pietro had been content for the company to follow a path of safe investments and carefully considered proposals, while he, Raul, had seen the potential for expansion and diversification. Admittedly they came with risks—but hadn't he proved, by amassing his own personal fortune on the stock market, that his gambles always paid off?

It was clear that his father had not trusted him. By awarding his mistress Gino's shares Pietro had found a way to control Raul from beyond the grave. The only possible solution, Raul realised, lay in the clause Pietro had added to his will stating that if Libby were to marry control of Gino's shares would pass to him. A clause that she was unaware of, because back at her flat in Pennmar she had not bothered to read the will in its entirety, pointed out a little voice in his head.

Madre di Dio! It was such an obvious solution and it would give him what he desired most in the world— complete control of the company he had been groomed to run since he was a boy. But marry his father's mistress?

It was absolutely out of the question, he assured himself firmly. The idea was inconceivable. He had experienced the delights of holy matrimony once, Raul thought sardonically, and had no intention of repeating the worst mistake of his life.

Not even if the prize was the thing he desired most in the world? his mind taunted. Not even if it would give him full control of CC and the opportunity to bed a woman who sent his libido into orbit every time he set eyes on her?

He did not envisage any difficulties in persuading Libby to be his wife. She had been willing to have an affair with an elderly billionaire and was not likely to turn down marriage to Pietro's other heir. And of course he would instruct his lawyers to draw up a pre-nup as watertight as a submarine, so that he could divorce her when he tired of her.

He stared across the room at Libby and desire jackknifed in his gut when he remembered how firm and yet deliciously soft her breast had felt in his hand. He wanted to rip off her clingy top, and the bra he could see outlined beneath it, and cup her naked flesh in his palms, stroke his fingers across her nipples and feel them harden. The chemistry between them was almost tangible. He knew with a primitive instinct that she would not stop him if he carried her into the bedroom and made love to her.

He was unbearably tempted, and it took all his willpower to force himself to step out of her room and close the door behind him. If he married her he could enjoy her delectable body *and* take control of CC. The idea was certainly worth serious consideration.

* * *

For several moments after Raul had gone Libby stood with her fingers pressed against her bruised mouth, still reeling from his kiss. How *could* she have responded to him so shamelessly? she berated herself disgustedly. His aunt had accused her of being a whore, and after her wanton behaviour Raul must surely agree with Carmina.

Sudden tears filled her eyes and she sank down onto the sofa and buried her head in her hands. For weeks Gino had woken her every few hours during the night with his cough, and she was so tired she could barely think straight. Today so much had happened in the space of a few short hours that her life seemed scarily out of her control. Raul had stormed into her life with the force of a tornado, but she had agreed to bring Gino to Italy because more than anything she wanted him to have the stability and security that had been lacking in her own childhood.

She had been unprepared for the violent sexual attraction between her and Raul. She knew she was ridiculously inexperienced for a woman of twenty-two—witnessing her mother's disastrous love-life had put her off dating and Miles had been her only serious relationship. But Miles had never made her feel the way Raul had done when he had kissed her.

She could still taste him. She traced her mouth with her fingertips and heat flooded through her when she remembered how he had ground his lips against hers and demanded a response that she had been powerless to deny. For a few seconds she indulged in the fantasy of him kissing her and caressing her, stripping her clothes from her body and pulling her down onto a bed…

Her eyes flew wide-open. That was never going to happen. She could never allow the fantasy to become reality, because Raul believed she was Gino's mother and she could not risk him discovering that she was a virgin. From now on she must ignore the sexual chemistry between them and hope that in the vastness of the Villa Giulietta their paths would not cross very often.

She glanced around the elegant sitting room which, like the bedroom beyond it, was decorated in muted shades and simply begged for splashes of colour to make it feel more homely. The prospect of eating dinner here alone was not inviting, but it was preferable to dining with Raul's unpleasant aunt.

She wondered where Raul would be spending the evening. With his mistress, perhaps? With his stunning looks and potent virility it was likely that he had numerous lovers. But his personal life was none of her business, she reminded herself, irritated because she could not get the image of him making love to some gorgeous woman out of her mind. Forget about Raul Carducci, she told herself. The only person who mattered to her was Gino who was asleep in his airy, *dry* nursery. She had done the right thing by bringing him to live in this beautiful house, and with her mind settled she went to check on him.

The following morning Raul's Lamborghini sped along the roads so fast that the fields and olive groves flashed past in a blur. Libby lifted her eyes from his tanned hands on the steering wheel to his hard profile, and sighed. He had not spoken to her since she had emerged from her bedroom dressed for their trip to Rome, but his silence as he had studied her appearance had thrummed with disapproval.

She did not know what he had expected her to wear, she thought irritably. She didn't own designer suits, or anything remotely suitable for a business meeting. Okay, so her denim mini-skirt was short, but it was perfectly respectable when she was wearing cropped leggings beneath it. Her cerise and purple top was admittedly pretty eye-catching, but the pink matched the colour of her flip-flops, and in an effort to look more elegant she had piled her hair on top of her head and tied the knot with a purple scarf.

But in comparison to Raul's superbly tailored char-coal-grey suit, navy blue silk shirt and grey tie she probably looked a mess, Libby conceded. He looked every inch a suave, billionaire businessman, and he was so drop-dead sexy her stomach lurched every time he changed gear and his hand brushed against her thigh.

Desperate to do something to break her intense aware-ness of him, she rooted around in her denim haversack for the tube of mint sweets she usually carried with her, and eventually unearthed an old packet of chewing gum. 'Would you like some?' She offered the packet to Raul.

'You chew *gum*?'

His expression of distaste was almost comical, but Libby flushed, acutely aware of the gaping chasm that separated their two worlds. Presumably the glamorous women he socialised with did not chew gum.

'It's not like I take heroin,' she muttered, stuffing the packet back in her bag. 'It's just sugar-free gum.' She shook her head disgustedly. 'Do you ever lighten up?'

Raul took his eyes from the road for a second and awarded her a sardonic glance. 'If by "lighten up" you mean do I ever dress like a circus clown, then the answer is no.'

'I am not dressed like a circus clown.' Libby breathed fire. 'I simply like to wear bright colours.'

'I'd noticed,' he said dryly.

'Well, it's better than being an old fogey. I bet you go to bed wearing a suit.'

'As a matter of fact, I always sleep naked.'

'Oh.' Libby made a choking noise which she quickly tried to disguise as a cough, blushing furiously as an image of Raul—stark naked and reclining on satin sheets—filled her mind.

It was a long time since he had seen a woman blush, Raul mused. But Libby's air of innocence must be an act, he reminded himself, his mouth tightening as he tried to dismiss the recurring image of her and his father as lovers. 'I have a feeling I'm going to regret asking this,' he murmured, 'but what *is* an old fogey? It is not a term I am familiar with.'

'Someone like my old headmaster,' she replied without hesitation. 'Stuffy, pompous, strait-laced…'

'You didn't like him, I take it?' Raul murmured, frowning at the idea that Libby saw him in the same unflattering light as her old schoolmaster. Why should he care what she thought of him? he asked himself impatiently. But her opinion of him rankled. Presumably she hadn't thought him stuffy and strait-laced when she had responded to him so enthusiastically last night.

'Mr Mills didn't like me.' Libby's voice broke into his thoughts. 'He accused me of being a rebel, and told me I wouldn't pass any of my exams. But I proved him wrong,' she said in a satisfied tone. 'I passed art.'

'Just art?' Raul had benefited from an excellent private education at one of Rome's top schools, and gone on to gain a Masters degree in business at Harvard. He could not hide his shock at Libby's lack of qualifications. How was he supposed to share the running of Carducci Cosmetics, which had a seven billion pound annual turnover, with a girl who was barely out of her teens and had a single qualification—in art?

'I assume you were educated in Ibiza, as you said you lived there. Did your parents own property on the island?' he asked her.

'No.' Libby hesitated. There was no reason why she should keep her background a secret, she told herself. 'I was brought up by my mother. I don't have a dad—well, I must do, obviously, but I don't know who he is. He abandoned Mum when she was pregnant with me. Mum was seventeen when I was born and she had a few problems.' She did not add that Liz had taken drugs for several years, or that life on the rundown housing estate where they had lived for the first few years of her life had been grim.

'Social Services eventually placed me with foster parents while Mum sorted her life out. It was fine.' Her voice faltered slightly. 'My foster parents were nice people, but they cared for seven other kids, and life with them was pretty hectic. I missed Mum terribly and I was glad when I was allowed to live with her again. That's when she took me to Ibiza, to live in a commune with artists and free-thinkers.'

For free-thinkers read hippies, Raul thought sardonically. Libby had clearly had an unconventional upbringing—the child of an unmarried mother and now a single parent herself. He hoped she did not harbour any ideas of taking Gino to live in a commune, because he would not allow it, he vowed. His father's son belonged at the Villa Giulietta. Raul suddenly realised he was glad Pietro had stipulated that the baby should grow up at the villa, where he would be safe.

Another thought occurred to him. If he married Libby, he could adopt Gino and claim custody of him should his mother decide to take off and live in an artists' commune. He forced the idea to the back of his mind and concentrated on the road that was filling with traffic as they headed towards the city centre. 'So, how long did you live in the commune?'

'Seven years. We went back to England when I was fourteen,' Libby explained. 'I'd had a few lessons from one of the commune members who had been a teacher, but when I went to the local secondary school in London I soon realised there were big gaps in my knowledge. I'd been allowed to run wild in Ibiza,' she admitted. 'I wasn't used to formal education, and I hated the lessons and the uniform.' And, even worse, the feeling that she was a failure, she reflected silently. 'The only subject I shone at was art.'

Now that she was an adult she bitterly regretted her poor education. She had adored her mother, but she knew that Liz had often been irresponsible—particularly when she had failed to provide proper schooling for Libby.

But she would still rather have lived with her mother than anyone else. Going into care had been a traumatic experience, which was why, after Liz had died, she had been so determined to keep Gino. He belonged to her, she thought fiercely. Raul was legally Gino's half-brother, but because Raul was Pietro's adopted son, he and Gino were not blood relatives, and he would never love the baby as she did.

Lost in her thoughts, she suddenly realised that Raul was speaking. 'How do you think you are going to be able to take an active role in running Carducci Cosmetics when you've admitted you have no business experience?' he demanded impatiently. 'Pietro must have been out of his mind when he awarded you control of Gino's shares. A lap-dancer with a qualification in art—' He broke off and growled something in Italian that Libby guessed was not complimentary.

'I may not have tons of qualifications, but I learned to be streetwise from an early age,' Libby retaliated. 'For years I used to help Mum run a market stall, and I'm confident I can tell the difference between a dodgy deal and a safe one. I'm determined to look after Gino's interests to the best of my ability, and keep his shares in the company safe. And I already told you I never worked as a lap-dancer,' she added tightly.

'So where did you meet my father?'

The question came out of the blue, and Libby froze, frantically trying to recall everything Liz had told her about her holiday romance with Pietro Carducci.

'We met on a cruise ship,' she mumbled. 'The *Aurelia*. It was a month-long trip, visiting ports around the Mediterranean.'

She could sense Raul's surprise. 'Do you often take cruises?'

Libby was not a natural liar, and she could feel her cheeks grow hot as she became more embroiled in the deception she had started when she had told Raul she was Gino's mother. 'No—it was my first cruise. I won the trip in a competition,' she added, relieved that that part of the story was true. Liz had been ecstatic when she had won the luxury holiday.

'So, you met my father on the ship?' Raul drawled. He remembered from when he had escorted Pietro aboard the *Aurelia* that most of the other guests had been elderly. Beautiful young Libby must have had rich pickings, he thought cynically.

'Yes.' Libby recounted her mother's story of how she had met Pietro. 'The *Aurelia* was huge. I took a wrong turn on my way back to my cabin one evening and ended up on the first-class deck. Pietro was returning to his suite, we got chatting, and…well,' she finished lamely, 'that's how we met.'

'It was certainly a fortuitous wrong turn you took that night,' Raul commented silkily.

Libby flushed at his sardonic tone. It was clear he believed his father had been targeted by a calculating gold-digger. But her mum hadn't been like that, she thought miserably. Liz had brought her up alone after being abandoned by Libby's father. Life had been tough, but Liz had been fiercely independent and would never have been attracted to a man for his money. Yet it would be impossible to explain that to Raul, Libby knew— especially as she had led him to believe that *she* had been his father's mistress. She had dug herself a hole and now she was falling ever deeper into it, but if she wanted to stay with Gino she could never reveal the truth.

Raul compressed his lips into an angry line, but did not say any more as he slotted the Lamborghini into his reserved parking space outside Carducci Cosmetics' office block. The building was a modern confection of steel, tinted windows and grey marble steps leading up to the front doors; the foyer was discreetly elegant, with marble pillars, black leather sofas and a reception desk staffed by women who looked as though they had stepped from the pages of *Vogue*.

She should definitely have worn make-up, Libby realised, after the lift had whisked them up to the top floor, where they were met by Raul's ultra-glamorous PA. Power-dressing and scarlet lipstick were clearly *de rigueur* for the female staff at CC, and when Raul ushered her into the boardroom she was conscious that her unconventional clothes drew glances of shocked disapproval from the eight male executives seated around the table.

Four hours later Libby had to concede that running a global company which boasted an annual revenue of several billion pounds and employed twenty thousand staff worldwide was nothing like selling souvenirs to tourists from a market stall in Ibiza.

Her head ached from trying to understand the discussions that had taken place—even though, out of deference to her, everyone had spoken in English rather than Italian. Now, finally, the meeting was over, and she closed her eyes wearily—but snapped them open again at the sound of Raul's terse voice.

'I realise you find the proceedings boring, but I'd appreciate it if you could at least remain conscious during a meeting.'

She flushed at his sarcasm. 'I wasn't bored, and I certainly didn't fall asleep, but I admit I didn't understand most of what was discussed.'

'Then for pity's sake sign over control of Gino's shares to me and allow me to get on with running CC,' Raul bit out savagely, his eyes darkening with fury when she shook her head. Jaw tense, he tore his gaze from Libby and resisted the urge to brush a stray flame-coloured curl off her face.

'Tonight's function starts at eight, which means you have plenty of time to find something suitable to wear,' he told her as he ushered her out of the boardroom and into the lift. 'Many of the top designer boutiques are in Via Condotti and Piazza di Spagna,' he added as the lift doors opened at the ground floor. 'I'll take you to your appointment with the personal stylist, but I'm due at another meeting so I will have to leave you with her.'

'Whoa!' Libby exclaimed as she raced across the marble foyer, trying to keep up with Raul's long stride. 'I don't need a personal stylist.'

He turned his head and ran his eyes slowly over her, from her unruly red curls, huge purple hoop earrings and psychedelic top, down to her minuscule skirt and shudderingly awful pink rubber flip-flops. And to his intense frustration realised that he still wanted her more than he had wanted any other woman. 'You most certainly do,' he assured her grimly. 'You are a representative of Carducci Cosmetics now, and I will not allow you to attend a prestigious dinner looking like someone who scrubs floors for a living.'

* * *

Two hours later, Raul strode into the five-star hotel where the dinner was to be held, and made his way to the bar where he had told Libby to meet him.

He might have known she would be late, he thought irritably as he glanced around the room and failed to spot anyone wearing a garishly coloured outfit. Presumably the queen of clashing colours would appear at any moment. He had explained to her that when she had finished shopping Tito, his driver, would take her back to his penthouse apartment so that she could change for the dinner, before the chauffer drove her to the hotel. So where was she? he wondered impatiently, when a glance at his watch revealed that it was ten minutes past the time he had arranged to meet her.

He moved his gaze slowly along the line of people sitting on stools by the bar, and his attention was caught by a shimmer of amethyst silk. The woman had her back to him, but as he lifted his eyes from the silver stiletto heels visible below her long skirt, up to her to her slender waist, and then higher to her milky-pale shoulders revealed by her strapless dress, he felt a jolt of stunned recognition. Her flame-coloured hair had been cleverly tamed and smoothed into loose, silky curls that rippled down her back, but he was not mistaken: it was Libby.

Hot, primitive desire kicked in Raul's gut as he stared at her reflection in the mirror behind the bar. Her make-up was discreet—just a hint of smoky grey eyeshadow which brought out the colour of her stunning blue-green eyes, a slick of mascara to define her long lashes, and a rose-pink gloss on her lips. The dress was a masterpiece of understated elegance that he knew would have come with an exorbitant price tag, but it was worth every penny, he decided, feeling himself harden as he noted how the superb cut of the bodice displayed her breasts like plump, velvety peaches.

Libby was naturally beautiful, but tonight she looked exquisite—and so incredibly sexy that his mouth ran dry as he strode over to the bar. She had dominated his thoughts and caused his body to be in a permanent state of arousal since he had first set eyes on her. Now he was not prepared to fight his urgent desire for her any longer.

CHAPTER FIVE

'CAN I get you a drink, *Signorina*?'

The barman gave Libby a polite smile, but it did not escape her notice that his eyes lingered boldly on the low-cut neckline of her dress. She was tempted to order an orange juice. At least holding the glass would give her something to do with her hands, and perhaps stop her feeling so horribly self-conscious while she waited for Raul. But as she was about to speak a familiar voice sounded from behind her.

'The lady will have champagne.'

It was a voice that never failed to send a quiver of reaction down her spine, as rich and sensuous as molten chocolate, and Libby's heart jolted painfully beneath her ribs as she turned her head and met Raul's dark gaze. His eyes gleamed like polished jet, and yet they seemed different, she noticed dazedly, no longer as cold as pools of black ice, but warm, and glinting with a sensual promise that trapped her breath in her throat.

'Raul,' she greeted him uncertainly, her voice emerging in a whispery breath, while a curious achy sensation unfurled in the pit of her stomach. No man had ever looked at her the way Raul was doing, and she had never expected *him*, of all men, to stare at her with such scorching desire blazing in his eyes.

'*Sei bellissima!*' he murmured in a velvet soft tone that brought her skin out in goosebumps. 'You look amazing in that dress, *cara*.'

She was drowning in his liquid gaze and had to moisten her lips with her tongue before she could speak. 'This old thing?' She resorted to flippancy in a frantic attempt to hide the effect he had on her. 'It's just something I slipped on to scrub the floor.'

Amusement glinted in his eyes, but to her amazement his smile was rueful. 'I can't believe I said that. You would look beautiful wearing sackcloth,' he astounded her by saying. 'But in that dress...' He moved his eyes slowly over her, leaving a trail of heat in his wake. 'You blow me away, *bella*.'

Not knowing quite what to make of this new Raul, who was no longer looking at her as if she were the most repugnant creature on the planet, Libby took a sip of champagne. It was deliciously cool and crisp, and she giggled as the bubbles exploded on her tongue. 'I've never tried champagne before,' she confessed, her pleasure fading when he looked amused. She bit her lip. 'But you already know that I'm not sophisticated, like the other women here tonight,' she said in a low tone.

Raul's smile faded and he stared at her intently. 'You are the most vibrant person I have ever met,' he admitted truthfully. 'You make me feel more alive than I have ever felt, and I regret that you find me stuffy.'

'I don't,' she denied swiftly, lifting her head so that their eyes locked. The electricity in the air around them was almost tangible and she knew that he felt it

as strongly as she. She did not know what had happened
during the two hours while he had attended a meeting
and she had been bullied by a glamorous personal stylist
into buying a whole wardrobe of exorbitantly expensive clothes; all she knew was that Raul was no longer
looking at her with anger and resentment in his eyes.
Incredibly, they no longer seemed to be enemies, they
were simply a man and woman drawn together by the
mysterious alchemy of sexual desire.

'I'm glad to hear it,' he murmured, moving imperceptibly closer, so that she breathed in the tantalising scent
of his cologne. She caught her breath when he ran his
finger lightly down her cheek. 'I have been thinking that
for Gino's sake we should make the effort to be friends.
What do you think, *cara*?'

Friends! She could not conceal her surprise. The
word conjured up an image of a comfortable, relaxed
relationship, like the one she had shared with Tony back
in Pennmar. But she could not ever imagine feeling relaxed with Raul. He dominated her senses and made
her so intensely aware of his raw masculinity that she
could think of little else other than her longing for him
to kiss her again.

Utterly disconcerted that he seemed to be offering
an olive branch, she watched him sip his champagne,
unaware of the wistful expression in her eyes as she
stared at his mouth. 'I think friends sounds a good idea.
For Gino's sake, of course,' she added hurriedly. An
unwelcome thought forced its way into her mind. 'That
doesn't mean that I will hand over control of Gino's
share of Carducci Cosmetics to you.'

'Of course not,' Raul assured her smoothly.

'I'm still determined to protect Gino's interests,' she warned him.

'I do not doubt your devotion to your son, and I understand your desire to do your best for him.' Raul's sexy smile stole her breath and melted the last vestiges of her resistance. 'I hope that in time you will come to trust me and realise that I want to build on CC's success for Gino's sake.' He touched his champagne flute to hers. 'Let us drink a toast, Libby. To a new beginning.'

She obediently took a sip of champagne, but the subject that had been bothering her since Raul had left her with Maria, the personal stylist, seemed likely to scupper their newfound friendship. 'This dress cost an absolute fortune,' she told him anxiously. 'Not to mention all the other clothes Maria the stylist insisted I needed. She explained that the bill was to be charged to your account, but I have no way of paying you back. The money I have in my savings account won't even cover one shoe,' she observed ruefully, glancing down at the exquisite three-inch stiletto heels that the personal stylist had selected for her to wear with the amethyst silk evening gown.

The shopping trip, during which Maria had whisked her into one designer boutique after another, had seemed surreal—especially as Libby had only ever bought her clothes in charity shops or discount stores. The shopping had been followed by a visit to a hair salon and beauty parlour, and later, when she had changed into the dress at Raul's luxurious penthouse apartment, the feeling that she had fallen into the pages of a fairytale had intensified.

Raul frowned. 'I have already explained that as you are now a representative of CC it is necessary for you to dress appropriately. You do not have to worry about paying for the clothes. Under the terms of my father's will all your personal expenses will be met by Pietro's estate.'

Guilt surged up inside Libby at Raul's words. It was bad enough that she was living at the villa under false pretences, but ten times worse to know that she was not entitled to a penny of the Carducci fortune. She bit her lip. 'I just don't feel comfortable about it,' she mumbled. 'It's fine that Gino's living expenses will be covered, but I feel it is morally wrong for me to live off Pietro's money.'

It was in Raul's mind to point out that it had been morally wrong of Libby to have had an affair with a wealthy man four decades older than her, particularly as he was convinced that Gino's conception had not been an accident. And yet her reluctance to allow him to pay for her clothes seemed genuine. Most women he knew would have been more than happy to flex his credit card, and he felt slightly irritated that Libby was not acting like the gold-digger he had assumed her to be.

He glanced at his watch, aware that the crowd in the bar was thinning as guests began to make their way to the banqueting hall. 'It's time to go in to dinner,' he said, proffering his arm to help her down from the stool.

'How many people will be at this dinner?' Libby asked nervously, gripping his arm as she struggled to balance on her vertiginous heels while he escorted her out of the bar and along a corridor towards a set of double doors which stood open to reveal long rows of white damask-covered tables set with gleaming silver cutlery and crystal glasses.

'Tonight's event is an international trade dinner, and I imagine a couple of hundred guests have been invited.' Raul glanced down at her tense face. 'What's the matter? You look as though you're about to be thrown to the lions.'

Libby bit her lip. 'People are looking at me,' she muttered. 'Do you think they know who I am—?' She broke off, flushing beneath Raul's sardonic glance.

'If you mean do they know that you were my father's mistress and the mother of his illegitimate child then, no, I have not advertised that fact,' he told her coolly. He had been conscious of the interested glances Libby was attracting, particularly from other men, and a primitive, possessive instinct made him move closer to her. 'People are looking, because your flame-coloured hair and English rose complexion make you very noticeable, *cara*. And in that dress you are incredibly beautiful.'

He meant it, Libby was stunned to realise, her heart racing when she glimpsed the raw hunger in Raul's eyes. No man had ever told her she was beautiful before, but as she caught sight of her reflection in one of the huge wall mirrors she could see that the amethyst silk dress suited her colouring and flattered her figure. It was almost impossible to believe that the elegant woman with the mane of tamed, silky curls tumbling down her back was really her, and without thinking she murmured, 'I wish Miles could see me now.'

Raul's dark eyebrows winged upwards. 'Who is Miles?'

'Miles Sefton—only son of Lord Sefton.' Libby grimaced. 'We met when I worked as a waitress at a very exclusive golf club where Miles was a member. I stupidly fell in love with him, and even more stupidly believed him when he said he loved me.'

'But something happened to make you realise he was not in love with you?' Raul murmured. The fact that Libby had been attracted to a member of the English aristocracy was more proof of her gold-digger tendencies. He must have imagined the note of hurt in her voice when she spoke of this Miles Sefton.

Libby nodded. 'When Miles invited me to lunch at Sefton Hall I thought it was because he wanted me to meet his family. But I found out later that his parents had been putting pressure on him to get married, and he'd found it amusing to introduce *me* as his girlfriend, knowing they would be horrified that he was dating a waitress. That lunch—during which Lord and Lady Sefton could barely bring themselves to speak to me—was one of the most humiliating experiences of my life,' she admitted. 'But not as humiliating as when I overheard Miles assure Lord Sefton that our relationship wasn't serious, and that he was only dating me because he wanted to take me to bed.'

She caught the expression in Raul's eyes and said bitterly, 'I know what you're thinking: why *else* would a member of the landed gentry have dated a waitress? Still, it proved what my mother always said—that all men are selfish and not to be trusted, and certainly not worth wasting your emotions on.'

Suddenly conscious that her raised voice was attracting attention from the other guests waiting to enter the banqueting hall, she took a deep breath, and moments later a footman appeared to escort her and Raul to their table.

'Your mother clearly has strong views on the inadequacies of the male species,' Raul commented dryly when they were both seated. Although perhaps that was not so surprising, he mused, recalling that Libby had told him her father had abandoned her mother before she had even been born.

'Mum had a lot of bad experiences with men.' Libby immediately sprang to Liz's defence. 'They always let her down.'

Including Pietro Carducci, she brooded, anger flaring inside her when she remembered how heartbroken her mother had been when her lover had failed to call her after the cruise. Admittedly Pietro had made provision for Liz and Gino in his will, but it was too late, she thought sadly. Liz had died believing that Pietro had abandoned her just as Libby's father had done.

'I won't make the same mistakes as Mum,' Libby said fiercely. 'Most of the men she dated when I was a child were creeps. I'm *never* going to put Gino through the misery of feeling that he has to compete with a new man in my life.'

Raul frowned. 'What do you mean?'

'I mean that until Gino is eighteen *he* is going to be the only man in my life. Romance is a fool's game anyway, and in my experience highly overrated,' Libby said bleakly, remembering the tears she had wasted over Miles.

'You can't seriously intend to remain single for the next seventeen years?' Raul could not hide his surprise at the vehemence of her tone. 'Wouldn't you like to get married one day? Perhaps have more children so that Gino grows up as part of a family?' He kept his tone deliberately casual while he digested the unwelcome news that Libby did not seem to have marriage on her agenda.

She shook her head. 'It's a nice idea, and I suppose if I'm honest a part of me wants to believe in the fairytale of falling in love with a man who would be a wonderful stepfather to Gino and all of us living happily ever after. But the reality is that something like one in three marriages end in divorce, and I'd rather concentrate all my energy on Gino than risk a relationship that may not work out.'

She paused, unaware of the wistful expression in her eyes as she added, 'I can't deny that I'd love Gino to have a proper family: a father, brothers and sisters. It was what I wanted more than anything when I was a child. But the fact is that Gino's father is dead. He only has me, and I will do my best to be a mother *and* a father to him.'

The arrival of a waiter to serve the first course put an end to the conversation. Raul sipped his wine and considered what Libby had told him. He was frustrated that she did not fit the image he had formed of her when he'd first realised that she had been Pietro's mistress. He had formed many unpleasant ideas of her, and had never expected her to evoke his sympathy. But now he recalled how Libby had said that when she had told Pietro she was pregnant with his child he had ignored her. She clearly believed that his father had let her down, as her own father had abandoned her mother. She had read in the papers of Pietro's death and must have known that she would have been entitled to a maintenance award for Gino, but instead of contacting the Carducci family she had disappeared and it had taken him months to find her.

The possibility that he might have misjudged Libby tormented Raul's mind throughout the dinner and the interminably long speeches which followed. But sitting beside her, inhaling her delicate perfume while his eyes strayed to the creamy upper slopes of her breasts displayed so tantalisingly above her low-cut dress, proved an even greater torment for his body. Lust was another emotion he had *not* expected to feel for his father's mistress, he thought irritably, shifting his position slightly to ease the uncomfortable sensation of his arousal straining against the zip of his trousers.

Libby was relieved when the after-dinner speeches finally came to an end. She had understood very little about EU trade policies or new business opportunities in China, and as her concentration had wavered she had grown increasingly aware of the man at her side. Raul seemed to have taken his suggestion that they should be friends for Gino's sake to heart, and throughout the meal he had subjected her to the full megawatt force of his charisma. He was a witty and entertaining companion, and every time he smiled she found it impossible to resist his sexy charm.

'What's happening now?' she asked him as they stood up from the table and joined the throng of guests walking out of the banqueting suite.

'Now everyone races towards the bar, desperate for a drink after sitting through two hours of dull speeches.' Raul glanced down at her, his eyes glinting with amusement and a latent sensual heat that made her heart race. 'Can I get you more champagne? Or would you like to dance?'

Libby glanced around and realised they were now in a vast ballroom. 'I don't think I'd better risk any more alcohol after the two glasses of champagne I had at dinner.' She caught her breath when Raul slid his arm around her waist and led her onto the dance floor.

'Wise choice,' he murmured, lowering his head so that his warm breath fanned her cheek. The feel of his lean, hard body pressed close against her warned Libby that he was a far greater risk to her equilibrium than another glass of champagne, but she told herself that she did not want to spoil their tenuous friendship by pulling out of his arms. 'Relax,' he bade her, his voice as sensuous as molten honey, and she could not prevent a quiver of reaction when he traced his fingertips lightly up and down her spine.

She lost all sense of time as they drifted around the ballroom, hip to hip, her breasts crushed against the steel wall of his chest as he imperceptibly tightened his arms around her. Other guests passed them by on the dance floor, but she was only aware of Raul. When he finally loosened his hold and eased away from her the dull ache in her pelvis had intensified to a hot, frantic throb, and she stared at him dazedly when he steered her towards the door.

'It's midnight, and we have a forty minute drive back to the Villa Giulietta,' he informed her gently. 'I assume you would prefer to go back to the villa, so that you are there when Gino wakes tomorrow morning, rather than spend the night at my apartment?'

'Oh, yes—definitely,' Libby agreed quickly, shame sweeping through her when she realised she had not thought about Gino for the past few hours. How *could* she have forgotten him so easily when he had been the most important person in her life for the past ten months? The truth was that Raul dominated her senses. Even now her treacherous body trembled at his closeness as he ushered her across the foyer and out of the hotel.

They were both silent on the journey from Rome. Raul appeared to be lost in his thoughts, and after one glance at his hard profile Libby closed her eyes in a desperate attempt to lessen her awareness of him. Eventually the crunch of the Lamborghini's tyres on the gravel drive told her they had arrived back at the villa, and as she lifted her lashes she could not restrain a gasp at the sight of the vast black lake spread out in front of the house, dappled with silver moonlight and reflecting a myriad diamond stars.

'It's so beautiful,' she whispered in an awed voice.

Too impatient to wait for Raul to walk round and open her door, she jumped out of the car and headed towards the lake. But walking in her high heels on the gravel was almost impossible, and she stepped onto the lawn and kicked off her shoes before running down to the water's edge. The damp grass was cool against the soles of her feet, and the soft breeze from the lake whispered across her skin like a lover's caress. She tipped her head back to stare at the stars and laughed in sheer delight at the beauty of the night.

'I love the way the moonlight casts a silver path across the black water. It makes you want to strip off and dive in.' She spun round to Raul, her face alight with pleasure.

Her boundless enthusiasm was irresistible, he thought, his mouth curving into a smile. 'I'm all for you stripping off,' he murmured dulcetly, 'but you may get a shock if you dive in. The water temperature drops considerably at night.'

Heat scalded Libby's cheeks. 'I was speaking figuratively,' she mumbled, her heart jerking unevenly beneath her ribs as Raul walked towards her, his eyes glinting with sensual promise. He halted in front of her, so close that she could feel the heat from his body, and her breath hitched in her throat when he slid his hand beneath her chin and tilted her face to his.

'What a pity,' he murmured, the amusement in his voice fading to be replaced with a stark hunger. 'There's nothing I would not do at this moment to see you naked in the moonlight, *cara*.'

'Raul…' Libby's faint protest drifted away on the breeze. She had wanted him to kiss her since he had walked into the hotel bar earlier and stared at her with undisguised desire blazing in his eyes. All evening she had ached for this moment. The chemistry between them was too overpowering to be denied, and now, as he slowly lowered his head, she trembled with anticipation and a wild, ferocious excitement that exploded in a starburst of pleasure at the first brush of his lips across hers.

Raul wanted to take it slow, to savour the moist softness of Libby's mouth in a leisurely tasting, but his plans were blown sky-high the moment he claimed her lips and felt her instant response. Passion did not simply flare between them, it roared into hot, urgent life, as untamed and out of control as a forest fire, consuming them both. He pulled her into the cradle of his hips and groaned when she moved sinuously against him, his erection so immediate and so shockingly hard that there was no way she could not be aware of it.

Her breasts were crushed against his chest, and he could feel the hard peaks of her nipples through his silk shirt. *Dio*, he had never felt such hunger for a woman. Desire pounded in his veins and demolished his ability to think. His usual cool logic had been replaced with primitive sexual need and he tangled his fingers in her fiery curls and tugged her head back to expose the slender column of her white throat.

Libby could not restrain a little moan of pleasure when Raul slid his lips down her neck. Every nerve-ending in her body was attuned to the brush of his mouth on her skin, and a tremor ran through her when he trailed hot, hungry kisses along her collarbone and bare shoulder. Held tightly against him, she was unaware that he had slid the zip of her dress down until the strapless bodice suddenly felt loose. Heart thumping, she tried to ease her mouth from his to protest, but he increased the pressure of his lips in a sensual assault that left her dazed with desire, and when he finally lifted his head she did nothing to stop him as he slowly peeled her dress down until her breasts spilled into his hands.

'You are exquisite,' he muttered hoarsely.

His voice was no longer coldly arrogant but rough with need, and Libby's faint spark of resistance melted away as he stroked his thumb-pads across her nipples so that they immediately hardened into tight, tingling peaks. Somehow, without her being aware that they had moved, Raul had guided her beneath the shadow of a tall pine tree, and she leaned back against the trunk, grateful for its support as he lowered his head and closed his lips around one nipple while he continued to roll its twin between his fingers.

The pleasure of his mouth on her breasts was indescribable, and she instinctively arched her back, no thought in her head other than that he should continue to stroke his tongue across each sensitive crest. Nothing in her life had prepared her for this clawing, clamouring need that caused her entire body to throb with desire. She wanted Raul with an instinctive, primitive hunger—wanted to feel his naked skin on hers and to take the solid length of his erection that she could feel jutting into her belly deep inside her.

He tugged up her long skirt until it bunched around her waist, and she trembled with anticipation when he slipped his hand between her thighs, forcing her to part them slightly, before he ran a finger over the lacy panel of her knickers. At the same time he drew one nipple fully into his mouth and suckled her. The sensual tugging sensation sent arrows of pleasure from her breasts to her pelvis. With a little sob she arched her hips towards his hand, and caught her breath when he slid his finger inside her knickers and discovered the slick wetness of her arousal.

She had never allowed a man to touch her so intimately before—not even Miles, whom she had been so sure she had been in love with. This hot, pulsing need that Raul was arousing in her was lust, not love—she knew that—but right then she did not care *what* the feeling was called. She was just desperate for him to assuage the burning ache between her legs. She closed her eyes and let her head fall back, unable to hold back a gasp of wanton delight when Raul ran his thumb-pad very delicately over her clitoris. The effect was instantaneous. Spasms of pleasure ripped through her, causing her muscles to clench; her legs buckled beneath her and she gripped Raul's hair as he cupped her bottom and lifted her, holding her tight against his rock-hard arousal.

'Please…' The spasms were fading, but instinct told her he could give her so much more pleasure.

'What are you asking for, Libby?' His voice was deep and harsh, slicing through the sensual haze that enveloped her. 'Do you want me to take you here and now on the damp grass, in full view of the house?'

Dear God, yes! That was exactly what she wanted. For a few seconds Libby stared at Raul's hard face, all angles and planes in the moonlight, and felt a frantic urge for him to lie her on the ground, strip off her knickers and plunge his swollen shaft into her moist, willing flesh. But the sound of his voice and the cold gleam in his eyes catapulted her back to reality. What was she *doing*? How *could* she have behaved with such wanton eagerness that she had practically begged him to make love to her?

'*Dio!* You said there will be no man in your life while Gino is a child, but clearly you will find it impossible to remain celibate until he is an adult. You are *desperate* for sex,' he taunted savagely. 'But I warn you now: I will not allow you to entertain your lovers at the villa. Gino is not going to grow up with a succession of "uncles".'

Libby shook her head, feeling sick as desire slowly ebbed and shame took its place. 'I don't have any lovers,' she said shakily. 'I've never felt like this before. You…' She closed her eyes to try and blot out the memory of how she had responded to him, and realised that honesty was her only hope of convincing Raul she was not the immoral slut he clearly believed she was. 'You make me feel things I've never felt for any other man,' she admitted huskily.

Raul's self-control wavered at Libby's breathy confession, and the temptation to seize her back in his arms and pull her down onto the grass—to take her hard and fast, as his body was screaming at him to do—almost overwhelmed him. Almost—but not quite. Nostrils flaring with the effort of dragging oxygen into his lungs, he stepped away from her and watched her dispassionately as she dragged the bodice of her dress up to cover her breasts. There was a way he could have everything his heart desired: control of Carducci Cosmetics, *and* this sultry green-eyed witch in his bed. He would be a fool not to seize his chance.

'In that case my proposition is even more tenable,' he said softly.

CHAPTER SIX

'WHAT do you mean?' Libby gave a sudden shiver, her skin quickly cooling now that she was no longer in Raul's arms. 'What proposition?'

He saw the tremor that ran through her and frowned. 'You're cold. Here—put this on.' He shrugged out of his jacket, draped it around her shoulders and caught hold of her hand to lead her firmly across the lawn. 'We'll continue this discussion inside.'

Libby would have preferred not to hold a post-mortem on the shockingly wanton way she had responded to him, but Raul's fingers were gripping hers like a vice and she had no option but to hurry alongside him. She burrowed into the jacket, which was still warm from his body and carried the faint scent of his cologne. She had forgotten to collect her shoes, but when they reached the drive and she picked her way cautiously over the gravel he scooped her into his arms and carried her up to the house.

He strode across the hall and into his study, and set her down on her feet before crossing the room and taking a bottle from the drinks cabinet. 'Would you like a whisky? It will warm you up.'

When she shook her head he poured himself a drink and swallowed the amber liquid down in one gulp. She sensed his fierce tension and stared at him in confusion. 'What proposition?' she asked again.

Raul swung round to face her, his dark eyes unfathomable. Ever since the idea of marrying Libby as a way to claim full control of CC had stolen into his mind he had thought of little else. The arguments for and against such a monumental decision had given him a sleepless night and had tormented him all day, so that he had barely been able to concentrate on the crucial board meeting.

He did not want to marry again. Once had been enough, he thought grimly, remembering his bitter divorce from his first wife. He valued his freedom, and was reluctant to sacrifice it, but he valued Carducci Cosmetics above anything—and there would be compensations to taking Libby as his bride, he acknowledged, as he slid his eyes down from her face to her pale shoulders and then lower still to the soft swell of her breasts revealed by the plunging neckline of her dress. She was so very lovely. Just looking at her evoked a dull ache in his gut, and he realised that he no longer cared that she had been Pietro's mistress; the chemistry between them was too strong to be denied.

And there was another important reason to marry her. Gino needed a father. Libby had stated that she would not bring him up with a succession of 'uncles', but it was unrealistic to expect that she would not have a relationship until the baby was older—and Raul found that he hated the prospect of watching from the sidelines while the little boy called another man Papa.

Libby's big blue-green eyes were locked on him, and he knew she was waiting for him to speak. 'I think we should get married,' he said abruptly.

'*What?*'

She must have misheard him, Libby told herself dazedly. Either that or this was his idea of a stupid joke. Perhaps it was wishful thinking? taunted a little voice in her head. Why had her heart leapt with excitement for the nano-second when she had thought he meant that he wanted to marry her? She wasn't in love with him, she wasn't even sure she liked him very much, and she could not understand why she felt drawn to him.

'I don't understand,' she faltered.

'I want to bring Gino up as my son.' The quiet intensity of his tone told her that this was no joke and that he was deadly serious. 'Let me explain,' he said when she gaped at him. 'When Pietro and Eleanora Carducci adopted me they gave me a life that I could never have imagined when I lived in the orphanage—not just wealth and education, but love, and the stability that comes from growing up with two parents. Gino will never know his real father, but if we marry and I adopt him he will grow up with a mother and father, and hopefully siblings,' he added, his eyes gleaming with a sensual heat that sent a tremor through Libby. 'Make no mistake: what I am suggesting is a real marriage,' he told her. 'I will love Gino as my son—just as Pietro loved me—but I have no blood relatives that I am aware of, and I would like to have children of my own.'

'Then surely it would be better to wait until you fall in love, marry a woman you care for, and *then* have children?' Libby argued. 'Heaven knows, enough couples who marry for love still end up in the divorce courts. What chance would a marriage between us stand when we don't even particularly *like* each other?'

Raul stared at her speculatively. 'I thought we had agreed to become friends for Gino's sake? And I have to say that tonight I thought we succeeded rather well,' he drawled, watching her face flood with colour when she remembered the feverish passion they had shared down by the lake. 'It is precisely the fact that we are *not* in love, and therefore have no expectations about our relationship, that makes me believe our marriage would work.'

He gave a bitter laugh. 'I have tried a conventional marriage, and paid heavily for my mistake. Three years ago I mistook the sexual attraction I felt for my PA for love. Dana assured me that she shared my desire for a family, and we had a great circus of a wedding. But once we were married she continually found reasons why we should put off trying for a child. She preferred to live in our apartment in Manhattan and party every night, and she complained that she hated the villa and found life here boring.'

Raul's jaw tightened as he recalled how his marriage had imploded.

'The only thing that made Dana truly happy was spending money—although she resented the hours I spent working to make it. At first I was prepared to fund her hobby, but she was a compulsive shopper, and if I ever suggested that she might like to control her spending she would become hysterical and accuse me of being a tyrant who wanted to keep her barefoot and pregnant. Not that her falling pregnant was ever likely,' he said flatly. 'After a year of increasingly bitter rows it was clear that the marriage was a disaster, and during one of our many screaming matches Dana admitted she had lied about wanting children, and had only married me because I was wealthy enough to give her the extravagant lifestyle she craved. We agreed to divorce and I offered her a generous settlement, including the Manhattan apartment. But that wasn't enough for my dear ex-wife. She wanted every last drop of blood she could squeeze out of me, and even made a claim on the Villa Giulietta.'

'But I thought you said she hated the villa?' Libby said faintly, stunned by the revelation that Raul had once been married. His past relationships were of no interest to her, she reminded herself, so why did she feel so stupidly jealous of his ex-wife?

'Dana knew I would pay whatever she demanded in return for her agreement to relinquish her rights to the villa. Her divorce settlement made legal history in the American courts—and I learned a very expensive lesson,' Raul said savagely. 'I will never fall for the illusion of love again, but I want Gino to have two parents, as I did when the Carduccis adopted me. You said yourself you longed to have a proper family when you were a child,' he reminded Libby when she stared at him in dumbstruck silence.

'I said I wanted to believe in the fairytale of a happy ever after family, but I'm not sure it really exists.'

'We can make it exist if it's something we both want.'

As Raul spoke he was startled to realise that he no longer only wanted to persuade Libby to marry him so that he could claim full control of the company. Everything he had said to her was true; he wanted to repay his adoptive father for all he had done for him by adopting Pietro's son, and he felt a fierce longing to hold his own child in his arms and finally have a blood link with another human being. Taking full control of CC until Gino was eighteen *was* important to him. But instead of divorcing Libby, as he had planned, he saw no reason why they should not have a successful marriage built on their mutual desire for a family—as well as their physical desire for each other.

Libby shook her head, trying to ignore the voice of her conscience which was whispering that Raul's suggestion made a crazy kind of sense. He was offering to be a father to Gino, and that alone demanded her serious consideration when she had spent her childhood wishing that she had a father.

If she married Raul she would no longer live in fear of him discovering that she was not Gino's mother and banishing her from the villa. But he had said it would be a real marriage. Her eyes were drawn to his hard body, and a quiver ran through her when she remembered how his bold caresses had taken her to such a level of excitement that she had been desperate for him to make love to her properly. Would he be able to tell that not only had she not given birth to Gino, but that she had never even had sex? Not if she pretended to be experienced, the voice in her head pointed out. But that would be another lie to add to all the others she had spun. Wouldn't it be better to admit the truth about Gino's parentage now?

She chewed on her lip, torn between her guilty conscience and her fear of losing Gino. Nothing had changed. If she revealed that she was Gino's half-sister and had no legal rights to him Raul would still fight her for custody of the baby—and if he won he might go ahead and adopt Gino, and send her back to England.

'It would never work,' she said abruptly. 'We're too different. Once this chemistry, or attraction, or whatever it is between us died out we would have nothing in common.'

'I'm not sure we are so different,' Raul mused. 'Our childhood experiences have made us appreciate the value of family life. We both think it would be best for Gino to grow up with two parents. Neither of us plans to marry anyone else, and yet we would both like to have children.'

Raul's deep voice was so softly persuasive that Libby found she could not come up with a single argument against his list of reasons why they should marry, and instead she pictured a scene in the future where she was cradling a newborn baby in her arms while Gino, now a toddler, met his little brother or sister for the first time. She could not deny that she would love to have her own baby some day—a little companion for Gino. But marry Raul! She must be mad to actually be contemplating it—mustn't she?

Wrapped up in her thoughts, she was unaware that he had moved closer to her until he lifted his hand and trailed his finger down from her collarbone to the vee between her breasts exposed by her low-cut dress. 'I don't think we need to worry about the chemistry fading, *cara*,' he murmured, his voice suddenly as rich and sensuous as molten chocolate. 'I'm so hungry for you that I'm unbearably tempted to push you down on the sofa and take you right now—and you would let me, Libby. Don't even think of denying it,' he warned her softly, placing his finger across her lips. Do you think I don't see the way your pulse races whenever I am near you? The way your eyes darken with desire and your lips part in readiness for my kiss?'

His mouth was so close to hers that Libby could taste his warm breath. How *could* she deny her desire for him when she was trembling with her need for him to close the gap between them? His tongue explored the shape of her lips before probing between them, pushing insistently into her mouth. Libby strained towards him, her pride discarded in her eagerness for him to kiss her with all the pent-up passion she could sense simmering between them. Her lashes drifted down, her whole being focused on the pleasure of Raul's wickedly inventive tongue.

But the sound of Gino's stark cry jerked her back to reality. Her eyes flew open and she gasped as she whirled away from Raul and stared towards the door, expecting to see Silvana standing there with the baby.

There was no one there. She stared at Raul, eyes wide with panic. 'I heard Gino cry.'

'The baby monitor,' he explained, nodding towards the device plugged into an electrical socket on the wall behind his desk. 'I've had them installed in every room in the house so that we can always be sure to hear him.'

Even in his study, Libby thought in amazement—which must mean that Raul would not mind being disturbed while he worked. 'I see,' she said slowly. 'That was very thoughtful of you.'

Gino's cries grew louder and he began to cough. Libby heard Silvana's voice speaking gently to the baby, but a strong maternal instinct drove her towards the door.

'I must go to him.' She hesitated, her eyes fixed on Raul's face.

'I would be a good father to him,' he said deeply. 'I swear I will care for him and protect him, love him as Pietro loved me.'

'Yes.' She could see the determination blazing in his eyes, hear it in his voice. 'I believe you would do that for Gino,' she whispered, moved to tears at the depth of emotion in his fierce avowal.

As a little girl she had dreamed that her father would one day find her, and that he would be strong and brave and would fight the monsters that lived under her bed. Didn't Gino need a father to fight his monsters?

But it was not necessary for her to marry Raul. Under the terms of Pietro's will Gino's future was secure, and he would one day inherit half of Carducci Cosmetics and the Villa Giulietta. But what about his emotional security? Didn't she, better than anyone, understand how important it was for a child to have a father? And Gino would need a positive role model to guide him as he grew into adulthood and inherited his share of the Carducci fortune.

'Marry me and allow me to take care of both of you, *cara*.'

Raul's voice was achingly seductive. He could have no idea how beguiling the concept of being cared for sounded after a lifetime of looking after herself, she brooded. She had adored her mum, but Liz had been too young to cope with motherhood, meaning that Libby had

had to learn to be independent from an early age. Now she was solely responsible for Gino. How much easier life would be if she could share that responsibility with someone else?

'I don't know what to do,' she admitted helplessly, terrified of the enormity of the decision facing her.

'Yes, you do,' Raul insisted. 'You must do what is best for Gino, and in your heart you know he needs me.'

He was so strong, so self-assured, and after months of worrying about Gino's health and struggling to cope with her grief at Liz's death, Libby felt so tired. 'Maybe you're right,' she said numbly.

'I am.' Raul's voice rang with conviction and a heady feeling of triumph swept through him. Libby need never know that his overriding reason for suggesting that they should marry was so that he could take full control of Carducci Cosmetics. He had not been lying when he had told her that he wanted to be Gino's father, or that he wanted them to have children together. Once they were married he would do his best to ensure she quickly fell pregnant; that way she would be too busy caring for a toddler and preparing for the arrival of another baby to realise that she no longer had control of Gino's shares in the company.

Raul could see the indecision in Libby's eyes and sensed the battle waging inside her head. He was re-nowned in the boardroom as a brilliant tactician, and, sensing victory, he deliberately softened his voice. 'It is in your power to give your son the stable family life you longed for when you were a child. Say yes for Gino's sake, *cara*.'

* * *

She couldn't do it. She could not marry a man who did not love her. Could she? Libby's eyes snapped open, and after hours of tossing and turning in bed she finally acknowledged that she was never going to fall asleep while Raul's astounding proposal was going round and round in her head.

She had fled from his study last night after telling him that she needed time to think, but in the pearly softness of dawn her emotions were still in turmoil. Wearily, she threw back the sheets and slipped out of bed, crossing to the window that overlooked the lake. The water was silvery-grey in the early-morning light, reflecting here and there the pink clouds above as the sunrise slowly stained the sky.

'*You must do what is best for Gino, and in your heart you know he needs me.*' Raul's words haunted her, for she could not deny the truth of them. Gino needed a father. She believed Raul when he had said that he wanted to adopt the little boy and care for him as Pietro had cared for *him*. Did she have the right to deny Gino what she had wanted more than anything when she was a child: a father, and the security of being part of a proper family, living in a proper home?

She had never felt secure when she and Liz had lived in the commune. When they had eventually moved back to England the other kids at school had been envious of her unconventional upbringing, but the reality was that she had never felt as though she belonged anywhere or to anyone. The adults at the commune had for the most part been absorbed in their own lives, and the children had been undisciplined and unruly, with the older ones frequently bullying the younger ones. Libby had learned to be tough to survive, but she did not want the same for

Gino. Children needed rules and boundaries as well as love to help them feel safe, and the fact that Gino would one day inherit a fortune meant that it was vital he had people around him he could trust.

She did not need to marry Raul for him to be a father figure to Gino. But he had told her he would like children of his own. He was embittered by his divorce now, but if she turned him down it was conceivable that in the future he would marry someone else and draw Gino into his new family. The idea of Gino having a stepmother made her blanch. What if Raul and his wife wanted to take Gino away on holiday? And what would happen at Christmas? Would she spend it alone, while Gino celebrated the day with Raul and his family?

She hugged her arms around her, trying to marshal her thoughts. Wouldn't it be better to agree to a loveless marriage and give Gino the stable family he deserved? When her mum had died she had vowed to devote herself to him and do what was best for him, and in a moment of calm clarity she accepted that marrying Raul and allowing him to be a father to Gino was indisputably the greatest gift she could give her orphaned baby brother.

Brilliant sunlight slanted across Libby's face and dragged her from sleep. She sat up, disorientated, and stared blankly at the clock, which showed that it was ten o'clock. She remembered now. Having finally made up her mind to accept Raul's proposal she had fallen back into bed, hoping to catch an hour's sleep before Gino stirred. But she had slept for much longer than she had intended. Gino should have had a dose of his antibiotic at seven, along with a bottle of milk and breakfast…

Heart pounding with panic, she jumped up and shot into the adjoining sitting room, stopping dead at the sight of Raul stretched out on the floor, building towers of wooden bricks which Gino delightedly knocked down.

Two sets of dark eyes focused on her: one pair flecked with amber, which lit up as she moved forward, the other pair as black as midnight and gleaming with sensual heat as they trailed over her wild hair and sunflower yellow nightshirt.

'I can't believe I slept so late,' she burst out, hastily dragging her gaze from Raul's mouth. She focused on Gino and was gratified when he greeted her with a beaming smile and crawled over to her with the speed of a missile. 'Hello, baba,' she murmured, her voice aching with love for the baby as she scooped him up and rubbed her cheek over his silky black curls. 'Has he been okay with you? I mean, he's only ever had me to care for him,' she explained, when Raul's eyebrows rose in silent query. 'He was due his next dose of medicine at—'

'Silvana gave it to him when he had his breakfast,' Raul interrupted her. 'The maid said you were fast asleep, so I sat him in his pushchair and took him for a stroll down by the lake.'

'Oh.' Libby stared at him, disconcerted by the idea of Raul taking Gino off without her. 'I hope he was warm enough. It's important to wrap him up while he has his cough.'

'The thermometer on the patio was showing eighteen degrees Celsius at eight o'clock this morning,' Raul in-

formed her dryly. 'As for Gino's respiratory problems—
I've made an appointment for him to see a specialist in
Rome next week.'

Relief flooded through Libby. 'Thank you. I've been
so worried about him,' she admitted. She bit her lip,
wondering how to broach the subject of Raul's marriage
proposal. Part of her still wondered if she had dreamed
the whole thing, and before she could say anything there
was a light tap on the door and Silvana appeared.

'I thought Gino might be ready for a nap,' the
nanny said with a smile. As if on cue the baby yawned
widely.

'I'm sure he is,' Libby agreed, her heart lurching
when Silvana took Gino through to the nursery, leaving
her alone with Raul. She tensed as he strolled over to
her, every nerve-ending in her body suddenly tingling
when he slid his hand beneath her chin and tilted her
face.

'Did you sleep well, *cara*?' As he spoke he lightly
touched the give-away dark circles beneath her eyes,
and Libby shook her head ruefully.

'No.' She did not explain the reason for her disturbed night, but the shadows in her eyes and the way
she tugged her bottom lip with her teeth told their own
story. An unbidden feeling of tenderness surged through
Raul. She was so young, and so fiercely protective of her
son, but there was a vulnerability about her that tugged
on his heart. He had expected her to jump at the opportunity to marry a billionaire, he admitted wryly. But
instead she had clearly been awake all night, debating
the best thing to do for Gino.

'Do you doubt that I will love Gino as much as if he
were my own flesh and blood?' he said softly.

Libby was drowning in the liquid warmth of his gaze. 'No, I don't doubt that,' she whispered, unable to tear her eyes from his mouth that was so tantalisingly close to hers. She forced herself to concentrate and voice her doubts. 'It's just that we don't know each other. We're practically strangers.'

Raul heard the note of panic in her voice and once again felt the curious sensation that his heart was being squeezed. 'That is something I intend to remedy over the next couple of weeks. I have arranged to work from the villa, so that I can spend some time with you and Gino, and I will only go to Rome when it is absolutely necessary for me to be at the office.'

'I see.' Libby wet her lips, and her heart began to pound when his head moved imperceptibly lower. 'That will be…good.'

The electricity in the atmosphere crackled, searing them both, and Raul could no longer resist the lure of her moist pink lips. 'Let me show you how good it will be between us,' he said hoarsely. 'I do not only want to marry you for Gino's sake. There is something powerful between us—attraction, chemistry, it doesn't matter what you call it—and it was there from the moment we laid eyes on each other. I challenge you to deny you feel it too.'

'I can't,' Libby admitted shakily, but her voice was no more than a fragile breath, lost beneath the hungry pressure of his lips as he caught her to him and brought his mouth down on hers in a kiss that plundered her soul.

She did not even try to resist. This was where she wanted to be, Libby accepted silently as she wound her arms around his neck to mould her body even closer to his. Her lashes drifted down, her senses focused on the slightly abrasive feel of his skin against cheek and the firm, demanding pressure of his mouth moving on hers in a slow tasting before he pushed his tongue between her lips and explored her with a bold eroticism that made her tremble.

When at last he lifted his head she stared at him dazedly, shaken not so much by his passion but by the faint tenderness she glimpsed in his eyes before his expression was hidden by the sweep of his thick black lashes.

'Will you be my wife, Libby, and allow me to be Gino's father?'

She suddenly felt so emotional that for a moment she could not speak. Maybe every woman felt the same way when faced with a marriage proposal, she told herself. But it meant nothing; Raul meant nothing to her, or she to him. The only reason to accept was an orphaned baby boy. She swallowed the lump in her throat and said steadily, 'Yes'.

His smile stole her breath, but to her disappointment he did not kiss her again, or carry her off to bed and make love to her as she had secretly hoped he would.

'I have some calls to make, so I'll leave you to get dressed, *cara*. Meet me on the terrace for lunch, and we can discuss the wedding.'

Two hours later Libby went to the nursery to collect Gino, and discovered that Raul had not wasted any time in announcing their engagement.

Silvana greeted her with a beaming smile. 'May I offer my congratulations, Libby? Signor Carducci told me that the two of you are to be married, and that he intends to adopt the *bambino*. He will be a wonderful father,' she said approvingly. 'I have seen how much he cares for Gino. I hope that you will be very happy.'

'Thank you.' Libby settled Gino on her hip and made her way along the rabbit-warren of corridors to the main part of the house. As she walked down the central staircase she saw Raul's aunt Carmina emerge from the dining room, and her heart sank when the older woman moved purposefully to the bottom of the stairs, clearly in a furious temper.

'You must think you are very clever.' Carmina launched into her attack as soon as Libby reached the bottom stair. 'First Pietro, and now Raul—both seduced by your youthful body and no doubt your expertise between the sheets. I credited Raul with more sense than to get involved with his father's whore,' she spat viciously. 'I can only think he has lost his sanity if he seriously intends to marry you.'

Libby was determined not to show that she was shaken by the vitriol in Carmina's voice, but she instinctively tightened her arms around Gino. 'I didn't seduce anyone,' she defended herself angrily. 'Raul was perfectly sane when he asked me to marry him—and why shouldn't I be his wife? You know nothing about me, and you have no right to make horrible insinuations about my character.'

'You are a cheap tart who deliberately went after my brother-in-law because you knew he was wealthy, and struck lucky when you conceived his child,' Carmina told her with icy contempt. 'Pietro and I...' Her voice quivered slightly. 'We should have been together—and would have been if he hadn't lost his head over *you*.'

Libby frowned. 'But I thought that Pietro's wife—your sister—died ten years ago? Surely if he had felt anything for you he would have told you in all that time?'

She bit her lip, feeling a pang of sympathy for Raul's aunt, who had clearly been in love with Pietro. No wonder Carmina hated her when she believed Libby had been Pietro's mistress. But even if she could reveal the truth Libby doubted Carmina would feel any happier that Pietro had had an affair with her mother.

'I'm sorry,' she murmured, and immediately realised that her apology had only fuelled the other woman's rage.

'You should not be here—you and your illegitimate son. The Villa Giulietta has been owned by the Carducci family for generations, and it will be a tragic day if a common whore becomes its mistress.'

Libby gasped in shock at the other woman's rudeness. 'Look, I realise you're upset, but you have no right to talk to me like that,' she said shakily. 'Raul—'

'Raul keeps his brains in his underpants, and all he is interested in is getting into your knickers. He has had hundreds of women, but he never keeps them for very long,' Carmina said contemptuously. 'Don't get too comfortable here, Ms Maynard, because he will soon grow bored with you—and then he will replace you in his bed.'

Carmina swung round and swept regally across the hall, leaving Libby feeling sick as she stared after her. 'She's a poisonous old bat,' she told Gino, and gave a rueful smile when he grinned at her, happily unaware of the unpleasant scene that had just taken place.

But she could not forget Raul's aunt's comments—
particularly the one about how Raul would grow bored
with her. The sexual attraction between them was white-
hot at the moment, but how long would it last? And what
would happen when it died? Would he take a mistress?
Perhaps conduct a discreet affair at his apartment in
Rome and return to the Villa Giulietta to play happy
families when it suited him?

The terrace extended out from one side of the villa
and overlooked the lake to one side and a long rectan-
gular swimming pool, set amid a lush green garden, on
the other. Tall marble pillars reached up to a roof formed
from the entwined stems of ivy, jasmine and climbing
roses, which created a fragrant shady bower.

Raul was seated at the table, idly skimming through
a newspaper. His hair gleamed like raw silk in the sunlight, and although his designer shades hid his eyes,
nothing could detract from the masculine beauty of his
sculpted features. Libby was conscious of a molten sensation between her legs as she walked towards him. It
was ridiculous to feel possessive of a man who, until a
few days ago, she had never even met. But the idea of
him making love to another woman was unbearable.

Could physical attraction alone be responsible for
the way her heart skittered in her chest when he got
to his feet as she approached and welcomed her with
a sensual smile that stole her breath? What else could
it be? she asked herself irritably. She might have been
mad enough to agree to marry him, but it was only so
that Gino would grow up with two parents. She would
never be so stupid as to fall in love with him.

Gino grinned when he spied Raul, and held out his
chubby arms to him, chuckling when Raul swung him

high in the air. The bond between man and child was already undeniable. Lauren suddenly felt ridiculously shy, and could not bring herself to meet Raul's gaze. 'It's so beautiful here,' she murmured, looking around at the expertly landscaped garden and the view of the lake beyond.

He nodded in agreement. 'I thought you might like to spend our honeymoon here at the Villa Giulietta, so that you can get to know the house and grounds properly. But of course if you would prefer to go away somewhere I will arrange it.'

Libby gave him a startled glance. 'There's no rush to plan the honeymoon, is there?'

'Certainly there is. We are to be married in two weeks' time. The necessary paperwork is already being taken care of.'

'Two weeks!' Shock caused Libby's voice to rise several octaves. 'That's too soon.'

Raul had strapped Gino into his highchair and the baby was now happily chewing on a rusk. 'I see no reason why we should wait,' he murmured as he moved to stand in front of her.

Her body instantly reacted to his closeness; her breasts felt heavy, and her nipples tightened and pushed against the restriction of her bra. She was embarrassed by the effect he had on her, but she could not prevent her eyes from focusing on his mouth, remembering how he had kissed her earlier and longing for him to do it again.

'We both agree that Gino's needs are paramount. And he needs both of us,' Raul insisted. 'The sooner we marry, the sooner I can start proceedings to adopt him. Who knows? Maybe his first word will be Papa!'

Emotion washed over Libby. Papa was going to be such an important word in Gino's vocabulary. She knew that marrying Raul was the right thing to do, but she couldn't forget his aunt's assertion that he had had countless mistresses. She stared at his handsome face and felt a sharp stab of jealousy at the thought of all the beautiful women he must have slept with.

'If this is going to work, there will have to be certain ground rules,' she said abruptly.

She flushed when Raul gave her a look of arrogant amusement. 'What kind of rules?'

'Well, fidelity for one. I think we should agree that we will both remain faithful within our marriage. Children are very perceptive, and I don't want Gino to grow up thinking that it's okay for his father to have affairs with other women. You are going to be his most important role model and you should set a good example...' She tailed off, her face scarlet as she wondered if she had revealed too much of herself and her insecurities. 'Your aunt says that you've had hundreds of mistresses, but none of your relationships last long and you'll soon grow bored with me.' The words spilled out in a rush.

Raul frowned. 'When did you speak to Carmina?'

'Oh, we had a run-in just before I came to find you.' Libby grimaced. 'She doesn't like me, and she made it clear that she disapproves of you marrying me.'

Having already been subjected to his aunt's views on his choice of bride, Raul was not surprised by the tremor in Libby's voice. What *did* surprise him was how angry he felt with Carmina, and the surge of protectiveness he felt for Libby. 'I'm sorry if my aunt upset you. She will not do so again,' he promised grimly. 'I will arrange for her to return to her house in Rome immediately. It is a move that is long overdue anyway,' he explained, when she looked worried.

He studied her speculatively for a few moments. 'As to my previous relationships—I am a thirty-six-year old red-blooded male, and I have not lived like a monk. But I certainly have not had hundreds of lovers.' Libby seemed to have developed a sudden fascination with the marble floor tiles and only reluctantly lifted her head when he cupped her chin and exerted gentle pressure. 'I agree with the fidelity rule. We may not be marrying for conventional reasons, but I am prepared to make a serious commitment to you as well as to Gino.'

It was ridiculous to feel so relieved by his statement, Libby told herself impatiently. And even more ridiculous to feel a little pang of regret because he had underlined the fact that they were marrying for convenience rather than love. She was too old to believe in fairytales, and Raul was not her prince.

He was still holding her chin so that her face was tilted to his. He brought his other hand up and tangled his fingers in her bright silky curls, the expression in his eyes causing her heart to miss a beat. 'I don't think there's a chance I will grow bored with you, *cara*. You are fiery and exciting and no woman has ever turned me on the way you do.' He stared down at her and desire coiled in his gut. 'I'm glad you decided to wear your new clothes,' he murmured. Her dress was a simple sheath of pale blue silk which moulded her breasts and the slight flare of her hips. She looked elegant and at the same time sinfully sexy—and he had never professed to be a saint.

After his disastrous marriage to Dana he had been adamant that he would never marry again, and his desire for full control of CC was the major factor in his decision to marry Libby. But it was not the only factor, he acknowledged as he brushed his lips across hers and felt her instant response. There would be compensations to taking Libby as his wife. Heat surged through his veins when she opened her mouth so that he could slide his tongue into her moist warmth, and he gave in to the temptation to slide his hand over her silky dress and cup one soft breast in his palm. Only the presence of Gino prevented him from pushing her skirt up and taking her on the table, and he was breathing hard when he tore his mouth from hers.

'Two weeks cannot pass quickly enough for either of us, *cara*,' he said thickly, satisfaction surging through him when she stared at him with dazed eyes and ran her tongue over her swollen lips. 'When you have had lunch I will take you to Rome so that you can choose a wedding dress.'

CHAPTER SEVEN

THE following days flew past with frightening speed. The wedding was only to be a small civil ceremony, and as Raul had taken charge of all the arrangements Libby felt strangely detached from it all—while at the same time it loomed on her horizon like a dark and ominous cloud.

'Do you wish to invite any of your family or friends from England to the wedding?' he asked during dinner one evening.

Since his aunt's departure from the villa they had taken to eating on the terrace rather than in the formal dining room. Dinner by candlelight with the view of the lake spread before them was romantic, and Raul was no longer a coldly arrogant stranger but such a charming and attentive companion that Libby looked forward to the evenings when they were alone together.

To her relief he never made any reference to her supposed affair with Pietro—indeed, he seemed to go out of his way to avoid the subject, and encouraged her to talk about her childhood living in Ibiza.

She turned her head from where she had been staring dreamily at the sun as it sank below the horizon, streaking the indigo sky and the vast expanse of water beneath it with crimson and gold. 'I lost contact with many of my friends when I moved from London to Cornwall,' she explained. 'My closest friend Alice would have come, but she's tied up in a big court case and can't get away.'

Raul was puzzled that she made no mention of her mother, but refrained from asking about her. He knew that Libby had had an unconventional childhood, living in the commune, and in his opinion her mother had been an irresponsible parent. He wondered if Libby had fallen out with her, but decided that it was none of his business.

She seemed to confirm his suspicions when she said cheerfully, 'There'll just be me and Gino on the Maynard side of the church. I hope you don't have hundreds of relatives, because I'll feel totally overawed.'

Beneath her breezy tone Raul heard the loneliness in her voice, and something tugged in his chest. Libby might act tough, but underneath she was achingly vulnerable. Perhaps she had sought a relationship with Pietro, who had been so much older than her, because she had hoped he would give her the security she had never had during her childhood? He brooded, startled by the unexpected surge of protectiveness he felt for her.

He had come to realise that, far from being the gold-digger he had first assumed, she had no interest in money. Indeed, his insistence that she should buy a wedding dress had resulted in a furious row, with Libby arguing that it would be a waste of his money and that she would wear one of the outfits she had bought when she had first arrived in Italy. Eventually, after much bullying, she had reluctantly agreed to choose a dress, but the bill she had presented him with had been small change compared to the forty thousand pounds his first wife's designer wedding gown had cost.

'If you have no close family members who did you appoint as Gino's guardian in the event of your death?' he asked her.

Libby gave him a startled look. 'I didn't. I mean, I'm twenty-two and perfectly healthy...'

'I appreciate that, but nothing in life is one hundred percent certain. I assumed you would have planned for Gino's care?'

It hadn't even occurred to her, Libby thought guiltily. And her oversight was all the more unforgivable when Liz's failure to appoint *her* as Gino's guardian was the very reason she had deceived Raul into thinking that *she* was the little boy's mother. Raul was right: life did not come with a guarantee. Supposing she had been killed in an accident? she thought, feeling sick. Gino would have been left all alone in the world and reliant on Social Services to care for him. The idea was too awful to contemplate, but fortunately she did not have to—because she was going to marry Raul, and he was going to adopt Gino, and whatever happened in the future he would be safe.

Libby clung to that thought a few days later, when she stepped into the dress she had chosen to get married in. It was not remotely bridal, she acknowledged as she twirled in front of the mirror and admired the way the multi-coloured silk skirt, overlaid with layers of chiffon, swirled around her legs. Aware that Raul disapproved of her favourite purple tie-dyed skirt and her penchant for green and orange, preferably worn together, she had planned to buy something elegant and sophisticated in a pastel shade, but the moment she had seen the dress she had fallen in love with its jewel-bright colours.

It was not as if theirs was a conventional marriage—there was no reason why she should wear a conventional wedding dress, she reassured herself. Raul was marrying her for the same reason that she was marrying him—for Gino. In all probability he would not care what she wore.

But despite her bravado her heart was thumping when she walked out of her bedroom for what, she realised shakily, was probably the last time. Her clothes had already been moved to the master bedroom that she would share with Raul, whilst another room further along the first floor corridor had been turned into a new nursery for Gino.

They might not be marrying for conventional reasons, but Raul had insisted that their marriage would be a real one, which meant that tonight he would expect her to join him in his huge bed and then he would—her imagination came to an abrupt halt. She only had a school textbook knowledge of what would happen next, and the realisation that she was going to have to act as if she knew what she was doing weighed heavy on her mind.

She rounded a corner and halted at the top of the great sweeping staircase which led to the marble floored hall below. Raul was there, looking so breathtakingly handsome in a dark, expertly tailored suit and white silk shirt that her heart thudded harder. He was unaware of her presence, and she studied him greedily, noting how his jet-black hair gleamed like raw silk in the sunlight, and how he moved with lithe grace for such a big, powerful man. He was holding Gino, who looked gorgeous in his new blue and white sailor suit, but when the baby squirmed restlessly in his arms he set him on his feet and hunkered down beside him, holding Gino's hands to help him balance.

Walking was Gino's new discovery, and although he could not yet take any steps unaided he loved being on his feet. He gurgled in delight as Raul patiently guided him across the floor, his little face alight with pleasure and trust in the man who was supporting him.

A lump formed in Libby's throat as she watched them. During the past two weeks she had become convinced that Raul would be a fantastic father. Every day he had visited the nursery to play with Gino, and the incongruous sight of him crawling around the floor with the baby, or patiently stacking bricks for him to knock down, had left her deeply impressed. There was genuine affection in his voice when he spoke to the little boy, and Gino patently adored Raul.

She moved to the top of the stairs just as Raul scooped Gino back into his arms, laughing as he said, 'Up you come, *piccolo*, before you wear those little legs out.' He glanced up and fell silent as Libby walked down the stairs, his expression unfathomable as he studied her appearance.

He hated her dress, she thought miserably. Why hadn't she chosen that cream silk suit that had made her look ultra-sophisticated?

'I realise it's probably not what you had in mind,' she burst out when she reached the bottom stair and he still made no comment.

'No,' Raul conceded, wondering what it was about this woman that caused fire to surge through his veins, not to mention other pertinent areas of his body, he thought derisively, supremely conscious of his rock-solid erection. 'But you never fail to surprise me, *cara*.'

'I did try on a cream outfit in the bridalwear shop, but it just wasn't me,' she told him earnestly. 'I love bright colours.'

'I realise that.' Raul swept his eyes over her, taking in her glorious red curls and the brilliantly coloured dress that moulded her full breasts and emphasised her tiny waist, while the floaty layers of the chiffon skirt drew attention to her slender legs. She was vibrant and intense, and he was climbing the walls with his ferocious need to take her to bed and enjoy the fiery passion she exuded from every pore. 'You look very beautiful,' he said deeply. 'You would not be you without your rainbow colours. And I have to admit that orange and green are growing on me.'

Startled by the serious note beneath his amused comment, Libby's eyes flew to his face, and she felt a curious fluttering feeling inside at the warmth of his gaze. A silent message seemed to pass between them, as elusive as a wisp of smoke. It drifted away before she could grasp it or comprehend it, but the fluttering feeling grew stronger when his mouth curved into a sensual smile.

'I made the mistake of thinking you would wear a conventional wedding dress and so I ordered flowers to match,' he said, taking a bouquet of pure white rosebuds from the dresser behind him and handing it to her. 'I hope you like them.'

The arrangement was starkly simple and yet exquisitely lovely, with the petals of the mass of rosebuds just beginning to unfurl to release their delicate perfume. Tears stung Libby's eyes and she dared not look at Raul in case he should see them. She had never expected flowers on her wedding day. 'They're perfect,' she said quietly. 'Thank you.'

His smile widened. 'Come,' he invited, holding out his hand to her. 'I believe we have a wedding to attend, Ms Maynard.'

Raul's mobile phone rang as they walked out of the villa. He frowned, knowing that it was likely to be a business call, and was tempted for the first time ever to ignore it. But the ringing persisted, and when he took his phone from his jacket he saw that the caller was his lawyer, Bernardo Orsini.

'I'm sorry, but I need to take this,' he apologised to Libby as they reached the car where his driver, Tito, was waiting to take them to the wedding hall in the nearby town.

'Bernardo?'

'I just wanted to let you know that everything is in place for you to be confirmed as sole chairman of Carducci Cosmetics once Elizabeth Maynard is married.' The lawyer laughed softly. 'I assume that *is* the reason for your hasty trip down the aisle? I congratulate you, Raul, for acting so swiftly. I presume you will allow a suitable amount of time to pass before you file for divorce? I hope the duration of your marriage will not be too disagreeable.'

Raul watched Libby as she bent over to strap Gino into his baby seat in the back of the car and felt an uncomfortable tightening in his groin as he studied the rounded curves of her bottom, moulded so enticingly beneath her silk dress. 'I'm sure I'll survive,' he assured the lawyer dryly.

But as he climbed into the car beside her and inhaled the delicate, floral fragrance of her perfume he was shocked to realise that his desire for control of CC had not been uppermost in his mind for days. It was his desire for Libby which dominated his thoughts.

The day passed in a blur, leaving Libby with a kaleidoscope of images that she knew would remain with her for ever. First there had been the ornate wedding hall in a beautiful *palazzo* overlooking Lake Bracciano, where she and Raul had made their vows. The ceremony had been witnessed by Tito and Silvana—who had somehow persuaded Gino to sit quietly on her lap—and Raul's close friends Romano and Flaviana Vincenti. Libby had met the couple and their two cherubic little daughters a few days before the wedding, and assumed Raul had told them that he was marrying her so that he could be Gino's father. But to her surprise they clearly believed that it was a love match.

'We never thought Raul would marry again after what he went through with Dana,' Flaviana said at the end of the ceremony, when she kissed Libby's cheek and offered her congratulations to the newlyweds. 'You must be very special to have stolen his heart.'

'Oh… But…' Libby was prevented from replying when Raul's dark head swooped and he claimed her mouth in a long, fiercely passionate kiss that left her dazed and hot-cheeked. When he finally released her she realised that a photographer had been busily snapping them.

'The reason for our marriage is a private matter between us,' he murmured as they filed out of the wedding
hall. 'Flaviana is an incurable romantic, and I see no
reason to shatter her illusions.'

And that, presumably, was the reason why Raul was
so attentive throughout the wedding reception: a celebra-
tory dinner at a charming little restaurant, followed by
a cruise along the lake, during which the adults drank
pink champagne and the Vincentis' little daughters
ran excitedly up and down the boat, much to Gino's
entertainment.

It had been an unexpectedly beautiful day, Libby
mused as she crept out of the nursery after checking
on Gino later that night. She stood in the doorway and
listened to the regular sound of his breathing for a few
moments, relieved that he no longer made the horrible
rasping noise in his chest. A few days ago she and Raul
had taken him to see a top specialist, who had given
him a thorough check-over, sent him for X-rays, and
finally assured them that the pneumonia had not caused
permanent damage to his lungs.

'You have a fine son, and I am confident he will grow
up to be a strong, healthy boy,' the doctor had said with
a smile as he handed the baby back to Raul.

As soon as the adoption process was complete Gino
would have a father and would grow up with the love
and security of two parents, Libby thought as she walked
down the corridor towards the master bedroom. It was
what she wanted—the reason why she had married Raul.
But now their wedding day was over and their wedding
night was about to begin. She felt sick with nerves, yet
at the same time she was conscious of a frisson of anticipation at the thought of Raul making love to her.

The chemistry between them was almost tangible; every time they were in the same room she was aware of the simmering sexual tension that made his eyes darken and evoked a restless ache deep within her. Her fear was not so much of losing her virginity, but the knowledge that she must fool him into believing that she had had sex before.

Perhaps she should tell him the truth? Her steps slowed and she gnawed on her bottom lip. Wouldn't honesty be the best policy now that she and Raul were married? Surely he would understand why she had pretended to be Gino's mother if she explained her fears that he might be taken away from her?

But what if Raul *didn't* understand? What if he was so angry at her deception that he had their marriage annulled, claimed custody of Gino, and banished her from the Villa Giulietta? The gamble was too great, she decided. She was not prepared to risk losing Gino, and so her secret must remain. Tonight she must play the part of sensual seductress and convince Raul that she was sexually experienced.

She pushed open the bedroom door. The bedside lamps had been switched on and the crisp white sheets turned back, but the room was empty. Grateful for the reprieve, she stepped out onto the balcony and took a shaky breath of the scented night air. The velvet darkness pressed around her, with stars shimmering like diamonds in the inky sky and the moon casting its silver gleam across the black waters of the lake.

'To me, this is the most beautiful view on earth.' Raul's deep voice broke the silence, and Libby stiffened when he came up behind her and slid his arms around her waist, drawing her against his chest so that she was conscious of the warmth of his body and the steady thud of his heart.

'The…the lake is especially lovely in the moonlight,' she agreed, her own heart thumping so hard that her voice emerged as a whisper of sound.

'I was not referring to the lake, *cara*.'

Hot, pulsing need coiled in Raul's gut as he pushed Libby's fiery curls aside and pressed his mouth to her slender white neck. He had wanted her the moment he had set eyes on her, and even the shocking discovery that she had been Pietro's mistress had not lessened his desire. He refused to dwell on the image in his head of her and Pietro together. She was his wife now, and he would make her forget all her previous lovers, he vowed fiercely, feeling the tremor that ran through her when he slid the zip of her dress down her spine.

Libby could hear the blood pounding in her ears, and trepidation and a fierce excitement corkscrewed through her when Raul pushed her dress over her shoulders and drew it lower and lower, until he had bared her breasts. She swallowed when he cupped each soft mound in his palms, and could not restrain a little gasp as he took her nipples between his fingers and tugged gently, so that they swelled and hardened into tight, aching peaks.

'Please…' The pleasure was indescribable. Arrows of sensation shot from her breasts to her pelvis and molten heat flooded between her legs, her arousal so swift and so shockingly intense that her nervousness was swept away by a tidal wave of need for him to touch her where she ached to be touched.

'You are so responsive, *cara*, and your eagerness is such a turn on,' Raul said thickly as he spun her round and lowered his head to capture her mouth in a hot, hungry kiss, sliding his tongue between her lips and exploring her with such erotic skill that Libby's legs buckled and she clung to his shoulders for support. 'I will please you; do not doubt it. I have never wanted any woman the way I want you,' he admitted harshly. 'The chemistry between us is too powerful to deny any longer.'

He swept her up into his arms and in a few strides had carried her from the balcony to the bed, scorching desire in his eyes as he dropped her onto the mattress and quickly removed her dress and shoes. His hand rested lightly on her stomach, and Libby caught her breath when he trailed his fingers down and hooked them in the waistband of her knickers. This was the first time any man had seen her naked, and she suddenly felt acutely vulnerable, her nervousness flooding back when she faced the fact that she was about to give her virginity to a man who believed she was sexually experienced. She had convinced herself that she could hide her innocence, but as he drew her knickers down her legs she instinctively tried to cover herself with her hands, her heart beating like a trapped bird in her chest.

Raul laughed softly. 'I see your red hair is natural,' he murmured. 'Don't hide yourself from me. Open your legs, *cara*. I want to look at you as I touch you. Do you enjoy oral sex?'

He watched her cheeks flood with colour, and was puzzled by the shocked expression in her eyes. She responded with such wild fervour when he kissed her that he had expected her to be impatient for sex. Instead she suddenly seemed shy and uncertain, and he was frustrated that she had made no attempt to touch *him*.

'I...I don't know,' she stammered in a panicky voice.

'Really? You've never...?' He couldn't hide his surprise—but nor could he deny a feeling of satisfaction that he would give her an experience she had never enjoyed with any of her previous lovers. 'Oh, *cara mia*, we must do something about that.'

Libby jerked as if she had been stung when Raul slipped his hand between her thighs. He frowned, and she forced herself to relax so that he would not guess that this was all new to her. Heart hammering, she spread her legs a little, and bit her lip when he pushed them further apart and ran his finger up and down the outer lips of her vagina in a butterfly caress that sent a quiver of pleasure through her. Heat unfurled inside her and built in intensity until she felt the wetness of her arousal flood between her legs. Nothing had prepared her for the exquisite delight of him gently parting her and sliding his finger a little way into her, and she moaned softly when he brushed his thumb pad lightly over the sensitive nub of her clitoris.

It was good—better than good—amazing. Her limbs felt heavy, and she put up no resistance when he pushed her legs wider apart. She sank deeper into the mattress and closed her eyes, so that she could focus on the new and wondrous sensations that Raul was creating with his deft fingers.

The feel of his warm breath fanning the tight cluster of curls at the junction of her thighs caused her lashes to fly open. Surely he wasn't really going to...?

She made a choked sound when he buried his head between her legs and replaced his finger with his tongue. 'No!' Mortified by the shocking intimacy of what he was doing, she caught hold of his hair and tried to pull his head up, but the sensual probing of his tongue was so amazingly good that her resistance melted away and she arched her hips, offering herself up to him and giving little yelps of incredulous pleasure.

A desperate yearning was building deep in her pelvis—a hot, achy feeling that she knew instinctively only Raul could assuage. Far from wanting him to stop, she was now frantic for him to continue his erotic caresses, and she muttered her protest when he moved and the heat of his mouth was replaced with cool air on her thighs.

'I know; I'm as hungry as you,' Raul growled as he stood up and began to strip out of his clothes.

He would have liked Libby to undress him, but he was so turned-on that it was doubtful he could have withstood her stroking her hands over his body. His trousers joined his shirt on the floor, and he saw her stare at the burgeoning length of his arousal straining beneath his boxers. He did not know why she felt it necessary to maintain the act of *ingénue* after she had responded with such eager enthusiasm to his foreplay. It was likely she'd had dozens of lovers. But he was hardly a saint himself, and he did not want to bed a timid virgin.

It was time he showed her what he *did* want, he decided, amused at the way her eyes widened with apparent shock when he stepped out of his boxers. His massive erection was not surprising when he was about to turn the fantasy of making love to her into reality, but he was burning up with frustration, and this first time was not going to be a leisurely sex session, he already knew. Desire jack-knifed through him as he nudged her legs wider apart and positioned himself over her.

Libby had watched, dry-mouthed, as Raul had undressed, blown away by the masculine beauty of his muscular chest with its covering of fine dark hairs that arrowed down over his abdomen. But when he had stripped off his boxers admiration had turned to astonishment at the awesome size of his arousal. There was no way she was going to be able to take him inside her, she thought fearfully.

Her heart jerked painfully beneath her ribs when he came down on top of her. The feel of his hard body pressing into the softness of hers was alien and frankly terrifying, and a strong instinct for self-protection caused her to tense beneath him. Panic-stricken, she brought her hands up to his chest to push him off her, but he laughed softly as he caught hold of her wrists and forced them above her head.

'I apologise if you find the missionary position boring, *cara*,' he muttered hoarsely, 'but I'm so hungry for you that I'm in danger of coming right now. We have all night to experiment,' he promised.

His words sounded more like a threat to Libby, but as she twisted and squirmed urgently beneath him Raul lowered his head to her breast and drew her nipple into his mouth, sucking and tugging on the taut peak so that sharp arrows of pleasure shot down to her pelvis. 'I love your impatience,' he groaned, mistaking the frantic bucking of her hips as an invitation.

Libby caught her breath when he moved his hand down and unerringly found the slick wetness of her womanhood. The feel of him touching her there, rubbing his thumb over her clitoris, drowned her fears in a swirling mass of sensations. He was driving her towards some magical place she could sense but could not reach, and she felt excitement rather than fear when he withdrew his finger and rubbed the tip of his thick, swollen penis against her.

He eased slowly into her and she let out a shaky sigh of relief. It was all right. It didn't hurt. The feeling of being stretched was strange but not unpleasant, and she relaxed, reassured that he would never know it was her first time. He lifted his mouth from her breast and stared into her eyes, the sinews in his powerful shoulders standing out as he supported his weight and remained poised above her.

'It has to be now,' he said harshly, and gripped her hips to hold her still as he drove into her with a powerful thrust.

His groan of pleasure was cut short when she gave a sharp cry of pain.

Raul stilled, paralysed with shock. *Dio!* It was impossible! He must have imagined the sensation of pushing through a fragile barrier. But she felt so tight around him. Heart pumping as if he had run a marathon, he drew back a fraction, stunned and uncomprehending when he saw that Libby was holding her knuckles against her mouth. Her eyes were dilated with shock. But she could *not* be a virgin, his brain pointed out, the idea was inconceivable.

He moved to withdraw from her, but her vaginal muscles gripped him in a velvet embrace. His blood was pounding through his veins, hot and insistent, and his desire was a pagan, primitive urge that was beyond his power to control. He gritted his teeth, the cords on his neck standing out with the effort of trying to fight it. But he could not hold back—could not prevent himself from sinking deeper into her hot, tight embrace. He let out a savage groan as the tidal wave overwhelmed him and he pumped his seed into her in a spectacular release that racked his body with exquisite aftershocks of pleasure.

CHAPTER EIGHT

LIBBY lay beneath Raul, frozen with shock. Her limbs trembled uncontrollably as reaction set in and she felt horribly sick. She pushed frantically against his chest, desperate for him to release her so that she could escape to the bathroom. His body was heavy on hers, his breathing fast and ragged. He rolled off her and snatched oxygen into his lungs. She could sense his stunned disbelief, and when he turned his head his eyes were as dark and fathomless as the lake on a moonless night.

'What the hell—?' He swore savagely in his native tongue.

Libby could not understand the words, but his meaning was clear. Undoubtedly he wanted an explanation, but she was in no fit state for a post-mortem, and as he reached out to capture her wrist she dived off the bed.

There was blood on the sheet. He stared at the small betraying patch, and then speared her with a savage glance. With a gasp Libby raced into the *en suite* bathroom, flung the door shut and locked it before she staggered over to the toilet and threw up.

Oh, God, what had she done? Even if she hadn't cried out like that when Raul had surged into her, the blood-stained sheet was tangible evidence that she had never given birth to a child.

She hadn't expected it to hurt so much. But, more than that, she thought numbly, she hadn't expected that giving her virginity to Raul would be such an intensely emotional experience. Libby sank weakly against the wall and buried her face in her hands. At the moment when Raul had joined their bodies as one it had hit her with the force of a lightning bolt that she wanted him to love her—as she loved him.

The words went round and round in her head. *She had fallen in love with him.* She couldn't say when exactly it had happened, but she had been drawn to him from the very start, she acknowledged wearily.

Oh, she'd fought him and stood up to him, and told herself she hated his arrogance and didn't care that he despised her for being, as he thought, his father's gold-digger mistress. But beneath her bravado, and despite the huge differences in their upbringing and lifestyles, she had been unable to dismiss the feeling that he was her soul-mate, and that they were somehow linked together by a higher force.

It had not only been his obvious affection for Gino that had prompted her to accept his marriage proposal. Yes, she had wanted him to adopt Gino, so that the little boy would have a father, but the truth was she had hoped that, in the tradition of the best fairytales, Raul would suddenly realise that she was the love of his life.

But when he had thrust into her so forcefully the pain in her heart had been a thousand times worse than the burning sensation caused when he had ripped the delicate membrane of her virginity. She had longed for him to whisper tender words of reassurance, but of course he hadn't. For Raul it had just been sex—and now, thanks to her stupid, melodramatic behaviour, he knew that she wasn't Gino's mother.

She flinched at the sound of hammering on the door and remained sitting on the cold marble floor, hugging her knees to her chest in an instinctively protective gesture.

'*Libby!* Open this damn door before I break it down.'

When she made no response Raul pounded on the door again until it rattled in its frame. She did not only have to worry about him smashing through the wood, but waking the whole house up. And she could not stay locked in the bathroom for ever. Taking a shaky breath, she forced herself to her feet and wrapped a towel around her shivering body. Her nipples looked starkly pink against her white breasts. They felt ultra-sensitive after Raul had lashed them with his tongue, and she was still conscious of a faint stinging sensation down below, but neither was as painful as the uneven thud of her heart as she unlocked the door.

He had pulled on his trousers but his chest was bare, and Libby felt a ridiculous urge to press her cheek against the whorls of dark hair that covered his gleaming golden skin, and listen to the steady thud of his heart.

Raul was glaring at her as if he would like to throttle her. 'Who is Gino's mother?' he thundered.

She bit her lip and tasted blood. 'Elizabeth Maynard.'

'Don't lie to me!' He fired the words at her like bullets from a gun, his eyes blazing. 'I saw your passport.

You are Elizabeth Maynard—a very virginal Elizabeth Maynard. Or at least you were until five minutes ago,' he growled harshly. 'You stupid little fool. Why didn't you tell me it was your first time? I would have—' He broke off and raked his hand through his hair, still barely able to comprehend what he had discovered far too late.

In his mind he heard again the thin animal cry of pain she had emitted when he had taken her, and guilt surged through him that he hadn't stopped. His body had betrayed him, he acknowledged bitterly. So greedy for the satisfaction it craved that instead of withdrawing from her he had thrust deeper and to his astonishment come instantly. It had never happened to him before. He prided himself on being a generous lover, and he had never before taken his pleasure with such selfish disregard for his partner. But then he did not make a habit of deflowering virgins, he thought grimly. He felt ashamed and somehow unmanned, and he buried both emotions beneath a torrent of anger.

'I would have taken more care,' he gritted as he stared at her chalk-white face which contrasted so starkly with her golden freckles.

Her eyes seemed too big for her face, and the betraying quiver of her lower lip evoked a curious pain in his chest—like a hand squeezing his heart. His jaw tightened and he dismissed the urge to pull her into his arms. 'Who *are* you?' he demanded savagely.

'I *am* Elizabeth Maynard.' Libby took a deep breath. 'And so was my mother. Mum met your father on the cruise ship and they had an affair. Gino is my half-brother,' she revealed quietly.

'*Your mother* was Pietro's mistress!' Raul swore again, unable to control the emotions storming through him. 'Then where the hell *is* she? Why did you go through the charade of pretending that Gino is your son?'

Libby's grief was still raw, and now it pierced her like an arrow through the heart. 'She's dead,' she said thickly, forcing the words past the constriction in her throat.

Raul stared sharply at Libby's white face, and despite his fury something stirred inside him when he saw the shimmer of tears in her eyes. 'I'm sorry,' he said tightly. 'Were the two of you close?'

'We were more like sisters,' she whispered. 'I miss her every day. For my whole childhood it was just me and Mum, you see. I have no idea who my father is because she didn't like to talk about him. All I know is that he broke her heart. He was married, but Mum hadn't known about his wife. When she told him she was pregnant with me he offered to pay for an abortion.'

She let out a shaky breath. 'Mum couldn't believe it when she found out she was pregnant with Pietro's baby, and when it seemed that he wanted nothing to do with her she felt that history was repeating itself and she had been abandoned by a lover again. But she adored Gino, and she was determined to give him the best childhood she could. That's why she decided to move to Cornwall; she thought it would be a better environment for him than the rough area of London where we lived.

'Then Mum collapsed suddenly and died from a blood clot on her lung,' Libby explained huskily. 'She hadn't made a will, and because she hadn't stipulated that I should have custody of Gino I was scared Social

Services would take him.' She darted a glance at Raul's face, but his expression was unreadable. She continued in a rush. 'So I pretended that he was my baby. I love him,' she whispered brokenly. 'He's all I've got—my only link with Mum—and he belongs with me. I know I should have told you the truth…'

'*Per Dio!* You say that now,' Raul flung at her bitterly. 'You lied to me and deceived me…'

'*I had to.*' Libby stared at him desperately, willing him to understand. 'Pietro stated in his will that he wished for Gino and his mother to live here at the Villa Giulietta. I was afraid that if you knew I wasn't his mother you would fight for custody of him and take him from me—and I couldn't bear that.' Her voice trembled and she forced back the tears that burned her throat, wishing that Raul would stop looking at her with such bitter fury in his eyes. 'You said that Gino needs both of us,' she reminded him huskily. 'That's still true. Liz—my mum—died when he was only a few months old, and I am the only mother he has ever known.'

'But you are *not* his mother,' Raul bit out savagely. Anger burned in his gut. He could not bear to look at Libby now that he knew she was a calculating liar—just as Dana had been.

He jerked away from her and strode across the bedroom and out onto the balcony. He did not know what to say, what to think. Learning that his adoptive father had had a child had been the biggest shock of his life, or so he had thought. But the discovery that the woman he had believed was Gino's mother was a virgin was so astounding that he was still struggling to accept the truth.

One thought stood out from the mass of emotions swirling in his head, and black rage choked him. It had not been necessary for him to marry her. Libby was not Gino's mother, which meant she had never been entitled to control the fifty percent share of Carducci Cosmetics that Pietro had left in trust for his baby son. If it had been known that Gino's mother was dead, control of the baby's shares would automatically have passed to *him*, Raul thought furiously, and he would not have needed to make Libby his wife in order to take full control of the company.

He sensed her behind him, and jerked his head round to find that she had joined him on the balcony. She had exchanged the towel for her robe. Not the elegant grey silk robe he had bought her, he noted, but the pink fluffy dressing gown she had brought with her from England that make her resemble a marshmallow. Her fiery curls tumbled around her shoulders and Raul thought how young she looked, and how innocent. But she was not quite so innocent now, he brooded grimly, remembering again her cry of pain when he had taken her virginity. For a moment his anger was overshadowed by guilt at the brutal way he had made love to her.

'You should have told me the truth,' he said tautly.

'If I had, you would have taken Gino from me. Wouldn't you?' Libby accused him shakily.

'Of course I damn well would.' He could not deny it. He would have claimed custody of his father's son and become sole chairman of CC until Gino was eighteen without the need for this farcical marriage. 'The hovel you lived in was no place to bring up a child. And what sort of upbringing would he have had with a lap-dancer?'

'I was *not* a lap-dancer—that was my mother,' Libby admitted in a low tone. She saw the look of disdain in Raul's eyes and her temper flared. 'Before you say another word, let me tell you something about Liz. It's true she worked in a grotty men's club, but she had no one to help her or support her, and she refused to live on benefits. I may not have had a conventional upbringing, but I never doubted that she loved me. She was heartbroken when Pietro didn't get in touch after the cruise. Not because she was after his money—she didn't even know he was head of Carducci Cosmetics when she met him—but because she really loved him, and he told her that he had fallen in love with her.'

Libby paused, her throat aching with tears. 'The truth is your father abandoned my mother. But despite that she adored Gino. She would have devoted her life to him, but her life was cut cruelly short...and so I took her place,' she said thickly.

Raul glared at her in frustration. She sounded so damned plausible, but he refused to be taken in by her now he knew how she had deceived him.

'Pietro suffered a stroke two days after he returned home from the cruise,' he said flatly. 'It was the first indication that he had a brain tumour, and it left him paralysed down one side of his body and affected his ability to speak. He was the most honourable, *honest* man I have ever known, and if he told your mother that he loved her then I am certain it was true. But perhaps he felt that she would be better off without him,' he said quietly. 'He did not know then that she was carrying his child, and he was ill and disabled. I'm sure he believed it was fairer to allow your mother to keep her memories of the happy time they had spent together rather than see him as a sick and dying man.'

Libby gripped the balcony rail and willed the tears that blurred her vision not to fall. She did not want to break down in front of Raul. 'It's a terrible tragedy that Gino lost both his parents without ever knowing them. Mum loved your father, and I know she would have cared for him during his illness,' she said thickly. 'She was a very caring person.'

The raw emotion in her voice caused a curious ache in Raul's chest, but he hardened his heart against her. She had proved that he could not trust her, and he reminded himself that her motives for pretending to be Gino's mother were questionable.

'What about you, Libby? Are you also a *caring person*?' he queried sardonically. 'Is that really the only reason you kept up the charade that Gino was your child?'

'Of course it is.' She stared at him in confusion. 'What other reason could there have been?'

Raul shrugged. His face looked as though it had been carved from marble: so beautiful, but so cold and hard. She wondered what had happened to the man who had smiled at her with such warmth when they had made their wedding vows, and whether he had been a figment of her imagination.

'I think you decided to fool me into believing you were Gino's mother because you knew you would be able to live a life of luxury at the Villa Giulietta. You used Gino as your meal-ticket.'

'*No.*' She shook her head fiercely, horrified by his accusation.

'Yes, he insisted grimly. 'But you knew you only had the right to live here while Gino was growing up. No wonder you jumped at my suggestion that we should marry. As my wife you would be financially secure for life.'

'That's not true,' Libby denied urgently. 'I didn't have any ulterior motive for accepting your proposal—any more than you did for marrying me. We both did it for Gino's sake, so that he would grow up with two parents.'

Raul speared her with a look of savage contempt. 'Do you really expect me to believe that the lure of money had nothing to do with your decision? You were presented with the opportunity to marry a billionaire and you seized it.'

He ignored the look of hurt in her eyes and pushed past her, unable to bear breathing the same air as her. History had a funny way of repeating itself, he thought bitterly. It was a pity he didn't feel like laughing. He had a reputation as a ruthless adversary in the boardroom, so how had he allowed himself to be taken in by a gold-digger—not once, but twice? Dana and Libby were two of a kind, and he was the biggest fool on the planet.

He pulled on his shirt and turned to find Libby watching him, her eyes huge in her white face. 'I thought my first marriage was short when it ended after a year, but twelve hours must be a record,' he said brutally.

Libby hugged her arms around herself, shivering despite the warmth of the night, and stared at Raul's hard face. 'Wh…what do you mean? And where are you going?' she asked shakily when he strode over to the door and pulled it open.

'I mean that I will see you in court when I divorce you, *cara*.' The sarcasm in the endearment made her shrivel. 'As to where I am going—hell seems pretty inviting at the moment, compared to being in the same room as you.'

Panic swept through Libby and she shook her head desperately. 'No, you can't mean that—you can't want a divorce. What about Gino? We married for him, re-member? To give him a stable childhood...'

'And that is exactly what I intend to give him. It will be better for him if I bring him up on my own than with a callous liar like *you* as his mother. There's not a court in the land that would award you custody of him after the stunt you've pulled,' Raul told her savagely.

Libby gasped and closed her eyes for a few seconds, willing the room to stop swaying. He couldn't mean it. Her mind whispered the reassurance over and over, but the cold fury in his eyes warned her that he would never forgive her for deceiving him. She needed to make him understand how much she loved Gino, and that everything she had done had been for the baby's sake. But he was walking out of the door. She took a jerky step forward and stretched out her hand. He *couldn't* leave her.

'Raul...please...'

He gave her one last bitter look that ripped her heart in two, and slammed the door before she could reach him. She stood trembling, willing him to walk back in, but the sound of his footsteps along the corridor told her he had gone. Suddenly the dam burst and she crumpled to her knees, tears coursing down her face. This was her wedding night, but thanks to her stupidity the honeymoon was over before their marriage had even begun.

* * *

Raul walked swiftly through the silent house and out of the front door, his feet automatically taking him to the place he always went when he needed to be alone. The lake gleamed silver in the moonlight, reflecting the dark shadows of the trees that lined the shore. An owl hooted somewhere, and his footfall thudded on the wooden jetty. It took him mere seconds to untie the mooring rope that secured his sailing boat and he leapt on board and cast off.

A breeze rippled the surface of the water and sent the boat scudding across the little waves. He focused on adjusting the rigging and headed far out onto the lake, the gentle flap of the sail and the lap of the water against the hull soothing his ragged emotions.

Libby was not Gino's mother. She had deceived him and made a fool of him. His nostrils flared as he sought to control his anger, and he sailed on through the velvet darkness, his way lit by the moon and the myriad stars that studded the heavens.

She had done it for money, of course. She had lied to him just as Dana had lied when she had assured him that she wanted children. Dana had been an avaricious bitch who had married him to get her hands on the Carducci fortune, and Libby was no better.

But that was not quite true, he brooded. Libby had shown none of his ex-wife's tendencies to max out his credit card or fill her days shopping for more clothes to cram into her overcrowded wardrobes. Nor had she shown any enthusiasm to visit nightclubs when he had suggested it on the two occasions before their wedding when they had stayed at his apartment in Rome. She would prefer to be at the villa with Gino, she had assured him.

Her dedication to the baby was indisputable; her love for him was absolutely genuine—Raul was convinced of that. He frowned as he recalled the grim, damp flat in Cornwall where he had found her. She must have made huge sacrifices—both materially and personally—for her little half-brother. He was under no illusions about the difficulties she must have faced as a single mother, trying to work and keep a roof over their heads while she cared for the baby. She was a beautiful young woman who should have been able to enjoy all the things that her peers took for granted: fashionable clothes, parties, socialising with friends—dating. But she had given all that up for Gino.

Could any woman love a child who was not her own with such generosity of spirit? he wondered sceptically. Dana would certainly not have done. But he knew of one woman who had. His adoptive mother had taken a feral, emotionally damaged seven-year-old boy into her home, and into her heart. Eleanora Carducci had loved him unconditionally, and he had adored her. But after his acrimonious divorce from Dana he had cynically assumed that all women had a hidden agenda. When he had discovered how Libby had tricked him his first reaction had been utter fury, but now his anger was cooling and he wondered if he had judged her too harshly.

'I didn't have any ulterior motive for accepting your proposal—any more than you did for marrying me. We both did it for Gino's sake.'

Her words hammered in Raul's brain, and guilt reared its ugly head—because he *had* had an ulterior motive, he acknowledged uncomfortably. He had married her to gain control of Carducci Cosmetics, and in truth had been just as guilty of deceit because he had not made her aware of that clause in Pietro's will.

Another thought slipped insidiously into his head. Libby had not been Pietro's mistress. She and his father had never slept together—in fact he had irrefutable proof that she had never given herself to any other man but him. For some inexplicable reason that fact filled him with a heady sense of triumph. He had always thought of himself as a modern guy, and he had absolutely no problem with a woman's right to enjoy a varied sex life with a number of partners—but Libby was his, and he was shocked by the primitive feeling of possessiveness that swept through him, the feeling that he wanted to keep her locked up in the high tower of the villa, away from the gaze of any other man.

There was a glimmer of pale light in the sky when at last he headed back to shore, feeling calmer and in control of his emotions once more, but still unable to answer the question of what the hell he was going to do now.

Shock jolted through him when he caught sight of a figure standing on the jetty. The fiery red hair was instantly recognizable, and as he took the boat closer he saw Libby was wearing jeans and a soft, silvery grey sweater. She looked very young and achingly vulnerable, and he felt a gentle tug on his heart.

'Catch this, will you?' he called to her, and threw a rope onto the jetty. After a moment's hesitation she picked it up. 'Tie it around that post,' he instructed as he brought the boat alongside and jumped out. She surveyed him warily, and he saw that her eyes were red-rimmed, her face so pale that she looked as ethereal as a ghost.

He glanced at his watch. 'It's four a.m. I wasn't expecting you to be up.'

She shrugged, and said dully, 'I haven't slept.'

Her tension was tangible, reminding him of a nervous colt poised to bolt if he came too close. But that was hardly surprising after he had subjected her to the full force of his hot temper.

She looked past him to the soft mist that was drifting across the lake. 'It must be so peaceful out on the water as the sun rises,' she murmured wistfully.

'To my mind it's the closest place to heaven.' He paused, and then said quietly, 'Maybe I'll take you with me some time.'

Her eyes flew to his face and her voice shook as she said desperately, 'Please don't send me away from Gino. I love him, and he loves me. It would be too cruel...'

'I know.' He exhaled heavily. 'I am not an ogre. I am fully aware of your devotion to him, and that in his eyes you are his mother.'

For the first time since he had slammed out of the bedroom Libby felt the terrible tension that gripped her muscles ease a little. 'I know what I did was unforgivable, but after Mum died I was so scared Social Services would take him. I had been in care myself. I know what it's like to feel that you don't belong anywhere or with anyone, and I was prepared to do anything to keep Gino with me.'

'Including sacrificing your virginity,' Raul said harshly. 'Did you really think you could hide your innocence from me?'

Colour flared in Libby's pale face. 'I hadn't expected the experience to be so traumatic,' she admitted ruefully.

Guilt kicked Raul in his gut. 'It should not have been. If I'd had any idea that it was your first time I would have been more patient.' He had probably terrified the life out of her, he acknowledged, looking away from her as he recalled how his hunger for her had made him plunder her untutored body with a savagery that now filled him with shame.

'I assure you I will be much gentler next time,' he promised tautly.

Next time! Libby bit her lip. 'Does that mean you intend for our marriage to continue? Even though I...?' She stumbled to a halt, and Raul's dark brows lifted sardonically.

'Even though you deceived me and married me under false pretences?' he queried coolly. 'I admit my first thought was to send you back to England, but apart from the fact that Gino needs you, it is also possible that you have already conceived my child. I realise that when we made love it was not a great experience for you, but it certainly worked for me,' he said self-derisively. 'I did not use contraception, and it is perfectly feasible that you are pregnant.'

Libby's heart clenched at the idea that she might be carrying Raul's baby. She seemed to be on an emotional roller-coaster, and she hugged her arms around her body as a little tremor of excitement ran through her.

Raul frowned. 'You're cold. Let's go back to the house.'

He walked beside her along the jetty, but Libby was so intensely aware of him that she stumbled, and would have fallen into the water if it had not been for his lightning reactions. He caught hold of her shoulder to steady her, stared at her white face for a second, and then scooped her into his arms, ignoring her protest as he strode towards the house.

'You can barely stand. You're wasting your energy fighting me, *cara*, because I'm not going to let you go,' he warned her, and he knew as he said the words that he meant them. Somehow Libby had crept under his guard, and to his surprise he was in no hurry to evict her.

CHAPTER NINE

THE steady thud of Raul's heart beneath her ear soothed Libby's ragged emotions, and the strength of his arms holding her felt comfortingly safe. Wasn't that what she had longed for when she was a child? she thought ruefully. To feel safe and protected? She had never doubted that her mother had loved her, but she had disliked most of Liz's hippy boyfriends, and had yearned for the security of a proper home and a family. Had she been drawn to Raul from the moment she had met him because her instincts had told her that he was a strong and powerful man whom she could trust?

He strode through the house, and her heart skittered when, instead of heading for his study or the sitting room, he carried her up the wide staircase to the master bedroom.

'We need to talk,' he growled as he lowered her onto the bed.

To her consternation he sat down next to her—so close that she could feel the warmth of his body and breathe in the intoxicating scent of his cologne, mixed with another scent that was intensely male.

She twisted her fingers together in her lap and said quietly, 'I don't suppose you'll believe me, but I felt really guilty about lying to you. You have every right to be angry.'

She sounded so convincing that Raul found it impossible to believe she was a clever actress. And even if she was, what difference did it make? He had married her to gain control of Carducci Cosmetics, and his other reasons were still valid: Gino, the desire for a child of his own, and his overwhelming desire for her that still burned with a white-hot flame.

He reached out and idly wrapped a flame-coloured curl around his finger. 'I suppose I understand why you did it,' he said heavily, and realised that it was true. He was still angry with her for her deception, but he could not help feeling a begrudging admiration that she had fought so hard to keep Gino. 'If I had been in the same situation I too would have done anything to prevent Gino from being taken into care. The memories I have of living in the orphanage are not happy ones.'

'How old were you when you were adopted?'

'Seven.'

'I was that age when I was allowed to leave my foster home and live with Mum again. We went to Ibiza soon after. Do you know anything about your real parents?' Libby asked him curiously.

'Only that they lived in dire poverty in the backstreets of Naples. My mother died shortly after giving birth to me, and for the first few years of my life I lived with my father.' Raul grimaced. 'My memories of him are of a big, brutal man—and the feel of his belt across the backs of my legs. He was an alcoholic, although of course I did not understand that then. All I knew was that he had an unpredictable and violent temper. He died when I was five. I don't know what happened to him, although I suspect he was a member of a criminal gang. One night he went out, leaving me alone as he often did, and later police officers broke down the door of our flat and took me to an orphanage.

'I was a difficult child, and the nuns who ran the orphanage struggled to control me. No one wanted to foster me, and it seemed likely I would spend the rest of my childhood in care. But Pietro and Eleanora Carducci were prepared to give me a chance. I don't know why they chose to adopt a feral street boy,' Raul said, his hard features softening as he remembered his adoptive parents, 'but I am thankful that they did. My life changed for ever because of them, and I will be eternally grateful for all they did for me.'

Libby nodded, her heart aching as she imagined Raul as the brutalised and unhappy little boy he must have been before he had been adopted. 'Life can be so precarious,' she murmured, 'and children are so vulnerable. All I want is for Gino to grow up feeling safe and secure and confident that he is loved.'

'Together we will do everything possible to give him a happy childhood,' Raul assured her. 'But is that really all you want, Libby? Was Gino's welfare truly the only reason you married me?'

She tensed as he slid his hand beneath her chin and tilted her face. He had moved along the mattress and was now so close that she could see the tiny lines that fanned out around his eyes. Last night those eyes had glittered with icy fury, but now, incredibly, there was a warmth in his gaze that gave her hope. 'I didn't marry you for financial gain, I swear,' she said urgently. 'I don't want your money.'

His sensual smile stole her breath. 'Then what *do* you want, *cara*?'

The atmosphere shifted subtly, and Libby's heart-rate quickened when he brought his other hand up and smoothed her hair back from her face. Suddenly shy, she dropped her gaze, but staring at his lap made her heart beat faster still. She had a vivid recall of what was hidden beneath his trousers: long, muscular legs, and strong thighs covered with wiry dark hair that grew thicker at the base of his masculinity. Hot-cheeked, she dragged her gaze away from that pertinent area of his body. But she could not forget his promise that the next time they had sex he would be gentler, and as she lifted her eyes to his mouth she couldn't help wondering when that next time might be.

The stinging sensation when he had taken her virginity had caused her to cry out more from shock than actual pain, but now she was aware of a restless ache low in her pelvis that grew stronger when she remembered how he had caressed her with his wickedly inventive tongue.

'I regret that losing your virginity was not the special experience it should have been. But I think you found some aspects of lovemaking enjoyable—am I right, Libby?' he queried softly.

'I...' Libby was transfixed by the sultry heat in his eyes that made her skin prickle and her nipples tingle.

Raul did not love her, and had never given her any reason to hope that he ever would. But he wanted them to remain married, and that was better than nothing, she told herself. He was going to be a wonderful father for Gino, and for any children they might have. She gave a tiny shiver of excitement at the thought that she might already have conceived his baby. A marriage of convenience might not be perfect, but she was a realist and accepted that few things in life were. After all, she had never expected to have a husband and children after she had vowed to devote herself to Gino. Raul was an unexpected bonus, and as long as she kept the fact that she loved him to herself, their marriage stood every chance of being a success.

'You don't seem very sure,' he murmured, his deep, gravelly voice whispering across Libby's skin so that she gave another shiver. 'I think it's time I showed you how pleasurable sex can be.'

Libby swallowed, her heart thudding so hard beneath her ribs that she snatched a shallow breath. He mistook the sudden tension that gripped her, and ran his fingertips lightly up and down her spine, as if he were soothing a nervous colt.

'Don't be afraid, *cara*. I will be gentle this time.'

And as if to prove his words the first brush of his lips across hers was as soft as gossamer, a delicate tasting that was sweetly beguiling and instantly left her aching for more.

When he kissed her again she opened her mouth and kissed him back. He framed her face with his hands, grazing his lips over hers until she gave a frustrated moan and curled her arms around his neck in a clumsy attempt to make him kiss her with all the wild, pent-up passion she sensed he was trying to control.

Libby's eagerness was irresistible, but Raul also found it strangely touching now that he knew how inexperienced she was. When she dipped her tongue tentatively into his mouth he groaned, his restraint pushed to its limits, and without lifting his lips from hers he tumbled them both backwards, so that they were lying on the bed.

He could not rationalise what was happening to him, he acknowledged as he drew her jumper over her head, startled to find that his hands were shaking. He had been furious when he'd realised that it had not been necessary for him to marry her, but since then he had been coming up with reasons why she should remain his wife.

He was not prepared to let her go—at least not yet. Maybe not for a very long time… The fact that she had not been Pietro's mistress made him happier than it had any right to, because of course it was only desire that pumped through his veins, nothing more. He had fallen in lust the moment he had laid eyes on her, and now that she was his wife he could enjoy the single most important benefit of being married as far as he was concerned: regular sex with a woman who could decimate his self-control with a single look from her blue-green eyes.

He stared down at her pale, slender body. Her breasts were surprisingly full and rounded, her pink nipples already puckering, inviting him to close his mouth around them. She was watching him warily, and he knew he must control his impatience and indulge in leisurely foreplay until she was fully aroused and ready for him to possess her. He kissed her again—a long, slow tasting that left them both breathing hard—and then deftly removed her jeans.

He stood up to strip off his trousers, and saw the doubtful glance she cast at the solid length of his erection. 'Trust me, *cara*, it will be good for you this time,' he assured her, and he stretched out on the bed and claimed her mouth with hungry passion. Her unrestrained response stirred his soul, and his hand shook again as he cupped her breast and gently stroked his thumb pad over its dusky crest.

Heat unfurled in the pit of Libby's stomach when Raul lowered his head to her breast and flicked his tongue back and forth across her nipple until it felt tight and swollen. The sensation was exquisite, and she arched her back, a sigh of pleasure escaping her when he transferred his mouth to her other breast and meted out the same delicious torture. The restless longing he had evoked the first time he had made love to her returned, and was even fiercer in its intensity. The slight soreness between her legs had faded, and she ached for him to touch her there, but he continued to caress her breasts, now sucking hard on one nipple while he rolled its twin between his fingers until the pleasure was unbearable.

Only when she made a guttural plea did he trail his hand lightly over her stomach and thighs, and she caught her breath when at last he threaded his fingers through the cluster of tight curls and slowly, oh, so slowly parted her, stretching her with infinite care so that he could slide one digit fully into her. She lifted her hips as he withdrew his finger a little way and then pushed deeper, in and out, with pumping little movements that caused a curious fluttering sensation deep in her pelvis.

Something was happening to her that she had no control over—a wondrous coiling sensation that grew tighter and tighter as his hand moved rhythmically, caressing her with delicate little strokes so that molten heat flooded between her legs. Frantically she curled her fingers into the sheet and closed her eyes, so that she could focus on the tiny spasms that were now rippling across her belly. Her breathing quickened and became sharp little gasps as he took her higher and higher to some unknown place that she was desperate to reach, and she gave a sob of protest when he suddenly withdrew his finger, leaving her bereft and empty.

'Please…' She could barely articulate the word, her limbs trembling, needing him to touch her again and take her to the end of the journey he had started. She felt him move, and her lashes flew open to see him position himself over her. The feel of the solid length of his erection pushing against her thigh made her heart pound.

'Try to relax, *cara*,' he said deeply, his voice shaking with his desire to sink his throbbing shaft into her, but recognising the importance to take it slow so that he did not hurt her. 'You are ready for me,' he assured her, but still he hesitated and rubbed his finger against the moist, swollen lips of her vagina.

Libby gasped when he found the tiny, ultra-sensitive nub of her clitoris, and she jerked suddenly, her eyes widening with stunned disbelief as the coiling inside her snapped. The spasms grew stronger, making her muscles convulse in wave after wave of indescribable pleasure, but she soon realised that this was just the beginning, for Raul was easing forward, and she instinctively bent her knees to allow him to penetrate her with one slow, careful thrust, sliding deeper, inch by inch, until he filled her to the hilt.

'*Oh!*' The feel of him inside her was so incredible that she could not restrain a soft moan, but he stilled instantly and rested his sweat-beaded brow against hers, his eyes dark with regret.

'Does it hurt? I'll stop...'

'No!' She clutched his shoulders as he withdrew a little, and urged him down so that he sank deeper once more. 'Don't stop.'

The first waves of pleasure were receding, but when he drew back again and then thrust forward, gentle at first, but then faster and harder, she sensed a new wave building, sweeping her inexorably higher and higher, so that she groaned and twisted her head on the pillows. Raul gripped her hips and held her while he continued to drive into her, each stroke more powerful and intense than the last. She was so nearly there. He paused, and she sobbed his name until he relented and stroked again, and then the world exploded in a series of exquisite spasms that racked her body so that she raked her nails down his back, utterly blown away by her first orgasm.

She knew from the harsh sound of his breathing that he was nearing his own nirvana, and her generous heart yearned for him to experience the same bliss that he had gifted her. Instinctively she lifted her legs higher and wrapped them around his hips, so that he could thrust deeper still. Now the feeling of him pumping inside her was even more intense, and impossible to withstand—for either of them. Raul threw his head back, his face a rigid mask as he teetered on the brink for as long as he could hold on to his self-control before it shattered spectacularly and he crashed over the edge, taking Libby with him and revelling in her cries of pleasure as she climaxed for a second time.

He had sensed that Libby was an intensely sensual and passionate woman, and now he had proof, Raul mused as he lay lax on top of her, utterly sated and so amazingly relaxed that he felt boneless and strangely complete—as if he had been waiting for this moment, with this woman, all his life. She had spoiled him for other women, and he almost resented the hold she had over him. The idea of having sex with anyone else was repugnant—and as for her ever giving her body to another man! Fire burned in his gut and a murderous black rage swept through him. He would tear the man apart with his bare hands. Libby was *his* woman, *his* wife, and he would never let her go.

Inferno! Where had that thought come from? he wondered impatiently. He had done the whole intense relationship thing once, and sworn that he would rather eat poison than repeat the miserable experience. Libby meant nothing to him. He viewed their marriage as a partnership based on their mutual desire to bring Gino up as part of a family—with astounding sex thrown in.

With that settled, Raul gently disengaged his body from Libby and saw that she had fallen asleep. She did not stir, simply snuggled up to him like a sleepy kitten, instinctively searching for warmth, her glorious hair spilling over the pillows and her long gold lashes fanning her velvet soft cheeks.

A partnership, he reminded himself firmly. Yes, she was very beautiful—even when she insisted on wearing all the colours of the rainbow at the same time. But he had learned that the best recipe for a successful marriage was one that did not include messy emotions, and he would *not* be moved by the flame-haired siren who was sleeping peacefully, with her head resting on his chest and her cheek pressed against his heart.

The sound of Gino's gurgling laughter roused Libby from a deep sleep. She stirred and stretched luxuriantly, wakefulness alerting her to the feeling of slight tenderness between her thighs. But that was only to be expected after Raul had made love to her so passionately in the early hours of the morning. She turned her head, and her heart flipped when he strolled in off the balcony, holding Gino in his arms.

Every time she looked at him she was struck anew by how gorgeous he was, and this morning, wearing a pair of close-fitting faded jeans and a black polo shirt, he stole her breath. He was laughing as Gino vigorously explored his ear with a chubby finger, and his tender expression as he smiled at the baby filled Libby with despair. How could she not love him? she thought helplessly. He was impossibly handsome, sinfully sexy, and heartbreakingly gentle with the little boy he intended to adopt as his son.

She quickly sat up, struggling to bring her emotions under control, and two pairs of dark eyes fringed with ridiculously long black lashes immediately turned to her.

'*Buongiorno, cara.*' Raul's grin revealed a set of very white teeth which looked even more blinding in contrast to his olive gold skin. A lock of hair had fallen onto his brow, and she remembered how she had threaded her fingers through its silky blackness and held his head to her breasts during their early-morning sex session.

She blushed at the sultry gleam in his eyes which told her that he was remembering it too. An elusive message passed between them that was gone before she could grasp it or understand it. But his gaze remained locked with hers, and her heart ached as it had done when he had made love to her a second time, with such surprising tenderness that afterwards tears had trickled from the corners of her eyes and he had gently kissed them away.

'Gino's had his breakfast and a bath, and I've taken him for a stroll around the garden,' Raul informed her. 'I think he'll be ready for a nap pretty soon.'

'It's nearly midday,' Libby murmured after a horrified glance at the clock. 'You should have woken me.'

'Silvana was happy to take charge of him. I think she expected you to be tired after your wedding night.'

'Oh, God!' Libby covered her scarlet cheeks with her hands. 'What must she think?'

'That you were worn out after a very energetic night with your new husband,' Raul said in a tone of extreme satisfaction. He sat on the edge of the bed and leaned forward to brush his mouth over hers in a lingering kiss that did not last nearly long enough. 'I'm sure she will understand that you may need to lie in and recuperate most mornings from now on.'

His grin was impossible to resist. Libby's lips twitched. 'You can take that insufferably smug smile off your face, *Signor* Carducci.'

'Make me, *Signora* Carducci,' he challenged softly.

He was prevented from kissing her again by Gino, who had grown bored with not being the centre of attention and now butted his head against Raul's shoulder. 'I'll take him to the nursery while you get up,' he said, getting to his feet and swinging Gino high in the air, much to the baby's delight. 'Silvana will mind him for a few hours. I thought you might like to come sailing with me.'

Libby threw him a startled glance. In the days leading up to their marriage he had spent many hours with her and Gino, but she had been under no illusion: the focus of his attention had been the baby. Her heart skipped at the idea that he wanted to be alone with her. She would fly to the moon with him if he asked, but she must not seem too eager or he might guess that her feelings for him were much more than lust and platonic friendship.

'Don't you have to work?' she queried.

True to his word, he had worked from his study rather than drive in to the Carducci Cosmetics offices in Rome each day, and on several occasions he had asked her to read through various documents and sign them. This had caused a certain amount of tension when she had questioned some of his proposals. Admittedly she hadn't really understood the finer details, but she could add up figures and was concerned by the level of risk in some of his ventures. To her surprise he hadn't argued with her, but simply filed the documents away, saying that perhaps she was right and he should be more cautious.

She hoped that her involvement in running CC would not create friction between them, she brooded. But all thoughts of the company, and indeed anything else, were wiped from her mind when his mouth curved into a sensual smile.

'Certainly not. This is our honeymoon, *cara*, and I think we should use the opportunity to get to know each other better. What do you think?'

I think I may have died and gone to heaven, Libby thought shakily. But somehow she managed a casual shrug. 'Sailing sounds good to me.'

It was beautiful out on the lake. The sun shone brilliantly in a cloudless sky, and a little breeze tugged the sails of Raul's boat and sent it skimming across the water. Libby sat with her arm propped on the boat rail and stared down at the crystal clear water.

'This is wonderful,' she murmured happily.

Raul was doing something with the sail. He had explained the technicalities of sailing to her, but she preferred to simply enjoy the scenery. The lake was a dense blue that reflected the sky, the green foliage of trees ringed the shore, and in the distance were the graceful turrets of the famous Odescalchi Castle.

'Have you never sailed before?' he asked her.

'I've never been on any sort of boat before—apart from a pedalo once. There's not much opportunity to mingle with the yachting fraternity at a South London comprehensive,' she said dryly. 'When did *you* learn to sail?'

'When I was a boy—Pietro taught me. I love the sense of freedom out here on the lake. It's where I come whenever I'm feeling tense.'

Libby digested this information and gave a faint frown. 'Does that mean you're feeling tense now?'

'Only certain areas of my anatomy, *cara*.' His eyes gleamed wickedly when Libby blushed, but she could not prevent herself from staring at the distinct bulge beneath his tight-fitting jeans.

'Oh!'

Raul was still grinning when he brought the boat up to a little wooden jetty which ran out from a secluded beach at the edge of the lake. An attractive summerhouse sat close to the water's edge, and tall pine trees provided shade and privacy.

'This land is all part of the Villa Giulietta's estate,' he explained to Libby. 'You can only reach the summerhouse by boat, and no one ever comes here but me.'

'A secret copse—how lovely,' she murmured, sternly telling herself that she must not read too much into the fact that he had brought her to his private hideaway. 'The trees shield the house so well that I doubt anyone sailing past would even know it's here.'

Her heart missed a beat when Raul came up behind her and slid his arms around her waist.

'Mmm... And as we are safe from prying eyes, there is no reason why I shouldn't do this,' he said softly, pushing her hair aside and trailing his lips up her neck before he nibbled her earlobe.

Tiny darts of pleasure shivered through Libby, and she made no effort to resist him when he tugged the straps of her sundress over her shoulders so that her breasts spilled into his hands. The feel of his warm palms cradling her naked flesh was intoxicating, and she gasped when he rolled her nipples between his fingers until they swelled into stiff peaks. Molten heat flooded between her legs, her desire for him instant and overwhelming. But even so she could not help feeling stupidly shy when he pushed her dress down over her hips so that it pooled at her feet and she was left standing before him in just skimpy white lace knickers.

'Raul…?'

'No one can see us,' he assured her thickly. 'I need you now, *cara*.'

His eyes blazed into hers as he pulled her pants down and slipped his hand between her thighs, and there was tenderness in his smile when he discovered the slick wetness of her arousal. He lifted her and carried her over to a patch of soft grass in the cool shade of the trees, stripping out of his clothes with flattering haste and coming down beside her to claim her mouth in a hungry kiss that demanded her eager response.

Fingers of sunlight filtered through the dense foliage of the trees and dappled their bodies. Libby could see tiny patches of blue sky between the green leaves, but as Raul lowered his head and suckled one taut nipple and then the other, she closed her eyes and gave herself up to the pleasure of his mouth. She bit her lip when he pushed her legs apart and flicked his tongue across her clitoris, back and forth, until she twisted her hips urgently, needing to feel him inside her. He was already massively aroused, but fascination made her bold, and she touched him, smiling at his swiftly indrawn breath when she closed her hand around the hard length of his erection and gently squeezed.

Raul withstood her ministrations for a few torturous minutes before he groaned and captured her hand, his breathing ragged as he fought to regain his self-control.

'Enough, witch…' he muttered hoarsely, and eased into her, pausing while her muscles stretched to accommodate him before he thrust deeper, again and again, in an age-old rhythm that quickly drove them to the edge. *'Tesoro...'*

The word was ripped from his throat as they climaxed simultaneously, Libby's vaginal muscles tightening and rippling around him, giving him the most intense pleasure he had ever experienced.

Afterwards, when they lay still joined, she wondered what the word meant, but she was afraid to ask in case she had imagined the closeness she sensed between them, the feeling that their souls as well as their bodies had merged.

CHAPTER TEN

AFTER that they went sailing regularly, and always stopped off at the hidden summerhouse. The glorious days of early summer slipped past, and before Libby knew it, it was June, and Gino's first birthday.

'I can't believe he's walking and saying a few words,' she said softly, when she and Raul tucked the worn out little boy into his cot that evening.

'He said Papa quite clearly when we lit the candle on his cake,' Raul said with undisguised pride in his voice. 'Did you hear him?'

Libby gave him a mock frown. 'I still think it sounded more like Mamma. Do you think he enjoyed his party?'

It had only been a small affair; the Vincentis had brought their two daughters, and several of Raul's other friends whom Libby had met at the dinner parties they had attended had also come with their children.

'One year old already,' she murmured, the familiar surge of love flooding through her when she stared down at Gino's flushed cheeks and silky black curls. 'I wish Mum could see him,' she whispered, tears filling her eyes.

Raul pulled her close. 'She would be very proud of you for being such a wonderful mother to him,' he assured her gently, conscious of the curious tugging on his heart that had caught him unawares so often recently. 'Don't cry, *cara*.' It tore him apart when she cried. 'Come with me. I've got something to show you.'

Puzzled, Libby allowed him to lead her out of the nursery and up several flights of stairs. 'We must be at the top of the tower,' she said breathlessly. 'Where are we going, Raul?'

'In here.' He pushed open a door and stood back for Libby to enter the room, grinning when her mouth opened in astonishment but no sound emerged. 'It's your art studio,' he explained unnecessarily as she stared around—at the large easel set close to a window which overlooked the lake, the stack of blank canvases, the shelves containing paints and other equipment. The paintings Libby had left behind in Cornwall were arranged around the room, and she felt a little swell of pride as she studied them. They really weren't bad, she decided.

'A friend of mine owns a gallery in Rome,' Raul told her as he joined her in front of a beach scene she had painted just before she had come to Italy. 'I showed him some of your work and he's very keen to organise an exhibition. What do you think of the studio?' he asked, concerned by her lack of response to something that he had taken great pleasure in organising for her. '*Cara*, why are you crying? If you don't like it…'

'I *do* like it—of course I do.' Libby sniffed inelegantly and gave him a blinding smile as she launched herself into his arms. 'It's the nicest, most wonderful thing anyone has ever done for me, and I love—' She stopped herself just in time and changed 'you' to 'it'. 'Oh, Raul, I don't know how to thank you.'

'I'll show you, *cara*,' he promised wolfishly. 'There is a very good reason why I had a sofa put up here—as I am about to demonstrate.'

Was it tempting fate to admit that she was the happiest she had ever been in her life? Libby mused a few weeks later, as she got ready for a dinner party that she and Raul were to attend that evening. Life couldn't be more perfect. Gino was a gorgeous, energetic little boy who was happiest toddling around the gardens of the Villa Giulietta. Libby adored being with him, but she appreciated the couple of hours a day when Silvana took charge of him, leaving her free to go up to her studio and paint.

Raul continued to work from the villa, and only drove in to his office in Rome when absolutely necessary. She loved the fact that she could pop in to his study and see him whenever she could think of an excuse, and he often invited her to join him to discuss plans and proposals for Carducci Cosmetics.

But if the days were good, the nights were heaven, she mused, smiling when she stared at her flushed cheeks in the mirror and realised that there was no need to apply blusher. Her fears that the sizzling sexual chemistry between her and Raul would die out had proved unfounded. They could not get enough of one another, and their lovemaking was more passionate and intense than ever. She loved the way he made love to her, Libby thought, feeling her breasts grow heavy at the memory of how he had joined her in the bath the previous night.

It had taken ages to mop up the floor after they had
caused a small tidal wave with the bathwater, she recalled with a smile.

'Libby, we have to go.'

She turned as he entered the bedroom, and held her
breath when he halted and studied her. 'I thought I'd tone
down the colour scheme for once,' she said doubtfully
when he seemed to be struck dumb. 'Do you think white
is a bit, well…virginal?' When she'd tried the dress on
she had thought that the simple white silk sheath overlaid with chiffon and decorated with tiny crystals on the
bodice and narrow shoulder straps suited her, but now
she wasn't so sure.

'It's rather too late for virginal, *cara*.' His eyes
gleamed wickedly, but his voice was curiously rough
as he said, 'You take my breath away.' He moved towards her and took something from his jacket pocket.
'My mother often wore this to parties,' he explained,
and Libby gasped when he held up a necklace of shimmering diamonds that sparkled brilliantly in the light.
'The Carducci diamonds are a family heirloom.'

'I can't wear it,' Libby protested in a panicky voice.
'It must be worth a fortune. Suppose I lose it? Really,'
she insisted, when he ignored her and fastened the necklace around her throat. 'I'm not a jewellery person.'

'I know,' Raul murmured dryly.

The only item of jewellery she wore was the plain
gold band he had given her on their wedding day. On
a recent trip to Rome he had taken her to an exclusive
jewellers and tried to persuade her to choose a bracelet
and perhaps matching earrings, but she had refused,

saying that there was no point in her having expensive jewellery when she spent most of her time playing in the sandpit with Gino.

Libby was so different from his first wife—from any other woman he had ever met. And to think he had accused her of being a gold-digger. He shuddered at the memory of how he had treated her when she had first arrived at the villa. His divorce from Dana had left him deeply cynical about relationships, but Libby had changed his attitude, changed *him*, and he wondered what had happened to his much vaunted idea of an emotionless marriage.

'Wear the necklace tonight and allow me to show off my Carducci bride?' he requested softly.

And, as usual, Libby found that she could not refuse him.

'*Zia* Carmina is looking forward to seeing you tonight,' Raul told Libby as he swung the Lamborghini onto the driveway of his aunt's house in a fashionable suburb of Rome.

Privately, Libby doubted that. On the previous two occasions when they had visited his aunt, Carmina had been polite to her in front of Raul, but cold and unfriendly the moment he was out of earshot. He was fond of his mother's sister, she reminded herself. And for that reason she was determined to try and get on with Carmina.

Raul's aunt greeted him with a kiss on each cheek, but she stiffened when Libby stepped towards her and her smile slipped. 'I see you are wearing the Carducci diamonds,' she commented tightly.

'Yes…' Libby hesitated. 'Raul asked me to wear them.'

Carmina gave her a strange look. 'Did he, indeed?' she said softly, and something in her tone sent a shiver down Libby's spine.

Dinner was an ordeal. Carmina was a patron of numerous charities, and a well-known figure among Rome's social elite, and Libby was sure she had deliberately invited guests who were either brilliant academics or stunningly beautiful models to emphasise Libby's lack of education and social graces. She felt hopelessly out of her depth as she struggled to join in the conversation around the table, and jealousy burned like corrosive acid in her stomach every time the gorgeous Italian television presenter sitting next to Raul leaned close to him and said something that made him laugh.

To her relief, coffee was served in the salon. She declined a cup when the waiter brought it round on a tray. For some reason she had gone right off coffee, the smell of it made her feel nauseous. Rather than watch Raul, who was still chatting to Miss Daytime TV, she wandered into the smaller sitting room next door to the salon—but immediately turned on her heel when she saw Carmina sitting on the sofa.

'I'm sorry… I—'

'Don't scurry away.' Raul's aunt gave her a cold smile, her eyes fixed on the necklace around Libby's throat. 'I wouldn't read too much into Raul giving you the diamonds,' she advised harshly. 'I had always hoped that one day *I* would wear the symbol of the Carducci bride,' she went on after a pause. 'After Eleanora died I thought that Pietro would turn to me. Not immediately, of course, but eventually. I loved him first, you see, before my sister had even met him. But when he saw Eleanora he chose her.'

'I'm sorry,' Libby said again, not knowing what else she could say.

'Pietro could have had me, but instead he chose a cheap little tart like you,' Carmina said bitterly.

'Actually, he didn't.'

Clearly Raul had not told his aunt that she was not Gino's mother, and that she hadn't been Pietro's mistress. Libby did not feel that she owed Carmina an explanation, but she'd had enough of the older woman's foul accusations. She opened her mouth to speak, but Carmina ignored her.

'And now you are a Carducci bride. I suppose you decided that losing control of your son's shares in Carducci Cosmetics was a small price to pay for becoming the wife of a billionaire?'

'Pardon?' Libby frowned as she tried to make sense of Carmina's statement. 'I don't know what you mean,' she mumbled, filled with a sudden sense of foreboding that made her heart thud painfully beneath her ribs.

There was a strangely triumphant expression in Carmina's eyes. 'Surely you read Pietro's will? It quite clearly states that if Gino's mother were to marry, his fifty percent share of CC would pass to Raul until the boy reaches adulthood. I had forgotten about the clause until I came across a copy of the will a few days ago, when I was tidying my bureau, and then everything made sense. Raul married you to claim full control of the company.'

The room swayed alarmingly, and Libby's legs suddenly seemed incapable of holding her. She sank down onto a chair. 'I did read the will,' she said shakily. But not properly, she thought, feeling sick, remembering how she been holding Gino when Raul had handed her the legal document. She had quickly skimmed down the first page and read the bit about Gino and his mother being able to live at the Villa Giulietta, but Gino had been squirming in her arms and she had handed the papers back because she'd been worried that the baby might tear them. It had all been so astounding and un-expected, and before she'd had time to blink Raul had whisked her off to Italy and she hadn't given the will another thought.

'Perhaps you would like to refresh your memory?' Carmina said softly. 'I was also a beneficiary of Pietro's estate—he bequeathed me some small items of jewellery—and I have a copy of the will here.' She crossed to the bureau, took some papers from the drawer, and dropped them in Libby's lap. 'The clause at the bottom of the second page is the one you should be interested in.'

Afterwards, Libby did not know how she managed to keep herself together for the remainder of the evening. Raul found her on the terrace, took one look at her white face and demanded to know what was wrong with her. She mumbled that she had a headache, hating him for playing the role of concerned husband when she knew it was just an act. At the beginning of the evening she would have been fooled by the compassion in his dark eyes, but now she knew what a snake in the grass he was. He had married her to get control of Carducci Cosmetics.

The words of the clause in Pietro's will swirled round and round in her head, and she could not stifle a little moan of pain.

'*Dio!* Why didn't you tell me your headache was so bad?' he demanded roughly.

'I didn't like to interrupt you when you were having so much fun with the queen of the chat show,' Libby snapped.

'Gianna Mancini's son was a year old last week, and we were swapping baby development news,' he said with a wry smile. 'Her husband is away on business.' He paused, and then added quietly, 'You must know I only have eyes for you, *piccola*.'

Her heart yearned for the tenderness in his voice to be real, but she knew his performance was worthy of an Oscar. She dared not meet his gaze, terrified that he would see the devastation in hers, and to her relief he left her to collect her shawl while he went to bid farewell to his aunt, then hurried her out to the car.

On the journey home she closed her eyes, to convince him that her headache was too severe for her to be able to talk. He could not know that it was not her head but her heart that felt as though it had been ripped open, leaving a raw, agonising wound that she feared was irreparable.

'I'm going to check on Gino,' she muttered when they entered the villa, and hurried up the stairs before he had time to reply.

The baby was sleeping peacefully, his arms outstretched and the covers strewn about the cot as usual, where he had flung them off. Her desire to give Gino a father was the reason she had married Raul, she reminded herself—and knew she was lying. For her it had been love at first sight. She had fallen for Raul from the moment he had stormed into her life, had been drawn to him by a force beyond her control.

Gino loved him too, she acknowledged, tears slipping silently down her face when she pictured how the baby's face lit up whenever he saw Raul. Gullible fool that she was, she had swallowed Raul's story that he wanted to adopt Pietro's son and be a devoted father to him, but now she wondered if Raul had lavished attention on Gino as part of his cold-hearted plan to persuade her to marry him and thereby gain full control of the company.

Numb with misery, she crept out of the nursery. Instead of walking down the corridor to the master bedroom she turned and ran up the stairs leading to the tower. Tears were streaming down her face. She hadn't cried like this since her mother's funeral—great, tearing sobs that racked her frame and made her chest burn. She couldn't face Raul tonight, she thought despairingly. If he realised how much his deception had hurt her, he would also realise that she was in love with him.

But it was likely that when she didn't come to bed he would search for her. She took a ragged breath and glanced wildly around the studio. There was no lock on the door, but maybe she could drag the cupboard across it to prevent him from entering…

'Here you are. I thought you were going to bed?'

She jerked her head around at the sound of his voice, and her treacherous heart performed its usual somersault at the sight of him lounging in the doorway. His jacket was unfastened, as were the top few buttons of his shirt, revealing several inches of tanned skin and silky dark chest hair. He was so beautiful it was hardly surprising she had lost her heart to him. But he didn't want her heart—he never had—and to be fair he had not tricked her into marrying him by pretending to love her. It was her own fault that she had hoped and prayed and looked for any tiny sign that she meant something to him. When he had created the studio for her she had thought he had done it because he cared about her, but now she wondered if he had hoped she would become so absorbed in her artwork that she would not realise she was no longer involved in running CC.

Pain ripped through her; and with it a burning, blazing, incandescent rage that she had been so stupid, and he was such a deceitful, lying—

'Have you taken some painkillers for your headache?' He took a step towards her, frowning when he saw that she had been crying. *'Cara…?'*

'Don't!' She put up a hand to ward him off. 'Don't *cara* me. Don't sound concerned when you couldn't give a damn.'

The tight band around her self-control snapped, unleashing her fiery temper, and driven by hurt and despair she snatched up the tub of orange paint she had blended from powdered pigment earlier that day and hurled it across the room. It hit him squarely on his chest, and he was instantly covered in liquid paint from shoulder to hip, while great splodges spattered both his legs.

For a few simmering seconds he stared at her in utter astonishment before he found his voice. *'Madre di Dio!* What's the matter with you? You crazy firebrand—have you gone mad?'

'On the contrary, I've finally come to my senses and seen what a sly, conniving, treacherous bastard you are.' Libby flung the words at him with the same force with which she had thrown the paint. 'Your aunt showed me the clause in Pietro's will—the clause on the second page that I didn't have time to read when you turned up in Pennmar and bullied me into agreeing to bring Gino to Italy.'

'I did not bully you.' Raul paused as the implication of her words sank in. He had completely forgotten that his aunt had a copy of the will. 'Why on earth did Carmina show you the will?'

'Because she hates me,' Libby told him flatly. 'She was in love with Pietro, and she still believes that I was his mistress. She must have guessed I didn't know about the clause stating that control of Gino's shares would pass to you if I were to marry.'

Panic churned inside her as she realised that Raul's aunt must have also guessed that she was in love with him. If she was that transparent, could Raul have guessed too? she wondered, feeling sick with humiliation.

She stared at him, and her heart splintered when she noted the faintly uncomfortable expression in his eyes. 'Can you deny that the reason you asked me to marry you was so that you would be able to claim full control of CC?'

'I don't deny that that was one of the reasons,' he said quietly. He gave a harsh laugh when she paled. 'What did you think, Libby? That I had fallen in love with you?'

'*No!* Of course not,' she denied instantly, colour storming into her cheeks. 'But I thought you loved Gino. You told me you wanted to adopt him.'

'Both those things are true.'

'Are they?' Now it was her turn give a mocking laugh. 'Maybe you just pretended to care for him because you knew how much I wanted him to grow up in a family and have a father, as I longed for when I was a child?' Her temper soared once more. 'I know I was wrong to pretend that I was Gino's mother, and I believe that I deserved your anger when you discovered the truth. But all the time you were furious with me for deceiving you, you knew—*you knew.*' Her voice rose shrilly. 'You were guilty of a far more cruel deception. You cold-bloodedly used my love for Gino to steal his shares.'

'I have not stolen his shares,' Raul said sharply. 'I admit I wanted full control of CC until Gino was eighteen, but only so that I could take the company forward and ensure that there *is* a company for him to inherit in the future.' He sighed. 'I don't wish to be disloyal about my father but he had allowed the company to stagnate. I knew we were in danger of losing our position as a world leader in the cosmetics market if we did not expand our product range and diversify into new areas of growth such as the perfume range we're about to launch, and I believed I needed to have full control of CC to implement my plans.

'*Dio*, Libby,' he growled savagely when she said nothing, just looked at him with angry accusation in her eyes. 'Can you blame me for wanting to protect the interests of the company I had expected to inherit? I was shocked beyond words when I learned that I would have to discuss every business plan with a woman who at that time I believed was my father's lap-dancer mistress. You were prepared to do anything to keep Gino, including deliberately fooling me into believing you were his mother. By the same token, when I realised you had not read that clause in Pietro's will, I seized the opportunity to claim Gino's shares.'

He paused, and felt as though his heart was being squeezed in a vice when he saw the shimmer of tears in her eyes. 'Like I said, gaining control of the company was *not* the only reason I married you. Gino was certainly an important factor—I love him as much as if he was my own child, and my greatest wish is to adopt him.'

'So you say,' Libby muttered scathingly. 'How can I ever believe you or trust you now?' She jerked backwards when he took a step towards her, closing her eyes in despair when the familiar musky scent of his cologne drifted around her. 'Stay where you are. I can't bear to be near you.'

Raul's jaw tightened. 'We both know that's not true. The sexual attraction between us was white-hot from the start. We've never been able to keep our hands off each other. Even when I thought I had good reason to despise you, I wanted you with a hunger I have never felt for any other woman. The prospect of having you share my bed every night was another very good reason for marrying you.'

He had married her for sex. Well, she'd known that, Libby reminded herself. So why did hearing him say it feel as if he had stabbed her through the heart? She stared at him wordlessly when he shrugged out of his paint-spattered jacket and dropped it on the floor, panic coiling inside her as he began to undo his shirt buttons.

'What are you doing?' she demanded shakily. Was he intending to prove that the sexual alchemy between them was as fierce as ever? However much she told herself that she hated him, her traitorous body was pathetically weak, and she was terrified she would be unable to resist him. 'As far as I'm concerned our marriage is over,' she flung at him bitterly. 'I won't be sharing your bed this night or any other.'

His trousers hit the floor, and she moved her eyes helplessly over his broad, muscular chest, covered in a mass of dark hair that arrowed down over his abdomen and disappeared below the waistband of his boxers.

His eyes narrowed on her flushed face. 'I could very easily make you eat your words, *cara*,' he drawled, but then to her surprise—and, although she despised herself for admitting it, her disappointment—he turned back to the door.

'Where...where are you going?'

'To have a shower. I can't walk through the house dripping paint everywhere. We will finish this conversation downstairs in ten minutes. Don't make me have to come and get you, Libby,' he warned her in a deceptively soft tone that made her realise his anger was tightly controlled.

What reason did he have to be angry? she brooded bitterly when she made her way slowly down the tower staircase a few minutes after him. He was the one who had deceived her; he was the one who had broken her heart. But of course he did not know that, and somehow she must hide her hurt from him.

To her relief the bedroom was empty, but the sight of the huge bed where he had made love to her so passionately, and lately with such tenderness, brought more tears to her eyes. How could she remain married to him, loving him as she did, but knowing that she would never be anything more to him than a convenient sex partner?

She could not sleep in here tonight. She dared not face him again until she had regained some semblance of control over her emotions. Brushing her hand impatiently over her wet face, she spun round—but before she could reach the door Raul appeared, his dark hair still damp from his shower, his black robe belted loosely around him.

'I'm going to sleep in one of the other bedrooms,' she said stiffly, and then gave a startled gasp when he scooped her into his arms and strode towards the bed. 'Put me down, Raul. Let me go.' It was a cry from the heart, and the wobble in her voice tore at his insides.

'I can't, *piccola*.' His refusal was heartbreakingly gentle, and her tenuous hold on her emotions cracked.

'You have to,' she wept, burying her face in her hands and rocking back and forth on the edge of the bed. 'I can't bear to be your wife any longer.'

Raul felt as though he had been kicked in the gut. Witnessing Libby's distress was sheer torture, but he knew that if he followed his instinct to haul her into his arms and kiss away her tears she would fight him like a wildcat.

'Listen to me,' he said urgently, hunkering down beside her. 'I need you to read something, and then, if you still feel the same way, I will—' He broke off, feeling as though an arrow had pierced his heart as he contemplated the utter bleakness of his life without her. 'I don't know what I will do, *cara mia*,' he admitted roughly.

Libby stared blindly at the document he had placed in her lap. 'I don't want to read it. I'll probably miss something important anyway—I'm good at that,' she said bitterly. 'You read it to me.'

'You don't trust me,' he said regretfully. 'I need you to see it with your own eyes.'

He moved to stand by the balcony window, staring out at the moonlight dancing across the lake, his heart slamming in his chest. Libby picked up the document and forced herself to concentrate on the few brief paragraphs.

'I don't understand,' she mumbled, after reading the page three times. 'It says that even though I am married you are returning control of Gino's shares in Carducci Cosmetics to me until he is eighteen.' She shook her head. 'If you went to all the trouble of marrying me so that you could claim full control of CC, why have you returned half the control back to me? It doesn't make sense.'

'Doesn't it, *cara*?' Raul's voice sounded curiously constricted. 'Can you really think of no reason why I might have revoked that damn clause? Look at the date at the top of the page.'

Libby stared at it uncomprehendingly. 'But that was two weeks after our wedding.' She stood up, her eyes locked on Raul's hard profile, and she suddenly had the strangest feeling that he was deliberately avoiding meeting her gaze. 'Why did you do it, Raul?' she whispered. 'You had full control of CC—the thing you wanted most in the world—so why give it up?'

'Because I discovered that I wanted something infinitely more precious than control of the company.' At last he turned to face her, and Libby caught her breath at the raw emotion blazing in his eyes. 'I discovered that I wanted you to love me—as I love you, *tesoro*.'

Silence stretched between them, simmering with tension. At last Libby shook her head. 'You don't.' There was no quaver of doubt in her voice. She could not allow herself to be swayed by the tenderness in his rueful smile, or the fierce urgency in his eyes as he strode towards her and caught hold of her hands. 'You said love is an illusion, and that you would never fall in love after your bitter divorce from your first wife. You married me to claim control of CC—and maybe because you do really care for Gino,' she acknowledged slowly.

'I swear that I love him, *cara*, and I will care for him and protect him as his father—*my* father—would have done. You stole my heart from the first, Libby,' he said roughly, his voice shaking with emotion. 'I was drawn to you from the moment I laid eyes on you, but I hated myself for wanting my father's mistress. Marriage seemed the ideal solution—it would give me control of the company and you in my bed—but even before our wedding day I knew it was more than that. You fill my world with colour and laughter and a joy that I had not known it was possible to feel. My life will be a grey and lonely place if you leave me.'

Could it be true? Could she believe him? Libby's heart was pounding so hard that it hurt to breathe and her hand trembled as she reached up and touched his damp eyelashes. 'Raul…?'

'I was planning to tell you about the clause in the will, and that I had reversed it,' he admitted gruffly. His throat ached, and it was hard to get the words out. 'I want us to make decisions about CC together, and build a successful company for Gino. But every day I kept putting it off. I was afraid you would realise I had fallen in love with you once you learned that I had returned Gino's shares to you, and I was scared you didn't feel the same way.'

'You? Scared?' Libby shook her head wonderingly, hope and a tremulous joy unfurling inside her when he lifted her hand to his mouth and pressed his lips against her knuckles.

'Oh, yes, *cara*. Scared stiff—because I knew that the only reason you had married me was to give Gino a father.'

Was this what sky divers felt as they were about to launch themselves out of a plane? Fear, excitement, and above all a desperate hope? Was she imagining the love blazing in Raul's eyes?

'Gino wasn't the only reason,' she admitted huskily. 'I love you, Raul. I can't remember a time when I didn't. Everything before I met you seems distant and colourless. I missed Mum so much…' she swallowed hard '…but you made me feel alive again—even when you made me angry, and especially when you made love to me.' Her voice cracked and the tears she had been trying so hard to hold back slipped down her face. 'I never thought I could be this happy.'

'*Tesoro*. Don't cry. *Ti amo*.'

The words were wrenched from his soul. Love—something he had never expected to feel for any woman until Libby had turned his world upside down. He drew her against him, his whole body shaking as he claimed her mouth almost tentatively; a tidal wave of emotion stormed through him when he felt her sweet response.

'You stole my heart, *cara*.' The words were muffled against her throat as he kissed her feverishly—her hair, her brow, the tip of her nose—and tasted the salt of her tears when he pressed his lips to her eyelids. 'Will you stay with me, my golden girl, the love of my life, my wife?'

'Just try to send me away,' Libby said softly. 'Oh, Raul, I love you so much.'

'And I love *you*—madly, my crazy little firecracker. You owe me a new suit, by the way,' he said, grinning when she blushed scarlet.

'I'm sorry,' she mumbled, thinking of his paint-spattered suit. 'I don't know what came over me.'

'I love your unpredictability, and your fiery temper, and your generous heart, *cara mia*. You and Gino are my world, and I could not ask for anything more than for the three of us to be a family.'

Her beautiful smile stole his breath. 'There's a chance that three will be four before too long. I don't know definitely yet, but I'm two weeks late,' she admitted softly.

'*Cara...*' Raul's throat worked convulsively as emotion overwhelmed him. For a moment he could not speak to tell her how much she meant to him, but when he claimed her mouth in a tender kiss he discovered that there was no need for words...

EPILOGUE

THE private art gallery was packed, the rooms buzzing with conversation as people crowded in front of the bold, brilliantly coloured paintings on display.

'Elizabeth Carducci is certainly a gifted artist,' an art critic from a national newspaper commented to the tall, handsome man who was standing at the back of the room. 'This exhibition is one of the most exciting I've ever attended. And of course the Galleria Farnese is one of the most prestigious contemporary galleries in Rome. There are several top collectors here`, and I've no doubt that Signora Carducci's work will soon be attracting international acclaim.'

'I am sure you are right,' the tall man murmured. 'And it is acclaim that is well deserved.'

The art critic glanced around the gallery. 'I've never met Signora Carducci, but I've heard that she is exceptionally beautiful. Can you point her out to me?'

'My wife is over there,' Raul replied, in a tone that caused the art critic to give him a nervous smile. 'In the green-and-orange dress,' he added dryly. 'As you can see, she is indeed beautiful.'

'What did you say to Carlo Vitenze that made him shoot off like a frightened rabbit?' Libby asked her husband when he strolled over to join her. 'He's a respected critic. I hope you haven't upset him.'

'I merely let him know that your husband is very possessive,' Raul said lightly. 'He seemed to get the message.' He dropped a kiss on his wife's soft mouth, his eyes gleaming when she immediately parted her lips. 'It doesn't surprise me that every man in this room cannot take his eyes off you. I can see I am going to have to lock you away in the highest tower of the Villa Giulietta.'

Libby gave him an impish smile. 'I already have two very special men in my life—and they are so incredibly handsome why would I be interested in anyone else? Careful, Gino,' she said gently as the energetic toddler rushed up to her. 'Mind the pram; your sister is asleep.'

'See Lissa,' Gino demanded.

Raul lifted him up so that he could look into the pram where three-month-old Elisabetta Rose was sleeping peacefully. 'There she is. You can give her a kiss when she wakes up,' he told the little boy.

His eyes met Libby's and his heart turned over when he saw the love that blazed in those blue-green depths. A love for him and their children which he returned a thousandfold.

'There are two very special ladies in my life—and they are so beautiful that they have captured my heart for all eternity,' he said softly. 'I love you, Libby.'

Three simple words that meant everything to her, Libby thought, blinking back the tears that filled her eyes.

Raul frowned in concern. 'Why are you crying, *cara*? The exhibition is wonderful.'

'Everything is wonderful,' she reassured him, wrapping her arms around his waist and smiling mistily up at him. 'I'm crying because I am the happiest woman in the world. You make me happy, Raul, you and Gino and Lissa, and I love you with all my heart.'

MILLS & BOON®

Want to get more from Mills & Boon?

Here's what's available to you if you join the exclusive **Mills & Boon eBook Club** today:

✦ *Convenience – choose your books each month*
✦ *Exclusive – receive your books a month before anywhere else*
✦ *Flexibility – change your subscription at any time*
✦ *Variety – gain access to eBook-only series*
✦ *Value – subscriptions from just £1.99 a month*

So visit **www.millsandboon.co.uk/esubs** today to be a part of this exclusive eBook Club!

EBOOK_SUBS_2014

MILLS & BOON®

Maybe This Christmas

Author of *Sleigh Bells in the Snow*

Sarah Morgan

Maybe this Christmas

COMING SOON
OCTOBER 2014

* cover in development

Let Sarah Morgan sweep you away to a perfect
winter wonderland with this wonderful Christmas
tale filled with unforgettable characters, wit,
charm and heart-melting romance!
Pick up your copy today!

www.millsandboon.co.uk/xmas

MILLS & BOON®

Why shop at millsandboon.co.uk?

Each year, thousands of romance readers find their perfect read at millsandboon.co.uk. That's because we're passionate about bringing you the very best romantic fiction. Here are some of the advantages of shopping at www.millsandboon.co.uk:

✶ **Get new books first**—you'll be able to buy your favourite books one month before they hit the shops

✶ **Get exclusive discounts**—you'll also be able to buy our specially created monthly collections, with up to 50% off the RRP

✶ **Find your favourite authors**—latest news, interviews and new releases for all your favourite authors and series on our website, plus ideas for what to try next

✶ **Join in**—once you've bought your favourite books, don't forget to register with us to rate, review and join in the discussions

Visit **www.millsandboon.co.uk**
for all this and more today!